Pretty Little Psycho
Original Story by K.C. Causer

Volume One
-Revised-

Note from the author,

If you have taken the time to read the initial release of my series, I'd like to thank you for your support and feedback on my first published work. I have opted to revise and redo the first three volumes of my series, and as such, some details have been changed.

Some character names are different, and some events have changed from the initial release. Book one has been completely rewritten. Hopefully this improves the overall experience while causing minimal confusion.

If this is your first time picking up one of my books in this series, then welcome, and I hope you enjoy the story and world that I've crafted for you. It's improved and grown thanks to feedback from readers like yourself, so please share your opinions if you feel inclined to do so. Criticism is the greatest tool an artist has to better themselves and their work.

~K.C. Causer~

Pretty Little Psycho is purely a work of fiction. Names and characters are products of the author's imagination and used solely in a fictitious manner and are in no way representative of similar real world counterparts. While businesses, places, brand names and events may mirror those of real life, this is merely done to add realism and familiarity to the story, and is in no way, shape or form meant to insult, undermine, make light of or present unfavorably any business, places, brand names or events represented within the story.

Copyright © 2021 by K.C. Causer
Cover illustration and original artwork by Christine Anne Morrill
Book production by Kindle Direct Publishing, kdp.amazon.com

Prologue

可愛いサイコちゃん

Standing in the bathroom of a small apartment in Shinjuku, Tokyo, a young girl with long, light brunette hair had just finished brushing her teeth after having enjoyed a peaceful dinner with her family. Her name was Makai Akira, named after her great grandfather, and only eight years old. After rinsing her mouth, she stored her toothbrush away in a colorful plastic cup, then made her way out of the bathroom, down the hallway towards the bedroom she shared with her older brother.

At thirteen, most would believe Shojiro would have little in common with his younger sibling, though the two were so close to one another that they naturally shared many hobbies. Shojiro, for example, loved baseball, and he shared that passion with Akira. The two of them would often play ball together, with Shojiro throwing pitches for his little sister to try and hit. On the other hand, Akira loved listening to music, frequently shared new tunes she'd hear on the radio with her brother, and even attempted to sing along with some of her favorites.

Laying on his futon bed, Shojiro was reading a manga that one of his friends from school had loaned to him and threw only a glance over to Akira as she entered the bedroom. She fished out a hairbrush from one of the plastic totes, then began brushing her hair. Shojiro watched her for only a moment before going back to reading his manga, for at least a few more panels, until he reached a good stopping point. Closing the book, he set it aside, then leaned up in his bed.

"Mom said for us to take the trash down before we head to bed," Shojiro said to his sister.

Akira looked to her brother and offered a cheerful smile. "Okay!"

Standing up from his bed, Shojiro walked over to the door, slid it open, then waited while Akira finished with her hair. She then raced over and passed him as she proceeded down the hallway, her brother following close behind, expressing far less excitement in their chores than she did. As they continued into the apartment's main room, which served as the kitchen, dining room, and tatami room all in one, they approached their mother, Ryoko, as she stood in the kitchen, washing the dishes from dinner.

Ryoko looked to her children as they approached her. She then gestured towards four tightly sealed bags of various organized trash. "Akira, Shojiro, could you take those bags down to the disposal area?"

Akira cheerfully nodded. "Sure!"

"Yeah, no problem," Shojiro unenthusiastically responded as he went to get the larger two bags, leaving the smaller ones for his sister.

Sitting at the table, reading his newspaper, their father, Demura, looked to his children as they began carrying the trash out. "Shojiro," he said, his deep voice capturing his son's attention. Demura then reached into his pocket and sat three hundred yen down on the table. "Get something for you and your sister."

Seeing the money, Shojiro set one bag down, then grabbed the cash, shoving it into the pocket of his shorts. "Thanks, Dad," he said before picking the bag back up, then moving to meet his sister at the front door.

Opening the door, Akira let her brother leave first, then followed behind him as she carried her two relatively light bags. Approaching the stairs, they each descended from the fourth floor to the ground level, where the disposal area was located.

Along the way, Shojiro could just barely hear two men talking to one another further down. Proceeding past the third floor, they crossed paths with the men Shojiro had overheard, who had since silenced themselves as they ascended the stairs, moving past the children. The man in front wore a sharp black suit, with medium-length black hair that was slicked back. While he appeared professional, there was a dangerous aura about him. His colleague who trailed behind him dressed similarly, only with his coat unbuttoned and no shirt underneath, which revealed a portion of the red and black dragon inked across his chest.

Shojiro stared briefly at the men as they passed by one another. Narrowing his eyes onto them suspiciously, he continued down to the second floor.

Akira to the men as they passed by, offering a smile as she followed her brother. "Hello," she politely said, though neither man gave her more than a glance as they ascended to the third floor.

Continuing further down, Shojiro sighed. "You shouldn't just greet everyone you see, Aki," he warned his sister, shaking his head afterward. "Those guys were yakuza. It's better just to avoid them."

She frowned as they reached the first floor. "Do they work with Dad?" she curiously asked.

Hanging a right at the bottom of the stairs, Shojiro opened a door that led to the outside alley, holding it for his sister. "Probably."

After stepping out, Akira carried her two bags over to a small alcove where other trash bags were sorted into old worn-out plastic bins. She sat her bags down in their designated containers, then looked to her brother, who casually tossed his into whichever ones he wanted, paying no attention to how they were labeled. He then moved to a nearby vending machine, fishing the money from his pocket as he approached it.

"You want a snack, Aki?" he asked as he looked over their options.

She excitedly ran to her brother's side. "Do they have fruit chews?" she asked before seeing a bag of chewy, kiwi-flavored candy. She gasped. "I want that one!" she said, pointing to the package on the other side of the glass.

Inserting the money into the machine, Shojiro picked out the fruit snack for his sister, then chose a candy bar for himself. After it deposited each of the snacks, Shojiro got them out and handed the package of fruit chews to his sister, which she gleefully took and wasted no time in opening. Shojiro couldn't help but smile at how happy this made her. Walking back over to the apartment building door, he opened it and beckoned her through it. Despite the late hours, the area was well illuminated by the street lights, but all the same, Shojiro didn't fancy them staying out here too long, as they didn't live in the best of neighborhoods.

Shojiro tore open his candy bar, then bit off a large chunk of it as they ascended the stairs. Akira hopped up every other step as she chewed up her candy, piece by piece, nullifying the efforts she put in earlier to brush her teeth. As they reached the fourth floor, they heard arguing coming from inside of their apartment. Though they hadn't spoken a word on the stairs, Shojiro knew that the unfamiliar voices were those of the men they passed earlier.

Shojiro reached out and took Akira by her arm, preventing her from going into the apartment. "Let's wait out here. It sounds like Dad's talking business with those guys we saw before."

Akira glanced back at him, still chewing up her candy. She nodded, then moved away, over towards the end of the hall, a short distance from the stairs, where she could look out of a window at the neon-lit streets.

Her brother stayed nearby, vaguely listening in on the conversation between those men and his father inside the apartment. One line stood out to him more distinctly than the others.

"I have betrayed no one!" Demura shouted. "A claim that you, for one, cannot make, Miyazaki."

Shojiro felt his shoulders tense up as he heard his father's angry voice. Whoever he was speaking to, this Miyazaki individual, their voice was more tempered and in control than Demura's, which almost felt desperate in comparison.

"Oh... that's so cool," Akira said as she saw a newly illuminated neon sign on a tall building several streets over. "Shiro, look!" she said to her brother as she held her hands onto the glass, leaning into it.

Shojiro looked at Akira, not wanting to ignore her but also wanting to listen to whatever was going on between his father and these men. His attention, however, was soon abruptly torn away from his sister as a loud gunshot echoed out from their apartment. His eyes shot back towards the door to their home, his heart stalling as his mind registered just what he had heard. Another shot followed the first, with a subsequent one right after.

The gunshots caused Akira to flinch as she held her hands close to her chest, crouching by the window. She looked to her brother. "Sh-Shiro... what was that?!"

As the realization of the situation began to set in, Shojiro felt his heart begin to race. He turned to his sister, then darted towards her, grabbed her hand, and forced her to follow as he pulled her towards the stairs. Akira followed her brother, being offered no other choice but to comply, as moments later, two more gunshots echoed out, now muffled by the floor that separated them. Descending another flight of stairs, they heard a door upstairs open. By the time they hastily reached the first floor, heavy footsteps thrummed out from the stairs above them.

Shojiro guided his sister over and through the door to where they had taken the trash. Just to their right were a series of vending machines, one of which they used moments ago. Shojiro led Akira over to the machines, pushing her behind the last one and up against the wall. He hid behind them as well, leaned up against it as he cautiously peeked around the corner.

Covering her mouth to keep herself quiet, Akira could feel her heart pounding in her chest as her mind raced to make sense of what was happening. Off in the distance, she could hear police sirens sounding off, likely responding to reports of gunfire. As the two of them huddled behind the machine, with Shojiro keeping watch, they each heard a set of doors open. He instinctively went to duck behind cover, though paused as he realized the men must have left out of the front doors of the complex. Moments later, they could hear an engine start, followed by a vehicle pulling away from the front of the building.

After staying hidden for a few moments longer, Shojiro cautiously stepped out from behind the machine but felt Akira lunge forward and grab his hand. She was still terrified, as was he, though he knew it was up to him to be brave. Cautiously, he led her back into the building, which seemed quiet enough. They then ascended the stairs, eager to check on their parents, who they hoped were safe.

Once they reached the fourth floor, Shojiro motioned for Akira to wait by the stairs while he checked the apartment. She did as he said, reluctantly so, as he approached and opened the door to the apartment. Stepping inside, he gasped as he saw both his mother and father lying on the floor, blood staining their chests and pooling beneath them. His breathing became staggered as he realized that those two men, the ones they had passed on the stairs, had just shot and killed their parents.

"M-Mom?! Dad?!" Akira said as she had moved into the apartment behind her brother. She rushed past him as she ran to her mother's side.

"A-Aki, no! Wait!" Shojiro said, moving to catch his sister, stopping her less than a meter away from their parents' lifeless bodies.

Her lip quivering, she shook her head as tears began to flood her eyes. She then felt as her brother forced her to face him, then held her in his arms, holding her head against his chest, preventing her from looking at what happened to their parents. She could barely wrap her mind around it. Her parents, each of whom she loved dearly, had been murdered by those men, the ones she so cheerfully greeted as they took the trash out. Now, she was all alone, with the sole exception of her brother, who did his best to try and console her after their horrific, mutual loss.

Chapter 1
Miserable Nirasaki

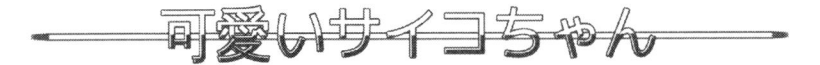

可愛いサイコちゃん

In the eight years since the incident that claimed the lives of her parents, Akira's life had changed in many ways; none of them positive. Every so often, she'd wake in a cold sweat, tears rolling from her eyes, as she relived vivid nightmares of that night. Horrible, reoccurring dreams that were, this morning at least, interrupted by an inappropriately upbeat yet irritating jingle that rang out from her cellphone.

With her head buried in her pillow, she groaned into it, then turned and gave a death-stare to her phone that sat atop her desk next to the old computer she occasionally used for schoolwork. Staring at the phone did little to silence its incessant tone, so Akira was left with no choice but to push her covers aside, then crawl over to her desk, where she reached up and haphazardly grabbed her phone. Squeezing the buttons on the sides, she silenced it, and for at least a moment, she felt a mild relief wash over her.

However, this alarm wasn't for naught, as this was the first day of her start in high school. Using her desk for support, Akira stood up and let out a deep, drawn-out yawn as she stretched her arms out to her sides and over above her head. Leaning over the chair of her desk, she opened the curtains to her window and saw that it was a beautiful day outside, though the bright sunlight stung her eyes as she squinted to see beyond the street outside of her house.

Moving away from her desk and window, Akira approached the antique oak dresser on the other side of her room, just beneath one of the many band posters she had hanging on the wall, and opened the top drawer. She then pulled out a pair of socks and underwear, then moved to another drawer to fetch the shirt and skirt that made up her uniform for school. She slid open the door to her bedroom with her clothes in hand and proceeded out into the hallway.

Making her way down the stairs and into the first-floor hall, she could smell that her grandmother was already cooking breakfast. She could also hear from the open door into their tatami room that her grandfather was up and watching something on the television. Akira turned down the hallway opposite the kitchen and stepped into the small bathroom, closing the door behind her. Setting her clothes aside, she tossed her pajamas off and into a small laundry bin before moving to the other section of the bathroom, where the shower and tub were.

After adjusting the water to her liking, she sat down on a small plastic stool and began to clean herself up, wasting no time relaxing or enjoying her time under the soothing water. Once she finished rinsing herself, she quickly dried off and hastily got dressed, donning her school uniform, a traditional white and blue sailor-inspired top, along with a medium-length navy blue skirt. Once fully dressed, she left the bathroom, her hair still damp from her shower.

As she made her way down the hallway to the kitchen, her grandfather, Watari Ryoma, glanced towards her as she walked by the open door to the tatami room, giving her a stern look, although he said nothing. Akira, on the other hand, didn't give her grandfather any acknowledgment as she continued to the kitchen, where she saw her grandmother, Watari Satomi, who was pouring herself a cup of freshly brewed tea. Akira threw her the briefest of smiles, then moved to the refrigerator.

Noticing her, Satomi smiled. "Good morning, sweetheart. Excited for your first day at a new school?" she asked in a loving tone.

Akira glanced over towards her grandmother, trying her best to hide her lack of enthusiasm. "I guess..."

"I'm sure your nervous. But don't worry. I hear there are quite a few more students at this school as opposed to your old one. So I'm sure that'll make it easier for you to make some new friends."

She rolled her eyes. *It's the only high school in the area, so, of course, there'll be more students... but that means it'll just be more of the same,* she thought before faking a smile at her grandmother's attempt to cheer her up.

Opening the door to the refrigerator, Akira pulled out the small bento box that she made the night before. Typically, she'd make her lunch for school from the previous night's leftovers, rather than anything fresh, as her mornings before school were seldom long enough to prepare anything to eat. Closing the door, she carried her bento box over to the small entryway near the front door, where she'd always remove her shoes before coming inside. Hanging on a nearby hook was her backpack, which she had already prepared for today's classes.

Akira unzipped her backpack enough to squeeze the bento box inside, then sealed it back before throwing the strap over her shoulder. Slipping her outdoor shoes on, she peeked back into the kitchen and threw Satomi a brief wave goodbye before heading out the door on her way to school.

"Have a good first day," Satomi said just before Akira shut the door.

Making her way along the stone walkway, Akira passed through the open gate of the chest-high concrete fence that bordered her house. They lived down a short, narrow street, barely wide enough for even one vehicle to drive through, in a neighborhood that would likely make anyone unfamiliar with the area uneasy. Aside from the claustrophobic street, there were also several old buildings nearby, of which not all were occupied. Near the end of her street, there was even a low-end apartment complex, a place where Akira often saw shady people loitering about, typically conversing over drinks, while throwing uncomfortable glances her way as she walked by.

Just passed the apartments, Akira followed alongside the old drainage canal that flowed through much of Nirasaki. It served to prevent flooding, as heavy rainfall would fill the canal and direct the water outside of the city. For Akira, all she knew was that between storms, the water from the canal reeked, and she could smell it, even just walking alongside it. She didn't travel very far before coming to one of the many bridges that crossed over the canal.

Just across the bridge, she couldn't help but notice the construction site that had been set up. It was right where an old music shop used to be, one where she'd been on more than one occasion to do little more than browse around, as she rarely had the means to purchase anything. The shop had been out of business for at least a year or more now. And judging by the chainlink fence that bordered the property, covered by a dark blue plastic tarp, they were completely rebuilding for whatever was to come next.

Continuing along the path parallel to the canal, the remainder of Akira's trip to school had far less to draw her interest. That was until she began walking alongside the large brick perimeter fence that bordered her school. As she moved around to the front of the building, she couldn't help but notice what appeared to be a shortcut of sorts. It was a secluded path that cut between the businesses and nearby buildings in front of the school and the brick fence she'd been walking alongside. It was shaded by the canopy of trees that hung over the fence, and there was just something calm and inviting about it.

A few other students were already walking along the path, so Akira took this moment to enjoy what appeared to be a soothing, relaxing moment before the misery that awaited her within the school's walls. Walking along, she stared at the canopy of trees above her, bathed in the rays of light that fell through the gaps between the leaves. She scarcely even noticed when she walked right into another student. As Akira bumped into her, she staggered forward slightly as the other girl stumbled off to the side. They each avoided falling, though that didn't lessen Akira's embarrassment after she just blindly walked into someone.

Turning to face the girl, Akira immediately bowed her head. "I'm sorry! I wasn't paying attention to where I was going," she politely said.

The other girl stared briefly at Akira before smiling and shaking her head. "I-I'm sorry too. I guess I shouldn't just stand around in the middle of a walkway while I'm on my phone?" she admitted, giggling afterward.

Akira raised her head and smiled at the girl. Though, that was when she noticed the unique blonde hair of the other girl. Something highly unusual for a student here in Japan. "Um... I like your hair."

Blushing, she awkwardly laughed. "Oh! Th-thank you."

Feeling as if she might have blurted out something weird, especially to someone she had just met, Akira fell a half step back as she inhaled sharply. "I, uh... gotta go!" she said, turning and hastily making her way off towards the main entrance. She felt so embarrassed for just randomly complimenting a girl after rudely bumping into her. It just made her curse herself under her breath for being so socially awkward all the time.

Once she arrived at the school's main entrance, Akira swung her backpack around enough that she could open up the side pouch and retrieve a folded piece of paper. On it was her class schedule, the numbers for both her shoe locker here in the main hall and the locker she'd use in gym class later today. Moving to her designated shoe locker, she stepped out of her street shoes and placed them inside. She then shuffled through her backpack until she found her old, worn-out pair of indoor shoes. Slipping them on, she began making her way towards what would be her first class of the day.

This was a strange change of pace, as at her previous school, all of her classes took place within the same classroom. But here, at Nirasaki High School, not all students had an identical class schedule, and they would move in between classrooms, each one designated for a different subject. It was an interesting change of pace and one that she hoped would alleviate some of the issues she had at her previous school with some of her fellow students, and in some cases, her teachers.

Making her way down the hall, Akira spotted the classroom she was looking for. Inside, she noticed several students in their seats, already waiting for the class to begin. Some were socializing amongst themselves, while others sorted through their school supplies, likely to ensure they had everything ready before class began. Seeing as she had arrived somewhat early, Akira secured herself a seat a few rows from the back, next to the window, which gave her an excellent view of the schoolyard outside.

Slipping her backpack off, Akira hung it by the top handle strap on a small hook on the side of her desk. Sitting down, she opened up her bag and pulled out her math book, a notebook, and an old cassette player, which had a pair of earbuds wrapped tightly around it. She never was very good at math or school in general, so she'd often retreat into her music, which was her primary escape from reality and all the misery that came with it.

While she had grown up in Tokyo, Akira had spent the past eight years living here in the small city of Nirasaki, in the Yamanashi Prefecture. And though it might have only been a thirty-minute drive to Yamanashi's capital of Kofu and a mere three hours from the outskirts of Tokyo, Nirasaki was a pitifully small city that had very little in the way of entertainment, at least in her eyes.

Although she had very little need for any form of entertainment outside of her music, as the vast majority of her time was spent slaving away with chores at home. Once they finished classes for the day, most students had social clubs or study groups to go to or friends to hang out with, Akira didn't. She instead had to rush home every day and complete a long list of chores. Even when she'd get done early, her grandfather would often find her other tasks to complete unless she had homework.

As she unraveled her earbuds and got ready to listen to some music, she watched as the classroom steadily filled up. She even noticed the girl she bumped into earlier; an easy task given her unique hair color, as most other students had dark brunette or black hair. Akira herself was a light brunette, which was uncommon enough, though it still stood out far less than such light and beautiful blonde hair did. She couldn't help but wonder if this girl had bleached her hair. Using cosmetic hair dyes and bleaches wasn't generally accepted in school, so the only excuse Akira could imagine was that the girl's hair was natural. Although, she certainly didn't appear as if she were an international student, her strange hair color aside.

Despite her curiosity, Akira's focus was abruptly shifted away from the blonde-haired girl when she saw an all too familiar sight. Stepping into the classroom were two girls, one slightly taller than Akira, the other just a bit shorter. The tallest of the two had shoulder-length dark brunette hair, a strong athletic build, and was the source of much of Akira's anxiety when it came to school. Her name was Nakajima Kana, and alongside her was her best friend, Hachi Miyoko.

While Kana was committed to maintaining peak physical performance in school and reclaiming her position as president of the athletics club here in Nirasaki High School, Miyoko played the game of popularity among her fellow students. She had long, perfectly straight black hair, was smart, charismatic, and, as Akira had discovered, was adept at manipulating the opinions of her peers, which led to most at their junior high school hating Akira and going out of their way to ignore or avoid her.

To know that her very first class of the day was shared with her two least favorite people in Nirasaki truly destroyed any hope Akira had for change here at this new school. Fortunately, it appeared that both Kana and Miyoko had someone else on their mind. They stopped by a student who Akira didn't recognize, a girl with soft black hair, tied back in a ponytail.

She was rummaging through her bookbag for something when Myoko moved to stand in front of her desk. Meanwhile, Kana got the girl's attention by smacking her ponytail aside as she stood next to the desk.

Akira had yet to see Kana and Miyoko harass other students, and being that she didn't recognize this girl from her junior high school, she wondered how they knew her. All in all, it didn't matter, so long as they weren't causing Akira herself any trouble. It did pique her curiosity, though, unfortunately, she couldn't hear whatever Miyoko was saying to this new girl, as they were on the other side of the classroom and were keeping their voices low.

While Miyoko spoke, Kana stood nearby, intimidating as always. She took a glance around the classroom, and as she did so, her eyes locked with Akira's. Feeling her heart race, Akira broke eye contact and looked down at her math book, hoping that Kana would be too busy with this other girl to bother her, at least for now. There was no such luck as Kana stepped away from the desk, weaving in between the rows of other students as she approached the desk Akira had sat down at.

"Well, isn't this a pleasant surprise?" Kana said in a deceptively friendly tone as she moved to stand next to Akira's desk. "I'm genuinely surprised to see you here, Makai. After how things ended last semester, I figured you'd have dropped out of school."

Keeping her head low, Akira didn't acknowledge her.

Abruptly leaning down, Kana slammed her hand firmly on Akira's desk with a dull thud, causing it to rattle, though making little noise. "Hey. It's rude to ignore someone who's talking to you," she said.

The sound of her voice alone made Akira tremble, as all too many times it was accompanied by physical reminders of how little Kana cared for her. Swallowing nervously, she looked out of the corner of her eye at her.

Kana cracked a half-smile, though she heard the door to the classroom close as she went to speak. Pausing, she glanced back and saw the teacher walking towards the front of the classroom. Looking back to Akira, she scoffed. "I guess we'll talk later," she said before looking to the old cassette player on the desk. Swiping it up, Kana unplugged the cable from it and grinned widely at Akira. "Drop by and see me later, Makai. There's something I need from you," she said before turning and walking away.

Akira watched as she could do little to stop Kana from taking her cassette player from her. It was one of the few positive things Akira had to hang onto, and losing it would completely isolate her from listening to the music she'd grown to love over the years. Kana knew this and knew that Akira would have to meet up with her to get it back.

Walking across the classroom, Kana passed by Miyoko, prompting her to follow as the two took their seats just a few rows in front of the girl Miyoko had been talking to. Judging by the look she wore, that girl was irritated and possibly upset by what Miyoko had been saying. She didn't appear to be afraid or intimidated, as Akira was of those two, but it was clear that they were not friends.

While not the biggest fan of it, Akira managed to make it through her math class by keeping her head down and taking what little notes she could. Math was by far one of her weakest subjects in school, and her grades showed it. In her old school, they refused to fail any student from any class, as having students who flunked out of their classes would make the school look bad by comparison. As a result, Akira's abysmal grades never led to her removal from school, though that didn't prevent her grandfather from punishing her for her educational shortcomings.

Once class concluded, Akira put her books away while keeping a close eye on Kana and Miyoko. They neither one paid attention to the girl they had been pestering before, though Kana did look to Akira and hold her cassette player up as a reminder that she still had it. She grimaced at the thought of having to retrieve her device but knew it had to be done, lest Kana decides just to ditch it somewhere, or worse, break it. Kana and Miyoko then stepped out of the classroom and out into the hallway.

Standing up from her desk, Akira slung her backpack over her shoulder and weaved through the classroom to follow Kana out. As she did so, she couldn't help but look to the girl they'd been talking to before class began. She looked frustrated, and it didn't appear on her notebook like she took many notes at all during class. After packing her things up, she hastily made her way out of the classroom. It was disheartening to know someone else was having to deal with Kana and Miyoko being cruel to them, but it wasn't as if Akira was in any position to help others with a problem she'd yet to find a solution for.

As she left the classroom, Akira looked around for Kana but didn't see her anywhere. Occasionally, when she'd steal Akira's things, she wouldn't immediately return them. This appeared to be one of those times, so Akira would likely need to try and catch Kana later on in the day if she hoped to get her cassette player back.

Letting out a deep sigh, Akira shook her head. "I hate my life..." she said under her breath before she turned and began moving through the students who were walking down the hallway.

As she approached her next class, she crossed her fingers, hoping and praying that she didn't share yet another class with Kana, even if she did still need to get her cassette player back. If math was a subject she hated, then this next one was one she loathed, physical education. As she arrived at the large gym hall, she noticed quite a few students already here and doing their exercises.

However, the first thing on Akira's mind as she entered the gymnasium was looking over the entire room to ensure neither Kana nor any of her friends were in here. At a glance, everything appeared to be clear. Amongst the students, Akira did notice a man who looked to be the gym teacher if she were to make assumptions based on his age and physique.

As she began to approach him, he turned and looked at her. "Are you with the nine o'clock class?" he asked in a stern tone.

Akira nodded but otherwise kept quiet.

He pointed off towards the west wall of the gymnasium. "Go ahead and get changed, then I'll give you the outline for your exercise routine."

"Oh, um... okay," Akira responded as she turned to follow his directions.

Across the gym hall, Akira could see the entrance to what must have been the entrances to the locker rooms. On the wall near each of the two open entryways was a sign dictating which was the boys' or girls' locker room. As she entered the girl's side, it was a short walk down a three-meter long hallway before an abrupt turn led Akira into the first section of the locker room. Walking past other girls who were getting changed, Akira was relieved to not see Kana or any of her friends in here either.

Checking the piece of paper from her backpack once more, Akira found her locker number and matched it up with a locker on the wall furthest from the entrance. Approaching it, she noticed that a short distance to her left was a room that led into the showers. This at least meant that she wouldn't have to go very far to change clothes once she got out of the shower. Turning back to her locker, she opened it up and set her backpack down inside of it. Unzipping the main compartment, she pulled out a fresh, new set of gym clothes; a white t-shirt with navy blue trimming along the neck and sleeves and a pair of matching navy blue shorts.

Changing into her new clothes, Akira haphazardly tossed her school uniform down on top of her backpack and closed the locker door after grabbing her old pair of gym shoes. Just a short distance away was a conveniently placed bench. As she sat down to put her shoes on, she threw a few more glances around to make sure Kana truly wasn't in this class with her, and that was when she caught a glimpse of another girl she recognized, Abukara Hideko. It was somewhat of a surprise to see her in this class without Miyoko or Kana, being as they were such close friends, but Akira had a hunch as to why she was here.

Hideko, unlike her friends, wasn't quite as horrible towards Akira, though she was always a willing accomplice to the misery Miyoko and Kana inflicted upon Akira. Gym class alone with her likely wouldn't be that bad, and so Akira was relieved to see that Hideko would be the only girl from Kana's small circle that she'd have to deal with.

Once she had her shoes on, Akira hopped up and returned to the main hall of the gym. She then spotted the gym teacher speaking to three other students, one of whom Akira recognized as the blonde-haired girl that she bumped into on the secluded alleyway outside of school. As she approached, the gym teacher glanced over to her, then paused his conversation with the other students just long enough to hand a sheet of paper over to Akira. He said nothing to her as he did this and then promptly returned to answering the other students' questions.

It irritated Akira that he was so short with her right off the bat, saying barely anything when she first came into class and now shoving her off with a sheet of paper to tell her what to do. As upsetting as this was, it hardly felt unusual to her. Most of her teachers blindly taught their students at her old school, paying little attention to any of them and even ignoring issues in class, such as Kana tormenting her even while the teacher continued with the lecture. Stepping away, she looked down at the paper that he'd given her.

Examining it, she saw it outlined different exercises that she needed to accomplish. She also noticed that it had her teacher's name listed near the top of it, which was Masaru Tenchi. Skimming over the exercises, Akira could tell some of them would likely take place outside. With how hot the summers typically got, she felt that she'd prefer to stay inside with the air conditioning on most days. Though for now at least, there was still plenty of spring left before the heat became unbearable.

Making her way towards the northern side of the gymnasium, Akira pushed open one of the double doors and stepped onto the field outside.

It was a fairly wide-open area with a track field for students to run on, though it lacked much else. Her old school featured a pool, and several other nice amenities, though during gym Akira never had a chance to enjoy them, thanks to Kana.

Still, she found the weather today very favorable, with a cool breeze and even a bit of cloud coverage, which provided a blanket of shade for her while she ran. Stepping out onto the track, Akira started with a brisk walk before steadily pushing herself up to a light jog. She noticed that there were quite a few students outside already, so she was far from being the only one to decide on running as her first activity.

While she wasn't opposed to exercise, Akira had always found physical education to be a class she'd dread. At her old school, she had it every day and always with Kana and her friends. Much like most of her other teachers in junior high, her gym teacher saw Kana as a model student based on her grades and physical performance, which led her to turn a blind eye to anything Kana did to Akira. Although this was a fresh start, she feared that her new gym teacher would soon fall into that same old song and dance with these so-called perfect students.

"Hey, Akira!" a male student called out from behind her. Moving to run alongside her, he smiled cheerfully. "I didn't know I'd be sharing gym class with you," he said in a friendly tone.

Akira cringed upon hearing his voice. She didn't even need to look to see who it was, as she was all too familiar with the boy who called out to her. While she did her best to ignore him, she knew that would do little to deter him from pestering her. As he moved to run alongside her, her suspicions were confirmed. His presence in this class came as no surprise to Akira, as she'd already spotted his step-sister, Hideko, in the locker room.

His name was Kenichi Takashi, and despite his step-sister being a willing participant in Akira's misery, he went above and beyond to be kind towards her. His kindness, however, wasn't out of any genuine goodwill. Ever since he first laid eyes on her, Takashi has harbored an unhealthy obsession with her; love at first sight, he calls it. Even with the rumors and lies Kana and her friends spread around their school about Akira, Takashi always remained friendly towards her, as if he believed his toxic form of kindness would win her over.

Setting her sights straight ahead, she tried to avoid making eye contact with him. "C-could you just leave me alone, Takashi?"

Laughing briefly, he shook his head. "Come on. I'm just trying to say hello and see how you've been doing. How was your break from school?"

Exhaling sharply, she ignored his question.

"What's the matter? Did you not have a good break?" he asked as a frown slowly formed across his lips, though he almost instantly turned it around and smiled once more. "Oh! What if I take you out for some ice cream after school? Maybe that would brighten up your day?"

Akira gagged. "Ugh... no. Pass."

Takashi frowned at her response. "Aw... well, what about some coffee or something? You know, there's this one place at the mall I went to with my family, and they had some interesting flavor choices. Maybe you'd like to go there with me?"

Slowing down, Akira looked to Takashi, taking a moment to catch her breath. "Could you please just leave me alone?" she pleaded.

"I'm just trying to make you feel better. I mean, it's the first day at a brand new school! You should be excited!" he enthusiastically stated.

"There's hardly anything 'new' about this school... it's just more of the same," she mumbled under her breath.

Moving closer, he reached up and brushed his messy, black hair behind his ear. "Come on. It's the perfect chance to change things up. And what better way to start things off than with a nice guy like me?"

His words sent a cold shiver down her spine as if death itself were breathing down her neck. "N-no, thank you!"

"Don't you think it'd be nice, though? Having a man like me there for you?"

Akira went to speak, though she bit her tongue. Shaking her head, she walked away from Takashi as if to start her run once more, though she felt his hand on her shoulder. Turning to face him, she pulled herself from his grasp and took a few steps back. "P-please! Don't touch me," she said in a shaky tone.

Moving closer to her, he shrugged. "I'm not trying to be mean or anything, Akira. I'm just trying to..." he paused, taking a moment to think about what to say. "Oh, hold on... that's right! You're more of a tomboy, so you probably don't want to go out and get coffee or ice cream," he said as he smiled at her. "How about we do something different then? We could go bowling, or maybe even hit up the batting cages? What do you say?"

She ran her fingers through her hair, wanting to just scream her frustrations with him away. "I... I don't want to go anywhere with you."

Takashi crossed his arms, looking as if he wasn't convinced. "Why not? It's not like you're seeing anyone."

Tensing up, she glared, "Just because I'm not seeing anyone doesn't mean that I want to see you."

"Oh, come on... won't you at least go out with me just once?" he pleaded.

She grit her teeth. "No! I'm not interested in–"

Abruptly moving forward, he took her hands into his own. "Akira, I know you don't think I'm your type. But if you just give me a chance, I promise I'll make you the happiest that you've ever been."

As she felt his hands on hers, unease quickly filled her mind. Doing her best not to lose her composure and just scream, she took a deep breath. "L-let go of me, Takashi..." she said as she attempted to pull away from him.

"You're blushing."

"I'm not blushing!" she snapped.

"You look so cute when your cheeks turn all red like that..."

Closing her eyes, she growled under her breath. "Let go..."

"I'll let you go if you promise to let me take you out on a date."

She glared at him. "No! Let go because I said so!"

He sighed. "Every day at school, Kana and her friends always make you so miserable. All I want to do is make you smile. I really wish you'd lower your guard and give me a chance," he said before offering her a gentle, loving smile. "I know, if you let me, I'll make you the happiest girl in Nirasaki. I'll treat you like a perfect lady, and–"

Akira and Takashi each paused as they heard a sharp whistle from off towards the gymnasium. Looking that way, they noticed the gym teacher, Masaru, standing by the open doors. He pointed directly at Takashi, then beckoned him over.

Disappointed that they were interrupted, Takashi looked back at her. "You should text me after school, okay?"

Akira did her best to conceal the disgust she held towards him after what he said to her and offered no response to his request.

Takashi smiled at her and let out a brief chuckle as he shook his head. "You're always playing hard to get. Anyway, I'd better see what the teacher wants. Talk to you later, Akira."

Letting go of her, Takashi turned and began walking towards Masaru. Akira nervously rubbed her hands over her arms, shivering at the thought of him touching her like that. It wasn't even the first time that he grabbed hold of her against her will, far from it. Fortunately, it appeared as if Takashi was being scolded by Masaru, likely for grabbing onto her. Public displays of affection weren't allowed on school grounds, and while there was hardly any romance between them, at least from her eyes, him grabbing onto her like that surely crossed that line. Although, given that Masaru was scolding only Takashi, it made Akira wonder if someone had seen her in distress and called for help.

Looking around, she couldn't see any student who was watching her with any degree of concern, so she was likely just overthinking things. If that were the case, she'd probably be given a talking to by Masaru as well. Rather than waiting her turn, Akira returned to the track and continued her run. If anything, this kept her away from Takashi. For the time being, she'd have at least some respite from the man who was unreasonably obsessed with her.

Chapter 2
Signs of Friendship

可愛いサイコちゃん

After finishing her gym class with no further interference from Takashi, Akira quickly changed back into her school uniform and began making her way to the school's cafeteria. At her old school, since they were in the same classroom throughout the entire day, students would enjoy lunch together. The food would be prepared by home economic students or school staff, then brought to each classroom by volunteers. Akira herself would often volunteer so that she'd have time away from Kana and her friends. It was a tradition that was intended to teach students to be kind and caring towards others.

Here at Nirasaki High School, things were handled differently. With students changing classrooms throughout the day, they would instead meet up at a designated time to eat lunch together in a cafeteria. It was a common practice in other countries' school systems, and while it wasn't an entirely foreign concept, it was strikingly out of place in a more rural city, such as Nirasaki. That said, Akira welcomed the change, as it meant she didn't have to carry heavy pots of soup up a flight of stairs and could instead focus her energy on avoiding Kana, Miyoko, and the others who tormented her.

Making her way into the cafeteria, Akira was surprised by how many students were here and struggled to spot somewhere she could sit alone. However, as she searched, she saw someone familiar to her, though in a somewhat positive light. It was the girl she'd seen in her math class, the one with her hair tied back into a ponytail. She looked far less irritated than she was back when Kana and Miyoko were bugging her, which was a relief. She was sitting mostly alone, with at least two seats between herself and other nearby students. Throwing another glance around, Akira saw that most empty seats were nestled in between other students, and she didn't fancy sitting down right alongside someone she didn't know at all. At least with this one girl, they had some common ground.

Taking a deep breath, as if to compose herself or maintain some degree of confidence, Akira approached the girl. She tried to think of the best thing to say to start a friendly conversation. She wanted to ask permission to sit down next to her, but she wasn't sure if it was best to lead with that. As she drew closer, her time was running out to decide what she'd say. Moving around to the side opposite of her, Akira stopped at the chair across from the girl.

Noticing her standing around awkwardly, the girl looked to Akira. It appeared she had been preparing a beautifully designed bento box of her own, mixing a bit of rice with egg and adding some soy sauce over the top of it. Akira could also spot a few pieces of fried pork that was mixed in as well, which only served to make her eager to dig into her own lunch.

Realizing she had been awkwardly lingering in silence, Akira finally spoke up. "S-sorry, uh... would you mind if I sat here?" she quickly asked, gesturing to the seat across from the girl.

"Um... sure, I don't mind," she said, motioning to the chair herself.

Akira offered a brief bow of her head, then pulled it out and sat down, placing her backpack in the adjacent seat as she unzipped it and pulled her bento box out. Setting it in front of her, she smiled awkwardly at the girl, then bowed her head once again. "M-my name is Akira, by the way. But, you can just call me Aki if you'd like."

The girl smiled back at Akira, far more naturally than her new, nervous acquaintance had. "Asano Tomoe. It's nice to meet you, Aki."

Realizing she forgot her surname, Akira let out a nervous chuckle, though she kept her voice down to not further embarrass herself. "Sorry... it's Makai Akira, I meant..."

Tomoe cocked her head curiously at her. "Makai? I don't know that I've met anyone with that name before."

She offered a wide, toothy grin. "I, uh... I get that a lot, actually," she said, biting her lip. "So, I couldn't help but notice that you were in my math class."

Thinking briefly on it, Tomoe nodded. "Yeah, I think I saw you in class. I remember seeing your hair and how it stood out," she said, frowning. "I didn't know that this school allowed students to dye or style their hair, but you're the second girl I've seen with light-colored hair."

Akira playfully stuck her tongue out as she reached up and tugged at her hair. "It's not dyed. This is my hair's natural color."

"Really?" she gasped. "You're lucky. It's a really beautiful."

Blushing, Akira stammered as she tried to speak. "S-so, um... I kind of couldn't help but notice that in math class earlier, those two girls were talking to you. Um... Kana and Miyoko?"

Tomoe sighed, then nodded. "Yeah... they were."

"Do you know them?" Akira asked, trying to be cautious not to dump too many of her problems in Tomoe's lap.

She nodded again. "Hachi Miyoko lives in the same neighborhood as me. Or... I suppose I live in *her* neighborhood if you were to ask her. My mother and I just moved here to Nirasaki about a month-and-a-half ago, and since then, Miyoko's been... less than welcoming."

Akira resisted the urge to smile, as Tomoe's gentle description was all too accurate to what she already knew of Miyoko. "Y-yeah... I'm not surprised to hear that. She's... not very nice. And, if you're not careful, she'll go around spreading rumors about you to everyone else at school."

Tomoe frowned. "Did she do that to you?"

She lightly grimaced as she thought back to some of the horrible rumors that were spread about her. "Uh... well, yeah... at our old school."

"I'm sorry to hear that, Aki..." Tomoe responded.

Biting her lip, Akira sighed. "It's... okay," she said. Not wanting the conversation to go south so quickly, Akira's mind raced to think of what to talk about instead. "S-so, you, um... said you moved here a while back? Where did you move from?"

Tomoe appeared hesitant to answer that; as if where she came from was to blame for Miyoko's harassment.

She grimaced. "U-uh... you don't have to tell me if you don't want to. Not judging, of course. I mean... I moved here from Tokyo, so I'm not from the area either, ya know?" she quickly explained, panicking over the fear that she might have touched on a topic she shouldn't have.

"You're from Tokyo?" Tomoe asked.

Akira nodded. "I grew up in Shinjuku. But, I moved here when my–" she began to say before stopping herself. "Um... I moved here to live with my grandparents when I was eight. What about you?"

Feeling more at ease, she offered a shy but proud smile. "I'm from

Fukuoka. It's really far away from here, but... I moved here with my mom, and, well..." her smile began to fade, "my dad stayed back in Fukuoka."

Akira frowned. "Your parents aren't together anymore?"

Tomoe lowered her head.

Realizing she had again clumsily asked a question she shouldn't have, Akira reached up and held her hand against her face in embarrassment. "I'm so sorry! I shouldn't have asked," she responded, though it didn't seem to help Tomoe's mood. Her mind raced to think of what she could say to alleviate the awkwardness she had created. "If... if it makes you feel any better, my family's kind of... well, 'fractured' too."

Looking to her, Tomoe stared briefly, though she didn't respond.

Akira bit nervously at her lip. "So, um... you don't have to feel like you're alone. I know it's not the same as your parents splitting up, but... I sort of know how you feel..." she said before an awkward silence began to fill the air between them. "So, um... is that why Miyoko was harassing you?"

"Y-yeah. When I first met her, she seemed nice... but then she somehow figured all of this out on her own... I guess secrets don't really stay secrets in a town this size, huh?" she asked as she let out a disheartened chuckle. She sighed. "In class, she was telling me that no one would like me, because I'm not from around here, or... because my dad left my mom and me."

Akira couldn't genuinely say she was surprised by Tomoe's words. If anything, she was amazed that Miyoko wasted so little time before jumping to something that cut so deep. Though, from her own experience, she knew it'd only get worse for Tomoe from here.

"That's... really cruel of her to say something like that..." Akira admitted.

Tomoe sighed. "It may have been mean... but that doesn't mean it's true," she said, forming a smile across her lips.

"What do you mean?" Akira curiously asked.

With a playful giggle, Tomoe's smile brightened. "Even though she said no one would want to be my friend if they knew those things, you're still being nice to me, even though you know about them," she said before offering a firm nod. "So, she can say what she wants, but that doesn't make it true."

Akira frowned. "Well... I mean, she's trying to bring up things about you that others would shun you for..."

She scoffed. "She's making a lot of assumptions. I'm not worried," she said before leaning in closer. "Say, Aki, would you want to be my friend?"

Akira recoiled in slight shock. "Wh-what? Really?"

Tomoe nodded. "Sure! You're the first person who's sat down and talked to me here at school, and you're nice, so... why not?"

A glimmer of hope filled Akira's heart briefly as she considered Tomoe's lighthearted offer, one that held so much more weight in Akira's eyes. As she contemplated it, though, she began to fear the rejection she'd soon experience if Tomoe heard some of the many nasty rumors Miyoko spread around her old school, of whose many students were now here at her high school.

Swallowing nervously, Akira lowered her head. "I... I don't know..."

Tomoe paused, a frown beginning to form across her lips before she shook it away. "Why not? I bet we have a lot in common. You know, aside from us each moving here from a big city. What kind of hobbies do you have? Do you like to watch television? Listen to music? Oh! Maybe you like video games?"

She felt overwhelmed by all of Tomoe's questions, almost to the point that she began to sweat as her face went flush. "I, um... well, I like music."

Tomoe cheerfully clapped her hands together. "Me too! What kind do you like?"

She's so full of energy, Akira thought to herself before sighing. "The music I like is... well, a lot of alternative rock and metal. Some pop is okay, I suppose. Anything with a catchy beat."

Tomoe rested her elbows on the edge of the table, just in front of her bento box. "What are some of your favorite bands?"

Akira blushed. "I... don't know if you'd know them, to be honest..."

Tomoe pursed her lips. "Why do you say that? My friends back in Fukuoka listened to a lot of different genres of music."

"Well... because I mostly listen to foreign bands," she explained.

"Foreign bands? So, the music is in other languages?"

Akira nodded. "Yeah... mostly in English. See, a friend of mine back in junior high school used to listen to American rock music a lot, a bit of metal too... and, when she saw I was struggling in our English class, she helped me learn by having us listen to the music and sing along. Honestly, it helped a lot in learning the language... not that I ever really use it..."

Tomoe's face lit up. "That's really cool, Aki! I think that sounds like such a fun way to learn another language," she said, shrugging her shoulders. "I lucked out in my English class since my mother works as an English and Japanese translator. So, she tutored me on everything I needed to know," she admitted with a playful laugh. "But I don't really ever use it either. We had a few foreigners visiting back in Fukuoka, but I only ever talked to one once. He needed directions, so I helped him out."

She smiled. "That was really kind of you," she said before letting out a subtle sigh. "You're... so nice, Tomoe..."

"Thank you. I try to be nice to everyone. When I was growing up, my mom always said, 'never judge others because you can't just assume the circumstances of their life.' Which I think is great advice," Tomoe said with a playful giggle.

Hearing those words eased Akira's fears she held before, fears of what might happen if someday Kana or Miyoko were to try and destroy whatever friendship may form between Akira and Tomoe. As a reluctant smile formed across her lips, Akira leaned forward. "You know what?"

"Hm?" Tomoe responded, cheerfully listening to whatever Akira had to share with her.

Taking a deep breath, Akira exhaled off to the side sharply, then looked to Tomoe with determination in her eyes. "You're right! We do have a lot in common, and... I think we should be friends too."

Her smile grew as she giggled. "Thank you, Aki. I know we'll be the best of friends. So long as we stick together," she said with an affirmative nod.

Akira smiled back at her new friend. "We'll stick together, no matter what. And... regardless of whatever rumors or lies Miyoko tries to spread about either of us, we'll only ever trust one another's word. Right?" she asked, trying her best to preemptively discredit Miyoko's lies, as she knew some of the horrible things said about her would resurface from those who hated her from Nirasakinishi.

Tomoe offered a firm nod. "Absolutely!" she said before looking down at her bento box. "Oh, but we should probably start eating before we run out of time," she said, picking her chopsticks up. Looking at Akira's bento box, she gestured towards it. "You haven't even started getting your's ready."

"Um... w-well... now mine will still be nice and hot, while your's is all cold," she responded in a teasing tone.

Tomoe puffed up her cheeks, feigning irritation. "I bet that was your plan all along," she responded as she began mixing up her rice, pork, and egg. "So, since you've lived here longer than me but also aren't originally from this area, I was just curious. Do you like it here?"

She scoffed as she popped the top off her bento box. "No... not really," she said as she stuck her finger in her food, reminding herself that it was always cold since she stored it in the refrigerator at home.

"Why's that?" Tomoe asked after having taken her first bite.

Akira shrugged her shoulders as she stirred her food around. "Mostly because I haven't had many good friends here... well, up until now," she said, smiling once again at Tomoe.

She smiled back before taking another bite of her food.

Sighing, Akira gathered up some food with her chopsticks. "That and... honestly, Miyoko has been bullying me a lot too... her and Kana both," she admitted before taking a bite of the cold teriyaki chicken she had.

Tomoe frowned. "Has she been picking on you because you're not from here either? Or, was there another reason?" she asked before pausing. "Oh, sorry... maybe I shouldn't be asking?"

Akira swallowed her food nervously. "It's, um... because they think I'm weird. I... guess I just don't fit in with what they expect," she said, feeling almost as if she were sweating as the subject even came up.

Seeing how bothered Akira was, Tomoe shook her head. "Don't let it upset you. There's that old, stupid adage of, 'the nail that sticks out, gets hammered down,' but in my opinion, that's just not the way to think nowadays, you know?" she said before dawning the same cheerful smile as before. "Think about popular musicians. They're famous because they stand out; because they're unique. If you're different, then... I know it might be tough, but you should embrace that, you know?"

Akira looked to Tomoe, once more shocked by her words. There had been a select few who had accepted her for the unique person she was, but none of them were in her life anymore. Staring at her new friend, she pushed back the urge to cry simply because she was so relieved to hear someone talk like that to her. "Th-thank you... it means so much to hear you say that," she responded.

"You deserve to hear it. Because it's the truth," she said before gesturing once more towards her friend's food. "Keep eating. You've barely even taken one bite of your food."

Sitting here, talking to Tomoe, while it may have just been for a moment, felt to Akira like the most phenomenal experience of the past few years. Even looking back, those she held most dear to her didn't even speak to her the way her new friend did. Tomoe's words stood out in ways Akira never imagined, and for the first time in years, she felt as if this new friendship that was forming would be one that was genuine and would stand the test of time. While Kana and Takashi reminded Akira that nothing had changed since Nirasakinishi, Tomoe proved that soon enough, Akira's life would undergo many wonderful changes.

Akira and Tomoe continued their idle conversation as they finished their lunches, shifting from topic to topic; such as television shows and movies they enjoyed. Soon enough, they took the last bites of their meals and cleaned their bento boxes up, returning them to their book bag and backpack, respectively. With only a few minutes remaining before going to their next classes, the girls said their goodbyes and parted ways, each visibly upbeat and cheerful over the time they had spent together.

The rest of Akira's day was admittedly rather pleasant compared to how it originally started. She spent much of her time in class thinking about her new friend, wondering what she could have done in life to deserve the attention of such a kindhearted person like Tomoe. Nearing the end of the day, Akira was walking towards the main entrance, somewhat pleased that she had such a great second half of her day, primarily thanks to Tomoe spending time with her during lunch.

As she approached the main entrance to the school, she eagerly looked around in hopes of finding her new friend, if only so they could talk a bit more before they parted ways as they each head home for the day. While she didn't spot Tomoe anywhere, she did see Kana, Miyoko, and Hideko standing together near the exit, casually talking with one another. Akira was promptly reminded that, while she may have been distracted by the blissful thoughts of Tomoe, Kana still had her cassette player, Akira's only real form of entertainment.

Reluctantly, Akira made her way over to the three of them, none of whom even threw a glance her way. Meekly standing nearby, she waited for a moment as the girls talked about their classes, even mocking a student in one of them and laughing over his misfortune. Akira timidly spoke up, though she didn't even get a full word past her lips before the three turned their attention to her, effectively silencing Akira of whatever she intended to say.

"What do you want, Makai?" Kana asked.

Swallowing nervously, Akira struggled to look Kana in the eyes as she held her head low. "Um... y-you still have my... my cassette player..."

Taking a step closer to her, Kana placed her hand against Akira's shoulder and shoved her a short distance back. "I'm up here, Makai. Stop staring at the floor and speak up!" she demanded.

Feeling her heart race, Akira took a deep breath and spoke again. "Can...

can I have my cassette player back... please, Kana?" she timidly asked.

"Your what?" Kana asked, raising her eyebrow. She lightly gasped. "Oh! That..." she said before looking to Miyoko, who pulled it from her bag. Kana took it from her friend and turned back to Akira. "You've got a class schedule, don't you?"

"Wh-what? Um... y-yeah, I do..." Akira reluctantly answered.

Kana held her empty hand out. "Hand it over."

Staring at Kana, she was hesitant to just give her schedule over. "But... it's my only one. I-I haven't made a copy of it yet, or anything..."

Exhaling sharply, Kana let go of Akira's cassette player, allowing it to fall onto the hard tile floor of the entryway. As it hit, it made a loud, snapping crack.

Akira gasped as she saw her cassette player fall, with the tape bay ejecting open and popping one of her mixed tapes out just enough that it could be easily removed. She quickly kneeled to pick it up, though Kana prevented this when she placed her foot on top of it and pushed down with enough force that Akira could hear the crack and crunch of plastic against the floor. She grimaced as she watched her cassette player steadily getting crushed underfoot.

"Your schedule... if I have to ask again, I'll just take your whole bag," Kana said.

Quickly pulling back, Akira took her backpack off, rummaged through it, and presented her schedule to Kana the moment she found it. Holding the paper out to her, Akira kept pleading in her mind for Kana not to break her cassette player.

Swiping the paper out of Akira's hand, Kana examined it to ensure it was what she wanted, then raised her foot off the device as she turned to her friends, waving the paper around victoriously.

Reaching out, Akira retrieved her cassette player, examining the damage that might have been done to it from the fall, alongside the weight pressed against it.

Kana glanced back at her. "Thanks, Makai. With this, we'll know just when we can hang out with you. It'll be just like old times. Now... you'd better run home. It'd be a shame if you fell behind on your chores," she teased before walking away with her friends as they left the school.

Standing up, Akira felt utterly defeated, though, at the very least, the only damage to her cassette player was a crack to the shell of it and a few minor scuffs. The tape itself wasn't as fortunate. The weight of Kana's foot against the device's door had pressed the thin plastic too hard and crushed it, preventing it from ever being usable again. With a deep sigh, Akira turned and walked over to her shoe locker to change into her outdoor shoes.

"Aki?" Tomoe called out in a gentle voice as she approached.

Akira nearly jumped at the sound of her friend's voice. She looked to her as she drew closer from the interior of the school. With a sigh, Akira relaxed her posture and pulled her backpack in front of her so she could put her cassette player away.

Tomoe stopped just out of arms reach as she watched her friend stuff a visibly damaged cassette player into her backpack. She frowned. "I'm sorry, I should have done something..." she admitted.

Akira shook her head. "It's... there's nothing you could have done," she began to say, having been made all too familiar to the feeling of everyone standing around watching her, yet no one ever intervening to help. Taking her indoor shoes off, Akira swapped them for her street shoes, then threw her backpack over her shoulder. "I'll see you tomorrow, Tomoe..."

Watching as Akira began to leave, Tomoe reached into a side pouch on her book bag and searched around. Finding a piece of paper and a pencil, she held the paper up against the nearby wall and hastily wrote something down. Putting the pencil away, she ran to catch Akira before she could leave the school itself.

"Hey, Aki!" Tomoe called out. As Akira turned to her, she held out the piece of paper. "If you have time later, you can text or call me if you'd like."

Staring blankly at her, Akira's eyes trailed down to the note, seeing a phone number scrawled out on it. She took it Reluctantly, seeing Tomoe also wrote her name on it, which gave Akira the proper kanji spelling of it. "I, um..." she began to say before looking back to her friend. "Thank you."

Tomoe nodded. "See you tomorrow, Aki," she said before returning to the shoe lockers so she could change her shoes out as well.

Watching her leave, Akira looked down at the note once more, then began to leave the school. As she stepped outside and made her way down the secluded alleyway, she couldn't help but stop and hold the note Tomoe gave her up to her chest as she hugged onto it. Her new friend gave her a phone number, so now they could talk outside of school as well. Akira practically squealed in excitement before folding the note up and stuffing it into the side pouch on her backpack before rushing home.

Akira raced down the pathway alongside the wall that bordered the school itself, then made her way out onto a small road, staying close to the edge as a few cars passed by. As she took a left, just before the small bridge that crossed over the drainage canal, Akira ran her hand across the railing while allowing her mind to wander. She continued to follow the canal into Fujimi, the neighborhood where she lived. As she did so, she tried her best to remain calm and pay more attention to her surroundings.

As she passed by a few people on the street, she kept her wits about her and her head down, to avoid attention, as her neighborhood wasn't exactly the safest in Nirasaki. Walking by the low-end apartment buildings near her house, she noticed the usual guys sitting outside, drinking beers and talking amongst themselves. They stared at her and even whistled as she passed by, though she avoided making any eye contact with them.

Arriving at her grandparent's house, Akira reached over and unlocked the small gate to the fence and let herself in. After reaching the front door, she stepped inside. Kicking her shoes off at the entryway, then making her way into the kitchen. She noticed her grandmother was baking fresh bread, filling the entire house with the scent of herbs and spices.

Looking over towards her, Satomi smiled. "Welcome home, sweetheart," she said as she took the loaf of bread out from the oven.

Akira smiled at her grandmother, offering only a casual wave of her hand before making her way down the hall. Passing by the open door to the tatami room, she saw her grandfather was seemingly still watching television, just as he was when she left. She could see he was watching a baseball game, and, judging by what he was saying under his breath, his team was losing. Moving further down the hallway, she hung a left and began ascending the stairs, though she barely even reached the third step before hearing her grandfather call out to her.

"Akira? Is that you?" Ryoma loudly said from the tatami room.

Pausing, she let out a deep sigh, then turned around and approached the open doorway to the tatami room. "I just got home from school, yeah..."

He looked to her from the short table, where they'd often sit and eat meals together as a family. "You're late. You were supposed to be home an hour ago," he pointed out.

Leaning against the doorframe, she groaned under her breath. "No... I said that my schedule had me at school later than at my old one..."

He eyed her suspiciously as if he were trying to peer through her lies.

Akira pushed off from the doorframe and held her arms out to her sides.

"I literally told you about it last week!" she said in disbelief.

"Don't get smart with me," Ryoma snapped.

"I'm not! I'm just saying that I–"

"You've already wasted enough time," he said, gesturing for her to go away with a wave of his hand. "Start with your outdoor chores while you still have daylight, then get the laundry started before it gets too late. And, if I catch you on that computer or listening to music before your chores are done, you'll go back to being grounded."

Exhaling sharply, she rolled her eyes, then turned and started down the hallway. "Fine, whatever..." she said under her breath.

"What was that?" he asked.

Stopping just down the hall, Akira groaned. "Yes, sir," she said, loud enough that he could hear her, though with no sincerity. She continued to the stairs, ascending to the second floor. "He never listens to a word I say..." she complained to herself as she stormed her way up the stairs, trying her best not to stomp her feet too hard.

Just down the second-floor hallway, she slid open a door on the left and walked into her bedroom. Closing the door behind her, she approached her futon bed, dropping her bag down onto the floor next to it, then flopping onto her thin mattress with an audible thud as she bottomed it out and hit against the floor. For a moment, she laid there on her stomach, with her face buried in her pillow.

While solely her own, Akira's room was a strange amalgamation of both a girl's and boy's room. Hung on the walls were posters of pop idols, many of which had on very flirtatious outfits. Alongside them were posters of western rock bands and a dartboard, along with various action figures and stuffed animals on a few shelves. On her desk sat an all-in-one computer, intended to help her with school, although more often than not, its primary use was helping Akira keep up with the bands she loved, and even listening to some of the songs she didn't have on cassettes.

Screaming into her pillow, she vented her frustrations with her grandfather, though she knew she'd only have more to deal with if she didn't tend to the chores he'd assigned to her. It was a little after five in the afternoon, an hour later than she typically got home from her junior high school, and so she now had the same amount of chores to do in less time. Rolling out of bed, she forced herself up and onto her feet, then began to change into more casual clothes so she could knock her chores out.

Throwing on a tank top and a pair of shorts, then grabbing her baseball cap, Akira proceeded back downstairs to tend to what she felt was her long list of mundane tasks that served no purpose other than to make her even more miserable. There was once a time when she shared these responsibilities with her older brother, but she was now left to handle all of them on her own. Everything from weeding the garden and watering the plants, to sweeping and mopping the floors and doing dishes, if it involved physical labor, it was Akira's responsibility.

Between these irritating chores, her grandfather always nagging her to do them the moment she got home from school, and the bullying she faced at school itself, Akira often questioned why she even bothered waking up in the mornings. Fortunately, today, she was given a great reason to crawl out of bed from now on, and that reason was her brand new friend Tomoe. There was so much Akira didn't know about her, and as she worked through her mundane chores, she couldn't stop thinking about how wonderful it would be to learn everything there was to know about Asano Tomoe, the one light in her otherwise dark and dismal days.

Chapter 3
The First Step

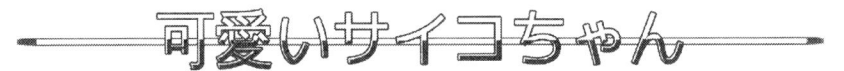

可愛いサイコちゃん

The following day, Akira was awoken once again by the sound of her phone's alarm going off. Crawling out of bed, she wandered over to her desk and turned the alarm off. Yawning sleepily, she opened her dresser and gathered up her clothes for school. As with the day prior, she descended the stairs and darted into the bathroom to get washed up and changed into her school uniform. The kitchen was her last stop before it was time to head to school. Sitting her backpack down on the floor near the refrigerator, she grabbed her bento box of leftovers and stuffed them inside of her bag.

Throwing her backpack's straps over her shoulders, she moved to the front door to change into her outdoor shoes, then left for school. As she did, she waved goodbye to her grandmother, who was tending to the garden outside. Slipping by the apartments along her route, Akira followed the drainage canal just as she had done on Monday. As she drew closer to the school, she passed down the secluded pathway and went to check her schedule to see which was her first class for the day.

Feeling around in the now empty pocket, Akira was promptly reminded that Kana had stolen her school schedule, and she had no copies of it. She thought back on that moment and felt as if she should have known better. Although, at her previous school, she only ever needed to know where her one classroom was, and that would be where she'd stay the entire day, physical education aside. So, this was an entirely new problem for Kana to create for her.

As she stepped into the school, Akira heard her name called out from behind her.

"Aki!"

Pausing, Akira turned and saw Tomoe approaching the front of the school, waving to her as she drew closer. Almost immediately, Akira's face lit up with excitement. "Hey, Tomoe! Um... h-how are you doing today?"

"I'm good. I got plenty of rest, and it's a beautiful day outside," she said with a smile before heading to her shoe locker. "You seem like you're in a better mood today too. I know yesterday didn't end too well for you," she said, sounding disheartened before gasping. "Oh! Was your cassette player okay?"

Akira nodded. "Yeah. It's scuffed up a bit, but otherwise, it's fine. I'll have to figure out how to fix the cassette... or maybe I could try moving the tape itself to a different cassette frame?"

Tomoe took her street shoes off and stepped into her indoor ones. "You know how to do that?" she asked, sounding rather impressed.

Akira lightly blushed at the idea of impressing her. "I, um... y-yeah, yeah! I've done it a few times before. It's not that hard at all," she said, lying through her teeth as she'd never tried to fix her broken tapes.

Tomoe giggled. "Just be careful. You don't want to break a second cassette while trying to fix the first one."

"Ain't that the truth?"

Putting her outdoor shoes away, she turned to Akira. "Oh... did you still have my number?"

"Your number?" Akira asked as she grimaced. "Yeah... I still have it. I'm sorry I didn't message you yesterday. Whenever I get home, I always have a lot of chores I have to do," she explained before pulling her cellphone from her skirt pocket. "Here, let me add it into my phone real quick..."

Tomoe smiled. "It's alright, Aki. I was just worried you might have lost it, that's all. I was going to ask you what classes you had today if you had messaged me... but I can just as easily ask now."

Akira sighed. "That's... kind of what Kana was harassing me about. She took my cassette player so she could coerce me into handing over my school schedule. So, I don't know what my first class is for the day," she admitted as she put Tomoe's cellphone number into her phone using the piece of paper she was given yesterday.

Tomoe gasped. "What? That's so mean. Why would she take your schedule from you?"

She slipped her phone back into her pocket. "So she knows which classes

I have. It makes it easier for her to know when and where she can push me around," she admitted, providing herself with yet another reminder that things here were going to be no different here than back at her junior high school.

"Well, do you know if your first class is gym? If it is, then we have the same class today as well," Tomoe said, offering a bright smile.

Akira frowned. "No, I had gym yesterday... dang it," she said, wishing that she shared gym with her new friend.

Thinking briefly on it, Tomoe smiled. "I know what we'll do. We can go talk to the gym teacher, and he should be able to print you off another copy of your schedule if he pulls your name up in his office."

Akira's face lit up as she heard her friend's solution to the problem Kana had created for her. "That's perfect! Tomoe, you are so awesome!"

She giggled. "I'm just happy to help out," she said before motioning downward. "Change your shoes out, and we'll head to the gym."

With an eager nod, Akira hastily made her way over to her shoe locker, stepping out of her shoes the moment she reached it. Swapping her street shoes out for her indoor ones, she quickly returned to Tomoe's side as the two of them began walking to the gym.

The halls were bustling with students as everyone made their way to their first classes of the day. As they walked together, with Tomoe in the lead, Akira's eyes couldn't help but gloss over her new friend. She could tell just by looking at Tomoe that she was almost as athletic as Kana, though not quite as muscular. Judging by her legs, it was clear that Tomoe did a lot of exercise at her previous school, which made Akira curious.

"Say, Tomoe..." Akira said, trying to think of how to word her question. "Did you, like.... play any sports or anything at your old school?"

Tomoe glanced back at her and smiled. "Yeah. I was on my school's soccer team. I've played since I was..." she began to say, pausing as she counted the years since she first played. "It has to have been at least six years now? So, I was around nine or ten when I first tried playing it."

"Oh, wow! So, you must love it, huh?" she responded.

Tomoe excitedly nodded. "I really do. It's so invigorating! Although, at my old school, I pretty much always got stuck playing the goalie since I was good at it."

"Is that stressful? Like, being responsible for guarding the goal?"

"At first it was, but once you get the hang of it, you start to learn that it's always a team effort. Even if you're stuck on the goal the whole game," she said before glancing back at her friend once more. "What about you? Do you play any sports?"

Akira grimaced. "N-not really... I'm not very athletic, if I'm honest."

"You don't have to be. That comes in time. The only thing you need to enjoy playing sports is enthusiasm. So long as you're having fun, that's all that matters," Tomoe explained.

"I dunno... I'd sort of like to win if I did play..." she admitted.

Stopping at the entrance to the gym, Tomoe giggled. "Winning is fun, and that's definitely my goal whenever I play. But, win or lose, so long as I have fun and tried my best, that's what's most important to me."

Akira smiled at her. "You're really amazing..." she blurted out before immediately blushing as she realized she thought that aloud to her friend.

Tomoe laughed. "I'm glad you think so. But, we should ask Mister Masaru about your schedule so that you won't be too late for your class."

She nervously nodded. "R-right. Sorry..."

Leading the way, Tomoe brought Akira over to their gym teacher, then explained the situation, citing that the schedule was lost rather than stolen. Much to Akira's surprise, Masaru appeared more than happy to walk with the girls just down the hall from the gym, where he stepped into his office and brought Akira's schedule up. Printing her out a new one, she now saw that biology was her first class of the day.

Thanking each of them, Akira hastily left to get to her class. Along the way, she couldn't help but feel so embarrassed for simply blurting out a compliment like that to Tomoe. Though it was true, she did feel as if her friend was amazing in virtually every regard. She was talented, kind, friendly, intelligent, wise, and incredibly pretty. While a part of her was jealous of how phenomenal Tomoe was, Akira felt admiration above anything else.

Arriving at her classroom, Akira took her seat just as the teacher came in and closed the door. Glancing around, she noticed both Hideko and Miyoko sitting together near the front of the class. *Oh, great... those two are in this class,* Akira thought to herself, taking a second glance around the room. *But at least Kana isn't in here too...*

As her class began, Akira found her focus wasn't on the subject, nor the presence of either Miyoko or Hideko, but instead on another girl at school. Tomoe had gone above and beyond to help Akira fix the problem Kana's behavior presented to her, and she accomplished it through the use of her knowledge and quick thinking. In so many ways, Tomoe was what

Akira hoped to someday be; strong, independent and confident. As it stood, she lacked each of those, while it appeared as if Tomoe had them in spades.

Paying minimal attention and mostly daydreaming about her new friend, Akira impatiently waited for the class to end. Once it had, she wasted no time getting to her next class, business ethics, followed by creative writing, the latter of which she was genuinely excited for, if only because it might allow her to express herself freely. All-in-all, she was more so excited to get to lunch so she could sit and talk with Tomoe some more, preferably about subjects unrelated to school or their homework.

Once her business ethics class concluded, Akira excitedly gathered her school supplies up and went to leave, though before she could, the teacher beckoned her to the front of the class. Approaching him, Akira checked to see what he wanted, though as she expected, all he did was lecture her over how it appeared that she wasn't paying any attention during class. He compared it to doing nothing in the workplace, how that type of attitude she had would get her in trouble once she was older, and how she'd end up working at a dead-end job for little-to-no pay. Akira nodded and agreed with him, paying no attention to what he was saying, and he could certainly tell that she was disinterested in his one-on-one lecture. Once he let her go, Akira checked her phone and saw she only had a couple of minutes to get to her next class.

Out in the hallway, most students were already in their classrooms, and while she walked by a couple of teachers, she didn't see many others out in the hall aside from herself. Taking the stairs, however, she heard talking between two girls. Ascending the first flight, she couldn't make out what they were saying, but she recognized each of their voices once she reached the landing. Checking around the corner and up at the top of the stairs confirmed her suspicions. It was Miyoko, and she appeared to be arguing with Tomoe.

"You heard me. The answer is no. Kana and I won't leave you alone because you don't deserve it," Miyoko responded.

Tomoe gasped in disbelief. "What have I done to deserve to be harassed by you and your friend?"

"For one, your attitude. Since you first moved here, you've acted as if you were so high and mighty. Probably arrogant from living in a big city, as if you think that you're better than us," Miyoko casually explained.

Akira peeked further up the stairs, seeing that the two stood face to face at the top, roughly a meter apart.

Tomoe almost laughed at how absurd Miyoko's claims were. "I've never felt like I was better than anyone because of where I'm from. I've tried to be as nice as I can to everyone I've met."

"That's a lie. You pretend to be nice. I can see through you, Asano... you're a very manipulative girl. The type who likes to sugarcoat every word because you think others will just fall in line with whatever you say," Miyoko explained.

Akira frowned. *No, she's not...*

Tomoe placed her hands on her hips. "No, I'm not."

"You're manipulative nature is probably why your father didn't want you around... I bet your mother is every bit the snake you are," Miyoko added.

"H-hey! My mother is a wonderful woman. You have *no* right to talk about her that way!" Tomoe snapped.

Akira grimaced as the two of them went back and forth, fearful of where this argument might lead them.

"I bet she has your temper too. It sounds like your father was lucky. Anyway, I need to get to class, so I'll see you around, Asano," Miyoko said as she turned to leave.

Tomoe puffed her cheeks up in anger. "You know, it's a good thing you wear so much makeup; otherwise, everyone could see how ugly you really are underneath," she retorted.

Stopping, Miyoko turned and glared back at her. "*What* did you say?!"

Worrying that things might escalate further, Akira moved further around the corner and moved up the stairs. "T-Tomoe!" she nervously called out as she ascended. "I... I can't believe I ran into you on the way to my class." Akira hesitantly glanced over at Miyoko, who appeared to be very irritated, likely more so now that Akira had interrupted them. She looked back at her friend. "M-maybe I could walk with you to your next class?"

"Shut up, Makai!" Miyoko snapped.

Tomoe glared at her. "Don't talk to her that way," she responded.

"N-no, it's fine. Tomoe, come on, we're going to be late for class," Akira said as she took her friend's arm and gently tried to coax her to walk down the hallway with her.

Miyoko scoffed. "Hideko said she saw you two sitting together at lunch. I guess you two are best friends now, huh?"

"Aki is a great friend. And, unlike *your* friend, she doesn't try to hurt anyone," Tomoe responded.

She laughed. "I'm not surprised you two are such good friends. I guess after your father abandoned you, it's pretty easy to sympathize with an orphan like Makai, huh?"

Tomoe recoiled in shock. "Orphan?" she asked under her breath.

Akira shook her head. "J-just ignore her. Come on, let's go," she said, worrying that if things kept on, then Kana might retaliate against one or both of them later.

Tomoe moved closer to Miyoko with determination in every step she took, practically dragging Akira along with her. "Talk about me all you want. But Aki is my friend. Leave her out of this."

"I'll talk about whomever I want, Asano," Miyoko responded.

Akira moved back around, placing herself almost between the two of them. "Tomoe, please? Let's go... we're going to be late for class," she said in a low voice.

Miyoko grinned widely. "You and Makai have so much in common. It's kind of fitting that you're both friends. Family disarray aside, you're both from big cities and with plenty wrong inside your little heads. You're manipulative and full of yourself, while Makai is a deviant little–"

Akira turned to her. "M-Miyoko, don't, please!" she pleaded.

"If you don't stop talking about Aki, then I'll..." Tomoe began to say before stopping herself short of making a threat.

"You'll what?" Miyoko fearlessly responded as she leaned in closer.

Akira moved between each of them. "S-stop, both of you, please!"

Irritated by Akira's involvement, Miyoko reached out and shoved her aside, forcing her to stagger back and up against the wall opposite of the stairs. "Butt out, Makai!"

Tomoe moved forward and pushed her hands against Miyoko's shoulders, shoving her back a short distance. "Don't push my friend!"

Growling under her breath, Miyoko rushed in and shoved Tomoe back, though not nearly as far.

Akira grimaced as she watched them push one another. Her heart raced as she knew where this was going and how it would ultimately end. No matter who won this altercation, Kana would hear about it, and no doubt she and Tomoe would both get beaten up as a result.

Miyoko moved to shove Tomoe once more, though Tomoe grabbed onto her arms instead. Twisting her arm to release Tomoe's grip, Miyoko reached out and grabbed Tomoe's hair, as well as the front of her blouse. She wrestled to try and get her to let go, but it was a struggle. They argued through grit teeth, insulting one another as they danced around amidst their attempt to overpower the other. Tomoe eventually managed to free herself from Miyoko's grasp and shove her back, though Miyoko wasted no time before charging back at her.

"S-stop! Please," Akira pleaded, fearing how bad it would be once Kana learned of this.

Shoving and grabbing one another, with a few light scratches, the two of them wrestled for several agonizing seconds before their fight brought them closer to the edge of the stairs. Akira saw this and feared they would both fall, though just as she pushed off from the wall and moved to try and intervene, Tomoe shoved Miyoko away from her. Staggering back, Myoko lost her footing at the top of the stairs and fell backward, hitting her head solidly against the concrete and tile steps as she tumbled down further to the landing between the two flights, where she hit the floor with a dull thud.

Tomoe covered her mouth as she gasped. "Oh no... M-Miyoko? Miyoko, are you okay?" she asked, panic clear in her voice.

Akira stood next to her, wide-eyed as she saw what happened. Her heart pounded heavily in her chest, feeling every pulse throughout her body. She knew this was bad, and that she and Tomoe were now as good as dead once Kana heard of this.

Without hesitation, Tomoe hastily moved down the stairs to where Miyoko had fallen. "Oh, no... Miyoko, I'm so sorry," she said as she covered her mouth at the sight of Miyoko's motionless body. "Please... please say she's okay," she pleaded in a low, barely audible voice.

Reluctantly, Akira began descending the stairs to the landing where Tomoe and Miyoko now were.

Kneeling, Tomoe gently shook Miyoko by her shoulder. "Miyoko? Miyoko, please, wake up. I'm sorry! I didn't mean to push you down the stairs," she desperately said.

Swallowing nervously, Akira stepped down onto the landing and moved around to where Tomoe was, closely observing Miyoko. She didn't budge a muscle, even despite the pain that fall no doubt caused. It was clear that she was unconscious, but that brought only dread into Akira's heart, not relief. As, while the fight between the two of them was over, Tomoe and Miyoko's argument would likely only lead to more severe pain and suffering once Kana learned of this. That alone was enough to put a sickness into Akira's stomach that twisted and turned into knots.

Tomoe looked to Akira, her heart racing after having shoved a fellow student down the stairs. "W-we... we need to go get a teacher."

Akira looked to Tomoe, momentarily speechless as her mind raced. "Wh-what happened? I thought you said, you had gym class?"

She stared at Akira, unsure of how to respond to such a strange question, given the situation. "I, um... I did, but I didn't realize that it drew blood when I scraped my knee in gym. I'd already begun walking to my next class when I noticed it, so I turned around to go to the nurse's office," she hastily explained.

Akira glanced down at her friend's knees, seeing that there was indeed a scrape across her right knee, a few small streaks of blood showing on the shallow cuts through her skin, though none that was flowing freely. She looked back at her friend. "I... I think you should just go to class... o-or, the nurse's office, or whatever," she said as she took a staggered breath. "And... and I need to get to my... my writing class. I'm already running late. We both are."

Tomoe's eyes widened slightly in shock. Given what happened, Akira's priorities were shocking. Tomoe stammered with her words as she tried to speak. "Wh-what about Miyoko? Aki, she just fell down the stairs, we have to help her, we can't just–"

"*Yes,* we can," Akira interjected. Silence filled the air between both of them before she grimaced as she looked back to Miyoko. "You two just had a huge argument and, trust me, that isn't a good thing," she said, her eyes returning to Tomoe. "Miyoko hit her head pretty hard... I mean, look! She's out like a light. With any hope, maybe she'll forget what happened?"

Tomoe frowned. "But, Aki... what if she–"

She moved closer to her friend, prompting Tomoe to take a half-step back. "Don't tell *anyone* about this..." she said in a panicked tone, fear clear in her voice. "If you tell a teacher, then you'll get into trouble, all for something that she started. And, if you tell another student, then word will get back to someone like Kana..." she turned fearfully to Miyoko, "if she doesn't tell Kana herself..." she added, swallowing nervously.

Biting her lip, Tomoe looked back to Miyoko, who still wasn't moving.

She turned back to her friend. "Just... go to the nurse's office, or your next class, it doesn't matter. But, just don't say a word to anyone about the fight or anything."

Looking back to Akira, Tomoe frowned. "Are... are you sure?"

She offered a firm nod. "If we're lucky, she hit her head hard enough that she forgot all about that argument and the fight. I think it's best to leave it that way."

Reluctantly, Tomoe nodded, then cautiously moved around Akira and started towards the stairs. She stopped briefly to look back at her friend and the damage she'd done, then hastily made her way down the stairs.

Akira watched as her friend as she left, though her eyes soon returned to Miyoko's motionless body. In her mind, she knew how furious Miyoko would be if she remembered all of this and how it was extremely likely that Tomoe would end up as a target of the same bullies who've ruined Akira's life for the past three years. This thought truly depressed her even to consider, and so as it stood, she felt them keeping quiet was their best option. Hopefully, Miyoko wouldn't remember a thing, and this would all blow over in no time.

Swallowing nervously, Akira stepped closer to the stairs, then rushed up to the second floor, walking as fast as she could down towards the far end of the hallway. Despite how calm and collected she was when speaking to her friend, she could feel now that her heart was racing at the thought of the absolute nightmare that would unfold should Kana hear about any of this. Approaching her next class, Akira gently knocked on the door and waited for her teacher to respond. After a moment, the door slid open.

Akira bowed her head. "I'm so sorry for being late, ma'am! Could I please come in?"

The teacher, an older woman, nodded. "Yes, come in. What's your name, young lady?"

She raised her head and entered the classroom as her teacher stepped aside. "Makai Akira, ma'am. Sorry again for being so late."

"It's alright, as long as you don't make a habit of it. Just find yourself a seat," she said.

Akira briefly bowed her head once more. "Yes, ma'am. Thank you."

Walking between the rows, Akira didn't even think to check if any of her least favorite people were in the class. She didn't even think about the class itself. As she took her seat, her mind just raced with thoughts of what happened. If Miyoko woke up and remembered anything, then there was no telling what she might do.

At the very least, she and Kana would most likely beat up both Akira and Tomoe for it, even if Akira herself was trying to keep the two of them from fighting at all. At worst, Kana might take it upon herself to ruin their lives. For Akira, she knew for a fact that Kana had the means to devastate her life. All Kana had to do was share a certain bit of sensitive information about Akira to her grandparents, and then it'd be all over for her. As for Tomoe, Miyoko alone had the means and experience to ruin someone's social standing at school and bury their chances of a peaceful or even tolerable life here. There was no telling what fuel Kana might add to that fire, though it likely wouldn't be pleasant for Tomoe regardless of what it was.

Akira then began to second guess her insistence that they just ditch Miyoko where she fell. If a teacher stumbled across her before she came to, then it's anyone's guess what could happen. There were no witnesses, aside from Akira, Tomoe and Miyoko, so it would still ultimately come down to their word against her's. But then, a fear began building in Akira's heart as she worried about how much trouble they'd be in if someone like the police were to get involved.

Barely twenty minutes into class, Akira's attention was torn from her thoughts when the intercom that hung on the wall in the class came on with a message that may have appeared odd and cryptic to some, but for Akira, it was all too clear what the message was regarding.

"Attention all students, staff, and faculty members. Please remain in your classrooms until further notice. For any students not in a classroom, please go to the nearest occupied classroom and wait inside until further notice. All faculty members, please dial extension one-six-one and wait for further instruction. That is all, thank you."

Biting her lip, Akira felt a cold chill wash over her. With a slow, deep breath, she reached inside of her backpack and pulled her cassette player from it. Nervously unraveling her earbuds and nearly dropping them from how her hands wouldn't stop trembling, she slipped one in and hit the play button. At times like these, when she just felt overwhelmed by the world around her, Akira often looked for any opportunity she had to escape into the one place she felt safe, within the sanctity of her music.

Even with one of her favorite songs playing in one ear, Akira couldn't help but sweat as she began to worry about why they'd make such an ominous announcement. Far as she could recall, there wasn't any blood or anything from Miyoko's fall, so perhaps she just hit her head really hard? Was she still unconscious, and a teacher found her? Or maybe during the fall, she severely injured herself? If she had a broken bone, that would be concerning for anyone attempting to help her, but not to the point of requesting everyone lock themselves in classrooms.

Watching her teacher pick up the phone from her desk only made Akira more nervous. What information could the teachers possibly need to all know if Miyoko had fallen? As Akira's mind began to trail to darker places, she eventually came to what was an inevitable conclusion, though an absurd one to be sure. Akira's heart sank when she began to consider it. What if Miyoko's fall down the stairs wasn't only painful, but fatal? Even as her mind barely glossed over the possibility, Akira felt her body turn frigid.

Meanwhile, the other students in the class began looking around curiously, talking amongst themselves as if to figure out what was going on.

The teacher looked to her students, seeing that they were gossiping. "Everyone settle down. I'm sure it's nothing to be worried about."

Akira shook her head in disbelief. *I'm just overthinking things. Miyoko is fine... she's probably just really pissed off and making a huge deal about what happened,* she thought, trying to calm her nerves.

Try as she might, Akira could do little to quell the fear that she may have witnessed far more than a mere injury of a classmate. And, while she may have grown to hate Miyoko for the things she had done, it was still difficult to believe and accept that she might be gone forever. The last time Akira experienced death in her life was when her parents were murdered. It took years for her to learn to deal with the trauma of seeing her parents lying in a pool of blood, and even now, it pained her to think back on it.

Chapter 4
Consequences of Action

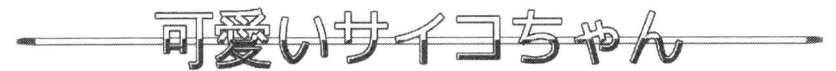

可愛いサイコちゃん

As she sat in class for the first few minutes, checking her phone occasionally to see the time, now only halfway through the hour, Akira felt her nerves and fears swelling up in waves. At times, it felt as if she were suffocating as she thought about what happened and the truth behind Miyoko's condition. With class on hold, most of the students around Akira quietly sat as they read from their textbooks, while others gossiped about what was going on, though they kept the conversation purely between themselves.

The teacher had since hung the phone up and moved to the door to the classroom, opening it up as she stood just outside, looking up and down the hall repeatedly. Nothing about her demeanor told Akira that she was alarmed, only that she was observant of her surroundings. After a moment, however, she slid the door closed while she stepped outside. Listening in carefully, Akira could vaguely make out the sounds of her teacher talking to someone out in the hallway, though it was entirely unclear who it was, as the walls muffled most of their speech.

As she opened the door back up, the teacher stepped aside and motioned with her hand into the classroom. Much to Akira's surprise, Tomoe stepped into the room, appearing pale as a ghost and visibly nervous. The mere sight of her friend shocked Akira, though not as much as Tomoe's fear, which was so obviously on display for anyone to see. She wasn't sure what her friend was doing roaming the halls, but she must have overheard the announcement and assumed the worst, judging by her demeanor.

Akira held her hand up and waved to her friend.

Tomoe appeared just as shocked to see Akira in this class as Akira was to see her. Nervously, she made her way over to the empty seat that was behind her friend, nearly tripping on another student's desk as she did so.

"A-Aki, what's going on? Why did they tell everyone to get out of the hallways?" Tomoe asked, her voice barely a whisper as she frantically looked around the classroom.

Akira turned around in her seat. "I don't know any more than you do. But, you need to calm down," she said, keeping her voice low. Throwing a glance over to her teacher, Akira could see she was standing in the doorway, on the lookout for any other students. She turned back to Tomoe. "I thought you were going to your class, or the nurse's office, or something?" she asked in confusion.

Tomoe swallowed nervously, appearing almost as if she were on the verge of tears. She nodded. "I... I did go to the nurse's office. Th-they cleaned my wound, then put a bandage over it. I was on my way back to my class when..." she said, looking to the teacher. "When she insisted I come in here."

She sighed. "Perfect timing then..."

"Aki... I'm scared. Do you think Miyoko woke up and told–"

"Shh!" Akira promptly responded, shushing her friend, as she feared that the situation might be far worse than Miyoko telling anyone anything. She then went to speak, though she couldn't find the words to share what was going through her mind. The more she thought about it, the more she felt it was better to assume the worst while hoping for the best. Sharing grim speculations with her already nervous friend was likely not going to help either of them.

Tomoe watched her, seeing how unsure and conflicted she was. "Aki, I think we're in trouble..."

"We... we're fine," she responded, trying her best to put forth a facade of confidence, something she had very little of at the moment. "A teacher must have found her lying there and called for help. I'm sure this is... all just protocol or something," she explained, following it with a nervous chuckle.

Tomoe frowned, clearly not falling for Akira's efforts to console her. "But, if that was the case, why would they make all of us..." she began to say before pausing as she heard something off in the distance.

As Akira carefully listened in, she could hear it as well. Perking up in her seat, she looked off towards the windows and listened closely; it was police sirens, and they were getting progressively louder. A few students looked curiously out of the classroom windows, seeing within a few moments, several police cars arrived, along with an ambulance.

Placing her knee in her seat, Akira boosted herself further to see better without standing up. Sitting back down, she looked to Tomoe, who was practically petrified with fear.

Tomoe's lip began to quiver, her whole body shaking nervously.

Akira could feel it in her gut. She knew that this was just yet another sign that pointed to the fear that she glossed over earlier. However, if her suspicions were well placed, it was even more important that they keep their mouths shut, or so she felt. "H-hey, calm down, okay?" she said with wavering confidence.

Still trembling with fear, Tomoe looked to her. "B-but... if she tells them that we had an argument, and fought... a-and that I..." she shook her head as she pushed her tears back. "Aki, I don't want to get into this much trouble, especially on my very first week at school!" she responded, in nearly a full panic with how worked up she was, though keeping her voice low enough that only a few students looked her way.

Motioning with her hands for her friend to calm down, Akira exhaled sharply, her breath staggering as she too was nervous. "Just try to breathe, alright? Take deep breaths."

"Everyone, please stay in your seats," the teacher stated, seeing that several students had moved curiously to the windows.

Akira frowned at Tomoe before relaxing back into her seat. "Just... try not to think about it. Let's talk about something else, alright?"

Tomoe held her head low, her eyes staring blankly down at the desk, wide, with shrunken pupils as her heart and mind each raced to make sense of what was going on.

Forcing a smile, Akira turned in her chair and rested her elbow on Tomoe's desk. "So, um... yesterday you told me you were from Fukuoka, right? It's a coastal city, isn't it? Did you live close to the water? Or further inland?"

Tomoe swallowed nervously as her eyes trailed to Akira, seeing how she was worrying far less over everything. "I, um... w-we lived kind of near the center of the city, I guess..."

"How long of a walk was it to reach the water? Did you have beaches there? Have you ever gone swimming?" Akira curiously asked.

"Wh-why are you asking me so many questions?" she nervously asked.

Akira's smile began to fade. "Because... I think you're cool, and I want to know more about you..." she said, her cheeks turning slightly red, adding at least some color to her otherwise pale complexion brought on by all of the fears and worries that dominated the back of her mind.

Tomoe let out a staggered sigh. "I... I never really went swimming. Sometimes I'd go shopping near the pier with my parents, but I've never gotten into the water."

Akira forced herself to smile once more. "What about boats? Have you ever been on one before?"

"Maybe once or twice," she admitted.

"Did you like it? Or... did you get seasick?"

Tomoe thought briefly about the question. "I mean, I guess it was okay."

Akira lightly giggled. "Guessing that you weren't crazy about it, huh?"

"I never really gave it much thought, honestly..."

"What about seafood? I bet there are some great places to eat at in Fukuoka, huh?" she eagerly asked.

Tomoe shrugged. "I guess so?" she said, her eyes trailing away as she looked around the classroom.

Akira gave a toothy grin. "I remember that there was this noodle shop not too far from where I grew up back in Shinjuku. We'd go there on weekends and eat so much ramen that... oh man, even as young as I was, I still remember that I felt like I was going to burst by the time we got done," she said with a genuine, lighthearted laugh as she recalled a wonderful memory of her childhood.

Tomoe's attention returned to Akira, finding it difficult not to smile at how happy this nostalgia made her friend. While she knew this was all more of a distraction than anything else, it did feel good to have this moment to get to know Akira a little better.

"You know... there were a lot of arcades in Tokyo, too, especially near where I lived. I used to be decent at a few games there. Although looking back, it was probably a huge waste of money," she admitted.

As Akira continued to talk about random things with her friend, time began to pass by. Before long, it had already been almost forty-five minutes since the police showed up. Though, little had changed since the school went on lockdown. As their discussions on random topics continued, the nervousness Tomoe first felt upon entering the classroom had faded significantly.

The teacher had been on the phone a few times throughout the class, though she had moved back to the door and waited since the most recent call. This drew Akira and Tomoe's attention, though for only a moment before they went back to their idle discussion. That discussion came to an abrupt halt when there was a gentle knock against the door to class. When the teacher opened the door, Tomoe's horrified expression told Akira that things were likely about to get far more tense for both of them.

Turning around in her seat, Akira saw a uniformed police officer speaking to her teacher. And, after only a moment, her teacher turned and looked directly at both Akira and Tomoe.

"Miss Makai, could you come here?" she asked.

Feeling her heart pounding in her chest, Akira didn't immediately move, though her teacher repeating the request prompted her response. "Y-yes, ma'am!" she nervously responded.

Standing up, Akira almost tripped as her foot got caught on the leg of the desk, though she managed to regain her balance. Feeling frigid and cold, though also sweating, she approached the teacher and officer.

"Are you Makai Akira?" the officer asked in a stern, disciplined tone.

She timidly nodded. "Yes, sir..."

The officer took a step back. "Would you please come with me? There are a few questions we'd like to ask you."

Akira wasn't sure how to respond. She looked to her teacher, then back to the police officer. "I, um... o-okay, but I... I need to get my bag before I leave."

The officer shook his head. "You can leave it here. After answering our questions, you'll be allowed to return to class."

Her teacher nodded. "I'll make sure your bag is fine, Miss Makai."

Swallowing nervously, Akira reluctantly nodded, keeping her head low, as she avoided eye contact with the police officer. Stepping out of class, she turned and moved off to the side.

The officer gave a bow of his head to the teacher, prompting her to close the door. He turned to Akira. "Now, Miss Makai, do you have anything on your person? Any small items? Pencils, cosmetics, anything of note?"

Akira thought briefly to herself, then checked the pockets in her skirt, though she only had her cellphone on her. Pulling it from her pocket, she showed it to him. "J-just this..."

He offered a firm nod to her. "That's fine. Now, follow me," he said as he began making his way down the hall.

Putting her phone back into her pocket, she began following the officer, though she wasn't sure what to make of this situation. She was being taken aside to be questioned, which told Akira that Miyoko wasn't awake and giving the police any details about who pushed her. If that were the case, they'd of come for Tomoe. That meant that Miyoko was still unconscious, or Akira's assumptions of the worst-case scenario were true and that the police weren't here to address accusations of assault but, instead, to investigate a murder.

Descending the stairs behind the officer, Akira did her best to maintain her composure. It was difficult, given what she could assume happened. She couldn't be sure what the police might already know, and that alone brought her more fear than the realization as to why they were even here at all. Her mind raced with what she'd say when they began questioning her, and it became clear that her time was running out as she was brought to one of the classrooms nearest the main entrance to the school.

Inside, there were four police officers, two of whom wore suits rather than uniforms, which, to her, meant that they were likely of a higher rank. She noticed that the desks had been moved aside and stacked in the room's corner. In the center of the classroom sat the teacher's desk, with chairs on either side of it.

Glancing over towards Akira, one of the higher-ranking officers gestured towards a chair at the desk. "Please, have a seat."

Akira cautiously sat down, her nerves fighting against her as she tried to maintain her composure. She nervously surveyed her surroundings, watching as the officer who escorted her here and one other left. Another uniformed officer brandished a notepad and stood nearby as if he was prepared to take notes of everything that was said between Akira and whoever began questioning her.

The man who had instructed her to sit down approached the desk and took the seat across from her. He leaned forward, resting his elbows on the desk as he interlaced his fingers, eyeing her intensely. "I'm sure you're probably a little confused. Let me explain. My name is Detective Yasuhida Masato. I'm the lead detective here in Nirasaki. We were called to your school today regarding an incident, and we hoped that you might be able to assist in shining some light on the situation."

Akira timidly nodded. "I... I can try, sir."

"We'd appreciate that. But first, before I ask you any questions regarding the incident, I'd like it if you could tell me a little about yourself," he said as he readied a pen alongside a notepad that was resting on the table.

"Uh... like what?"

Yasuhida offered a brief shrug of his shoulders. "Whatever you'd like to share. If you're not sure where to begin, just start with the basics. Your name, hobbies, what schools you've attended, then just go from there."

Swallowing nervously, Akira inhaled sharply. "Oh... um, okay. Well, my name is Makai Akira. And as far as hobbies... I guess I listen to a lot of music. The last school I went to was Nirasakinishi Junior High..." she said, noticing that the one officer was taking notes as she spoke. This led her to believe that his responsibility was to notate every word she shared, while the detective had his notepad ready for important details.

Yasuhida nodded. "Go on."

She shrugged. "I don't know what else to say... I don't really talk about myself to anyone..."

"I see. So you're somewhat of a loner?" he asked.

"N-not, really. I just kind of keep to myself."

Yasuhida jotted something down on his notepad, then turned his focus back to her. "How well would you say you do in school?"

"I dunno... I guess I'm pretty mediocre as far as grades go."

"Mostly Bs and Cs then?" he asked.

She nodded. "More Cs, if I'm honest..."

Crossing his arms on the table, he looked intensely at her. "So, would you say your school life has been more so positive or negative?"

Akira couldn't help but lightly chuckle under her breath at the very idea of her school life being defined as positive, especially following today's encounter with Miyoko. Slowly, she shook her head. "I'd, uh... say it was somewhere in the middle," she said, not wanting to give out too much information.

Yasuhida narrowed his eyes on her. "Would you say you've had any difficulties with other students here at this school? Or at previous ones?"

Although subtle at first, Akira saw the signs of where this was going. A student had been injured, possibly even killed. So, why not find out if they had any enemies, then question them? If so, then the police must have spoken to Kana or Hideko, who no doubt pointed a finger firmly at her as the culprit.

It was now that Akira wasn't sure if she needed to continue to tell the truth or if she should lie. The truth wasn't that she had hurt anyone at all; she only witnessed the incident. However, the one who she witnessed committing it was also the only person who had been nice to her in years. The last thing she wanted to do was to throw someone like Tomoe under the bus. Biting her lip, Akira knew she needed to keep her new friend safe. If they looked out for one another, then things would have to be all right, or so she hoped.

"Miss Makai?"

Akira abruptly shook her head. "S-sorry... what was the question again?"

Yasuhida exhaled sharply. "I asked if you've had any difficulties at this or the previous schools you've attended."

"Difficulties? Not... really. I mean, I'm p-pretty terrible at studying, but I've made it through most of my classes all right," she said, trying to speak more confidently; if only to hide how nervous she was. Though, she still couldn't help but stammer as she spoke, regardless of her efforts.

"What about with other students?"

Akira could feel her heart throbbing heavily in her chest as if she were doubting every word she spoke, though she continued. "I was picked on a lot in junior high... b-but it was mostly because I didn't have any friends."

"That must have been difficult for you."

"I, um..." she shook her head. "N-not really! I've always been too busy to hang out with friends, anyway..." she responded, a subtle, albeit nervous chuckle following.

He eyed her suspiciously. "I see. Then what would you say has occupied a majority of your time?"

Seeing how he was looking at her, Akira swallowed nervously. "Um... well, after school, I a-always go straight home. B-because, I live with my grandparents, and they have a lot of chores that I, um... I help them out with. You know, because of their age? I like to help out around the house whenever I can," she explained, hastening her speech as she tried to go into more detail for the detective. Although, she quickly realized that she must have sounded so nervous or even panicked as she spoke.

Yasuhida leaned back, appearing as if he were thinking intensely on what she said. "So most of your time is spent at home?"

"Mostly... unless I had errands that my grandparents asked me to run for them in town," she responded, trying to speak more naturally to appear as if she were calm.

Approaching from behind Yasuhida, a tall man, who immediately drew Akira's attention, leaned down and whispered something to the detective. Observing the man, Akira saw that he wore a similar suit to Yasuhida, only it was of a dark tan color. She also noticed that he didn't look Japanese in even the slightest. He had short dark blonde hair and the facial structure of a foreigner, likely from far to the west. His unique appearance reminded her briefly of the girl who she bumped into on her first day of school, although she was hard-pressed to believe they were related, as that girl seemed to be Japanese, and yet this man was clearly a foreigner.

Nodding to his colleague, Yasuhida turned his attention back to Akira. "I'd like for you to tell me if you're familiar with any of these names."

"Um... okay?" Akira said, feeling a bit confused.

"Is the name Abukara Hideko familiar at all to you?"

"Y-yes, sir."

"What about Hachi Miyoko?"

Akira swallowed nervously. "Um... yeah."

"And Nakajima Kana?"

She nodded. "I... I know her, yes."

"Do you have any notable relationship with any of these students?"

Hesitantly, Akira nodded once more. "Those are the names of the, um... the girls who picked on me a lot in junior high," she answered honestly, knowing that such information would be far too easy for anyone to discover, let alone law enforcement.

Yasuhida stared briefly at her before inhaling sharply. "Would you mind going into more detail regarding what they did to you?"

Akira shrugged. "I mean... it was the typical teenager stuff, I guess? They teased me a lot, called me names, and sometimes took my belongings."

Yasuhida reached up and held his chin briefly, offering a subtle nod. "Nothing physical then? No fights between you or any of these students, nothing violent?"

Akira hesitantly shook her head. "N-no, sir, not... not really."

"Do you have any negative feelings towards any of these students?"

"No, sir."

He nodded. "And where would you say you were between ten-forty-five and approximately eleven o'clock?"

"Today?" she asked.

Yasuhida nodded.

"Uh, well... ten-fifty would have been right when my business ethics class ended. After class, my teacher held me for a bit to go over a few aspects of what we covered in class, and then I got to my creative writing class a bit late."

"How late?"

Akira shrugged. "Maybe... five or ten minutes?"

"Was your teacher made aware of your late arrival?"

She nodded. "Yes, sir."

"I see. Wait here for one moment then, Miss Makai."

Standing up, Yasuhida stepped out of the room briefly. While gone, Akira looked around the room and noticed the blonde-haired man from earlier was watching her closely. He and Akira locked eyes before she looked down, breaking eye contact with him, as the way he was staring at her made her feel very uneasy. Several minutes later, the detective walked back into the room and approached her, standing next to the desk.

"I appreciate you taking the time to speak with us on this matter. Now, before we escort you back to your classroom, was there anything else you wanted to share with us?" Yasuhida asked.

Akira shook her head. "N-no, sir."

He nodded. "Alright then, but before you go," he gestured towards the man who was staring at her, "Lieutenant Yakovna will need to take your fingerprints."

Her eyes trailed back towards the lieutenant briefly, then shot back to the detective. "M-my... fingerprints?" she nervously asked.

"Yes. Following these types of incidents, it is standard procedure for fingerprints to be taken, as it helps us exclude you from the investigation."

Biting her lip, Akira swallowed nervously. "Oh, um... o-okay..."

Turning away, Yasuhida left the room once again while the lieutenant he referred to as Yakovna approached the table and sat down. Placing a box on the table, he pulled out a few things and began to take her fingerprints. Akira avoided eye contact with him as he took her hand and pressed her fingers into a thin ink sponge one by one, then marked the paper he had with each of her fingerprints. Once finished, he handed her an alcohol wipe, which she used to get the remaining ink off her fingers. The one time she allowed her eyes to trail up to his, she noticed how intense his stare was. It was as if he knew beyond any doubt that she was guilty, even though she knew she had done nothing wrong.

It was at this moment that Akira realized that the police weren't letting her go because they believed that she was innocent, but instead because they likely just needed more time to prove her guilt. This wasn't the end of this incident for her, but rather the beginning of a struggle between two aspects of her life that now felt as if they were mutually exclusive to one another. She could either tell the truth, freeing her from these accusations and plunging her back into the life she once lived, or she could hold steady with these lies and protect Tomoe, which could cost her the freedom and joy that she had only experienced these last two days.

Chapter 5
In The Aftermath
可愛いサイコちゃん

Once Lieutenant Yakovna dismissed Akira from her interrogation, she was escorted back to her class by the same officer who brought her down in the first place. During the walk back, her mind scrambled to make sense of everything she shared with the police, as she now realized it could all come back to haunt her if there were any inconsistencies in her story. As she arrived back at her classroom, Akira quickly moved to take her seat next to Tomoe, doing her best to maintain her composure after the questioning she had just endured.

Looking to her friend, she offered a smile, although it was forced and straining on her even to present it. Tomoe could tell, and it seemed to worry her, so Akira formed a V with her fingers as if that might help convey that everything, at least on the surface, was alright. It did no such thing, as Tomoe sighed, lowering her head as she feared that she might be called next. Seeing her friend worried, Akira tapped her finger on Tomoe's desk to get her attention.

"Say, um... if school lets out early, did you want to hang out?" she asked.

Tomoe went to respond, though she stopped and thought about it for a moment longer before nodding. "Yeah, actually. If you don't mind?"

Akira shook her head. "Not at all. I think it'd be... fun," she responded. Although, in truth, she just desperately wanted a chance to talk in private with her friend about the realization she had come to earlier.

Tomoe attempted to crack a smile, but even that proved difficult for her.

Time steadily passed by until it was already almost twelve-thirty. Having not had anything for breakfast, and it being half-passed lunchtime, Akira felt her stomach grumbling. She was starving, but it seemed rude to eat in the middle of the classroom when that wasn't the designated place to do so at this school. Writing a few oddball things down on her notepad to pass the time, Akira watched as Tomoe nervously thumbed through her phone, perhaps hoping to find something to distract her. Though, before she could, the intercom came on again with the same familiar chime, drawing everyone's attention to it.

"Attention, students. The remaining classes for the day have been canceled. Club activities on school grounds have been suspended for the remainder of the day," it said before repeating the message once more.

Akira looked over at her friend. "I... guess that's good news, huh?"

Tomoe lowered her head. "Tell me about it," she said as she watched her hands. "Ever since we got in here, I haven't been able to stop shaking..."

Staring at her, Akira frowned. "Well, hopefully, once we're on our way out, your nerves will relax a little?"

"I hope so," she responded.

Putting her supplies away, Akira threw her backpack on and waited for Tomoe to get up from the desk. Together, they followed the other students into the hallway, down to the first floor, and out of the school. The walkway just in front of the school was densely packed as everyone left at once. Avoiding the crowd, the girls moved down the secluded alley that Akira typically took to get home, where they at least had some privacy to talk.

"So, are your hands still shaky?" Akira asked.

Tomoe reluctantly shook her head. "No... I think the fresh air is helping me calm down."

"That's good... because, I, um... there's something I kind of wanted to talk to you about," Akira admitted.

"Same, honestly..."

Stopping, Akira turned to Tomoe. "Well, mine is about Miyoko..."

She nodded. "Mine too."

Akira glanced around the area, seeing a few other students walking along, though none of them were specifically making their way down this secluded alley. "I mean... the signs were pretty obvious, so I'm not surprised we both came to the same conclusion."

Tomoe cocked her head curiously at her friend. "Conclusion?"

Akira reluctantly nodded. "About Miyoko..."

Frowning, Tomoe shook her head. "I didn't really come to a conclusion.

I just thought that it'd be best if I told the police what happened. I don't want to drag matters out and make this worse than it has to be, you know?" she admitted before sighing. "I know I'll get in trouble... but my mother always told me it's better, to tell the truth rather than to hurt others with a lie."

Akira grimaced. "I, um... think it might be better if you give that some more thought..."

"The longer I wait, the more trouble I'll probably be in, Aki."

"I just think you're rushing things... that's all."

Tomoe shook her head. "I want to do what's right. I appreciate you trying to help, but it's wrong to hurt someone and then hide the truth. Besides, even if Miyoko doesn't remember the incident, it's bound to come up again, and when it does, she'll probably recall what happened."

Akira bit nervously at her lip. "F-fine... if that's what you want. But, first... can you at least hear the conclusion I came to?"

Tomoe sighed. "I don't know what kind of 'conclusion' you're talking about. That Miyoko doesn't remember a thing? Is she still unconscious? Or did they say she–"

"Miyoko's dead..." Akira said, pausing afterward as she inhaled sharply, then turned away, pacing a short distance as she came to accept this herself.

Tomoe stood, unmoving, as she stared blankly ahead, feeling a cold chill wash over her. "Sh-she's..." she began to say before looking to her friend. "H-how... how could you possibly know that?"

Sighing, Akira glanced back at her. "Because of the way the police questioned me, the way they spoke... the severity of the situation was clear in their voices. On top of that, they took my fingerprints and asked about my relationship with Miyoko, Kana, and Hideko. There's no reason they'd ask any of that if she wasn't..." she paused, taking a deep breath as she shook her head. "I don't want to talk about this out here."

Tomoe's eyes trailed around the area aimlessly as she tried to think about what she'd just been told. Taking a few steps forward, she placed her hand against the nearby wall before slowly falling to her knees, then sitting on the cold, stone walkway. Her mind raced with the thought that she hadn't just hurt someone but instead ended their life.

Looking back to her friend, Akira frowned. It was clear that Tomoe was taking things very hard, which she couldn't blame her for at all. As she tried to think of what to say to help her friend, she glanced back towards the school and noticed a sight that hardly put her mind at ease. The man who'd taken her fingerprints earlier was standing outside of the school's main entrance, smoking a cigarette as he watched them from afar. Swallowing nervously, she quickly moved to Tomoe's side.

Kneeling, Akira placed her hand on her friend's shoulder. "I, um... think it might be best if we head back to my house and talk about this."

Tomoe frowned, appearing almost as if she were on the verge of tears. "Aki... I... I can't believe that I... did I... did I really just... k-kill someone?"

She shook her head. "We can talk about it at my house. For now..." she paused, glancing back towards the lieutenant at the entrance to the school. "I think we should go..."

Hesitantly, Tomoe looked to her friend and then followed her eyes towards the man, eyeing them closely. "Oh no..." she stammered under her breath.

Akira looked back at her friend. "Come on. Let's go to my house. We can talk about this more there," she said, pulling on her friend's upper arms, urging her to stand up.

Tomoe reluctantly stood up, trembling in fear as she stared at Yakovna, though she was fortunately guided away from looking at him by Akira, as her friend gently pushed her down the walkway.

As they walked along, Tomoe was at a complete loss of words, unsure of what to say. They continued on the way towards Akira's house, following the canal, crossing over near the construction site, just as Akira had done before. Upon arriving at her grandparent's house, Akira checked to see if her grandfather's truck was there, and unfortunately, the vehicle was parked in its usual spot. It wasn't until they approached the front door, with Akira leading the way, that a word was spoken since the news of this revelation was brought to light.

"A-Aki, wait," Tomoe said as she stopped on the walkway.

Turning back to look at her, Akira frowned. "What's wrong?"

She shook her head. "I... I d-don't know if I can do this..."

"This?" Akira curiously asked.

Tomoe gestured towards the house. "Meeting your family after... after hearing what you... you said to me earlier..."

Biting at her lip, Akira reluctantly nodded. "I don't want you to think that I don't have a lot on my mind too. I do. But, before we do anything, I think we need to talk about this. And before we do that... you're going to have to meet my grandparents, and we'll probably have to do chores."

"I don't know..." she responded, shaking her head in disbelief. "If what you said is true, then I..."

Akira took a step closer towards her friend, placing her hand on Tomoe's shoulder. "Just don't think about it. We can talk later, I promise. But, just like... hold it together until then... okay?"

Staring at Akira, Tomoe reluctantly nodded. "I'll t-try my best..."

Offering a smile, if only to instill confidence in her friend, Akira turned and continued towards her front door. Reaching down, she picked up the false rock, then pulled the key from it. Unlocking the door, she stepped inside, holding it open for her friend.

"I'm home!" Akira called out.

Taking their shoes off, Akira led Tomoe into the kitchen, then down the hallway and stopping at the open door to the tatami room, where both of her grandparents were sitting, watching an old television show while enjoying freshly brewed tea. They each turned to look at her, surprised that she was home so early, even more so when they saw she had a friend with her. Though, Ryoma quickly scoffed and went back to his television show.

"Welcome home, Akira. Did school let out early?" Satomi asked.

Akira nodded. "Yeah. They cut classes short because of an incident at school," she said before stepping aside and gesturing towards Tomoe. "I hope you don't mind, but I invited my new friend over."

Tomoe respectfully bowed her head. "M-my name is Asano Tomoe. It's, um... it's a pleasure to meet you both," she nervously said.

Satomi bowed her head. "It's nice to meet you as well, Miss Asano. My name is Watari Satomi, and this is my husband, Watari Ryoma."

"You kids better keep it down. If I have to come upstairs and say it a second time, there'll be trouble," Ryoma firmly stated.

Tomoe looked nervously at Akira, though she just rolled her eyes.

"We'll be quiet; no worries there. Come on, Tomoe. My room is just upstairs, she said with a wave of her hand, beckoning her friend to follow.

As the two of them ascended to the second floor Tomoe noticed just how quaint and traditional the house was. It had a warm feeling that reminded her that despite having grown up in a larger city like Fukuoka, Nirasaki was a more rural and traditional city.

Sliding the door open, Akira allowed Tomoe to enter first, then followed her inside and shut the door behind them. Looking around her friend's bedroom, Tomoe saw the posters on the wall and noticed how things weren't exactly tidy. Akira had a hamper overflowing with dirty clothes, her bed was a mess, and her nightclothes still laid on the floor from earlier this morning. There were a few interesting pieces, such as a lava lamp that rested atop her dresser, and the dartboard that had a few darts littered across the surface, as well as the various action figures and stuffed animals that sat on scattered shelves.

"Your room is very... cute," Tomoe reluctantly admitted.

Akira scoffed under her breath. "Thanks."

She dropped her backpack onto the floor, sat on her bed, then waved her friend over. "Have a seat, and we'll talk... quietly."

Approaching Akira's bed, Tomoe hesitantly sat down on her knees just in front of her friend.

"Alright. So..." Akira pulled her legs up, crossing them as she placed her hands firmly on her knees and leaned forward slightly. "Miyoko's gone... or at least that's what it appears like."

Tomoe nervously bit at her lip. "I can't believe that I... how could I do this, Aki? I know she was harassing me, and she said horrible things, but... how could I just...?" she asked on the verge of tears.

Akira frowned. "Tomoe, stop. You can't blame yourself."

She shook her head in disbelief. "What do you mean? This is all my fault. If I hadn't started a fight with her then–"

"You didn't start anything," Akira interjected. "Miyoko was the first to get aggressive. She pushed me, and you defended me," she explained, blushing slightly. "Which... th-thank you for that. No one's ever defended me before, well... not since..." She shook her head. "It's been a long time since anyone stood up for me, Tomoe. But, you did... and, I know it turned out like this, but it's not your fault."

"It *is* my fault. If I hadn't escalated things, then she and I never would have fought with one another." She exhaled sharply. "I mean... I didn't, like, go out of my way or anything to argue with her. I was walking to the nurse's office, and she was standing in the hallway, texting on her phone," she explained, shaking her head in disbelief. "I... I just wanted to talk to her about how she's been treating me lately. To tell her to stop, you know? That's all I wanted..."

Akira slowly nodded. "Miyoko's not well known for her... compassion towards others."

"Honestly, you showed up just as I started talking to her. And you saw how everything just deteriorated into... well..." Tomoe said as she lowered her head.

"Were any of her friends around? Kana, Hideko... anyone?" she asked.

Thinking back on it, Tomoe shook her head. "I... I don't think so. But, I can't remember for sure..."

"Ideally, we can hope that no one saw you two talking. Otherwise, they might piece together what happened..."

Tomoe buried her face in her hands. "I can't believe this. All I wanted to do was ask her to leave me alone... I never meant to..."

Akira reached out and placed her hand on her friend's knee. "Don't blame yourself, Tomoe. You weren't trying to fight with her, and even I was trying to help break things up between you two. This is all her fault."

She sighed as she looked back at her friend. "Maybe I should have just ignored her? If I had, then she'd still be alive right now..."

Akira puffed up her cheeks, irritated that Tomoe kept blaming herself for something that was entirely Miyoko's fault. "Like I just said, she's to blame for her ending up at the bottom of the stairs. Trust me, I've known her for years. She's a complete and total bitch. This is *all* her fault."

Tomoe frowned. "But... if I hadn't argued with her, then–"

"Blaming yourself isn't going to help anyone!" Akira snapped.

The two stared at one another in a brief silence before Tomoe lowered her head and let out a deep sigh.

Crossing her arms, Akira shook her head. "This *whole* accident could have been avoided if Miyoko wasn't such a bitch... regardless of who you want to believe started the fight..."

Tomoe's eyes slowly trailed back up towards her friend. "Accident?"

Akira stared oddly at her friend before nodding. "Yeah. I mean, you didn't intend to push her down the stairs, and you damn well didn't mean to kill her."

"That's... true, I guess..." she admitted in a low voice. "But even so, I still think that I should turn myself in."

Akira shook her head. "You shouldn't."

Tomoe looked at her in shock. "B-but, why not?"

"Because! If you confess to the police, they'll slap you with the harshest penalty they can. You'll be arrested and probably even thrown in jail," she said before sighing. "Not to mention, your mom will probably be really upset... and I'd lose my only friend," she admitted in a sad voice.

Tomoe frowned. "But... they're going to find out eventually, right?"

Akira scoffed. "The police? Not necessarily. Honestly, those idiots couldn't find a light switch in a dark room, let alone a criminal in this shitty little town."

"A... a criminal?" she responded in fear.

Pausing, Akira let out a deep sigh. "Don't... look too much into it. For now, I think the best thing for us to do, is to keep our mouths shut and not say a word to anyone about anything. If anyone asks, just play dumb."

"We'd have to lie to everyone?"

She shook her head. "We don't have to lie. We just don't tell the truth."

Lowering her head, Tomoe stared blankly at the foot of Akira's bed before another question crossed her mind. "Say, um... Aki? What kind of questions did the police ask you when they pulled you aside earlier?"

Akira shrugged. "They asked me for my name, my experience at school, how I felt about the people who bullied me and... I answered all of their questions pretty neutrally. I didn't lie about Kana and her friends being assholes, but I didn't make a huge deal about it either."

Tomoe nodded. "Were you scared?"

"Maybe a little..." Akira responded, looking away to better conceal her true feelings on the matter.

"I think I'd be terrified if they questioned me..." she admitted before pausing. "One thing that confuses me though... is, why did they even pull you aside?"

Akira scratched the back of her head. "I, uh... sort of get the feeling that Kana probably told them I did it. That sounds like something she'd do."

She gasped. "What?! But why would she assume you were responsible?"

"Because she hates my guts?" Akira chuckled, shaking her head.

"She hates you enough to blame you for something like this? But why?"

Akira stopped, biting her lip as her eyes trailed away from her friend.

"Should I not have asked? I'm sorry if I'm being too nosy..."

Akira sighed, looking back at her friend. "It's not that; it's... let's just say that Kana doesn't like me... because of a misunderstanding she and I had."

She nodded. "I see. Sorry for asking such an uncomfortable question."

Scoffing, Akira dismissively waved her hand. "Don't worry about it. But, hey! I wonder if classes will be canceled tomorrow too?"

Tomoe sighed. "Somehow, I doubt it."

"I hope it is. Because the last place I want to be is at school, with Kana blaming me for what happened and giving me so much shit for it."

She frowned. "Um... hey, Aki?"

"Yeah?"

"I... I didn't notice it when we first met, or even much earlier at school... but why do you use such vulgar language?" she timidly asked.

Akira shrugged her shoulders. "I don't know... it's just the way I talk. I try to watch what I say at school and around my grandparents since I've gotten in trouble for it, but outside of that, I just sort of talk however I want."

"Oh..." she responded, expecting to hear a more reasonable explanation.

Knocking at the door gently, Satomi slid it open and peeked into the bedroom. "Were you girls hungry?"

"Uh... oh, shoot! I completely forgot about how starved I was earlier!" Akira said before laughing. "You wanna get a bite to eat, Tomoe?"

"That would be really nice, actually," Tomoe responded.

Satomi smiled. "Come downstairs, and I'll make a snack for you girls."

Excitedly, Akira hopped up from her bed and rushed past Satomi, hastily making her way downstairs as she felt her hunger coming back in full force. Tomoe followed behind her friend, though far more slowly, as she didn't want to run in someone else's house. Downstairs, Satomi prepared a rather simple lunch for the two of them, though soon after they were done eating, Ryoma began dishing out chores for Akira to do. He insisted that since she had a friend, she should accomplish her tasks faster and more thoroughly.

Akira protested to her grandfather that Tomoe shouldn't have to help with the chores. However, Tomoe reassured her that she didn't mind. In truth, Akira knew that her friend likely just welcomed them as a distraction from what happened earlier, which she couldn't fault her for wanting. They began by taking care of the dishes from lunch and cleaning up the kitchen. The girls then dusted all of the main rooms in the house, with Tomoe choosing to sweep, while Akira handled mopping behind her on the hardwood floors. Afterward, Akira proceeded to gather up all of the dirty clothes in the house, then left Tomoe to load the washing machine while she changed into a pair of jean shorts and a tank top so she could tend to the garden.

Once the clothes were finished, Akira and Tomoe stood together in the laundry room, folding and sorting the laundry out as they spoke to one another about various subjects, never deviating too closely to the incident earlier today at school. Primarily, they discussed where they each used to live before moving here to Nirasaki. Akira reminisced about her foggy memories of Shinjuku, which were few and far between, as she left there at such a young age. At the same time, Tomoe led much of the conversation by speaking at length about Fukuoka and the life she used to have there.

Akira learned that the reason they left and why Tomoe's parents split up was due to her father's gambling addiction. He was, as she explained it, a wonderful, caring, and loving husband and father, but he would often squander much of his paycheck at pachinko parlors or gambling in games of mahjong or shogi with acquaintances of his. Her mother eventually had enough, and they left. She had chosen Nirasaki due to the low cost of living and its reputation for being such a quiet and peaceful city.

Soon enough, they were finished with chores, and Tomoe was ready to return home herself, as she knew her mother would probably be worried about her. Despite having to do chores the entire time she was here, Tomoe graciously thanked Satomi and Ryoma for allowing her to hang out with Akira, then said her goodbyes to her friend before leaving just before dinner time. As she left, Akira couldn't help but feel hopeful for their future, as, in her eyes, Tomoe felt as if she were an ideal friend. Kind, intelligent, polite, and from what it felt, very understanding and reasonable.

Chapter 6
Unavoidable Accusations

可愛いサイコちゃん

Wednesday morning, Akira awoke to her alarm, restless from nightmares she had throughout the night. Her dreams were filled with the varied scenarios her imagination could muster over Tomoe and her being caught by the police or even by Kana alone. Akira was certain that Kana was the one who directed the police towards her, prompting the interrogation that brought about so much anxiety for her the previous day. And, with the police letting her walk, even if they didn't exclude her as a potential suspect, she now had a fear of what might happen if Kana were to take matters into her own hands.

At the best of times, Kana was a condescending, controlling, and sadistic person, for her to now possibly be under the belief that Akira had shoved Miyoko down the stairs and likely killed her, the thought of what she might do sincerely terrified Akira. Regardless, she knew for sure that she'd be in trouble if she didn't go to school and that aside, she wanted to see Tomoe again. As was her morning ritual, Akira cleaned herself up, then left for school with everything she needed in her backpack.

Arriving at the school itself, Akira nervously glanced around the area, searching not only for her friend but for Kana as well. Fortunately, she found Tomoe walking among a group of other students first. Her head was held low, and it was clear that she still had a lot on her mind. Akira put on her best smile and moved to meet with her friend.

"Tomoe! Good morning," Akira enthusiastically greeted her.

As she approached, it was clear that Tomoe must have had more on her mind than Akira had first assumed, as it appeared she had quite a rough night's sleep, if she even slept at all. She appeared exhausted and looked as if she were still wearing makeup from the previous day, which, while functional, was hardly flattering on her.

Akira frowned. "Uh... rough night?" she cautiously asked.

Covering her mouth as she yawned, Tomoe nodded. "I don't think I got even a solid hour of sleep..."

"That... sucks. I'm sorry to hear that," she responded, glancing around the area cautiously for Kana.

"On top of that, I unintentionally worried my mom last night," Tomoe admitted with a deep sigh. "I left my phone in your room while we did chores, and it slipped my mind to call or text her after school."

Looking back to her friend, Akira grimaced. "Sorry about that. You had so much on your mind yesterday, and I should have reminded you."

She shook her head. "You don't have to apologize. It's my fault."

Glancing behind her friend, Akira noticed Kana approaching the school with her friend Hideko. Even from this distance, she could tell Kana had her eyes fixated on her, which meant trouble. Swallowing nervously, Akira looked to Tomoe. "W-well, we'd better head inside and get our shoes changed so we can get to class," she said with a forced laugh as her eyes trailed briefly back to Kana.

Akira led the way into the school as Tomoe followed. The two then began swapping their shoes out. While changing, Akira threw several glances over towards Kana and Hideko, seeing the two talking, and, by the looks of it, Hideko was visibly upset. However, Kana seemed to be comforting her. After a moment, however, Kana stepped away from her friend and began approaching the two of them. Akira nervously looked to Tomoe, who was just now putting her street shoes away.

"O-okay, let's go," Akira eagerly said, as she wanted to avoid Kana at all costs.

"Hey, Makai," Kana called out as she drew closer.

Pausing, Akira glanced back towards Kana.

She appeared oddly calm and somewhat less hostile than she typically was, at least towards Akira. She gestured towards the main entrance to the school. "I want to talk before class. Could you step outside with me?"

Akira looked briefly at Tomoe before her eyes darted back towards Kana. Swallowing nervously, Akira shook her head.

Surprised by Akira's response, Kana exhaled sharply as she glared at her. "I'm asking nicely, Makai. All I want to do is talk. Now, come on."

"N-no..." Akira timidly responded.

Taking a deep breath, Kana grit her teeth as her glare intensified. A clear sign of how little patience she had for Akira at this moment.

Seeing how concerned Akira was, and knowing that Kana often bullied her, Tomoe gently placed her hand onto Akira's upper arm. "Come on, let's get to class before we're late."

Akira looked briefly to Tomoe, offering a nod, though her eyes soon trailed back towards Kana. This girl terrified her, but at least with her friend nearby, Akira knew that she was somewhat safe. Turning around, she walked away with Tomoe, and the two made a beeline for their math class, taking a set of seats right next to one another. As the girls pulled their books from their bags, Kana entered the classroom and approached the two of them. Standing next to Akira's desk, she towered over her as she stared down, a presence that was impossible for anyone to simply ignore.

"I'm not playing around, Makai. I want to talk to you. Alone. *Now*," Kana firmly stated.

Akira kept her head held low, her eyes fixated on her notebook.

Kana glanced back at Tomoe, who was staring at her. With another deep sigh, Kana moved forward, placing one hand on the edge of Akira's desk and the other on the back of her chair. "You already know what I want to talk about, so stop making things look worse for yourself and come with me," she said before leaning in closer. "I will *not* hurt you, but if you don't come talk with me, then I can promise that you'll regret it later," she said in a low voice.

"She doesn't want to talk to you," Tomoe pointed out.

Looking back to Tomoe once more, Kana locked eyes with her briefly, then went to speak before she heard the door to the classroom shut.

"Everyone take your seats, please," the teacher said as he walked towards the front of the class.

Kana pushed herself off Akira's desk and immediately walked away, taking her seat on the other side of the classroom. She sat in the same spot she did on Monday, the desk in front of her where Miyoko sat, now empty. Akira kept looking over at Kana throughout the class and noticed that she wasn't paying attention to the teacher's lesson. When she wasn't holding her head and visibly struggling to not sob while staring at the now-empty desk her best friend once sat, she was looking over at Akira, locking eyes with her as she struggled to contain her anger.

As class ended, while everyone else was gathering their things up, Kana stood and made her way back across the classroom, approaching Akira once more.

"Makai..." Kana said, clearly still wrestling between her mixed emotions.

Akira timidly looked up at Kana.

Taking a deep breath, she kneeled, so she was more-so at Akira's current height. She lowered her voice. "A-Akira... please. I know I've hurt you in the past... but I need to talk to you," she said, in an almost deceptively polite tone. "I know you know something about what happened... you have to. I just want to talk. Please..."

Akira stared at her, a part of her aching and wanting to talk to Kana, while the other part of her knew that nothing but pain would come of it. Biting her lip, she shook her head. "I... I have to get to my next class," she timidly responded.

Kana allowed a moment of silence to fill the air as she struggled with her emotions. Her focus drifted over to Tomoe, who was looking back at her with a mild fear lingering in her eyes. Kana's body began to tremble before she stood up, and as she did, she swiped Akira's backpack from the hook where it hung on the edge of the desk, then promptly unzipped the main compartment of it and dumped everything out onto the floor. Kana then threw the nearly empty backpack harshly into Akira's arms and turned away, marching towards the exit to class, her fury visible in every step she took.

Akira and Tomoe were left speechless at Kana's outburst, one that the teacher glanced back to see the aftermath of, though he simply shook his head and went back to helping another student. Akira, however, knew that Kana's outburst was incredibly mild, given the circumstances.

Tomoe got up from her desk and kneeled, picking up several of Akira's items from the floor and setting them onto her desk.

Hesitantly, Akira got up and held her backpack open as she began putting her things back inside. "That... went better than I expected."

"Better?" Tomoe asked in shock, though she then flinched, as she knew they shouldn't be talking loudly about this in class. "She looked really upset, Aki... I thought she was going to cry."

She shook her head. "If I had gone with her, I'd of been the one crying... and probably bleeding too," she said before letting out a deep sigh. She then looked at her friend. "Hey, Tomoe? Would you, um... mind walking with me to gym class? Just in case Kana is still around?"

Tomoe could see the concern in her eyes. She timidly nodded. "Y-yeah. Sure. I'll walk with you."

"Thank you..." Akira responded, offering a slight bow of her head. She then hastily stuffed the rest of her things into her backpack, then zipped it up, and slung it over her shoulder.

Grabbing her bookbag, Tomoe gestured towards the door with a nod. "We'd better head that way now. Otherwise, I'll be late for my next class."

Together, they left the classroom and walked down the hallway towards the gym. Akira kept glancing around, though try as she might, she couldn't spot Kana or any of the others anywhere. She knew she'd have to put up with Takashi and possibly Hideko in gym class, but at least Kana wasn't there to harass her. Arriving at the doors to the gymnasium, Tomoe walked in with Akira long enough to see that the gym teacher was here and that plenty of students had already shown up for class.

Akira graciously bowed to her friend and thanked her repeatedly. Tomoe could only smile and reassure her that she was just happy to help. Once Tomoe left, Akira went straight towards the girls' locker room and began changing into her gym uniform. As she did so, she threw several cautious glances around, watching for anyone who might harass her. She didn't spot Hideko, which was odd, and she assumed that Kana wouldn't go out of her way to skip classes simply so she could further harass her.

Letting out a sigh of relief, Akira left the locker rooms and made her way towards the double doors at the end of the gymnasium. Some fresh air and a bit of cardio would likely do well to get her mind off everything that felt as if it weighed her down. As she got outside and made her way onto the field, she was once again approached by her least favorite person, which was even more irritating, considering how much she had on her plate already.

Running up to walk alongside her as she approached the track, Takashi smiled. "Good morning, Akira."

She sighed, rolling her eyes. "Go away, Takashi."

"You sound like you're in a bad mood. Has Kana been bothering you again?" he asked before shaking his head. "She really doesn't waste any time... but, at least, she's not in gym with us. And, hey! Yuuki isn't here either. I guess we're both lucky, huh?" he asked with a light chuckle.

'Lucky' would be if you'd piss off and leave me alone, she thought to herself before hastening her pace as she made her way out towards the track field.

Takashi moved to keep up with her. "Was there anything on your mind that you wanted to talk about?"

"If I did, it wouldn't be with you," she responded.

He frowned. "Oh... I guess you must already know then?"

She reluctantly glanced over at him several times, then slowed her run until she could stop and turn to face him. "Know what?"

"About what happened yesterday. I'm guessing that's why you're in a bad mood," he said before glancing around.

Akira grimaced as she realized what he was referring to. "I... I d-don't know what you're talking about."

Takashi recoiled in slight shock. "Huh? Really? You don't?" he asked, to which he received no response. "Oh, sorry, I thought that, well..." he let out a subtle sigh, then shook his head. "It doesn't matter. I shouldn't be the one to tell you, but... we were all sent home early yesterday because a student fell down the stairs and..."

Listening to him, she couldn't help but look away from him, lowering her sights as she avoided eye-contact with him.

He stared at her for a moment before nodding. "I see... I guess Kana did tell you then," he said, prompting her to return her focus to him. "The girl who fell down the stairs was Miyoko."

A moment of silence elapsed before Akira bit at her lip, then exhaled sharply. "H-how... how would you know that?"

"Hideko told me. When the police showed up yesterday, she, Kana, and Yuuki were all asked a bunch of questions about it. She said they wanted to know if anyone frequently fought with Miyoko or got into arguments with her," he admitted before sighing. "She told me that Kana was quick to blame you for it, which I thought was dumb... I mean, you've never really been into any arguments with Kana or Miyoko," he said before cupping his chin. "I mean... you did punch Miyoko that one time..."

"Sh-shut up!" Akira responded in a mild panic. "Why do you always have to constantly run your mouth?!"

"Huh? Did I say something wrong?" he asked.

Exhaling sharply, she held her forehead.

Takashi lightly gasped. "Oh, dang! Wait a second. You really didn't know? Sorry... the way you acted, I thought Kana would have told you. I mean... I guess I can see why she hasn't yet; since she thinks you shoved her friend, but–"

Akira abruptly turned and began walking away from him.

"H-hey! Wait up," he said as he ran to catch up with her. "Sorry if I said something to upset you, Akira. But... if it makes you feel better, you can vent your frustrations to me. I'm a really good listener."

It'd make me feel better if you'd get lost and leave me alone, she thought to herself as she let out a deep, irritated sigh.

He continued to follow alongside her, thinking of what he might say to pull her mind away from the sad news he'd just shared with her. Then, it hit him. "Oh! I noticed the last couple of days; you were sitting with someone in the cafeteria. I've never seen her before. Is she new?"

Akira angrily grumbled incoherently under her breath.

"She's pretty cute. She's also in one of my other classes. The teacher had us each go up to the front of the class and introduce ourselves. When she went up front, I could tell she was the athletic type. I'd say she's probably in as good of shape as Kana. A bit shorter, maybe, but she's got better curves," he explained as he trailed alongside her.

Stopping in her step, she clenched her fists and turned to Takashi, glaring at him angrily. "T-Tomoe is my friend! Don't you *dare* creep on her! If you do, I swear, I'll..." she said, tears forming in her eyes.

Takashi frowned. "I'm not 'creeping' on anyone, Akira. I'm just saying that I can see why you'd want to be friends with her," he said, his smile returning. "I don't mind, by the way. You know, the only thing that I care about is your happiness. Which is why my heart belongs to you and no one else," he said as he placed his hand solemnly over his chest. "I don't even watch dirty movies or obsess over girls in anime or manga."

Akira could practically feel her skin crawl as she listened to him speak. With a deep sigh, she abruptly turned and began walking away from him.

Following her, Takashi closed the distance and looked at her with concern. "Honestly, I swear that I haven't betrayed you, Akira. You're the only girl in my heart. I wouldn't even fantasize about any other girl. Even if your friend is hot."

Abruptly stopping, Akira froze briefly before turning and glaring at him again. "Kenichi Takashi! Would you please get the *hell* away from me?!"

Takashi frowned. "I can tell you're frustrated... it'd probably make you feel a lot better if you had someone to vent to. I know she probably just makes you want to scream. My ears are always open... and so is my heart."

Akira could feel her eye slightly twitch at his incessant persistence. She had plenty of irritations, but the problem was that she didn't want to vent any of them to one of the primary sources of her daily annoyance. She held her index finger up in front of her. "If there were anyone I'd want to vent to... it wouldn't be–"

He reached out and wrapped his hands around hers as he moved slightly closer. "I know you always worry about others judging you... but, I just want you to know that I'd never judge you, Akira. Not for anything. So whatever is on your mind... or in your heart, I promise, I'd be more than happy to listen to you."

She felt yet another cold chill wash over her as she felt his hands on hers. *If you could listen, you'd of heard the literal hundreds of times I've asked you not to touch me.* She exhaled sharply, then pulled unsuccessfully on her hand. "L-let go of me!"

He smiled. "But, I like holding your hand. Your skin feels so soft. You must take good care of yourself, Akira. I mean," he let out an exasperated sigh, "your beautiful face is absolutely radiant today. It's shimmering in the soft sunlight."

She gagged. *Shimmering in the soft sunlight? Just when I think he's run out of gross shit to say, he comes at me with that.* She shook her head. "Just, let go of me already!"

He leaned in a bit closer, prompting her to stagger half a step back to maintain her distance. "You do look a bit paler than usual. You're not getting sick, are you?" he asked, frowning. "If you are, you should stay home. I could bring you soup, medicine, some manga to help pass the time. Anything you need, I'd be happy to bring it over."

Akira grit her teeth. "The last time you tried to come over, you got me into a ton of trouble with my grandfather. I'd appreciate it if you'd stay away from my house... and *me!*"

Takashi frowned. "Aw... it's not my fault he thought I was your boyfriend. I mean," he chuckled, "we would make such a great couple."

She immediately gagged. *I think I'd rather die...*

"Hey!" a girl shouted out from off towards the gymnasium.

Takashi and Akira both froze. Turning towards the sound of her voice, Akira saw the girl she bumped into on her first day of school, the one with the short blonde hair, approaching them. She appeared angry, though her focus seemed to be on Takashi, not Akira.

He swallowed nervously. "Uh... y-yes?"

Crossing her arms, the girl stared Takashi down. "Weren't you told by Mister Masaru to not put your hands on girls? *Specifically* her?"

Pausing as he tried to think, he recalled the incident during their last gym class. Immediately, he let go of Akira and backed away from her. "I, um... sorry!" He quickly bowed his head to the girl before turning and walking away hastily.

Watching as Takashi fled, Akira wished that she had that kind of power. Returning her attention to the girl, Akira noticed her approaching.

She smiled. "Are you okay?"

Akira reluctantly nodded. "I... I'm fine. Thanks."

Turning to watch Takashi from a distance, the girl sighed. "If he keeps grabbing onto you like that, tell Mister Masaru. He got onto him Monday for it. But if he keeps it up, then I bet Mister Masaru will do more than just scold him."

"You're right. I probably should. I'm just not used to teachers doing anything about shit like that since they never did at my junior high."

She looked curiously at Akira. "Really? That's shocking. It's a teacher's responsibility to protect their students. Where did you go to junior high at? If you don't mind me asking."

Akira shook her head. "No, it's fine. I went to Nirasakinishi. Oh, and my name is Makai Akira, by the way. But, you can just call me Aki."

She smiled. "It's nice to meet you, Aki. My name is Yasuhida Ikumi. I'm not very familiar with Nirasakinishi, but I'm from Shiritsu Higashi Junior High School."

"Shiritsu Higashi? I've heard that's a really popular school."

Ikumi giggled. "It is, but it's a lot further away from my house than this one. With how close this one is, I can just walk to school instead of having my dad or uncle give me a ride," she said before examining Akira, almost as if she were studying her. "So, um... do you remember me, by chance?" she asked with a hint of nervousness in her voice.

"Remember you?" she responded before slowly nodding. "Y-yeah. I do. You're the girl I bumped into outside of school on Monday morning."

Ikumi's smile brightened as she excitedly nodded. "Uh-huh! I remember you told me that you liked my hair," she said, her cheeks reddening slightly. "I didn't really have a good chance to tell you, but I think your hair is really cute too."

Akira awkwardly chuckled. "O-oh... thanks," she said as she reached up and ruffled her hair. "I don't do much to it. Wash, rinse, dry, and just sort of call it good from there."

She let out a disheartened sigh. "You're so lucky... if I did that, my hair would be so frizzy. Especially with the humidity around here."

"I guess I should count that as a blessing then, huh?" Akira responded.

Ikumi nodded. "Yeah!" she said before an awkward silence filled the air between them. Biting her lip, she glanced briefly around, then looked back to Akira. "A-anyway... I think it'd be best if I head back inside and finish my exercises, since... I've kind of done everything Mister Masaru had for me out here," she said before bowing her head. "It... it was nice talking to you, Akira." She gasped. "Oh! Err... I mean, Aki."

Akira smiled. "Yeah... nice talking to you too."

Ikumi offered another quick bow of her head before turning and hastily making her way back towards the doors that led into the gym.

Watching her leave, Akira reached up and playfully scratched at her cheek. "She was... a bit odd. I wonder why she was so nervous?" she asked herself before glancing over towards Takashi. "Even if she's odd... if she can get him to leave me the hell alone, it might be worthwhile to talk with her during my gym classes. Maybe she and I could exercise together, and then I wouldn't have to worry about him anymore?"

With Takashi now keeping his distance, Akira was able to peacefully return to her exercises. While out on the track field, she had far too much time to allow her mind to wander to places she didn't need it at. Such as what kind of violent retaliation she would receive from Kana, what information she may have accidentally shared with the police, or what would happen if she was convicted of killing Miyoko, a crime she didn't even commit. It terrified her to think she could spend the rest of her life behind bars for something someone else did, though she had to weigh that against going back to how things were before she and Tomoe became friends, where life itself felt like a prison.

Chapter 7
No Escape

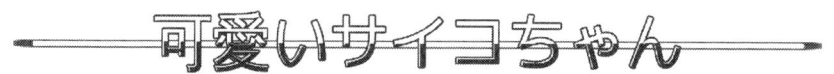

―――――可愛いサイコちゃん―――――

Washing up in the showers, Akira hastily changed into her school uniform and cautiously left class. It was nearing lunchtime, and she was ready to eat some food and relax with Tomoe. Not that they'd had much time to relax since the incident from the previous day. Although, this was when she realized that she had forgotten to pack any food for lunch when she left this morning. The school did provide food for students if they neglected to bring their own, though Akira would have preferred to choose her own meal rather than be given one by the school.

While walking down the hallway, with multiple students around her, she noticed Kana and her boyfriend, Yuuki, walking towards her. Freezing, Akira swallowed nervously before turning and walking back the other way. Cursing her poor luck under her breath, she just wanted to avoid whatever Kana might have had planned for her. Though before she could get far, she felt resistance from her backpack. Glancing behind her, she saw how Yuuki had a grip on the handle atop her backpack.

He was more than a full head taller than Akira, and far more built than even Kana, as he was among the top players of their baseball team back in Nirasakinishi. Despite his popularity and success in school, Akira knew all too well how volatile Yuuki could be. He'd frequently get into fights with other boys at the school, and often he would be the one to come out on top. He'd been dating Kana for as long as Akira had known either of them and as bad as he could be, he was always at his worst when Kana was around to encourage him to indulge in truly sadistic punishments for those she didn't like.

Kana moved around in front of Akira. "Going somewhere, Makai?"

Akira timidly shook her head. "N-no... I just... I forgot something in the gym, th-that's all."

"You forgot something? Interesting... I wonder what else you've forgotten in that," she pressed her finger against Akira's forehead, "empty little head of yours? Like, maybe everything that's happened in the past eight years since you first moved here?"

"Wh-what? I... I d-don't know what you're talking about," she said as tears slowly began to form around her eyes.

"You don't?" Kana asked in shock before lightly chuckling. "Did you hear that, babe? We must be mistaken... it seems Makai doesn't know anything," she said before rolling her eyes.

She swallowed nervously, feeling her heart pounding away in her chest.

Moving uncomfortably close, Kana narrowed her eyes intensely on Akira. "Do you think I'm some kind of idiot, Makai?"

She shook her head.

"Good, I didn't think so," Kana calmly responded. "So. Let's cut to the chase. Just answer one very simple question for me. Were you the one who shoved my best friend down a flight of stairs?"

Akira reluctantly shook her head once more.

Kana grit her teeth angrily. "Don't lie to me, Makai!" she angrily said before exhaling sharply. "Do you think you were justified in what you did? Do you think that us pushing you around for something you deserve gives you the right to kill my best friend?" she asked in a low voice as she leaned in closer.

"I... I-I don't know wh-what you're... t-talking about...." Akira timidly responded, trying her best to feign ignorance, though lacking any confidence in her words.

Kana scoffed. "You've always been a terrible liar," she said before thinking briefly before exhaling sharply. "I saw you made yourself a new friend. That new girl, Asano Tomoe? The girl from out of town? Moved here around a month or two ago?" she asked before rolling her eyes once more. "Ya know, Miyoko didn't like her at all. We pushed her around so she'd know not to try and mess with us," she said before reaching out and grabbing the front of Akira's shirt. "Is that why you did it? To 'protect' the newest object of your perverse obsession?"

Akira swallowed nervously, shaking her head yet again. "N-no... Kana, I didn't have anything to do with what happened. I swear. I never... I never even saw Miyoko yesterday, I don't think..."

Gritting her teeth, she moved in closer, less than a breath away from Akira. "There's not a soul in this school who hated Miyoko... *except* you. I know you shoved my friend down the stairs. Maybe you didn't intend for her to die from it, but that's what happened," she said in a low voice, raising it only for emphasis. "You want to 'pretend' your mistake away... fine. Have fun pretending it didn't happen. Because, if you don't own up to what you did, then I swear... I'll make everything we ever did to you before pale in comparison to what I'll do to you from now on. Every. Single. Day."

Akira could feel her heart pounding away inside her chest as she locked eyes with Kana. Everything else around her felt as if it didn't even exist, and the only thing she could hear was the very real threats Kana handed her without even a hint of hesitation.

Pulling back, Kana kept her eyes on Akira before abruptly throwing a hard punch into her stomach. Yuuki released his grip from the backpack, allowing Akira to double over and slump against the wall as her stomach ached from the hit. With little more than a scoff, Kana moved around her and began to walk back the way they had come from.

Pain from the sharp jab aside, Akira felt a sickness in the pit of her stomach. Kana blamed her for Miyoko's death, even though it genuinely wasn't her fault. Hesitantly turning to look over her shoulder, Akira saw Kana didn't even glance back at her. She didn't know what the consequences would be to not confess to something she didn't do. But in her heart, she honestly suspected that prison time for a crime she wasn't responsible for might be easier to live with.

On her second attempt to get to the cafeteria, Akira was met with little resistance. As she arrived, she scanned the room searching for her friend and found Tomoe sitting at the same place as on Monday, with a textbook out as she wrote a few things down in her notebook. Approaching the table, Akira moved to the opposite side as her friend and sat her backpack down, then took the seat right across from Tomoe.

"Hey..." Akira said in a low voice.

Tomoe looked up at her friend and noticed that something seemed to be wrong. "Are you alright?"

Akira sighed as she shook her head. "Not really." She paused, gathering her thoughts. "Kana caught me on the way here. Right in the middle of the walkway with students passing by us. Nobody said a word... they just ignored us."

Tomoe's mouth hung open, somewhat in disbelief that their fellow students would do nothing to deter the bullying. "What did she do?"

Akira glanced around. Taking a deep breath, she leaned in closer to whisper to her friend. "She thinks I was the one who pushed Miyoko down the stairs. And apparently, she wants me to confess to it..."

Tomoe's eyes widened. "Wh-what? But why?"

"Because she hates my guts? I told you that before."

"Yeah, but... I don't understand. Why would she try to force you to admit to doing something that you didn't do?"

Burying her face in her hands, Akira groaned. "I don't *freaking* know."

Tomoe frowned. "I'm sorry she's being like that."

Akira slouched back in her seat. "The worst part is, she said if I don't confess to what she believes happened, then she's going to make my life, well... a living hell. As if it hasn't been shitty enough already."

Lowering her head, Tomoe felt terrible about the pain Akira now had to endure, all because of something that she had done. "Say, Aki?" she asked, looking to her friend. "Why don't I walk you home after school? Then... if Kana tries something, maybe I can intervene, or at least get help?"

Moving her eyes up to look at her friend, Akira saw Tomoe offer a comforting smile. "You... you wouldn't mind?"

Tomoe shook her head. "Not at all. I'm happy to be there for you, Aki. Especially since I feel like this whole mess is all my fault."

"Don't say that," she said before sighing. "So... how have you been holding up throughout the day?"

"It's been difficult, but I guess the good news is that nobody has said anything about what happened. It's like they don't even know..."

Akira nodded. "That's what it sort of seems like."

Tomoe frowned. "Aki, how long do you think all of this will go on? All of this anxiety, the fear... not to mention Kana accusing you."

Akira rolled her head back. "Knowing her, it'll either be graduation or until she just says 'screw it' and kills me in some blind rage..."

"Please, don't say that," she said in a saddened tone.

"Well, she's been tormenting me since I was thirteen. She's never once let up. Only now, she's got an even stronger vendetta against me."

"Maybe if you make more friends, she'll leave you alone? Strength in numbers, you know?" Tomoe suggested.

Akira forcefully chuckled before shaking her head. "There's no way. If she's not dissuaded from bullying me in front of a group of students and teachers, then me having friends isn't going to stop her. Especially if she thinks I killed her best friend."

Tomoe frowned. "I just can't believe that she'd be so bold as to bully you in front of other students and even teachers," she said before a thought crossed her mind. "If you don't mind me asking. What kinds of things has she done to you?"

Akira crossed her arms. "Well... I'd rather not go into detail about some of the shittier things she's done. But she's broken and stolen my belongings, locked me out of my locker before, beaten me up on multiple occasions. Oh! And she's dragged my reputation so far through the mud that I'd bet most everyone from my old school hates my guts."

She gasped. "Oh, wow... I'm so sorry that she was so mean to you."

Akira reached up and frustratingly held her temple. "It's nothing you've got to apologize for. I just wish she'd leave me alone. I can't even be myself when she's around."

"Hey, Aki," Tomoe said, drawing her friend's attention. Smiling, she nodded. "So long as we're friends, I promise I'll do whatever I can to keep people like Kana away from you."

Despite it being a struggle, Akira smiled. "That's really... it means a lot to hear that, Tomoe. Thank you."

She lightly giggled. "It's what friends are for."

"I wish I had more friends then. Either way, I'm going to go get some food, so I'll be right back."

Walking up towards the line of students waiting to get their food, Akira found a spot at the end and waited patiently for her turn. After getting a meal, she returned to her table. While she ate, she mostly kept quiet so Tomoe could study. Once she was done eating, she did some writing for her class, and before long, lunch was over. Parting ways, Akira and Tomoe each went to their respective classes.

Although she spent the rest of her day constantly looking over her shoulder, Akira was fortunate enough to avoid running into Kana again. Even with this as a silver lining, she was still terrified of the walk home, as she knew that would be when she'd be most vulnerable. As her last class came to a close, Akira rushed to the main entrance and met up with Tomoe. She expressed her fears and concerns, though her friend reassured her that she would do whatever she could to prevent Kana from hurting her.

Leaving the school, they went along with the flow of the other students before branching off and following the drainage canal. There was some idle conversation about classes between them, though Akira kept looking around nervously. Passing by the construction site on their left, they took a right and crossed over the canal. As they did so, Akira couldn't help but vaguely hear the subtle sounds of a bicycle. Glancing around once more, she caught a glimpse of Kana, riding on her bike towards the two of them. Immediately, Akira moved around behind Tomoe, almost as if she were a terrified child, hiding behind their parent for protection.

As Kana drew near, she reversed her pedal, forcing her bike to screech to a halt. She had stopped just a short distance away from the two girls, certainly no further than three meters at most. Hopping off her bike, Kana flipped the kickstand down and ensured her bike was stable. She then turned her focus towards the two girls.

"You know, I thought I was generous. I asked you again and again when we were at school for us to talk... just to talk," Kana said.

Akira nervously swallowed as she cowered behind Tomoe.

Crossing her arms, Kana exhaled sharply. "I even pleaded... no, I begged you to talk to me. Instead, you ignored me, pushed me away, and went on, acting as if nothing was wrong," she said, shaking her head. "And now, you've left us with no choice..."

"Us?" Akira wondered aloud.

Kana lightly scoffed before gesturing behind them with a nod.

Both Akira and Tomoe glanced back, seeing Yuuki on the other side of the short canal bridge. He'd just hopped off his bike and threw the kickstand down himself, then began to approach them over the bridge.

Moving around to position herself between the two girls and the street to Akira's house, Kana glared. "This is your last chance to talk, Makai."

Looking quickly between both Kana and Yuuki, Tomoe exhaled sharply, setting her focus on Kana. "Leave her alone. Aki hasn't done anything wrong," she said, trying to maintain her courage, despite knowing this was all due to her own mistake.

Kana exhaled sharply. "I'd shut up if I were you, Asano. After what Makai did, I couldn't care less about you. In fact, you'd be doing yourself a favor if you just ditched her here and left," she said before narrowing her eyes onto Tomoe. "But, if you do want to defend this little psycho here, then I have no qualms about giving you the same treatment as her."

Tomoe briefly glanced back at Akira, who was still cowering behind her, clinging loosely onto the sleeve of her uniform in fear. Sighing, Tomoe returned her sights to Kana. "Aki is not a 'psycho.' In fact, she's probably the nicest person I've met since I moved here," she responded.

Akira lightly blushed. "R-really?" she quietly asked.

Kana rolled her eyes. "Give me a break," she groaned before shaking her head. "Last chance to walk away, Asano. Take it, or leave it."

Tomoe sighed. "This is stupid... come on, Aki, let's just go," she said as she began to walk towards the street Akira's house was on, undeterred by Kana or Yuuki.

Reluctantly, Akira followed her friend, still clinging to her shirt sleeve.

Standing her ground, Kana watched as the two of them walked right past her. She didn't allow her sights to leave them until they were a short distance past her. Exhaling sharply, she looked to her boyfriend and offered a nod of her head.

Wasting no time, Yuuki hastily walked towards the girls. Tomoe was keeping her sights forward, ignoring them, while Akira trailed directly behind her, with her eyes closed as she repeatedly pleaded in her head for Kana and Yuuki to leave them alone. Unfortunately, her pleas would go unanswered as Yuuki grabbed onto Akira's backpack, then after giving a swift tug, he forced her back and away from her friend.

Feeling herself being pulled, Akira staggered back before feeling Kana catch her, placing her hands firmly on Akira's upper arms as she held her from behind.

Turning around, Tomoe gasped as she saw what happened. "Hey! Leave her alone!" she shouted, stomping her foot.

Kana pat her right hand against Akira's upper arm. "You're trembling, Makai. It must be from all those heavy burdens you're carrying..."

Reaching out, Kana pulled the straps of Akira's backpack down, slipping it off, though not allowing her even a moment to slip away. Kana then tossed it over for Yuuki to catch as she maintained her grip on Akira to prevent her escape.

"There. You must feel better without all that weight on your shoulders," Kana said, comforting Akira before her voice took on a far more serious tone. "Maybe there's something you'd like to get off your chest as well?"

Akira shook her head as tears began to run down her cheeks.

"Nakajima Kana, leave her alone!" Tomoe repeated.

Yuuki turned to Tomoe. "Keep talking. One more word and this backpack will go for a swim."

Kana lightly gasped. "Oh! Now, there's an idea," she said, forcing Akira to walk with her back to the bridge that ran across the canal.

Scoffing at Tomoe, Yuuki followed Kana over towards the bridge.

Tomoe went to speak, though she didn't want to urge Yuuki to throw Akira's things down into the water, as it would ruin all of her school supplies. Reluctantly, she followed them over towards the bridge. As she approached, she noticed Kana had forced Akira up against the railing, holding her by a handful of hair as she positioned Akira to stare down into the water.

Leaning forward, Kana gave Akira a cold stare. "My best friend is dead, Makai... and I know damn well that it wasn't an accident. You're the only one who had a beef with any of us. So, quit hiding the fact that you shoved her. Admit it, and I'll stop."

As best she could, Akira shook her head. "K-Kana... I d-didn't do it, I swear!" she explained in a whimper.

Exhaling sharply, Kana rolled her eyes. "Confess to what you did, and I promise I won't hurt you. Just admit to it, and then we'll let the police do their job. Now... you pushed Miyoko down the stairs, didn't you?"

"How many times does she have to tell you that she didn't do it before you believe her?!" Tomoe shouted.

Yuuki turned and looked at her before exhaling sharply. "You're every bit as dense as she is. Did you already forget what I said?" he asked before rearing back, then throwing Akira's backpack as hard as he could, out and over the railing, where it plummeted down into the meter deep water.

"H-hey!" Tomoe responded as she moved to reach out, almost as if she felt she had some hope in catching the discarded backpack that was well beyond her reach.

Akira watched in horror as her belongings were thrown away, landing with a moderate splash in the murky canal waters.

Pulling Akira off the railing, Kana turned her around and pushed her back up against it, gripping the front of her shirt tightly. "You want to keep up this charade? Fine. But things are about to get *much* worse for you from here on out, Makai. I swear... until you confess to what you've done, I'm going to make every single day for you *significantly* worse than any of the ones before it. Count on that."

Rearing back with one hand, Kana formed it into a fist, then threw it into Akira's abdomen, stunning her and nearly causing her to collapse onto her knees. Before she could, however, Kana lifted Akira over her shoulder. Heaving with all of her strength, Kana threw her over the railing of the bridge and down into the waters where her backpack now resided. However, unlike her bag, Akira landed with a loud splash as she submerged immediately into the filthy depths of the stagnant water.

Tomoe reached up and covered her mouth, gasping in disbelief that anyone would ever do something so cruel to someone else.

Shaking her head, Kana let out a deep sigh before looking at Yuuki. "Go grab your bike, babe," she said, gesturing with a nod behind her.

He offered a nod and then began moving towards his bike at the other end of the bridge.

Meanwhile, Kana began approaching Tomoe, who was still stunned and left almost speechless at their cruelty.

"H-how could... how could you do something like that?!" Tomoe hysterically asked. "I just don't get it... Aki is such a kindhearted and sweet girl. Why are you so hateful towards her."

Kana scoffed. "She's far from it," she said before taking a deep breath, then sighing. "You're gullible if you believe Makai is kindhearted or sweet. But, maybe you're just ignorant?" She shrugged her shoulders. "Or maybe you're just trying to be a good person. I mean, after all, you see a girl who's all alone, has no friends, and gets pushed around a lot... so you befriend her, you're nice to her, and then you try to defend her. For a lot of people, it might be the right thing to do... but, even under the best circumstances, I wouldn't trust Makai as a friend. Not anymore."

Tomoe growled under her breath at Kana. "You'd never trust her because you've probably never taken the chance to get to know her!"

"You have no idea what you're talking about, Asano," she snapped. Gesturing off the edge of the canal bridge towards Akira, she shook her head. "Makai was once my best friend. For five years, she and I were so close that we were practically like sisters."

Tomoe recoiled in shock upon hearing this. "Wh-what?"

She nodded. "Yeah... I guess she neglected to share that detail, huh? She probably also didn't tell you about how I have an actual sister too. Her name is Ina, and she's a year younger than me," she said, exhaling sharply. "She and Makai were really good friends too... up until Makai tried to force herself on Ina."

"She... Aki did what?" Tomoe asked as her eyes widened.

Kana narrowed her eyes on Tomoe. "You heard me. Makai doesn't like boys like a normal girl... instead, she tries to seduce and prey on other girls. That's what she tried to do to my sister," she said, gagging in disgust. "If you had a younger sibling, then you'd understand why I do the things I do to her. But being a degenerate isn't enough for her," she said before shaking her head once more. "Whether she intended to or not, Makai killed my best friend. And... if you're willing to be her friend when she tried to molest my sister, then murder Miyoko... then you're every bit the degenerate that she is."

Tomoe stared at Kana, unsure of how to respond.

Looking at her boyfriend, Kana nodded. "Let's go," she said before walking past Tomoe on her way towards her bike. "I'd suggest you distance yourself as much as you can from Makai, Asano," she said as she got on her bike, kicking the stand back up, then rolling it around to ride back in the direction of the school.

Tomoe watched as they left, her mind racing with so many thoughts. Her focus was broken, however, when she heard coughing from down below in the canal. Remembering that Kana had thrown Akira into the waters below, Tomoe ran as quickly as she could onto the bridge, then looked down. She could see Akira standing up in the water, her clothes completely drenched, her hair soaked while she was coughing as she no doubt swallowed some water amidst her panic during the situation.

"Aki?! Are you alright?" Tomoe called out.

Blowing her nose to get the water out, Akira let out a deep sigh before speechlessly looking up at Tomoe on the bridge.

Frowning, Tomoe glanced around before noticing a couple of men standing just outside of the construction site. She wasn't sure how long they'd been standing there, but she knew she needed help if she wanted to get her friend out of the canal. Turning back to Akira, she motioned for her friend to wait, then quickly stepped away, rushing over towards where the men were.

Approaching them, Tomoe asked for their help, and judging by their confusion, they must have not seen what happened. She explained the situation, and then one of the men stepped back inside the construction site, returning with a rope, along with two other workers. The four men all followed Tomoe over as she led them back to the bridge.

Wasting no time at all, they dropped the rope down and pulled Akira back up onto the bridge. Thanks to the water, her clothes were completely soaked and smelled of mold and mildew. The construction workers asked if they needed more help, but Akira just wanted to go home. She was practically crying as she and Tomoe continued the short distance towards her house. She was soaked to the bone, one of her shoes had fallen off, and she couldn't find it, and all of her belongings in her backpack were gone.

Arriving at her house, Akira just sat down on the edge of the concrete bricks that bordered the garden. Reaching up and covering her eyes, Akira sobbed nonstop for several minutes. Tomoe could do little but watch with a broken heart as she was powerless to help her friend. Even when she said she'd keep her safe, as she promised, she could do nothing but watch as Kana ruined so many of Akira's things. Wiping her tears out of her eyes, Akira just shook her head in disbelief.

"I can't believe her! I can't believe she'd throw me in there like that!"

Tomoe moved over and sat down next to her friend. "I'm... sorry I couldn't do anything to stop her."

Sniffling, Akira shook her head. "It's not your fault. It's hers! She's a fucking plague. I hate her so much! She's done nothing but made my entire life a living hell."

Tomoe lowered her head. "I'm sorry..."

"I wish..."

Tomoe looked at Akira, seeing how upset her friend was.

Akira wiped the tears from her eyes. "I wish it were... I wish it were Kana who fell down the stairs and died... then maybe my life wouldn't be so miserable anymore."

Tomoe's eyes slowly widened, hearing her friend wish for something so horrible, something that she wished had never even happened in the first place. Burying her face in her hands, Akira continued to cry. Tomoe couldn't help but feel terrible, as, in her eyes, she felt like this was all entirely her fault. Although, in the back of her mind, she couldn't help but think back on what Kana had told her, about how Akira was supposedly some sick, demented girl who was best avoided, despite everything Tomoe had come to know about her.

Chapter 8
Past Mistakes

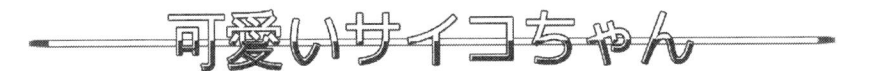

可愛いサイコちゃん

Rather than going home after ensuring her friend made it back to her house safely, Tomoe stayed with Akira, as she was worried about what happened. Akira's grandparents weren't home, and according to a note they had left on the kitchen table, they were running errands and getting groceries. Akira stood by the sink, pulling her waterlogged phone out from her skirt pocket and setting it on the counter, then removing her shirt and skirt, each of which she wrung out over the sink. Tomoe stood nearby, trying to think of what she could do or say to help her friend after such a horrible turn of events.

Twisting her school shirt tightly, Akira squeezed it as hard as she could, forcing as much water as possible out of it. Upon unraveling it, she pulled it close to her nose and cautiously sniffed it. The water from the canal reeked of mold, mildew, and the general nastiness one would expect from water that was so stagnant. What's worse was the fact that it wasn't just her clothes that smelled so terrible; her whole body did as well.

With a deep sigh, Akira shook her head. "I need a hot shower..."

Tomoe looked up at her friend, wishing she knew what to say.

Staring down at her shirt in her hand, Akira angrily raised it into the air and threw it into the sink with an audible splat as the damp fabric hit the metal sink. "Fuck Kana! She's the absolute worst person in the world!"

Tomoe frowned. "Aki..."

"I can't believe she'd throw me into the canal!" Akira turned to look at her friend, resting back against the edge of the kitchen counter. "She calls me a psychopath, and yet she's the one who goes out of her way to ruin my life every goddamn day!"

Tomoe lowered her head as she sighed.

Reaching up, Akira held her wet, clumped together hair, frustratingly pulling at it. "I just wish she was out of my freaking life!"

Still unsure of what to say, Tomoe remained silent. It almost felt as if a few minutes passed before anything was said between the girls.

"So, um... what did they do to you after she threw me into the water?" Akira reluctantly asked.

Tomoe's eyes darted up towards her friend, contemplating whether she should admit to what she was told.

Akira sighed. "I hope they didn't beat you up at all. If they did that just because you stood up for me, then... I don't know what I'd do."

Tomoe nervously bit at her lower lip as she took a deep breath. "Well... they didn't really do anything. Kana just told me that I shouldn't be your friend anymore."

Akira scoffed. "Figures. She's probably trying to get you to ditch me; that way, I'm an easy-ass target again. Not that she was dissuaded at all by your presence."

"Sorry about that..."

Akira quickly looked at her friend and shook her head. "It's not your fault. You tried to help me, and I appreciate it, I do... but Kana and Yuuki are brutes. I'm just happy that you didn't get hurt."

Taking a deep breath, Tomoe put her attention fully on her friend. "So, um... Kana did tell me about something. And... I'd be lying if I said I didn't want to hear the truth about it..."

Akira's eyes locked with Tomoe's, an uneasiness washing over her, like the feeling of an impending disaster.

"She mentioned that the two of you used to be best friends before, well... something happened..."

Akira let out an exasperated sigh. "Shit..."

Tomoe paused as she noticed Akira's reaction.

"It was about her sister, wasn't it?" she asked, sounding as if she were on the verge of tears.

Tomoe reluctantly nodded. "I... I take it that it's true then?"

Sniffling, Akira wiped the budding tears from her eyes. "If she said that I tried to force myself on her sister... that's a goddamned lie, and she knows it!" she said, more tears forming. She let out a deep sigh as she shook her head in disbelief. "Fuck... I know you'll hate me for what I am... but," she looked back to her friend. "I didn't do the shit that she's accusing me of. She's lied about this to other people too, and I'm so sick of it!"

She motioned for Akira to wait. "Aki, please. Just... just tell me what happened. I promise I'm listening to what you have to say."

Taking staggered breaths, Akira could feel herself trembling as she nodded. "A-alright... well, the truth is, I used to be friends with them. Kana, Ina, Hideko and... yeah, even Miyoko. They were so kind to me when I first moved here, especially Kana," she explained, sniffling once more as she shook her head in disbelief. "We used to spend almost every weekend at each others' house."

Tomoe nodded as she continued to listen closely.

"A-anyway..." Akira said, clearing her throat. "Over time... I kind of realized that I, well... I kind of preferred girls, from a romantic standpoint, I mean. I don't really like guys at all, I mean... they're okay as, like, friends. But I just can't imagine being with a guy romantically. But a girl," she paused, letting out an exasperated sigh as she shivered. "Even the thought of it makes my heart flutter..." she said before her eyes trailed back to Tomoe. "But, um... th-that's not the only thing Kana accused me of, I'm sure..."

"Aki," Tomoe said, drawing her friend's attention. She offered a comforting smile. "I'm not judging you... remember what I told you before? My mom raised me not to judge others. So, don't feel as if you should be nervous around me, okay?"

Taking a deep breath, Akira nodded. "A-alright... um, anyway. More than just liking girls, I specifically had a crush on Kana's sister, Ina. She was... about six months younger than me, and... one night, when we had a sleepover, I built up the courage to tell her that I had a crush on her," she explained before sighing once more. "Before I did, I kind of brought up the subject of 'girls liking girls' to her, and... I was shocked. She didn't immediately think it was disgusting or anything."

"Did she feel the same way then?" Tomoe curiously asked.

Biting her lip, she shook her head. "No... she didn't. But, she was at least kind of curious about the idea. And, so... she and I kissed. I remember being so embarrassed, and my face was probably so red at the time," she admitted, blushing at the thought of that pleasant memory.

Tomoe smiled at her friend's reaction.

Reaching up, Akira ran her fingers through her hair. "S-so, um... while we were kissing... I thought everyone was asleep. I had moved from my makeshift bed on the floor into Ina's bed, which was next to mine. And, while we were kissing... Kana turned the lights on," she said, all joy from this story fading from her as she mentioned that detail. She trembled. "When she caught me lying in bed with Ina, with us kissing, she assumed I was doing something far worse," she said, abruptly shaking her head. "Ina even defended me, saying that all we were doing was hugging. But... Kana knew we were kissing and just assumed I was trying to..."

Tomoe frowned, feeling genuinely bad for Akira.

Reaching up, she wiped more tears from her eyes. "Kana kicked me out of her house right then and there. She... fortunately, only told our friends and never mentioned it to her parents... or my grandparents. But, ever since then, she's been bullying me non-stop for what she thinks I did that night and told me that if I ever retaliate... that she'd out me to my grandparents, and tell them what I 'did' to Ina."

Staring at her friend, Tomoe could see how genuinely disheartened Akira was. While she didn't have extensive experience vetting people's emotions, she felt that her friend was speaking from her heart and was being honest about what happened that night.

Nervously biting at her lip, Akira sniffled once more. "And, just so you know... I understand if you don't want to be friends with a girl who... is a lesbian," she admitted, timidly looking back to Tomoe. "B-but... I just want you to know that... I n-never hurt *anyone*. Not like Kana accuses me of..." she said before she hung her head low once more. "I could never do something like *that* to anybody. Especially not my best friend at the time."

Tomoe took a brief moment to gather her thoughts before she nodded. "I have to admit... when Kana accused you of trying to force yourself onto her little sister, the news shocked me. That doesn't sound like something you'd do. Honestly, you're just too nice," she said, offering a smile to her disheartened friend.

Akira hesitantly looked back to Tomoe, feeling somewhat encouraged by her words.

"As for you being a lesbian..." Tomoe said before shaking her head. "Like I said before. My mother taught me never to judge others. Actually, one of my friends back in Fukuoka was, well... I did promise him that I wouldn't say... but it's not like you'll meet him anytime soon. He came out and told me that he liked boys," she said, giggling lightly. "As long as it made him happy, I didn't mind at all. And, so long as you're happy with how you feel, then I don't mind either."

"S-seriously?" she asked in disbelief. "So... you don't think I'm a freak or anything?"

"Not at all. I think you're nice, and..." Tomoe snickered, "you're pretty funny too."

Akira offered a slight smile at her friend's comment. "That's... sweet of you to say. Well, I'm sorry I wasn't up-front with you about all of this. It was probably weird to hear it from someone like Kana first."

"You don't have to apologize. None of this is something I'd expect anyone to share with someone they just met," she responded.

Akira awkwardly chuckled. "Y-yeah... I guess that's true..." she said before letting out a deep sigh. "I'm, um... going to go take a shower and change into some dry clothes," she said as she turned and got her clothes out from the sink, then grabbed her phone from the counter. "I don't know when my grandparents will be home, so it's probably best if you wait in my room," she said, turning to face her friend.

"Alright. But, if you want to take your time and enjoy the water, then feel free. I'll be fine," Tomoe said as she offered a comforting smile.

"I might just do that. Thank you, Tomoe," Akira said before making her way down the hallway, passing the bathroom by so she could dump her soaked clothes into the washer.

Returning down the hall, Akira ducked into the bathroom and got some warm water running as she took her seat on the small stool and began washing herself up, working diligently to remove the putrid smell of the drainage canal's waters. While cleaning up, she heard the door to the bathroom open, which drew her attention towards the glass door that separated the two sections of her bathroom.

"I hope you don't mind, but I brought you some clean clothes," Tomoe said.

Akira blushed. "O-oh! Um... th-thank you," she said, feeling flustered at the notion of Tomoe going to that length for her.

"If you feel up for it, you should soak for a bit in a hot bath. I think that would help you feel better," she suggested.

"I, uh... I might. Thank you, Tomoe," Akira shyly responded.

"Enjoy your shower, Aki," she added before closing the door behind her as she left.

Letting out a deep sigh, Akira turned back around to face the shower. "She brought me clothes to wear? That's..." her cheeks reddened further, "so considerate of her..."

Allowing the water to wash over her, Akira momentarily lost herself as she couldn't help but look far too deep into the kind actions of her friend. After returning to her senses, Akira quickly rinsed off and got out of the shower. Despite Tomoe's insistence, she didn't want to leave her friend waiting any longer than she had to, although a part of that was simply due to how desperately Akira wanted to spend time with her as well. After getting changed into the shorts and t-shirt Tomoe left for her, Akira raced upstairs to her bedroom.

"Hey, I know you said I could relax if I wanted to, but... I figured I could always do that another time, while I might not always be able to hang out with you as easily," Akira said with a light chuckle as she stepped inside.

Tomoe looked at her as she sat in the chair at the computer desk. Judging by the expression she wore, she had a lot on her mind.

Exhaling sharply, Akira offered a brief nod before approaching her friend. Tossing her ruined phone into the trash can near her desk, Akira sat down on the edge of the desk itself. She interlaced her fingers as she slumped forward slightly. "Um... is there anything on your mind?"

She let out a deep sigh. "I just... I feel like all of this is completely my fault, and I don't know what to do," she said as she leaned forward, crossing her arms on Akira's desk, then laying her head down, forehead resting against her arms as she felt herself on the verge of tears.

Frowning, Akira placed her hand on her friend's arm. "Please... don't blame yourself for everything, Tomoe."

"Why? It's all my fault!" she responded amidst her tears.

Akira shook her head. "No, it's not," she said before forcing a smile. "Don't forget, it was my idea for us to leave her there on the stairs. If not for that, then none of this would be happening," she explained before reaching up and scratching the back of her head. "I mean... if you'd of told someone, then you'd probably be in jail right now... but," she shook her head, "that doesn't discount that I'm partially responsible for this too!" she explained, hoping to uplift her friend's spirits, even if just a little.

Reluctantly, Tomoe looked up at her.

She continued to smile, offering a nod to affirm further what she said before. "We're in this together, Tomoe. Just you and me. So long as we remember that, and work together, then... then everything will be alright."

"But now, all because of me, Kana's going to do things... like *that* to you," Tomoe explained as she wiped her tears away.

Akira shrugged her shoulders. "Honestly, the absolute worst Kana could ever do... doesn't bother me one bit, so long as I know I have a friend like you in my life," she said with a smile. "All this time, Kana's been bullying me, treating me like shit... and I've been all alone. But, not anymore."

"Aki..." Tomoe said before leaning back, sitting up properly in the chair as she wiped her remaining tears away.

Brightening her smile, Akira lightly giggled. "So, do me a favor. No more crying. No more worrying. Sooner or later, this will all be over, and then things will go back to normal. And, when they do... you and I will both be up one friend, right?"

Tomoe nodded. "Y-yeah... so, um... I hate to bring up something bad again, but what all was in your backpack?"

Akira sighed. "Pretty much everything. My books, which were rentals, by the way, all of the school supplies that I use every day, not to mention my cas–" she started to say before reaching up and slapping her hand against her forehead. "Fucking hell..."

Tomoe's eyes widened as she recoiled, shocked at her friend's sudden outburst. "Wh-what's wrong?"

Exhaling sharply, she shook her head in disbelief. "My cassette player and *all* of my mixed tapes were in there!"

"Your... mixed tapes?" Tomoe curiously asked.

She nodded. "Yeah. They were cassettes that my friend gave to me. They had a bunch of awesome foreign songs on them. I always kept all of my cassettes on me, so I could cycle through them if I wanted."

Tomoe frowned. "Aki, I'm so sorry..."

Burying her head in her hands, Akira groaned in frustration. "I can't believe it... hours of my favorite music washed down the fucking canal, like garbage left on the street. Fuck my life."

Reaching out, Tomoe placed her hand on her friend's knee. "Hey, it'll be okay... maybe we can go out and look for it?"

Akira shook her head. "We won't find it. And even if we did," she paused, sniffling as she shook her head, "the water would have ruined all of the cassettes, not to mention the player itself..."

Tomoe sighed. "I wish there was something I could do to make everything better... I really do."

Taking a deep breath, Akira slowly looked over at Tomoe, tears in her eyes.

"I can't do much about your cassette player or tapes... but you're welcome to borrow my books for any of the classes we share," she said with a soft smile.

Staring briefly at her friend, Akira shook her head. "No. You need them to study. You're way smarter than me; you deserve a good education. I'm not stealing your books and forcing you to handicap yourself."

Holding her hand up to her chin, Tomoe contemplated an idea. "If that's how you feel, then why don't we spend this weekend together and study?"

"Like... over at your place?" she timidly asked.

Tomoe nodded and offered a bright smile. "Sure! I bet my mom wouldn't mind!"

Akira sighed. "Yeah, but my grandfather wouldn't allow it. I have extra chores on weekends... he'd kill me if I didn't get them done."

"Would it be better if I spent the night over here instead?" she asked.

Akira frowned. "My grandfather probably won't let you spend the night. It was always like pulling teeth to ever have any of my old friends over."

"Well, it never hurts to ask. Plus, you can tell him the truth. Well... maybe not about the backpack thing, but that we're spending the weekend to study," Tomoe suggested with a smile.

She thought briefly on it as she slowly began to nod. "Maybe... honestly, my grades in school are... pretty terrible. So, I could argue that you found out about that and wanted to tutor me. My grandfather won't let me join any clubs because he thinks all I'll do is goof around in them, so having you tutor me on the weekend would probably work as an excuse."

Tomoe giggled. "It's not an excuse if I actually *do* tutor you. If your grades are poor, I'd be more than happy to help you improve."

Akira pursed her lips. She didn't care about her grades. Though, the idea of spending an entire weekend with Tomoe genuinely excited her. Eagerly, she nodded, then smiled. "I like it! And, I think that should work. I can't imagine why they'd say no to me trying to improve my grades."

"You said that they just went out on some errands, right? Maybe we can ask them when they get back," Tomoe cheerfully suggested.

Smiling, Akira nodded. "Y-yeah... and, if I ask while you're here, you can help me explain what we'll cover. This might actually work!" she admitted with a light giggle.

Tomoe smiled brightly, giggling along with her friend.

With their new plans for the weekend formulated, Akira and Tomoe left the bedroom and began working on chores. Once her grandparents returned home, Akira took the first opportunity she had to ask if she and Tomoe could have a sleepover next weekend. At first, Ryoma was staunchly opposed to it. Though, once they emphasized how Tomoe wanted to tutor Akira to help improve her grades, Satomi helped to convince her husband to allow Tomoe to spend the weekend over.

After some negotiations between Akira and her grandfather, she was able to get his permission to allow Tomoe to spend the weekend. The only requirements were that they don't get too loud and that Akira still completes her chores in a timely manner. Tomoe graciously thanked both Ryoma and Satomi for allowing her to come over, then helped Akira finish what chores she had for the evening. Once they finished, she bid her friend farewell just before dinner and made her way home. This left Akira with only dishes to do after dinner and the rest of the night to kick back and relax, albeit without her music.

The following day, Akira aimed to try and get to school as quickly as possible to avoid Kana. Using an old ragged backpack of her's that she had laying around, she packed up what little school supplies she still had, alongside some leftovers in her bento box, and left for school. Along the way, she kept an eye on her surroundings and felt fortunate once she made it to school without running into Kana or Yuuki. She looked around for Tomoe upon her arrival, spotting her friend already inside the school with her shoes changed out.

Tomoe appeared to be in a better mood than she had been all week, given everything that had happened. The two enjoyed a relatively brief conversation before parting ways with one another as they left for their first classes of the day. If memory served, Akira knew she wouldn't see Tomoe until lunchtime. Her classes before then were biology, business ethics, and creative writing, the class she was in when the police first showed up at school on Tuesday.

Akira felt fortunate that today, she could make it through her classes without any ominous messages echoing out from the overhead intercom system. Once each of her classes were over, Akira left and made her way down the hallway to where she recalled Tomoe's class being. Since their classrooms were so close, there was no reason they couldn't meet up and then walk to the cafeteria together. And, as she drew closer to her friend's class, seeing a steady flow of students leave the classroom, she saw Tomoe. Though excited herself, Akira saw that her friend looked deeply troubled, as if she'd just learned of new information that made their lives more difficult.

Akira threw her a quick wave to get her attention. "Hey, Tomoe," she said, moving in closer. "Is everything cool? You look like you're worried about something," she asked, keeping her voice low as she approached her friend.

Tomoe nervously looked at the students around her, none of them paying any attention to her as she and Akira drew closer to one another. She turned to face her friend. "A-Aki... when you left with that police officer on Tuesday... who was it who asked you all of those questions?"

"Huh?" Akira responded, unsure as to where this was coming from. "Um... some detective, I can't remember his name."

"Did he have short black hair, a mustache that went down into a goatee, and wore a dark grey suit? Spoke in a gentle but confident and professional tone?" Tomoe asked as she explained the man in detail.

Staring at her, Akira reluctantly nodded. "Yeah... that was the guy who questioned me. Why? Was he here at the school again?"

Tomoe nodded. "During my second class, the principal came by and brought me back to his office. That guy, the detective, was waiting for me there," she said as her eyes began to swell with tears, though she pushed them back and wiped away the few that escaped. "He asked me a lot of questions about what happened that day, and he..." she grimaced, "he asked about you."

Akira swallowed nervously. "Wh-what did he ask?"

She glanced around as other students made their way throughout the hall. "Maybe... we should go somewhere we can talk in private?"

Biting her lip, Akira nodded, then beckoned her friend. "Yeah, follow me," she said as she turned and began making her way towards the nearby staircase.

Descending to the first floor, Akira led her friend against the flow of students and towards the main entrance to the school. Because it was still in the middle of the school day, this area was empty, giving Akira and Tomoe a perfect opportunity to talk about whatever the detective had questioned her about. Turning around, Akira leaned back against the nearby wall and crossed her arms before nervously glancing around.

"So, um..." Tomoe began to say, drawing her friend's attention back to her. "The detective... he asked me about where I was on Tuesday during the time of the... 'incident.' That's what he referred to it as."

Akira nodded. "And what did you tell him?"

"I told him the truth about scraping my knee and how I was on my way to class, then stopped so I could go to the nurse's office... but, obviously, I didn't tell him about what happened on the way there. I just said that I went there, got checked in, and then when I was walking back, I heard the announcement and got pulled into your classroom," Tomoe explained as her erratic breathing proved just how nervous she was.

"So... did he buy it?" she asked.

Tomoe frowned. "I think he did. I know he asked the principal about us signing in whenever we go to the nurse's office, which I did have to do when I went there. So, I'm kind of hoping that works out to make the detective think that I didn't have anything to do with all of this, but..." she let out a deep sigh, then shook her head. "Aki, I was so nervous when he was talking to me. I swear, I thought I was going to start crying..."

"It's terrifying, I know... I was scared too," Akira responded. Reluctantly, she relaxed her posture and stepped forward, closer to her friend. "You said he asked about me, right? What did he ask?"

"Um... he asked if I knew you, and I told him that we were friends," she said, lowering her head as she looked off to the side. "He also asked me if you had expressed any anger or violent tendencies... or if I'd noticed any signs of you harboring any malice towards anyone," she said, looking back to her friend. "He never once mentioned Miyoko or Kana's names during the whole conversation."

Akira slowly nodded. "Maybe that means he doesn't think that you were directly involved? If so, then that's good news... he might have just asked you shit because you and I are friends," she said as she began to think about how this might affect everything in the long run.

Tomoe frowned. "If they don't think I had anything to do with it, does that mean they're certain you're responsible for it? B-because... he asked me a lot of questions about you."

She bit her lip. "M-maybe..." she said before abruptly shaking her head. "But, I'm just relieved that they're probably not suspecting you. That means all we have to do is worry about–" she said before cutting herself off as she stared down the hallway furthest from them.

Tomoe followed her friend's eyes and saw the very detective they were just talking about. It appeared as if he were leaving the school, though he looked directly at each of them. Judging by his stare, he knew precisely what they were talking about, or so it felt. The girls each watched him as he turned and began making his way out of the main entrance, looking back at neither of them as he left the building. They closely watched him as he made his way towards a solid black sedan parked just out in front of the school.

"You said he called you to talk during your second class, right?" Akira asked, her eyes remaining on the detective.

Tomoe timidly nodded. "Y-yeah..."

"Did he keep you long? Or... like, you made it to your last class, right?"

She looked at her friend. "I made it back to my second class just as it had ended..."

With a deep sigh, Akira turned to her. "Then, he was here long after you, and he talked," she said, lightly grimacing. "He was talking to another student... at least one. Had to be," she said, shaking her head. "Probably Kana or someone..."

"What are we going to do, Aki?" Tomoe asked.

"Nothing. The worst thing is, he saw us talking... and I'd bet money that he knows exactly what we were talking about," she said before crossing her arms. "My bigger concern is Kana. Yesterday, she threw me in the canal. I'm hard-pressed to imagine what else she'll do... but, I'd say at the very least, she'll probably beat the shit out of me."

Tomoe forced a comforting smile for her friend. "I'll walk home with you. And if Kana tries to stop us again, I'll... I'll keep her from following you while you run home."

"And if Yuuki's with her like before?" she asked.

Tomoe grimaced. "I'll, um... just have to do my best to try and give you an opportunity to get away."

"Only for them to just beat *you* up? Not a chance. I don't know what we'll do. But, we've gotta figure out something..." Akira said, sighing deeply. "For now, I'm starving. So, let's go sit down and eat before our lunch period is over."

She nodded. "Alright. And, maybe one of us can come up with an idea after school to get out without Kana catching us."

"We can hope," Akira said before beckoning her friend to follow as she turned and started towards the cafeteria.

As Akira and Tomoe left, they each had yet more on their shoulders than before. It was beginning to feel as if the weight of their lie was going to crush them if they didn't do something to prevent it. The problem was, neither of them could think of what could alleviate all of this from their lives. At least for Akira, the easiest route was just to tell the truth and leave Tomoe to face the consequences of her actions. But, to do that would plunge Akira back into the life she lived before Tomoe came along.

While she wasn't in constant peril before this semester, she was all alone with a bleak future awaiting her. Kana would torment and harass her regardless of Miyoko's death, so the only real difference would be the ongoing investigation into the girls from law enforcement. For what little she had before, Akira was willing to risk the freedom she now had if it meant fighting to maintain that very same freedom.

Chapter 9
Unintended Repercussions

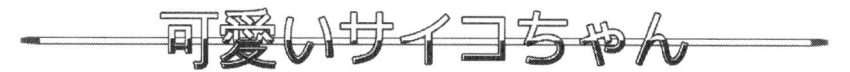

可愛いサイコちゃん

Once their day at school concluded, the girls made their way back to Akira's house, fortunately without any intervention by Kana. For Akira, it was a relief that this long first week was almost over, and she could finally breathe a sigh of relief, if only for a couple of days. Before then, she would have to survive just one more day of school. Waking up bright and early Friday morning, Akira crawled out of bed and gathered up her clothes for her morning shower.

Descending downstairs, her clothes in hand, she overheard her grandmother speaking to someone in the kitchen. It didn't sound as if she were talking with Ryoma, judging by the tone of her voice, and Akira's assumption was proven true the moment she heard an all too familiar voice. Despite just being in her pajamas, she hastily made her way down the hallway and into the kitchen, where she saw Tomoe speaking with her grandmother while Satomi made her morning tea.

"Wh-what are you doing here, Tomoe?" Akira asked in confusion.

Tomoe turned and smiled cheerfully. "Well, I woke up kind of early, so I thought that maybe we could walk to school together?"

Akira's mouth hung slightly agape as she stared in disbelief, shocked that her friend would drop by and walk to school with her, likely just to help her feel safer on her way there.

Satomi turned and looked at her granddaughter. "She was just telling me about how you two first met. I'm proud of you, Akira. Seeing that someone was having a rough first day, and so you sat with her and helped cheer her up. No wonder she wants to return the favor by tutoring you."

Tomoe smiled. "It can be really difficult to adjust to a new school. So I'm grateful for her kindness."

Akira blushed. "I... just did what I thought was the right thing to do."

"So, what time do you usually leave for school, Aki?" Tomoe asked.

Reaching up, she playfully scratched at her cheek. "Um... usually right after I wake up and get ready, so... if you can give me about twenty, I'll be good to go."

Tomoe nodded. "That's fine. We should be able to get to class with a bit of time to spare."

Satomi looked at her. "I do apologize, Miss Asano. If I knew you were going to come by, I'd of made breakfast a bit earlier. Akira so seldom eats before school, so it didn't even cross my mind to have anything prepared for you girls."

Tomoe bowed her head. "That's very kind of you to say, Miss Watari. But, my mom made me some breakfast before I left, so I'm okay."

"Hey, let me go get washed up and changed real quick, and we can leave for school," Akira said to her friend before turning and darting down the hallway.

Rushing into the bathroom, Akira hastily tossed her clothes aside, then cleaned up and changed. She was in such a hurry to not make Tomoe wait on her that she barely even dried her hair off before she was back out to meet her friend. Tomoe was shocked at how quickly Akira cleaned herself up but was happy to set off on their way to school.

Along the way, they tried to maintain a more optimistic conversation, though it was clear to each of them that they were struggling to stay positive. After arriving at school, they each began changing into their indoor shoes. It was still early, and so there weren't as many students here as the previous days, though it still felt quite busy in the main entryway. Akira and Tomoe stood around with a bit of time to waste and began discussing what they'd do this weekend, studying aside.

Akira cupped her chin. "Unless you're into, like, board or card games, all I really have for entertainment is my music. I have an old game console somewhere in my room, but I'll be damned if I know where it is..."

Tomoe smiled. "I wouldn't worry about that. I'm not really into video games. A few of my friends tried to get me into them back in Fukuoka, but I honestly prefer just playing sports or something."

"Oh, right. You mentioned you were the goalie for your school's soccer team, yeah?" she asked.

Tomoe offered a wide grin as she nodded. "That's right. And, I'd love to get back into it if our school has their own soccer team, that is."

Akira sighed. "I'll be honest; I've never really played soccer before. The only sport I've ever played was baseball, and even then, I was a pretty lousy pitcher. Although, I did have a pretty damn good swing with the bat. I could hit virtually any pitch, even my brother's *stupid* curve balls..." she said, rolling her eyes.

Pausing, Tomoe looked curiously at her friend. "Brother? I thought that you were an only child?"

"Huh?" she responded, looking back to her friend. She sighed. "Y-yeah... I have an older brother. But, he's not around anymore."

Tomoe grimaced as she covered her mouth. "Oh... Aki, I'm so sorry... I didn't mean to bring up such a terrible memory..."

Akira raised her eyebrow in confusion before gasping. "*No,* no... my brother isn't dead or anything. When I said he's not around anymore, I mean he moved away awhile back."

"Oh!" she responded, letting out a deep sigh of relief. "I was so scared that I brought up a terrible memory for you..."

"It's alright..." Akira said before sighing. "It'll come up sooner or later, but... just for the sake of transparency. My parents died when I was eight years old. That's why I live with my grandparents."

She stared briefly at her before slowly nodding. "I... remember Miyoko calling you an 'orphan' before she and I..." she said, inhaling sharply. "So, I sort of knew your parents weren't around anymore. Especially when I saw you lived with your grandparents... oh, and you told me the day we met that you knew how I felt, what with my parents being split up."

Akira looked at her and smiled. "I do know how you feel..."

A moment of silence passed before Tomoe spoke up again. "So, your brother... you used to play baseball with him?"

She nodded. "Yeah. He taught me a lot of things before he moved away. Taught me how to play ball, how to throw darts... we also went bowling once in Kofu, that was fun," she said, lightly chuckling. "He also taught me a lot of shit he shouldn't have. Like, how to steal and not get caught, or the right way to throw a punch," she added, jabbing briefly into the air.

Tomoe frowned. "Well... I'm glad you don't steal or get into fights." Her smile returned. "But, the other things he taught you seem nice."

Akira scoffed. "They might be nice, but... I really don't give a shit about him anymore," she said with a deep sigh. "When I was thirteen, he left to go to the police academy in Tokyo. The plan was; he'd graduate and get a job in Shinjuku, then... he was *supposed* to come to get me, and I'd just transfer to a school in Tokyo."

"So, what happened then?" she timidly asked.

"Fuck if I know," Akira said with a roll of her eyes. "My brother left, he finished at the academy, and now, all he's done is sent letters to us about how things are going. Every one of them full of some bullshit excuse for me about why our plan hasn't worked out," she said before growling under her breath. "It's been almost three years since he left, and I'm still stuck here in this shitty little town. It pisses me off, and as far as I'm concerned, my brother's as good as dead to me."

Tomoe frowned once more. "Don't say that... I'm sure there's a reason that the plan you two had didn't work out... or, hasn't yet."

Akira forcefully laughed. "Oh, there's a reason, alright. When he moved away, his girlfriend moved with him. I'll bet he got a place with her, and they don't want me around for fear that I'll... I don't know, 'kill the mood' or some shit."

Staring at her friend, Tomoe wasn't sure what to say. Though, her attention was soon diverted away as she noticed a somewhat worrying sight. Akira soon saw her friend's troubled expression and followed her eyes to see Kana and a man who Akira recognized as Kana's father, Nakajima Senzo, approaching the two of them. They both nervously watched as Kana drew closer to them. She appeared angry, furious at them, yet doing her best to hide it behind a facade of kindness.

"Miss Makai," Kana politely said, begrudgingly so.

"Huh?" Akira asked, glancing confusingly towards Tomoe, who shrugged. Turning back to Kana, Akira hesitantly spoke up. "Um... y-yes?"

With her father standing right behind her with his arms crossed, Kana took a deep breath, then bowed her head. "I am deeply sorry for the way I mistreated you this past week."

Akira's eyes widened in shock, turning again to look at Tomoe, who appeared every bit as speechless.

Raising back up, Kana turned to her father and was handed an envelope. Turning back around to Akira, Kana bowed her head once more, holding the envelope out, gripping one end loosely with both hands as she presented it to her.

"I humbly request that you kindly accept this small token of my most sincere apologies," Kana said.

Akira reluctantly shook her head. "N-no... no, it's fine. It's t-totally fine. I'm not even upset about it..." she said as her heart began to race.

"Miss Makai," Kana's father said, drawing Akira's focus to him, "it has come to my attention that my daughter has not only destroyed your belongings but also actively harassed and even assaulted you. Her actions have brought a great deal of shame to our family, and for that, I would offer my deepest apologies. It would do well to help right the wrongs my daughter has committed if you were to accept this offer from our family to you," he said with a bow of his head.

"B-but..." Akira began to say as she grimaced.

Kana glared at her as she lowered her voice to a whisper. "If you don't take this envelope, Makai... I *swear* I'll..." she said, biting her tongue before she finished.

Swallowing nervously, Akira hesitantly took the envelope, though she didn't feel comfortable even holding it.

Both Kana and her father raised their heads.

"I believe you have a class to get to, Kana," Nakajima said.

Kana exhaled sharply as she threw Akira a look that told her precisely how much pain and suffering she'd soon experience as a result of the trouble this incident had just caused.

Akira watched as Kana left, terror filling her heart.

"Miss Makai," Nakajima said, drawing her attention back to him. "I'm not sure why it is that you and Kana stopped being friends. She's never spoken of it to me. However, regardless of the reason you're no longer friends with her, that's no excuse for her behavior," he said before offering another bow of his head to her. "I'm sure you still have our home number. If Kana ever causes you trouble again, I encourage you to call and speak to me, and I will make sure that her behavior is corrected."

She shook her head. "R-really, Mister Nakajima... it's nothing, I..."

"I know you two have a lot of history together, but don't let that stop you from reaching out to me," he said, glancing off in the direction his daughter had left in. "For her actions, I've grounded her. And, since it appears Taichi Yuuki was involved in what she did to you, I've forbidden her from seeing him while she's grounded," he looked back to Akira. "Perhaps that will help her understand why it's important *not* to conduct such delinquent behavior."

Akira could practically feel herself sweating as she heard him speak. "Please... Mister Nakajima, I know Kana didn't mean it. She's just... she's been under a lot of stress lately, and... what she did, it was hardly a bother at all, really!"

"I appreciate you being so humble and considerate of others. But, I spoke to Detective Yasuhida, and I heard what she did to you. She's lucky the police themselves didn't charge her for attacking you like that," he explained before offering one more subtle nod of his head to her. "Now, I've taken up enough of your time, Miss Makai. You should probably get to class. But, do remember to call me if Kana causes you any further trouble," he said before turning and leaving.

Watching him leave, Akira turned to Tomoe. "You told them what she did?!" she asked, trying her best not to scream, as she feared how badly this would come back to hurt her.

Tomoe frowned. "I'm... I'm sorry, Aki. I completely forgot that I told the detective about Kana throwing you into the canal. I don't even remember how... but the conversation just sort of went that way, and I wasn't sure if I should lie or not," she said before bowing her head. "I'm so sorry."

Reaching up, she held the sides of her head as dread filled her mind. "Kana was so pissed... Tomoe, she might end up outing me for this. And, if she does, I am *so* fucked," she said, abruptly shaking her head. "I have to give this money back!"

Without hesitation, Akira began hastily running off towards their math class, with Tomoe following behind her. As she did so, she noticed the teacher approaching the class as well. He paused, allowing the two of them the opportunity to head into class before he closed the doors. However, Akira knew that she'd now have to wait until the end of class to give Kana back her money and apologize for what happened, lest her old friend makes good on her threat to expose Akira's secret to her grandparents.

Taking their seats in their usual spots, Akira found her loathing that she chose a seat so far away from Kana. While everyone focused on the lessons being taught, Akira spent much of the period staring at Kana, who was texting under her desk constantly. Once class was over, however, Akira got up and prepared to catch Kana in the hallway, where she could apologize and return the money. Tomoe stuck by her friend as the two of them left and weaved through the flow of students to catch up with the girl they had up until now been avoiding.

"K-Kana! Kana, wait up!" Akira pleaded, though her old friend didn't listen. Quickening her pace, she managed to catch up to her. Walking alongside her, Akira bowed her head repeatedly. "I am so, *so* sorry about all of this, I *really* am! I swear, I didn't tell a soul about what happened. I didn't! A-and... and you can have this back. I don't want it. After all of the trouble this has caused you... it's the least I can offer," she frantically said as she kept pace with Kana.

Stopping, Kana turned to Akira and glared. "You think this is about the money, Makai? You think this is about my father punishing me?" she asked, fury building in her voice. "I don't care about that money. Not at all!" she said before she stifled her anger. "You know what really hurts?"

Akira swallowed nervously as she listened.

"What hurts most is that, honestly... I used to look up to you when we were friends," she admitted.

Akira recoiled slightly in shock.

Kana nodded. "It's true. You lost your parents when you were just a kid. Even considering that... losing my mom and dad... it'd make me cry just thinking about it. But, you *lived* it... and yet you were so strong. Strong enough that you'd smile, laugh and joke about things with us... like there wasn't anything wrong. I remember thinking how jealous I was that you had that kind of strength... that willpower just to keep pushing forward..."

Akira frowned as she listened to what her old friend shared with her. "Kana... I..."

She shook her head. "These last few days, Makai... no... Aki... they've been so hard on me. You and I used to be close... really close. You were like a sister to me. Miyoko too... I loved her like family. I loved you like family," she said, inhaling sharply. "What you did to Ina... that's between you and me. No one else. But... everything now, with what happened to Miyoko..." Tears began to form in Kana's eyes, though she quickly wiped them away. "I'd like to believe that of all the people in Nirasaki... you'd be the one to understand the pain of losing someone you love dearly. And yet... you just stand here, playing games with my emotions as you just drag all of this on."

Akira bit at her lip as she lowered her head.

Sniffling, Kana took a step closer to her. "It's not too late, Aki. Just... just tell the truth. It doesn't matter how or why it happened. Accidents aren't from malice or hatred; they're just... horrible moments we never intended to be," she said, struggling to try and offer a comforting smile to her. "So... just tell me the truth... tell me what you did to Miyoko. Please..."

Staring down, Akira's mind swirled with so many thoughts, and beyond that, many different scenarios that could follow how she handled this situation. Hesitantly, she looked back to Kana. "I'm so sorry. I really, *really* am... but, the truth is," she paused, taking a deep breath, "I don't know what happened to Miyoko... I really don't..."

Kana's eyes were locked on Akira's as she spoke, though once those final words were spoken, that stifled anger began to fill Kana once more. Abruptly, she swiped the envelope from Akira's hands. She then began ripping it to shreds, destroying everything inside it before throwing it in Akira's face, the scraps of paper scattering everywhere.

Akira's eyes widened as she saw her old friend's response. It was both terrifying yet relieving that it was only the envelope and its contents that suffered.

Kana glared at her. "I was *hoping* that you'd have a heart, Makai," she said, making no effort to keep her voice down. "Your parents died right in front of you... but you just go off and *murder* my best friend and pretend like *nothing* is wrong?!" she shouted, ensuring anyone nearby could hear what she said. "No wonder you were never hurt by your parents dying! You're incapable of it! You're a *monster*, Makai Akira! A psychopath! A horrible, terrible person who *raped* my little sister and *murdered* Hachi Miyoko!" she yelled out before turning and running away.

Stunned by her outburst and all of the information she so blatantly shared with everyone in earshot, Akira's face burned a horrible red tint as she tried to maintain even a minor semblance of composure. Tomoe, too was shocked, though she, at least, didn't have the embarrassment of being the subject of Kana's ridicule. However, she was able to see other students nearby, who were staring at Akira, already gossiping and talking amongst themselves about what information was shared. Up until now, most students didn't even know Miyoko had died, and now they learned of it from a girl who wished to place the blame for her death squarely on Akira's head.

Tomoe moved to Akira's side and held onto her arm as she leaned in. "W-we should probably leave, Aki... come on, I'll walk you to the gym," she said, urging Akira to walk along with her.

Akira said nothing in response to her friend, though she did allow Tomoe to guide her away from the students who had observed the sudden outburst of Kana's.

Once they were far enough away, Tomoe stopped and looked back at her friend. "Aki... are you okay?" she hesitantly asked, concerned for her friend after such a display.

"I can't believe this... this feels so unreal," Akira said, shaking her head in disbelief. "I can't believe that she'd just shout all of that out..."

Tomoe went to speak, though she found it difficult to know what would be appropriate to say to comfort her friend.

Reaching up, Akira frustratingly ran her fingers through her hair. "This is just like back in junior high, when she and Miyoko spread so many horrible rumors and shit about me that nobody wanted to even look at me, let alone speak to me," she said as tears began to form in her eyes.

"Aki, I'm... I'm so sorry," Tomoe began to say as she reached out to put her hand on her friend's shoulder as a show of support.

Glancing further down the hallway, Akira let out a deep sigh, then returned her attention to Tomoe. "We're probably nearly late for our next classes. I don't give a shit about mine, but... you should go. I don't want you to fall behind in class because of this."

She frowned. "I don't want to just ditch you after... *that* happened."

Akira shook her head. "I'll be okay. We'll talk more at lunch..."

"Are you sure?" Tomoe asked.

She nodded and offered a painfully forced smile as reassurance. "I'm alright. I'm sure once I get out on the track field and start running, I'll forget all about what she said. You just... go to your class, and... and be sure and take notes. After all, you're tutoring my dumb ass this weekend," she said with an awkward chuckle.

Reluctantly, Akira turned and began to make her way to gym class. Her mind filled with terrible memories of her time back in Nirasakinishi, where Miyoko and Kana spread awful rumors about Akira that destroyed her reputation among her fellow students and even soiled her in the eyes of her teachers. Back then, she found her only blessing was that word of these rumors had mostly not come to the attention of her grandparents. The few that did left a disheartening mess for her to clean up at home as she struggled to disprove fabricated lies about her.

Once she arrived at the gym hall, Akira kept her head down and made her way into the locker room. As she began to change, she threw a few glances around to see whether or not Hideko was in class today. She hadn't seen her since Miyoko's untimely demise, and given how reliant Hideko was on both of her closest friends, it made sense for her to miss so many days of school as she mourned Miyoko's death. Not that Akira could relate, as her only pain that came from that tumble down the stairs was in the form of Kana's own unique form of justice.

"Aki, hey!" Ikumi said as she approached.

Slipping her gym shirt on, Akira glanced back and noticed Ikumi, who was smiling cheerfully at her. *Her again... she's always in such a good mood. I feel like I've never seen her do anything but smile...*

"After math class, I was going to see if you wanted to walk to gym together... but I kind of got lost during the lesson, and I needed to ask the teacher to explain something to me," she admitted with a giggle. "I guess I was just daydreaming too much in class, huh?"

"Y-yeah... I guess," Akira responded, feeling at least mild relief that Ikumi, who had been kind to her so far, likely didn't overhear what Kana had shouted to everyone in the hall.

Ikumi lightly blushed, appearing as if she were awkwardly looking for the words to ask a difficult question. "So, um... hey! I was curious if... if you wanted to, maybe... do our exercises together? I've been doing them alone, but it'd be nice to have some company, you know? Someone to talk to, to help, maybe?" she nervously asked.

Akira was hesitant to answer, as she just wanted this time to clear her head and not be distracted by any conversation or company. Still, Ikumi had been so kind to her, so she didn't want to push her offer away so carelessly. "I... honestly, I have a lot on my mind and... I'd enjoy the company but don't... don't take it personally if I don't say much. I'm just dealing with a lot of shit right now..."

She appeared surprised by Akira's words, though her smile soon returned as she offered a nod. "I understand. You don't have to talk or anything. It'd just be nice to have some company, you know?" She shyly bit at her lip as she seemingly struggled to come up with what to say next. "If... if you do want to talk to someone, though, I'd be happy to hear you out. I promise I won't tell anyone."

A slight smile fought to form across Akira's lips, twitching at the corner of her mouth before she nodded. "I'll keep that in mind... thanks, Ikumi."

She offered a comforting smile to her, then glanced over towards her locker. "I'll go get changed real fast, and then we can go start with whatever exercises you'd like to do first."

"Sure thing," Akira said, feeling somewhat better about not declining Ikumi's offer to exercise together.

While she might not have felt the best right now, Akira had to admit that it was nice to know someone like Ikumi wanted to keep her company and help her feel better. Even if her offer initially had nothing to do with

Akira's current hardships. It did provide her with some hope; hope that once she got out on the field and began running, or doing squats over on the mats, that she might feel better about everything Kana shouted out to, what felt like, the whole school.

After they had each changed into their gym clothes, Akira led the way for them to each go outside to run on the track field. As they ran together, side-by-side, Akira was relieved to see that Ikumi was simply matching her pace and not attempting to push them to run faster. Throughout their run together, they barely spoke at all. Akira's mind was too focused on what Kana had shared with so many people and how she felt as if this next week would only devolve into something far worse than mere words.

Once they finished their laps, the two of them stopped off by an area with benches and a cooler filled with water bottles. Akira had worked up a sweat while running, and so a fresh bottle of water was precisely what she felt that she needed. As she quenched her thirst, she couldn't help but noticed Takashi watching her from afar. Almost as if he were afraid to approach her while Ikumi was nearby.

Looking towards him, Ikumi sighed. "He seems like a bit of a creep."

Akira nodded. "He really is..."

"I'm guessing that the 'likes' you, or something?"

"So he says..."

Ikumi shook her head. "He sure doesn't act like it from what I've seen."

Sitting down on the bench, Akira took a short drink of her water. "From what you've seen? That makes me wonder how much you've noticed."

Ikumi shrugged. "I've just seen him in gym class. On Monday, I saw you two, and at first, I wasn't sure if he was like, your boyfriend or something, and you two were just messing around. But when I saw the look on your face, I knew you were uncomfortable, and that's when I got the teacher."

Akira smiled. "Thanks for that... you really saved my ass that day. You also saved my ass on Wednesday, which I *also* appreciate, by the way."

Ikumi giggled. "You're welcome. But, it's not like I could just stand there while some creepy guy grabbed on you."

She frowned. "You wouldn't be the first if you had..."

Ikumi looked to her friend with concern. "Why do you say that?"

Akira shook her head. "At my old school... no one really liked me at all. Whenever I'd get bullied, or someone like Takashi would grab hold of me, everyone would just ignore it," she said with a deep sigh as she lowered her head. "There were times I honestly felt like I didn't even exist..."

"What? That's... that's horrible. No one ever stood up for you? Not even the teachers?" Ikumi asked in shock.

She lightly scoffed. "Even the teachers hated me... this one girl from my school, Kana, she hates my guts and had spread a ton of rumors to ruin my reputation. She's here at this school too... already doing the same things she did back then... sometimes even worse," she admitted, somewhat venting her frustrations with Kana, though unsure as to why she was trusting all of this to someone aside from Tomoe.

Ikumi frowned as she listened to Akira. "Well... I can't do anything about someone spreading rumors about you... but, I can promise you that no matter what kind of rumors people try to spread, I'll only ever judge you by your own actions," she said, offering a supportive smile.

Hesitantly, Akira looked to Ikumi and found herself fighting the urge to smile back at her. "Thanks... it means a lot to hear that," she said before sighing. "You're a good friend, Ikumi."

Lightly blushing, Ikumi giggled. "I... I t-try my best," she responded.

"Come on. Let's head back inside and finish our workout routine. I can already feel my skin burning from the sun," Akira said as she stood up, throwing a glare up towards the bright skies above.

Ikumi offered a firm nod as she stood up. "Yeah! And, we can talk some more about random things while we work out," she excitedly said. "Oh... um, if you want to, of course. I know you have a lot on your mind."

Akira smiled at her. "I do... but we can talk a little while we work out. Just... nothing too heavy, alright?" she said with a light chuckle, as she knew she still had a lot of thoughts to sort out in her head.

Chapter 10
Benefits of Friends

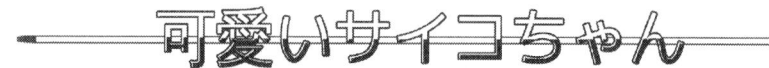

可愛いサイコちゃん

Throughout the remainder of gym class, Ikumi continued to keep Akira company, which was appreciated since it kept Takashi from bothering her. Once they finished with their exercises and got cleaned up, they left the gym together. It was lunchtime for each of them, and given that she had been kind enough to work out with her during gym class, Akira just didn't feel right in telling Ikumi to sit alone. After all, it wasn't as if she and Tomoe couldn't wait until after school to discuss whatever might have been on their minds.

As they walked down the hall, Akira couldn't shake the feeling that every stare she got from passing students was a direct result of what Kana had shouted out earlier. It had been almost three full hours since then, and no doubt friends had shared the rumor amongst themselves and with their classmates. Fortunately, Ikumi appeared oblivious to whatever was on the minds of other students. Instead, she was texting on her phone as the two of them walked side-by-side.

Entering into the cafeteria, Akira led Ikumi to where she and Tomoe always sat. As they approached, Akira offered a friendly wave to Tomoe, though her friend's attention was immediately drawn towards the girl she didn't recognize. Stopping across the table from her, Akira smiled, then gestured towards Ikumi.

"This is my classmate from gym. She's also in math with us. She and I worked out together in gym class, and she's been pretty awesome, so... would it be cool if she sat with us?" Akira asked.

"O-oh... um, yeah... I don't have any problem with her joining us,"

Tomoe said, caught off-guard by Akira suddenly showing up with a new friend, especially given how things played out earlier in the day.

Ikumi bowed her head graciously. "Thank you."

Akira pulled her chair out and took her seat as she took her backpack off and began fishing out her bento box.

"My name is Asano Tomoe, by the way," Tomoe said, introducing herself.

Ikumi smiled. "It's nice to meet you, Tomoe. I'm Yasuhida Ikumi," she said with a cheerful giggle as she sat down next to Akira.

Pausing, Tomoe stared at Ikumi momentarily before her eyes widened in shock.

She looked to Akira, then back to Tomoe. "So, have you two been friends for a long time, or...?"

"Nah, we just met on Monday," Akira said as she put her bento box down and looked at her new friend. "She's in the same math class as us. I don't have any other classes with her besides that one, but that hasn't kept us from getting to know one another."

"I see," Ikumi said before noticing how pale Tomoe had become. "Is everything alright? You don't look so well," she said in a concerned tone.

Akira looked to Tomoe, seeing the fear in her eyes.

"I'm... I'm o-okay..." Tomoe nervously responded. "S-so, um... Ikumi, your name... it's kind of f-familiar. Have we met before, by chance?"

Thinking briefly on it, Ikumi shook her head. "I don't think so? Maybe my name sounds familiar because my dad is in the newspaper fairly often? He's pretty well known here in Nirasaki. Yasuhida Masato, lead detective of the Nirasaki Police Department," she said, sounding very proud of her father's work.

Akira looked to Ikumi in shock, though she tried to conceal it. Her eyes trailed over to Tomoe, who so very clearly figured out who Ikumi was the moment she introduced herself. As Akira's eyes shifted back to Ikumi, she began to put the pieces together. *Her father is the detective?! Wait... oh, shit! I bet that she's also related to that guy who took my fingerprints. That blonde-haired foreigner...* she thought to herself.

"I... I-I see," Tomoe responded. "I can tell you're really proud of him."

Ikumi eagerly nodded. "I'm very proud of the work my father does. It's thanks to him, alongside the other men and women of the Nirasaki Police Department, that our city is as safe as it is," she said, looking to Akira with a smile. "You know, I've lived here my whole life, and I could probably count the number of major crimes on one hand," she added with another cheerful giggle.

"Th-that... sure is awesome, Ikumi..." Akira said, trying her best not to grimace at the realization that she'd been hanging out with the daughter of the very man who is attempting to find out whether or not she was the one to kill Miyoko.

Turning to glance up towards the front of the cafeteria, Ikumi then looked back to her new friends. "I'm going to go get something to eat. My bag isn't really big enough to bring anything to eat for lunch, so I have to get mine from up there, so... I'll be right back," she said as she stood up.

"S-sure, no problem," Tomoe said. She then watched closely as Ikumi left, then looked back to Akira in shock. "She's that detective's daughter?!" she asked, trying her best to keep her voice down.

Akira exhaled sharply as she ruffled her hair in frustration. "I... d-didn't even realize it... goddammit, I'm such a fucking idiot," she groaned.

Tomoe looked back to where Ikumi was now standing in line. "We have to distance ourselves from her, Aki. If she overhears anything strange that we say, she could tell her dad, and it could come back to bite us..."

"Yeah, no kidding," she agreed before an idea crossed her mind. "Or..."

Tomoe turned back to Akira. "Or what?"

"Hear me out," she said, offering a sly smile. "What if we become friends with Ikumi, like... good friends, and we use that to figure out what information her father has on us? She could let us know whether or not he suspects it was foul play or an accident. Ya know?"

Tomoe shook her head. "N-no way. Aki, it's *too* dangerous. What if she hears or sees something, and then she tells her father? It could point him directly to us..."

"I don't think we have anything to worry about there. We just don't talk about it, except when it's just us, ya know? If we keep our mouths shut on the matter when she's around, then just imagine what we might learn," Akira eagerly suggested.

"I don't like this... it's too dangerous. We should just politely avoid her and not risk it," Tomoe said.

She frowned. "I'd rather not. Honestly, her old man aside, she's been really kind towards me, and... that's not something I'm used to getting from anyone but you."

"That could be a ruse for all you know. What if her father asked her to be your friend so she could eavesdrop on us?" Tomoe asked.

"You're overreacting," Akira said before gasping. "W-wait... you aren't, like... jealous of her, or something, are you?"

She recoiled in shock. "J-jealous? Why would I be jealous of her?"

Akira grinned widely. "Because she's being friendly towards me, and..." she glanced off towards where Ikumi was in line to get her lunch. "She's pretty cute too..."

Tomoe pursed her lips as her eyes trailed over to Ikumi as well. "I mean, she is very pretty," she admitted, her focus returning to Akira. "So, is she like... the type of girl you're interested in?"

"Huh?" Akira asked, looking back to Tomoe. She awkwardly chuckled. "I... I mean, she's really... really cute, but... I don't know. Our situation aside, I don't know that I'd ever want to date someone whose parent is a cop. As you can imagine, I don't have the best of opinions of them."

"Because of all the anxiety and stress they're causing us?" she asked.

Akira sighed. "Not... entirely," she said, shaking her head. "Do you remember when I told you my brother taught me how to fight and steal? Well... he did a lot of both of those things before he moved away." She cracked a half-smile. "So because of that, I have a lot of 'experience' dealing with the police."

"O-oh! I see. You don't like them because they harassed you and your brother a lot?" Tomoe asked.

She nodded. "Yeah. He'd been arrested a couple of times, but I think the longest he stayed in jail was like, over a weekend. I've never even been handcuffed, myself," she said, glancing over to ensure Ikumi wasn't anywhere nearby. "And, I mentioned my parents died when I was just eight years old, living back in Shinjuku," she said, her focus returning to Tomoe. "The truth is... my father was a member of the yakuza. And, as you might imagine, that meant that we had quite a few run-ins with the police. Local cops knew who our parents were, and so my brother and I got harassed by them a lot. Even here in Nirasaki, we have been. So, because of that, I don't really have the best experience when it comes to cops."

Tomoe grimaced. "Th-the... yakuza? Aki... you really shouldn't admit that to anyone. A lot of people would probably judge you harsher for that than you being... well, interested in girls."

Akira scoffed. "I'm not ashamed of my sexuality or my father's legacy," she said, lightly chuckling. "Would it be wrong to say that I think it's kind of cool that he was a gangster?"

She frowned. "Yes, it would. Well, whatever you do, definitely don't tell Ikumi about your parents. The last thing we want is for the detective to know something like that when he's already keen on assuming you're the one who... well, shoved Miyoko down the stairs..." she said, feeling odd at just how casually she mentioned having killed someone.

Akira crossed her arms. "I wasn't going to tell her, geez... give me some credit. I'm not that stupid," she responded. Pursing her lips, she sighed. "Either way... I'm not a fan of the cops. So, going back on what you said... I don't think I'd ever date a girl like her. But, the chances she's even into girls is like... slim-to-none. I doubt there are any other lesbians here in Nirasaki," she said before lowering her head. "I'll probably be single until I graduate..."

Tomoe offered a comforting smile. "Don't be discouraged, Aki. Most students wait until they're done with school before they date anyone. Really, who has time for dating, you know? Sure, things are slow now at the start... but, before long, we'll have tons of homework, clubs to attend, and maybe even extra classes on the weekend," she said, sounding almost excited at the idea of being swamped with school work.

Akira forcefully laughed. "Change those extra classes and clubs to 'chores,' and you have my life as it is right now. And, it'll stay that way until I move out. I hate it... but I can't exactly afford my own place," she said before slumping forward, crossing her arms in front of her as she rested her head. "I just wish I had a girlfriend who I could hang out with. We could hold hands, hug, kiss, and cuddle together on the couch while we watch a movie or two..."

Tomoe stared at her, feeling bad for her lovesick friend and knowing that as negative as she was being, she was right. Nirasaki wasn't the most diverse area to live in, and Akira would likely not have a girlfriend until she moved to a big city like Tokyo. Her focus shifted away from her friend as she noticed Ikumi returning to the table with a small tray.

Seeing Akira slumped forward on the table, Ikumi frowned as she set her tray down. "Are you feeling okay, Aki?"

Akira mumbled something incoherently into her arms. Exhaling sharply, she leaned up. "My life... frickin' sucks..."

Sitting down in the chair, Ikumi gently pat Akira on the shoulder. "It'll be okay, Aki..." she reassured her friend before picking up a small red bean mochi that she had on her tray. "Would this cheer you up a little?" she asked, offering it to Akira.

Looking at the sweet snack, she reluctantly smiled, then took it. "Thank you, Ikumi... this does help," she said, popping it into her mouth. "These are so delicious," she moaned as she chewed it up.

Tomoe sighed. "Aki... it's rude to chew with your mouth full..."

Ikumi giggled.

Akira swallowed her bite, then grinned. "It's also rude not to admire perfection when you taste it," she said, her eyes trailing over to Ikumi's plate.

"I just had the one, sorry," Ikumi responded.

"You gave me your only one?!" she asked in shock.

Blushing, Ikumi nodded. "You looked frustrated, so I wanted to give you something sweet to cheer you up."

With a light chuckle, Akira scratched her head, ruffling her messy hair. "Well, thanks for that. It definitely helped," she said before pursing her lips. "I'll have to get you back for it sometime."

Smiling, Ikumi nodded. "If... if you feel you really want to, then I don't mind," she said as she shyly lowered her head.

"We should probably hurry up and eat, though. Otherwise, we might not finish before our lunch period is over," Akira said before digging into her food.

Tomoe offered a firm nod, then began to eat her lunch.

Looking between her two new friends, Ikumi reluctantly indulged in her own meal as well, though she threw several glances over at Akira as she dug into her rice and salmon.

Once the girls finished their lunch with minimal conversation, as Tomoe didn't want them getting too cozy around Ikumi, they each parted ways as they went off to their next classes. Akira knew she wouldn't see either friend until the end of the day, which gave her time to consider what Tomoe had said. It was true that Ikumi was unusually kind and friendly towards her, for virtually no reason whatsoever. And, while they could potentially exploit Ikumi for information on the investigation, it was far more likely that she would instead hear something that would seal Akira or Tomoe's fate, should she share it with her father.

With her last class from the day over with, Akira made her way to the school's main entrance, eager to meet up with Tomoe and ideally leave before they ran into Kana, Yuuki, or, at this point, Ikumi. As she arrived at the shoe lockers, she saw her friend waiting patiently for her, already on the lookout for those whom they would be best off avoiding. She hastily changed out her shoes and approached Tomoe, glancing around briefly herself, if only to ensure they were safe.

"I didn't expect you to beat me down here," Akira admitted.

"My class let out a bit early. Apparently, my teacher had an appointment she needed to make," Tomoe explained before sighing. "I haven't seen Kana or Yuuki yet. I think we should probably start towards my place before either of them show up. After her screaming at you in the hallway earlier, I'm a bit worried about what she might do next."

Akira nodded. "Me too. And, we should also leave before–"

"Aki, Tomoe!" Ikumi called out as she cheerfully approached.

Glancing back, Akira let out a deep sigh. *Before Ikumi shows up...* she thought, finishing the sentence she could now no longer share.

Moving closer, she offered a cheerful smile. "I meant to ask earlier, but I forgot. Did either of you have any after-school clubs that you've signed up for?"

Tomoe frowned. "Not yet."

"I don't really do after-school clubs," Akira retorted, her eyes scanning the area nervously.

"Aw... why not? They're a lot of fun, and they're really good for you. You can learn all kinds of new things, get tutored, and sometimes even get some amazing things for a resume once you graduate," Ikumi excitedly stated.

Akira nodded. "That might all be true. But I don't really have time. Like, I don't even really have time for friends, if I'm honest. I wake up, come to school, then I have to rush home to do chores all day. Then I sleep and do it all over again," she said before glancing back at the entrance, then shifting her focus onto Tomoe. "Speaking of which, I'd better get going, or else I'm gonna be in deep shit at home."

"You're right. You don't want to get grounded or anything, Aki," Tomoe added before looking to Ikumi and offering a slight bow of her head. "See you next week."

Ikumi felt taken aback by how suddenly her friends were in a hurry to leave. "I, um... w-well, maybe I can walk with you, and we could talk some more? I... I j-just need to change my shoes out, I won't take long, I promise," she said before turning around in a fluster and rushing to her locker to change her shoes.

Tomoe leaned in closer to Akira. "We should go."

Akira nodded once more, then turned and made her way out of the school, with Tomoe following closely behind her. As they left, they took the secluded pathway, if only so it'd be less likely that Ikumi would follow them.

"Once we cross over the canal, we should head the other direction. My house is west of the school," Tomoe explained.

She gasped. "Oh, that's right. You told me before that you live in the same neighborhood as Miyoko, yeah?"

She nodded.

"Wait, does that mean that you walked all that way to my house this morning?! Tomoe, that's like a thirty-five-minute walk, at least," Akira said in disbelief.

Tomoe abruptly stopped.

Staggering to a halt alongside her, Akira saw her friend looking ahead of them with fear in her eyes. Following her sights, she noticed Kana and Yuuki approaching them from near the end of the secluded alleyway. She grimaced, then turned and hastily began walking, then running in the other direction.

Tomoe quickly turned and ran after Akira, trying to keep pace with her, which was easy to do, given how much more athletic she was than Akira.

Running to catch up with them, Yuuki managed to grab Akira by her backpack. Though this halted her for a brief moment, she knew her life was more valuable than what little she had in her bag. Akira slipped the straps off and began moving away from him, though Kana managed to close the short distance between them. Grabbing Akira by her hair, Kana turned and shoved her up against the brick wall, pressing her firm against it, allowing her no hope of slipping away.

Throwing the backpack aside, Yuuki moved to stand between Tomoe and Akira, ensuring she wouldn't have a chance to intervene.

"Trying to sneak off the second school's out, huh, Makai?" Kana angrily asked. "I knew you'd try to run away like the coward you are."

"Leave her alone!" Tomoe shouted.

Yuuki moved closer to her, prompting her to stagger back reluctantly. Reaching out, he harshly shoved Tomoe, knocking her back and down onto the walkway. "Get lost. Despite your insistence, this doesn't involve you."

Kana scoffed. "I can't believe after what I told you that you'd still be friends with this psychopath, Asano."

"H-hey! Stop that!" Ikumi shouted from the end of the walkway as she ran towards them, tucking her phone away in her bag as she drew near.

Yuuki exhaled sharply. "This is already beginning to irritate me..." he said under his breath.

"What are you doing to my friend?!" Ikumi added as she began to approach Akira, though Yuuki moved to stand between the two of them.

"I'll tell you the same thing I told Asano. This doesn't involve you, so get lost," he firmly stated.

Kana rolled her eyes. "You're just manipulating every girl you can, aren't you, Makai?" she asked as she set her focus purely onto Akira, pressing her face harder against the wall.

"Ah! Stop it, Kana!" Akira cried out in pain.

"I'll stop when you stop playing games with people's lives, Makai!" she responded before pulling back, turning Akira around, then shoving her up against the wall. No sooner than she had her back against it, Kana threw a quick punch into Akira's abdomen, causing her to double over in pain, though Kana didn't let her slump or fall down.

Ikumi gasped. "S-stop it!" she said as she tried to move around Yuuki, though he quickly grabbed onto her arm and pulled her back, shoving her back down the way she'd come from.

"You're pushing your luck, blondie," Yuuki responded.

Composing herself, she glared at him as she put her foot down firmly against the walkway. "You're hurting my friend! She hasn't done anything to deserve to be treated this way, and... i-if she has, then it's the job of law enforcement to punish her, not you two!"

"Go preach somewhere else. The police haven't done a damn thing about the crimes your 'friend' here has committed," Yuuki responded.

Ikumi began approaching him once more, undeterred by him pulling and shoving her aside. "Then that means she's innocent of whatever you think she's done. The police don't make mistakes. They act on hard evidence. If they don't act, then that's because there is an absence of any actual evidence to convict an individual of a crime."

Tomoe staggered onto her feet as she moved towards her, reaching her hand out in an attempt to urge her to stand down. "I-Ikumi..."

He loudly groaned. "What? Are you an aspiring lawyer or something? Just shut up already."

Kana watched the two of them with mild interest as she continued to hold Akira, who was still reeling from the hit.

"I will not! What you two are doing is illegal," Ikumi firmly stated. "This is assault, and... probably several other crimes as well. You accuse Aki of having committed some horrible crime, yet you're both standing here committing a crime in front of multiple witnesses!"

Growling under his breath, Yuuki looked away briefly, then abruptly threw a quick punch into Ikumi's face, forcing her back and down onto the ground as she covered her injury. "Would you please just shut the hell up already?"

Tomoe rushed to Ikumi's side, kneeling next to her. "Ikumi! Oh my goodness, are you okay?"

Sniffling, Ikumi lowered her hand from her left eye, a clear redness forming around it, no doubt soon leaving it black in the wake of the hit. She appeared as if she were on the verge of tears.

Kana lightly chuckled. "Serves her right, babe," she said to him before looking back to Akira. "Now... where were we, Makai?"

Yuuki narrowed his eyes on Ikumi. "I suggest you both get lost."

With Tomoe's help, Ikumi stood up on her shaky legs, then turned, hastily running back down the secluded alleyway and hanging a left, going opposite of the school building.

He exhaled sharply. "At least one of you broads has half-a-brain," he said, looking to Tomoe. "Well? Are you not going to join her? I won't hesitate to knock your ass to the floor either, Asano," he warned her.

Swallowing nervously, Tomoe fell back a couple of steps, distancing herself from Yuuki. "Aki... is my friend. I'm not going to abandon her..."

"Then watch from a distance. I couldn't care less," Kana shouted in response before cupping Akira's face to force her to look at her. "If you don't want me to start breaking bones, I suggest you start talking."

Akira swallowed nervously. "I... I d-didn't do anything, Kana... I keep–"

Kana threw another punch into Akira's abdomen, refusing to wait for her to finish with her lies. "Stop this innocent act, Makai! You killed my best friend! Now, admit to it!"

Tomoe frowned as she watched Akira being beaten over what was completely her own fault. The longer she continued to carry on with this lie, the longer Akira would suffer as a result. Although it pained her, she knew that sooner or later, she'd have to come clean with what happened.

Taking a deep breath, Tomoe timidly stepped forward. "K-Kana, stop it! Aki didn't do anything."

Yuuki moved closer to her, glaring intensely down at her. "Back off, Asano... or else I'll do to you what I did to your bleach-haired idiot of a friend."

"B-but... Akira didn't do anything... she... she just," Tomoe began to say before hearing a sharp whistle.

Hearing the whistle as well, Kana and Yuuki each looked further down the walkway, seeing a man approach them. Akira too hesitantly looked, though she was shocked by who was drawing near them. Standing even taller than Yuuki himself was a man whom Akira could never forget, even despite only seeing him on one occasion. Lieutenant Yakovna, the man who took Akira's fingerprints the day of the incident, walked up to the group of high school students, his focus heavily on Yuuki. Behind him, a fair distance back, was Ikumi, timidly watching as she held her hand over her wound.

Yakovna looked briefly to Akira, his stern expression portraying none of the emotions he harbored inside. He then looked back to Yuuki. "What's your name, boy?"

Yuuki scoffed, then looked him up and down. Yakovna was wearing a sharp suit, but there was no badge visible on his person. "Who are you? That blonde girl's father?"

"She's my niece. As for who I am," he said, reaching behind himself, then pulling a folded leather case out, which opened to reveal his police badge. "My name is Lieutenant Yakovna Isaak, of the Nirasaki Police Department. Now... answer my question. What is your name?"

Hearing who he was, Kana released Akira, then stepped off and to the side, putting her slightly further away from Yakovna than she was before.

Yuuki glared at him, then gestured towards Akira. "If you're a cop, then you should do your damn job and arrest her!"

Yakovna exhaled sharply. "If I have to ask a third time, then that girl will be the least of your worries. Your name."

"It's Taichi Yuuki!" he angrily responded.

"I appreciate your cooperation, Mister Taichi," Yakovna responded before taking another step closer, prompting Yuuki to back away. However, he wouldn't distance himself enough before Yakovna reared back and threw a heavy hit at Yuuki's face, hard enough to knock him flat down against the walkway.

Akira, Tomoe, and even Kana each responded with shock at the sight of Yakovna, a veteran police officer, throwing such a heavy punch into Yuuki. And, while Akira was excited to see a thug like Yuuki getting what he deserved, Tomoe was instead fearful of this man, as he stood firmly on the opposite side of the law as them.

With a gasp, Kana stared at him in disbelief. "Wh-what are you doing?! You're a police officer! You can't punch a high school student like that!"

Yakovna looked at her and scoffed. "I stand to protect the people of Nirasaki," he said, approaching Yuuki, who was struggling to even lean up after the hit he took. Pulling a pair of handcuffs out, Yakovna kneeled and began to restrain him. "That hit, however, didn't have a damn thing to do with enforcing the law," he said, pulling Yuuki up and onto his feet. "Anyone who lays a finger on my niece will answer to me long before any legal system has a shot at them," he warned.

Kana grit her teeth angrily, then gestured towards Akira. "If you want to arrest anyone, you should arrest Makai! She... she murdered my best friend in cold blood. Because of her, Hachi Miyoko is... she's dead!" she said, on the verge of tears.

Yakovna looked at Akira, smirked at her, then returned his attention to Kana. "All in due time. However, I'd advise against going around and spreading rumors of crimes that have allegedly been committed or who has committed them. It taints the information we can attain from potential witnesses and further hinders the investigation. It'd be in your best interest to not scream it to the heavens... no matter how good that might make you feel."

Tears forming in her eyes, she grit her teeth. "You... you know she did it, and you're not going to do *anything* about it?!" she asked before looking to Akira. She growled under her breath. "I'll make you pay for this, Makai. Forget the police. Forget you confessing to anything! I'll make you regret dragging me through this *hell* if it's the last thing I ever do!" she warned before turning and bolting off down the alley.

Watching her leave, Tomoe looked to Yakovna. "Sh-she just threatened Aki... shouldn't you do something?" she timidly asked.

Yakovna looked at her and scoffed. "I'm afraid I have my hands full. However, if she does try something, you're welcome to contact law enforcement," he said, grinning at her. "Remember to provide as much information as possible so that we can properly investigate the matter," he said before shoving Yuuki forward as he began walking him back towards the school.

Passing cautiously by her uncle, Ikumi began approaching her friends. He glanced back at her. "Ikumi, you're coming with me."

"I-I'll be right there, sir," she responded before hastening her pace to approach her friends, primarily Akira. "Are you alright?"

Akira awkwardly chuckled, though it was difficult to do so. "I should be asking you that. H-how... how the hell did your... uncle get here so fast?"

Ikumi smiled. "Uncle Isaak has been giving me a ride home from school since Wednesday. I think it has something to do with what happened the day before. You know, whatever sent us all home early that day."

"O-oh... so, he's always picking you up from school now?" she asked.

Ikumi nodded. "Yeah. I told him I'd be fine, but he insisted. Between the three of us, I think something bad happened on Tuesday. I've heard a few rumors... but, I hope they're not true. I'd be so sad if they were..."

Akira stared at her, shocked that Ikumi appeared to genuinely have no idea as to what happened on Tuesday, even more so that she didn't overhear Kana's accusations made moments ago. "Y-yeah... well, it's always better to hope for the best, right?"

"I agree. You have to stay positive," she said before sighing. "So, um... will you two be alright walking home? That girl ran off, and she seemed really mad."

Tomoe approached the two of them. "I think we'll be fine. R-really, it was her boyfriend who was the real threat. I doubt she'd try anything on her own while I'm with Aki, so... I'll walk her home."

With a reluctant nod, Ikumi smiled. "Okay... if you're sure. I just–"

"Ikumi!" Yakovna called out from out in front of the school.

She looked back at him. "I'm coming!" she responded, turning back to her friends. "Sorry, I've gotta go. But, I'll see you two on Monday, right?"

Akira nodded. "Yeah. Monday morning in math class."

"And then gym!" Ikumi added with a giggle.

"Yasuhida Ikumi," Yakovna called out once more, his patience waning in his voice.

She lightly flinched. "I'd better go. Uncle Isaak sounds a little irritated. Have a wonderful weekend, you two!" she said as she threw them a wave, then ran off to meet back up with her uncle.

Akira watched as she left, then looked to Tomoe. "She... just saved our asses..."

Tomoe sighed. "She did... we're lucky that she was so persistent and that her uncle was nearby."

"Yeah..." Akira responded.

A brief silence filled the air before Tomoe spoke. "He's... kind of scary, isn't he?"

She nodded. "Terrifying, if I'm completely honest," she admitted before shaking her head. "But, let's get going. We still have to go to your house, then get back to my place in time to at least get some chores done."

"Alright. I'll lead the way," Tomoe said, moving down the secluded alleyway with Akira alongside her.

Despite the hits she took, Akira didn't find it too difficult to walk, though the dull pain in her stomach was uncomfortable, to say the least. What she did find difficult was coping with that ominous threat Kana gave her before disappearing. Moments before Yakovna showed up, she said she'd start breaking Akira's bones, and now supposedly she wasn't even going to wait any longer for the police to do anything? Kana threatened to take matters into her own hands, which could mean Kana might go as far as trying to severely injure or even kill her. With Yuuki arrested, she was at least on her own, but even by herself, Akira was deathly afraid of Kana, now for good reason.

Chapter 11
Home Run
可愛いサイコちゃん

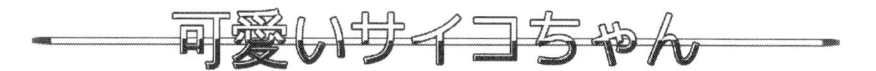

Following their encounter with Kana and Yuuki just outside of school, Akira found herself far less excited for this weekend that she was going to have alone with Tomoe. Originally, she was beside herself with what might happen over these next two days, but now, she found herself more-so fearful of what Kana might do to her the next time their paths crossed. Though, if not for her friend, Ikumi, that would have been the least of Akira's worries, as Kana would have surely put her in the hospital otherwise.

Once they'd gotten far enough from the school, Akira glanced around, ensuring that there wasn't anyone close enough to eavesdrop on their conversation. Most students, by this point, had broken off on their way home, and the nearest ones were so far away that Akira had no fear of them overhearing anything that was said.

With a deep sigh, Akira looked to Tomoe as they walked. "So, um... I think we should keep Ikumi around as a friend."

Tomoe reluctantly sighed, then nodded. "I agree."

"It might be risky, what with her father being the detective who's working on the case... and, her uncle being... terrifying. But, I think having her around will significantly deter Kana from coming after us," she added.

"I agree completely," Tomoe said, looking to her friend. "I'll be honest... if she hadn't gone and gotten her uncle... I was prepared to tell Kana that it was me who shoved Miyoko..."

Akira stopped and looked at her in shock. "W-wait... what?!"

She nodded as she turned to face her friend. "They're hurting you so much... and it's all my fault. I don't want you to suffer because of my mistake. I really am considering just coming clean to the police about all of this. If I do, I know I'll be in so much trouble... but I don't want anything bad to happen to you."

Akira lightly blushed. "You... you were so worried about me... that you'd go that far?" she asked in a low voice before shaking her head. "I... I don't want you to do that, Tomoe... ever."

"Huh? Why not?"

"B-because, I..." she began to say, her cheeks reddening further. She let out a deep sigh, then looked away. "Because... I r-really care about you a lot. And, I don't..." She shook her head, looking back to Tomoe with determination. "I don't want you to go away for something that was all Miyoko's fault. I don't want to... to not have you around anymore..."

Tomoe stared at Akira, listening to her words. She bit at her lip before slowly nodding. A momentary silence filled the air before she spoke up. "You... like me, don't you, Aki?"

Akira's blushing intensified as she diverted her eyes once more. "O-of course I do... you're my best friend."

"You know what I meant," Tomoe responded with a sigh. "I mean, you have a crush on me, don't you?"

Swallowing nervously, she looked back at her. "Is... is it that obvious?"

Tomoe smiled. "Maybe it wouldn't be if I didn't know you were into girls, but... knowing that, yeah, it's kind of obvious."

Reaching up, Akira nervously scratched at her neck as she offered a nervous smile. "Y-yeah... I guess it's not that difficult to put two and two together, huh?"

"Not really," she said before moving a bit closer and offering a smile to her friend. "I'm flattered that you find me attractive, Aki. Just knowing that... it does make me happy," she said before biting her lip. "I don't want to hurt you or anything. But, I'm not... I'm not interested in girls myself. There's nothing wrong with the way you feel... I just don't feel the same way. That's all."

Staring at her, Akira let out a deep sigh. "I... could have assumed as much," she said, sounding severely disappointed. "Like I said earlier... I doubt there's another lesbian in this whole town... and even if I were to move to the big city, I doubt I'd find many my age, who have similar interests to me," she said before holding her head in frustration. "Ugh! I don't want to date some girl who's five, ten, or even *twenty* years older than me, just out of some stupid desperation to find love!"

Tomoe's face contorted with mild embarrassment as she glanced around the area, then looked back to her friend.

Akira exhaled sharply. "Sorry, I'm just being dumb," she said, looking back to her friend and forcing a smile. "We should keep heading to your house, though."

Hesitantly, Tomoe turned and continued on their way down the street. As they walked side-by-side, she looked to Akira. "I do think that you are great in a lot of ways, though, Aki."

Akira lightly blushed. "R-really?"

She nodded. "Yeah. I mean, you're kind, thoughtful, funny, smart–"

Akira laughed. "I am *not* smart."

Tomoe rolled her eyes. "Maybe you're lacking in academic studies, but you make up for it with knowing a lot about the world around you."

"In other words, I have common sense and street smarts?" Akira asked with a toothy grin.

"When you put it like that, it makes it sound bad. A lot of people don't think about things the way you do. They don't see the world the way you do. You've been through a lot, and that changes the way you see the world around you," she explained.

Listening to her, Akira reluctantly nodded. "I suppose that is true..." she said before a smile formed across her lips. "Thanks, Tomoe."

With a playful giggle, Tomoe smiled back at her. "And... don't be too discouraged when it comes to finding love. I'm a firm believer in fate... and, when the time comes, I'm sure you'll meet the girl of your dreams."

Akira continued to smile at her friend, though it became progressively more difficult as she considered Tomoe's words. Turning her focus ahead, she let out a subtle sigh. She was right, fate would bring Akira to the girl of her dreams, and truly, she felt as if it already had. In every conceivable way, Akira truly liked Tomoe. Before, with her feelings towards her friend Ina, it was more affectionate and alluring, yes. But, the emotions she was developing towards Tomoe felt so much more genuine.

Everything from her voice, to the way she wore her hair, to her laugh, which settled Akira's heart as it graced her ears, even to the subtle scent of the various sweet fragrances Tomoe would wear, it all made Akira feel as if she were floating amidst the clouds while in her presence. There wasn't a single aspect about Tomoe that Akira could find that bothered her. In every way, this girl was absolutely perfect. The only flaw was that she had blatantly stated that she didn't feel the same way towards Akira. Words that were beginning to haunt her mind as she thought about them, wondering if there would ever be a circumstance in which Tomoe's opinion would change.

As the two of them walked down the street together, Akira began to recognize the neighborhood they were now in. It was one she'd visited on many occasions, as she and her old friends used to frequently spend time together at Miyoko's house, which wasn't far from here. It was a far nicer area than Akira's neighborhood and even slightly better than where Kana lived. The homes were all more modern, very spacious, and surrounded by larger lawns than anywhere else in Nirasaki. Following her friend, the two of them stepped off the sidewalk and made their way towards a two-story, grey-colored home with a blue roof.

Rather than taking the front door, Tomoe guided her friend under the carport and by a brand new silver-colored sedan that sat under it. Approaching the back door alongside her friend, Akira couldn't help but notice the many flower pots near the door and even a garden that occupied a small plot in the backyard. Much like her grandparents, Tomoe's mother appeared to enjoy gardening, which led Akira to wonder if Tomoe was as equally responsible for maintaining the garden as Akira was for her grandparents. As they walked inside, leaving their shoes by the door, Akira was surprised by just how tidy the house was. It was a larger house than the place she lived at with her grandparents, and everything seemed so modern.

"Mom! I'm home! And I brought my friend!" Tomoe called out as the two of them walked down the hallway.

Walking further along, they turned and entered the kitchen, and Akira couldn't help but admire just how luxurious it was. Modern appliances, more countertop space than she could ever imagine, and even a full-sized dining room table.

Turning to look at the girls, an older woman with short dark brunette hair smiled at them. "Welcome home, sweetheart," she said to her daughter before her attention was drawn towards Akira. "Oh? And this must be the new friend from school you've been spending so much time with."

Blushing, Akira immediately bowed her head. "M-my name is Makai Akira. It's an honor to meet you, ma'am."

She offered a welcoming smile. "Well, it's wonderful to meet you as well,

Miss Makai. My name is Asano Mari."

Akira raised her head back up, then nervously smiled. "L-likewise, ma'am... err, I mean, Miss Asano."

Tomoe giggled. "You're so flustered, Aki," she teased.

Mari lightly chuckled.

"Oh! By the way, Mom, I wanted to know if it'd be alright if I spent the weekend over at Aki's house?" Tomoe asked.

"The weekend? So, would you be back on Monday then?" Mari asked.

Tomoe nodded. "Yeah. I planned to come home after school."

She smiled. "That's perfectly fine, sweetheart. I don't mind you staying over at your new friend's house for the weekend."

Tomoe excitedly bowed her head. "Thank you, Mom!" she graciously said before turning to Akira. "Let's go upstairs and get my stuff packed up, then we can head to your place before it gets too dark out," she said before beckoning her to follow as she walked back into the living room, then over towards the stairs.

Akira offered a bow of her head to Mari, then hastily ran to catch up with Tomoe as she ascended to the second floor, then down the hallway into her bedroom. No sooner than she got there did Akira find herself immediately distracted by how amazing Tomoe's room was. She had a more European-style bed, rather than a futon one like Akira had, and also a much nicer looking desk, on which a brand new laptop sat atop. The room was far larger and more girly than Akira's, with bright, cheerful colors, frills on almost everything that could have it, and a general sense of girlish innocence.

After everything she'd need for the weekend, as well as Monday, was packed up in her bookbag, Tomoe threw it over her shoulder. Returning down to the first floor, they said goodbye to Mari, then left to try and get back to Akira's house in time to do some chores. The sun was just beginning to descend over the horizon, so they still had plenty of time before it was too late, and they were at risk of getting into trouble. Walking down the street, they spoke of just what they'd try to accomplish over this weekend.

For Akira, she was hopeful that she could follow her heart and open Tomoe's mind a bit more to the idea of dating a girl, namely her. Although, with how timid she was, she knew the conversation would be difficult for her to try and have. Tomoe, who led their discussion while Akira lost herself in her thoughts, was set on them improving Akira's pathetic academic performance. She had several ideas of how to tutor her friend, though it would all be down to how willing Akira was to learn the material and apply herself in school.

Walking alongside the canal, then crossing over the bridge where Akira had been thrown off, they approached the low-end apartment buildings, and Akira's eyes trailed over towards where the young men usually sat outside. They weren't there tonight, though judging by the lights that were on inside the apartment and the loud noises, the men were not only home but hosting a party of some sort. Even out on the street, both girls could hear the music playing, alongside shouting between party-goers.

Tomoe shook her head. "I feel so sorry for their neighbors."

Akira lightly chuckled. "Yeah... not to mention their livers. You just know those guys are probably chugging beers, hoping to impress girls."

"I don't see how that could ever be impressive to any girl," she admitted.

Akira shrugged her shoulders. "I think it's kind of a 'heat of the moment' sort of thing. Like, they aren't thinking straight, and so they're impressed that some guy chugged ten beers in a row or something."

"Ten?!" Tomoe asked in shock. "I don't know if that would be safe..."

"I mean... it depends on the beer. You'd probably piss like crazy, though," she admitted with a light chuckle before turning to smile at her friend.

As she did so, Akira caught a momentary glimpse as someone hastily approached the two of them. Akira gasped, prompting Tomoe to follow her vision, though before either of them could react, Tomoe felt a sharp pain as she was jabbed in her stomach by the pommel of a baseball bat. Immediately, Tomoe staggered back a step and fell to her knees, coughing as she held her stomach in pain. By now, Akira could see all too clearly who this attacker was. Turning to face her, wearing the same furious expression as earlier in the day, was Nakajima Kana.

Akira's eyes went wide as she took a half-step back. "K-Kana?!"

"I warned you, Makai... I warned you that I'd make you pay for killing my best friend," Kana angrily said as she moved to stand between Akira and the path to her house. "And I intend to do *just* that. I don't care if you confess to what you did or not. It makes no difference to me. After all that you've done to me and the people I care about over the years... enough is *enough*," she added as she tapped the baseball bat against the palm of her off-hand.

Swallowing nervously, Akira didn't want to abandon her friend, who was now injured, though it was clear that she needed to run, or else things were going to be significantly worse for her. Following her instinct, Akira immediately turned and tried to run back the way they came, not even thinking of where she was going, her only thought being that of how she might get away.

Seeing Akira fleeing, Kana exhaled sharply before glancing back at Tomoe. "If you know what's good for you, Asano, stay here or get lost; I don't care which, just don't interfere with me again, or else..." she said before promptly running after Akira.

A short distance ahead of Kana, crossing over the drainage canal bridge where she'd been thrown off, Akira frantically looked around for anyone who could help her. Up ahead, she saw the construction site and immediately recalled the men who were so quick to help her. Glancing back, she saw Kana running down along the canal, bolting towards her. Pushing herself as fast as she could go, Akira moved towards the construction site.

Upon reaching the entrance to the site, Akira pushed on the chainlink gate, which had a tarp covering it, preventing her from seeing anything inside. Slowly, the gate opened, and as she stepped inside, she frantically looked around. Aside from the construction equipment and building materials left behind, the lot was empty. This, unfortunately, made perfect sense, as it was already dusk, and the workers had likely all gone home for the evening.

Stepping further into the construction site, Akira looked around for somewhere she could hide, though she wouldn't have an opportunity to do so. With a loose, metallic rattle, the gate was haphazardly slammed closed, prompting Akira to turn and look behind her, seeing Kana approaching her slowly, baseball bat in hand. With panic setting in, Akira steadily began to back away, trying her best to keep her distance from Kana.

"There's nowhere for you to run this time, Makai..." Kana said as she swung the bat around in a circular flourish on her right-hand side.

Swallowing nervously, Akira took another glance around the area, realizing that there was nowhere else for her to go, other than through Kana. Taking a deep breath, she screamed as loud as she could. "Help! Someone! Please help me!"

The moment she heard Akira begin to scream, Kana ran forward, closing the distance. Seeing this, Akira tried to turn and run away, though

Kana was able to swing her bat low and hit Akira in the back of her knee, forcing her down onto the ground, where she landed on her hands and knees. Before even having a moment to allow the pain to subside, Akira felt as Kana stomped her foot into her back, forcing her down onto the loose dirt below.

Kana glared down at Akira, foot pressed against her back to prevent her from going anywhere. "A part of me... really wants to make you suffer for everything you've done, Makai... the other part," she held her baseball bat down in front of Akira's face, "just wants to beat you with this bat until it breaks... or my anger subsides, whichever comes first."

Akira stared at the bat, the fear of death washing over her as she could do little but cower. "K-Kana..." she said, her eyes trailing up to her old friend. "P-please... I swear, I didn't hurt Miyoko... I didn't!"

"Shut up!" she yelled. "I'm so sick of your lies! You're *not* the victim here; I am! You took advantage of Ina! You murdered my best friend! Because of you, Yuuki got arrested and probably thrown in jail. If anyone should be in jail, it should be *you!*"

Akira felt her tears running down her cheeks. "I didn't... I didn't do any of those things, Kana. Please... I'm sorry that... that all happened to you, but please! I didn't do it! It isn't my fault!"

Growling, Kana took half a step back and slammed the bottom of her foot against Akira's side, forcing her to roll over and onto her stomach. She then straddled Akira's abdomen as she pinned her to the ground, the baseball bat held firmly and pressed against her upper chest. "I'm so tired of hearing all of your lies, Makai! I'm done with it!" she said, gritting her teeth furiously. "And... you know what? If you're so dedicated to wasting your breath... maybe you shouldn't have any at all."

Moving the bat onto the ground just above Akira's head, Kana then placed both of her hands around Akira's neck and began to squeeze against her throat, applying an increasing pressure as her anger steadily built. "This is for Ina... this is for Miyoko! This is for all of the pain and suffering you've brought into my life! For betraying my trust and destroying my life, piece by piece!"

With her arms pinned under Kana's legs, Akira could only struggle, though she was far too weak, even with her adrenaline, to force Kana off of her. Breathing wasn't difficult for her, as much as it was simply impossible. She tried to gasp for air but couldn't. She attempted to speak, though what little came out was throaty and incoherent.

Kana's fingernails began to dig into Akira's neck as her grip tightened. "I used to look up to you, Makai... you used to be my best friend! How could you have become this horrible... this evil? So much so that you'd kill Miyoko and then pretend you did nothing wrong?!"

Tears ran down Akira's cheeks as she felt her vision getting blurry. She squeezed her eyes shut, feeling completely helpless as she knew her life was truly in Kana's hands, and it appeared as if she genuinely intended to put an end to Akira's life for all of the things she was accusing her off.

"K-Kana! Stop it!" Tomoe shouted in a panic as she ran over.

Glancing off towards her as she approached, Kana cursed under her breath. She released Akira, then stood up, grabbing her bat as she moved to stand between the two of them. "I'm getting tired of you always interfering, Asano."

Tomoe staggered to a stop a short distance from Kana, her heart racing. "P-please, don't hurt her. Aki is completely innocent."

Gritting her teeth as she growled under her breath, Kana took a step closer. "She's not innocent of *anything!*" she shouted before pointing the bat back at Akira, who was gasping for air on her knees as she held her neck, which was red from where Kana had been strangling her. "Makai deserves to die for what she's done. And if you don't get lost, you'll join her!"

Tomoe's eyes widened in shock. "You'd... y-you'd really do that? You'd go so far as to... to kill her?"

Lowering her bat, Kana exhaled sharply. "You don't have *any* idea how much pain she's caused. Whatever lies she told you to convince you that she was innocent, they're just that; lies."

She shook her head. "I don't believe that. Akira is a kind, thoughtful and wonderful girl... she's not the monster you make her out to be."

"K-Kana..." Akira groaned, her throat sore from being strangled.

Pausing, Kana looked back at her and glared.

Tears still flowing from her eyes, Akira frowned. "I'm sorry... I'm so, *so* sorry... for everything that's... ever happened to you. But... I'm telling you the truth, I... I didn't hurt Miyoko. I didn't do *anything* to her."

Gritting her teeth, Kana turned and held the bat out to her side, ready to swing. "Shut up, shut up, *shut up!*" she shouted. "I'm so tired of hearing your hollow apologies!"

Akira held her arms up, shielding her head as she cowered in fear.

Tomoe gasped. "Kana, stop!" she said, her mind racing as she thought of what she could possibly say. "She... she didn't push Miyoko down the stairs... I did!"

Stopping, it took a moment for Tomoe's words to sink into Kana's mind, though as they did, she turned and looked back at her. "Wh-what did you say?"

Swallowing nervously, Tomoe took a step back. "A-Aki... didn't push Miyoko down the stairs... it was me. I pushed her," she stammered out as her heart throbbed heavily in her chest. "I a-asked for her to stop trying to bully me all of the time... and I... sh-she and I got into an argument... and, Aki tried to get us to stop fighting... b-but, Miyoko shoved her, and I–"

"You... you shoved my friend down the stairs?" Kana asked in disbelief.

Pausing, she reluctantly nodded. "Y-yes... I did..."

An eery silence filled the air as Akira hesitantly lowered her guard, staring up at Kana as she stood speechless at Tomoe's words. Akira's eyes shifted to her friend, then back to Kana again, unsure of what would happen next.

Gritting her teeth, Kana's anger steadily began to flow back into her as she clenched her fists. "It was you... this *whole* time?" she asked in a low voice.

Tomoe grimaced as she took another step back, feeling her whole body began to shake.

Without warning, Kana charged after Tomoe with her bat. Closing the short distance, she swung it wide, though she missed as Tomoe ducked down and immediately began running towards the gate. Reaching out, Kana grabbed onto the back of Tomoe's blouse, dropped her bat, then pulled Tomoe back and into her grasp. Throwing her off to the side, Kana ran at her and shoved her up against the wall. Rearing back, she began repeatedly punching at Tomoe's head. Though Tomoe did well to try and shield herself with her arms, she couldn't escape.

"You stupid, hateful bitch!" Kana shouted as she continued to pummel Tomoe. "It was all your fault! It's been your fault this whole time, and you said nothing?! *Nothing?!*" she screamed.

Akira looked on in horror as Kana relentlessly beat on her friend, the girl she'd grown so fond of, and even began developing feelings towards. Mere moments ago, Kana was strangling Akira, and so she knew she had to do something to stop her, or else she'd likely kill Tomoe in her blind rage. Pushing herself up and onto her feet, Akira ran over to Kana and grabbed her arm, preventing her from striking Tomoe again. With little more than a brief glare, Kana pulled her arm free from Akira, then drove her elbow back, hitting Akira in the face and sending her staggering backward.

As she stumbled, Akira stepped onto the discarded baseball bat, causing her to lose her footing and fall onto the ground. Although the hit was painful, as was the fall, Akira wasn't worried about herself, but instead, Tomoe. Her heart was racing in her chest as she looked back at how Kana furiously attacked her friend. She had to do something to stop her, but Akira knew she was far too weak to stand up against someone like Kana. To have any shot at intervening, she'd have to have something to give her an advantage over Kana's significant strength.

As she went to push herself back up onto her feet, Akira saw the bat that had been discarded, the one she had just tripped over. Reaching out, she took the baseball bat and stood back up. Holding it firmly in her hands, she looked to where Kana and Tomoe were. Taking a deep breath, Akira conjured every ounce of courage she had, knowing full well that she would once again be at the center of Kana's attention once she intervened, but also that she had to do something, or else Tomoe might die.

Approaching them, she could feel her legs quivering with fear, her hands were shaking, and she could feel her teeth chattering as if she were freezing cold. Upon reaching them, Akira raised the bat into the air on her right side, and with all of her strength, she swung, aiming for Kana's head. The hit was hard, its force resonated through the bat, causing a shock to Akira's hands, but Kana shouldered the brunt of the impact, knocking her over and onto the ground, on her back, next to Tomoe. Reaching up, Kana held her head and cried out in pain. Akira stood there, fear holding over her as she looked at her friend, who hesitantly lowered her guard to see Akira. The two locked eyes in silence.

Hearing Kana's cries, Akira turned to her, the girl who had caused her so much pain, and watched as she held her head, likely trying to recover from the concussion Akira no doubt gave her. A strange feeling washed over her, and soon, she stopped shaking, she couldn't hear Kana's voice anymore, and she didn't feel fear nor courage within her. She moved closer to Kana with staggered breaths, raised the bat into the air, then slammed it again against Kana's head.

Tomoe's eyes widened as she pushed herself back against the wall, attempting to distance herself from what was happening. Kana held her arms up and pleaded for her life, but there was no response from Akira.

She continued to batter Kana, with every hit transforming the emotionless expression on her face into a look of pure anger, of hatred, of furious rage for everything this girl had forced her to endure. Gritting her teeth, she used every ounce of her strength to swing the bat, her mind flooded with painful memories of the suffering Kana forced not only her to endure but now Tomoe and Ikumi as well.

Tomoe watched, almost in horror, as Akira kept hitting Kana, again and again, blood from the wounds staining the wood of the bat, spattering from each hit back onto Akira's hands, clothes, and even her face. Feeling herself quiver at the sight of what laid before her, Tomoe forced herself to speak.

"A-Aki..." Tomoe said, gaining no response from her friend, whose assault didn't halter at all. "Aki," she tried again, to no avail. *"Akira!"* she shouted.

Stopping mid-swing, Akira froze for a moment, her expression changing, appearing almost worried or shocked by what she had done. Her hands were sore and shaking. Staring down at Kana's brutally battered body, Akira hesitantly let go of the bat, allowing it to fall, landing on Kana's shoulder, only to fall off and roll to the side.

"Akira?" Tomoe hesitantly asked.

Looking down at the palms of her hands, Akira saw the blood that was staining them, the only untouched portions being that which was shielded by the bat she held. Her hands were shaking, a single thought echoing through her mind, muttered under her breath. "Did... did I just... kill Kana?"

Chapter 12
Mixed Feelings

―――可愛いサイコちゃん―――

Her hands were soaked with blood, while her vision beyond them was blurred as she stared in disbelief at what she'd done. After all of these years, after all the torment Kana had put her through, it was finally too much. Seeing Tomoe hurt was the last straw; she had to stop it; she had to rescue her friend; she had to protect this girl who meant so much to her. Though in the process, Akira found herself crossing far beyond the line, a line that any reasonable person would never cross, and yet here she stood in this eerily quiet lot in Nirasaki, over the motionless, blood-soaked body of someone she'd known for years.

Akira's vision began to focus, putting into perspective the damage she had done to Kana. She laid motionless on the ground, her clothes tinged with blood, the features of her face now disfigured beyond recognition, with her hair, a matted mess as it clumped together with the blood from the assault. Even the dirt was dark with the blood that had spilled out from Kana's injuries. Looking towards her friend, Akira saw as she stood a short distance away, staring at her with wide eyes and her mouth held agape as she struggled to make sense of what she'd just witnessed. Akira turned her attention once more to Kana.

"She's... she's dead..." Akira said, her voice cracking as she spoke.

With her hands covering her mouth, Tomoe stared on, her eyes shifting back and forth between Kana's lifeless, mutilated body and her friend, whose clothes were soaked from the blood-spatter that flew off with every hit of her relentless assault. The sight of the vivid red that stained the front of Akira was terrifying, akin to something from the worst horror movie

Tomoe had ever seen, though this was no work of fiction that stood before her.

"Hello?! Is anyone there?" a man called out.

Both girls immediately turned and looked to where the voice came from. It was on the other side of the fence, the far side, opposite the entrance.

"I heard shouting! Is someone hurt?" the man called out again.

Looking around in a panic, Akira turned to her friend. "We... w-we've gotta get out of here."

Trembling, Tomoe looked to Akira, her heart pounding in her chest as she wasn't quite sure what to say.

Backing away, Akira hesitated. She noticed the bat lying next to Kana, the bat that no doubt had her fingerprints all over it. Thinking fast, she picked it up, then began making her way towards the entrance, motioning for Tomoe to follow her, which she did with great reluctance. Moving past the partially open gate, the girls ran towards Akira's house. Their minds were racing, they knew they probably forgot something, but at this point, they simply hoped that no one would see them or the blood that stained Akira's skin and clothes.

Crossing over the bridge, Akira slowed as her focus drifted towards the railings as she thought of what she could do to rid herself of the weapon she'd just used against Kana. Moving further ahead, Tomoe stopped, then glanced behind her, seeing Akira standing in the center of the bridge, staring aimlessly off into the distance. Looking around the area, she grimaced at the thought of them being spotted out here, her entire body quivering as she turned to face her friend.

Akira moved closer to the edge, placed her free hand on the railing, then looked down into the murky waters below. From her own recent experience, she knew that the water was nearly a meter deep and would likely do well to conceal the bat. With her hand still shaking, she raised the bat up and over the railing, then let go, allowing it to plummet down into the canal, where it landed with a splash that was far louder than she expected it to be. Stepping back from the edge of the bridge, she turned to Tomoe, who was petrified with fear. Offering a firm nod, Akira returned to her friend's side, then beckoned her to follow as she led the way back to her grandparents' house.

As the girls scrambled to get home, the time was nearly six-thirty, and the sun was already setting over the horizon. This didn't cause Akira to shy away at all when it came to stripping off her bloodied clothes the moment she reached the garden on the side of her house, where she used the water hose to desperately rinse herself off. While Akira vigorously scrubbed her arms, legs, and face to try and get rid of the evidence of what she'd done, Tomoe looked around the area in a panic, paranoid that they'd be seen.

Sitting the hose aside, Akira gave herself a once over before looking to Tomoe. "Did I... d-did I get everything?" she stammered as she held her arms out to her side and turned around so Tomoe could see if she missed any spots. After a moment with no response, Akira dropped her arms to her sides. "Tomoe?"

"Y-yes?" Tomoe nervously responded, staring at her friend with wide eyes as her heart and mind continued to race.

They stared at one another in silence for a moment before Akira sighed. "Did I miss any blood or anything?"

Tomoe reluctantly shook her head.

Akira let out a deep sigh. "Good..." she said, glancing over towards a window that was just slightly further down the house from where they were. "My grandparents might still be awake... but they should be in our tatami room, winding down for the night..." she said before returning her focus to her friend. "We need to get inside, and I need to get to the bathroom without them noticing me..."

Tomoe didn't respond; she only continued to stare at Akira.

Exhaling sharply, she stood up and walked past her friend, beckoning her to follow. Making their way inside, through the front door, Akira opened the door as quietly as possible. She took her shoes off in the small entryway, which still had visible bloodstains on them. Wrapping them up in her bloodied clothes, she cautiously peeked into the kitchen, seeing that it was empty. She once more motioned for Tomoe to follow as she carefully moved into the kitchen.

Taking slow and steady steps, Akira's primary focus was on making as little noise as possible. As she neared the open door to the tatami room, she could hear the television. Peeking just through the doorway, she could see her grandmother and grandfather sitting together, watching an old television show. Their empty teacups sat on the small tray in the center of the table, a sign to Akira that they would be going to bed soon. Turning back to Tomoe, she held her finger up to her lips, motioning for her to be quiet.

Reaching out, Akira took her friend's hand, then guided her silently past the open doorway and towards the bathroom just down the hall. As they moved, Tomoe took a step on one of the many old, creaky boards that lined the floors of this nearly century-old house. Hearing the board creak, Akira hastily pulled her towards the bathroom.

"Akira, sweetheart, is that you?" Satomi called out.

Stopping near the doorway to the bathroom, she glanced back. "Y-yes, ma'am. Tomoe and I... j-just got back from... from h-her house," she shakily said.

"That's alright, sweetie. I made some cake earlier today, you and your friend are welcome to it. Your grandfather and I will be going to bed soon, though," Satomi said.

"Um... cool! Th-thanks, grandmother. I, um... I'm going to grab a shower real quick, then start on my chores. I..." Akira looked at the clothes in her hands. "I n-need to do some laundry too, I think."

"I put some clothes in the washer earlier. Feel free to just add to those if you want. And, tell your friend to make herself at home. We're happy to have her over," Satomi added.

"Y-yeah, I'll tell her," she said before looking to Tomoe and motioning for her to hurry into the bathroom.

Stepping into the first room of their bathroom, Akira closed the door shut, then walked over to the sink, where she sat her clothes down on the floor nearby. Looking into the mirror, Akira could see where her face was still stained with a significant amount of blood. It was clumping up in her hair and already drying on her skin. The amount of it was shocking to Akira, especially given that she already tried washing her face off outside.

She looked to Tomoe, ready to ask why she didn't tell her, though her friend was leaned up against the wall, pale as a ghost, her face emotionless as she no doubt struggled to comprehend what they had just done. Akira took a deep breath, pushed off from the sink, then moved towards the other section of their bathroom. "I, um... I'm going to wash up real fast... d-don't, um... don't go anywhere, okay?" she asked in a low voice, though Tomoe didn't respond at all.

Reluctantly, Akira continued into the other room, sliding closed the textured glass door they had for a bit of privacy, then discarding what few clothes she still had on. Starting the water, she sat down on the small stool and began to wash herself off. Running the soap across her arms, she found herself just staring in disbelief at the tile wall in front of her. There was a faint red hue mixed in with the soap bubbles, especially when shampooing her hair, as well as on the soap in her hands when she began washing her face.

As she rinsed off, she watched the water swirl into the drain below her, a vivid red hue that steadily faded from it. That helped provide her with some confidence that the evidence of what she had done was washed away. Her mind still struggled to come to terms with what happened, however. So much so that she barely even noticed how red her skin was from the scalding hot water. Turning it off, she sat there on the stool for a moment, leaning forward, resting her elbows on her knees as she held her forehead, staring down at the floor.

"Did... did I really just do that?" Akira asked herself. Letting out a staggered sigh, she closed her eyes tightly. Opening them, she looked down at her open hands, staring into her palms. "Did I really... just kill Kana? She's dead... because of me?"

Bringing her hands up closer, she examined them in more detail. After all of the years of pain, torment, and suffering Kana had inflicted upon her; it was finally over. And, it wasn't just that the misery she'd endured for years had come to an end; it was that she was the one who ended it with her own two hands. Now, she'd no longer be living in a world where Kana was constantly making her miserable; it was this way now because of what Akira herself had done. She was the one who killed Kana. For years, she'd been terrified of Kana, petrified with fear whenever she was around, and yet now, Akira not only stood up against her, but she fought back.

A vast majority of her mind was still stuck with fear and uncertainty over the fact that she had just taken another person's life. But, at least in some small way, she was also proud of herself for standing up to Kana.

Reluctantly, Akira approached the door, then slid it open slightly. Just out in the adjacent room, Tomoe was still waiting. While she appeared as if she were still horrified over what happened, it did seem that she had calmed down, at least slightly. Tomoe noticed Akira standing behind the textured glass, her figure little more than a blur beyond it, as she peeked through the opening.

"Could I have a towel?" Akira asked in a calm, quiet voice.

Hesitantly, Tomoe offered a shaky nod. She then began to look around for where the towels were.

"Um, on the shelf. Just behind you," Akira said, pointing to the towels.

Turning to the shelf, Tomoe went to pull just one-off, though her nerves led to her pulling the whole stack off and into the floor. She gasped, then muttered under her breath, sounding as if she were about to cry.

"I-it's okay... just bring me one," Akira said, not wanting her friend to stress more than she already was.

Tomoe picked one towel up with a staggered sigh, then brought it over, holding it out for her friend to take.

Akira grabbed the towel, then stepped back away from the door, turning to face away from Tomoe as she dried herself off. An awkward silence filled the air between them as Akira ran the towel over herself, seeing that there were no red spots anywhere on the white fabric. "How are you holding up?" she asked, continuing to dry herself off.

Tomoe was oddly shocked to hear that question. She wasn't even sure that she was prepared to answer it. "I don't know..." she admitted in a low voice.

Akira wrapped the towel around herself, appropriately covering her upper and lower body. Moving back to the door, she slid it open and saw Tomoe standing with her head held low. "My grandparents are probably in bed by now, I'd imagine. So... we can go up to my room and talk if you want."

Tomoe reluctantly shook her head. "I don't know..."

Akira frowned. "I... I'm sorry, Tomoe..."

She looked back to Akira as if she were unsure what the apology was intended to be for.

After another moment of silence, Akira bit at her lip, then moved past her friend. "I should probably go change," she said as she approached the door that led out of the bathroom. She glanced back at Tomoe. "Did... you want to talk in my room? Or... maybe outside? I think we should talk outside. The fresh air would probably help..."

Tomoe stared at her with concern. "Aki... are... are you okay?"

Thinking briefly on it, she nodded. "I think so... you stopped her before she really started wailing on me," she admitted with an awkward chuckle. "I owe you for that, by the way... I still can't believe that you–"

"N-no... I mean..." Tomoe said, pausing as she inhaled sharply. "Y-you just... wh-what happened, I mean... you..."

Staring briefly at her, Akira contemplated how she could answer that. She offered a reluctant nod. "I'm... I'm alright."

"Alright?" Tomoe asked.

Akira nodded once more. "Yeah... I'm still... I guess, wrapping my head around what... what even happened. Ya know? It all happened so fast that, fuck... I don't know. It's like it's all a blur, ya know?"

Tomoe stared in disbelief at Akira, though it wasn't as if any answer her friend had would have sufficed when it came to explaining what had just happened.

"L-listen, I'm going to go get changed... wait, um... wait outside for me. Like, just outside the front door. I promise I won't belong. I'll change super fast," Akira said as she opened the door and went to step out into the hallway.

"A-Aki, what about your..." Tomoe began to say, her eyes trailing to the wad of blood-soaked clothes that laid on a pile on the floor.

Looking back at them, Akira nodded. "I'll... throw them in the washer and get it started before I meet you outside," she said before continuing out into the hallway.

Passing by the tatami room, Akira was relieved to see that the lights were off inside. The kitchen was dark as well, a clear sign that both of her grandparents had gone upstairs to turn in for the night. Heading up to the second floor herself, Akira slipped into her bedroom and scrounged up the first few articles of clothing she could find. Hastily getting dressed, she moved to her desk and slid open the bottom drawer, quickly grabbing a small box and slipping it into the pocket of her shorts.

Making her way back downstairs, though doing her best to keep quiet, she returned to the bathroom, where Tomoe was thankfully no longer lingering, and grabbed her clothes. Wrapping them up in her towel, she took them to the washing machine and dropped them inside. Adding a generous amount of laundry detergent, she then began the wash cycle, then held her hands together, praying that they would come out clean and without any remnants of the blood that currently stained them.

Making her way to the front of her house, Akira slipped on a pair of shoes she had sitting near the door, then stepped outside. For whatever reason, there was something oddly calming about tonight to her. She could hear the various crickets and other insects that were calling out into the night air, the distant sound of a few stray cars traveling down the nearby streets, alongside different yet subtle sounds that provided an atmosphere that put Akira's mind at ease.

Sitting at the end of the short walkway, where it stepped down into the loose gravel driveway, sat Tomoe. She had been staring blankly out into the distance, though her attention soon shifted to Akira the moment she heard the front door open.

Akira approached her friend, choosing to stand rather than sit, as she leaned back against the nearby fence. A moment of silence elapsed as they stared at one another, as well as in the area around them. As Akira's eyes settled on Tomoe, she could see just how distraught her friend still was over what happened.

"So, um... how are you holding up?" Akira reluctantly asked.

Tomoe continued to stare blankly ahead, offering no immediate answer. With a deep breath, she shook her head and stifled her tears as she spoke. "I... feel sick..."

She grimaced at her friend's words, knowing it was her own actions that led to that feeling. "Y-yeah... me too..." she lied.

Letting out a deep sigh, Tomoe held her head in her hands. "What... what even happened? How did things... go that far?"

Akira bit at her lip as she thought of how to choose her words. "It's just, you know... the same shit as before..."

She looked at her friend. "Wh-what do you mean?"

"Don't you remember? Miyoko started a fight with us, and shit went south." Akira felt the corner of her lips form into a very slight smile. *More like shit went 'downhill,'* she thought to herself before shaking her head and looking to Tomoe with more focus on her words, rather than her devilish thoughts. "But, the same thing happened with Kana. She attacked us, just like Miyoko had, and... we defended ourselves."

Tomoe stared in disbelief at her. "Y-you killed her..." she bluntly stated.

Akira pursed her lips. "You killed Miyoko."

"Th-that was an accident!" she retorted.

"Yeah, well..." Akira looked away. "It's not like I meant to beat the fuck out of her. It just sort of happened..."

Tomoe continued to stare, speechless at her words. "Aki... if... if I hadn't yelled at you... I... I don't even know if you would have stopped," she said, swallowing nervously. "You looked... so angry... so possessed with rage... it was... terrifying..."

Biting her lip, Akira reluctantly looked back at her friend.

"What... wh-what you did... that wasn't normal..." she struggled to say.

Akira went to respond, though she hesitated as she gave more thought to how exactly she would ask what she wanted to. "Why'd you tell her?"

"Huh?" Tomoe asked. "Tell who what?"

Akira gestured off towards where they had come from. "Why'd you tell

Kana that it was you? Why did you tell her the truth?"

Tomoe frowned, lowering her head. "B-because... she was going to... she would have seriously hurt you if I hadn't..."

"She'd of killed me if you hadn't," she clarified.

Sighing deeply, Tomoe nodded. "You're probably right..."

Akira pursed her lips. "And she'd of killed you if I hadn't of intervened." Tomoe looked back at her.

"Just... just sayin'..." she added.

"Aki... even though that's true, you... you still shouldn't have... there's no reason you should have hit her as hard as you did... as much as you did," Tomoe responded.

Shaking her head, Akira reached up and placed her hand firm against one eye and groaned. "Fuck... I need a moment. I feel like I can't even breathe," she said, turning and moving around the fence, back out onto the street.

Tomoe perked her head up as she saw Akira leaving. "A-Aki? Where are you going?" she asked, though she heard nothing in response.

Walking down the street, Akira passed by the apartments and almost began following the path back to the very scene they had just left behind. Stopping at the canal, Akira leaned onto the railing as she stared across and towards the construction site. Reaching into her pocket, she pulled out the small box that she'd taken from her room, a pack of cigarettes.

Opening the pack up, she took one out, along with the lighter that was stowed away inside. Lighting it up, she sat the pack and lighter down on the flat top of the railing and took a long, steady drag off it. Blowing the smoke out across the canal, she shook her head.

I'm not fucked up for the way I feel... or for what I did. Kana would have killed us both if I hadn't killed her. *Even if I knocked her out and we ran off... it'd just be a matter of time before she, and probably Yuuki too, caught us and finished what she started,* she thought to herself as she enjoyed her cigarette, tapping the ash off into the canal below. "Why can't she just see the obvious?" she asked herself.

"Aki?" Tomoe asked as she walked up behind her.

Pausing, Akira glanced back and saw her friend timidly approaching her. She sighed, then looked back out across the canal. "Sorry... I guess it was sort of childish to just run off like that... but I just needed a moment."

Tomoe approached her, frowning at both her behavior as well as what she was now doing. "You're smoking?"

Akira looked down at the cigarette in her hand, then nodded. "It helps calm my nerves. I used to just do it whenever Kana and my grandfather both stressed me the hell out," she said, lightly chuckling in disbelief. "I never thought I'd need it for something like this..."

Moving to stand next to her, Tomoe too stared out across the canal at the construction site no more than fifty meters away.

Exhaling the smoke up into the air, away from her friend, Akira closed her eyes, then crossed her arms in front of her on the railing as she leaned forward.

She looked at her, then sighed. "I'm... sorry if I upset you... and that's why you ran off," she said, drawing Akira's attention to her. "I'm just... I'm worried. I've never seen anything like that before. I don't know what to think, what to feel... I'm just really scared," she said, shaking her head. "This isn't how things are supposed to be, Aki... it's only been one week since school started, and... and I've seen two girls lose their lives... because of us," she said, tears forming in her eyes as she lowered her head.

Akira stared at her friend, her own sadness brought on by the tears in the eyes of the girl she'd grown to care so much for. Looking back to the cigarette in her hand, which was nearly half-burnt, she tossed it down into the murky waters of the canal. "I don't know what to think or say either..." she admitted, looking back to her friend. "Other than, you risked your life to save mine."

Taking a staggered breath, Tomoe looked back to Akira.

"And, when I saw Kana attacking you... I feared that she might kill you if I didn't do something. So, I did," Akira said, shaking her head. "I tried to grab her and make her stop, but she easily overpowered me. So, I did the only thing I could think of. I grabbed the first weapon I could find and attacked her..." she explained, her eyes trailing across the canal.

Swallowing nervously, Tomoe nodded. "But... but, why did you take it so far? Why did you... have to kill her?"

She continued to stare out for a moment before a subtle smile began to form across her lips, one she quickly wiped away. She looked back to Tomoe. "I don't know why... if I were to try and guess, I suppose it's just because she's been a constant fear in my life for the past three years. She's always gone out of her way to make me miserable, ruin my life, my reputation, and even threatened to out me to my grandparents..." she admitted before reaching up and holding her forehead in frustration. "I know that doesn't justify what happened, and I didn't intend for it to, but..." she looked back to her friend, "I'm not some monster who took her life because I wanted to... I barely even remember what was happening after I hit her off of you..."

"So, you just sort of blacked out?" Tomoe asked.

Thinking on it, Akira shook her head. "I don't think I really 'blacked out' or anything, but, like... I just wasn't me for a moment... you know?" she asked, looking back to her.

"I'm not so sure I understand..." she responded before sighing. "You and she used to be friends. I know she did some horrible things to you, but... aren't you sad that she's... that she's dead?"

Akira lightly scoffed under her breath. Not really, she thought. With a sigh, she forced herself to nod. "I guess it still hasn't completely set in..." she said as she watched the construction site from afar. What the fuck am I going to do when the police find her? They're already suspicious of me, and I don't have any way to prove that I'm innocent.

Tomoe could see the troubled look on her friend's face. It reminded her of how she felt the day she pushed Miyoko down those stairs. While Akira's actions felt incomprehensible at the time, Tomoe was beginning to see that she was merely viewing the same events as before, only from her friend's perspective. When Miyoko died, Akira had no investment in the situation, she could have easily told someone what Tomoe had done, but she didn't. Now, Tomoe was the witness to a horrific crime Akira had committed, one that, much like the one that preceded it, had taken the life of someone they both knew.

Chapter 13
Wavering Confidence
可愛いサイコちゃん

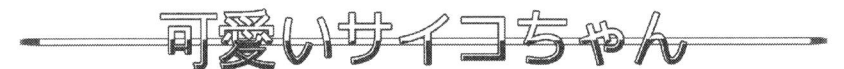

After returning to the house, Akira and Tomoe reluctantly went up to Akira's room and prepared to turn in for the night. Fortunately, they had a spare futon bed in one of the closets from when Akira's brother lived here, so Tomoe wasn't left to sleep on the bare floors. Though, even with a comfortable bed to sleep in, it took some time for Tomoe herself to fall asleep. Akira was out like a light when her head hit her pillow, but, for Tomoe, she struggled to get the imagery of Akira repeatedly bashing Kana out of her mind.

Up until now, Tomoe had always felt that Akira was just an awkward, misunderstood girl. Under the surface, she was kind, caring, and funny, albeit a little strange at times. But now, Tomoe wasn't quite so certain that Akira didn't have something wrong with her, though she had to ask the same question of herself. Tomoe had, with great reluctance, accepted that they were hiding the truth behind Miyoko's death. Now, it appeared they would be doing the same with Kana's, to whatever end that would bring them to.

The following morning, Akira laid sprawled out on her bed, snoring loudly with her covers kicked half-off, as she slept like a rock. A short distance away, Tomoe was curled up in her own bed, clung tightly to her pillow, which was lightly saturated with a mix of tears from sporadic crying throughout the night, and drool from her drifting off into an exhaustion-induced deep sleep. While the sunlight gently peeked through the curtains of the window, neither girl stirred until they were each abruptly shocked back into reality by shouting.

"It's seven-thirty! I don't care if you have a guest over. You have chores to do, young lady!" Ryoma shouted from the other side of the door.

Akira rubbed her eyes with a groan, then let out a deep yawn as she stretched her arms out above her head. Lazily she looked over at her friend, seeing Tomoe perked up in bed, clearly sprung to life thanks to Ryoma's rude awakening.

Akira smiled at her friend. "He does that whenever I sleep in on the weekend. You sort of get used to it," she reassured her.

Tomoe turned to Akira and frowned. "I didn't know what that was at first... he startled me..."

She nodded. "Yeah, it happens..." she said before sighing as she sat up in her bed, crossing her legs. "I'd ask how you slept, but judging by your eyes... I'd say you barely slept at all."

Tomoe lowered her head. "I couldn't stop thinking about last night..."

"Me either," Akira admitted.

Her eyes trailed back to her friend, recalling that every moment that she struggled to sleep, Akira was snoring in the meantime. "Did you wake up much throughout the night?"

Akira nodded. "Yeah... but I just kept rolling over and going back to sleep. After everything that happened yesterday, I just felt so mentally exhausted, you know?"

"R-right. It was... exhausting..." Tomoe said.

"But," Akira began to say with a grunt as she got up from her bed. "Now we've got a plethora of chores to take care of before we can do anything," she said as she stood up and looked to her friend. "I know shit played out differently than we intended to, but... were you still going to tutor me this weekend? Or, did we just wanna hang out and have fun?"

She let out a staggered sigh, shaking her head. "I... I don't know..."

Akira pursed her lips. "Well, we can't do either until my chores are done, so you have time to think on it. But, I'm going to go brush my teeth. I'll be right back," she said as she began making her way over to her bedroom door.

Watching her friend leave, Tomoe wrestled with her emotions. She knew Akira was lying about how she slept, and to Tomoe, that felt like a clear sign of just how little empathy Akira had towards the girl she had just killed. The thought of Akira putting everything all behind her and moving forward with their original plans for this weekend disturbed Tomoe, though she couldn't fathom how she could ever bring something such as that up to her friend.

Leaving her bedroom, Akira descended the stairs, where she passed by her grandmother in the hall on the way to the bathroom.

"Good morning, sweetheart," Satomi said as she turned to allow Akira plenty of room to walk by.

"Hey, grandmother," Akira sleepily responded as she turned to head into the bathroom.

"Oh, before I forget. I saw you had started a load of laundry last night, but you didn't move the clothes over to the dryer. I went ahead and ran them through another wash cycle, then put them into the dryer. Hopefully, once they finish, they won't have any lingering smells, but... try not to forget when you start the laundry, alright, Akira?" Satomi said in a calm, understanding tone.

Akira nodded and proceeded into the bathroom before stopping. Her eyes immediately widened as she abruptly stepped back out into the hallway. "W-wait, you did the laundry?!"

Satomi nodded. "Yes, sweetheart. I'm not upset with you for forgetting it. After all, you had your new friend over, so you were probably just distracted. All I ask is that you're more mindful about it in the future."

"R-right... th-thank you, grandmother," Akira nervously responded.

Turning around, Satomi continued down the hallway towards the kitchen.

Hastily, Akira made her way down the opposite end of the hallway and into a small storage room where the washer and dryer were. The dryer was still running, and it appeared as if Satomi had also started a second load of laundry in the washer. Opening the dryer door, Akira began rummaging frantically through the laundry for the clothes she'd left in the washer the night before. Finding her school blouse, she pulled it out and saw the faded red bloodstains all across the front of it and on the sleeves. The wash had done little more than dull the color of the blood and nothing to remove it.

Feeling her heart race, Akira bundled her blouse up in her arms and searched for the towel she had used. Upon finding it, she discovered that it too had light bloodstains on it. Pairing it with her shirt, she found her socks and skirt, each of which were also still stained. Other articles of clothing appeared to be fine, thankfully, but Akira could tell that her uniform was ruined and she needed to destroy or hide it. Wrapping the clothes up in the towel from last night, she tried her best to ensure that there were no bloodstains visible; Akira hastily ran back down the hallway and up the stairs.

"Don't run in the house!" Ryoma shouted from the tatami room.

"S-sorry!" Akira responded in a panic as she reached the top of the stairs. Opening the door to her bedroom, she stepped inside and looked at Tomoe. "Okay... so, just sharing some good information... blood doesn't come out in the washer," she said, her voice shaky as she showed the ruined clothes to her friend.

Tomoe gasped. "Wh-where were those? I thought you said you were going to wash them last night?"

She nodded. "I did. Or at least, I meant to. My grandmother said she washed them and put them into the dryer, but... I don't think she saw the bloodstains. Or, at least, that's what it seems like..."

Holding her head in her hands, Tomoe exhaled sharply.

"I know. What a relief, right?" Akira said with an awkward chuckle.

Her eyes trailed back to her friend, seeing the forced smile she wore, truly relieved that her grandmother didn't see the stains. Meanwhile, Tomoe was left to wonder just what other close calls were left for them to make and how much more Kana's death would prolong the misery and anxiety that they'd been facing over this past week. This wasn't a step in the right direction, but instead just another step into the despair that they'd introduced into their lives by lying about Miyoko's death.

Akira let out a deep sigh, then scratched playfully at her hair. "Well... if you're good to get started, we might want to get a jumpstart on the chores we have this morning. Should be able to get a handful done before we need to stop for breakfast."

Biting her lip, Tomoe inhaled sharply. "Aki... what are we going to do about... about what happened?"

"What do you mean?" Akira asked.

She shook her head. "After... last night, we just left her there. We did... we did the same thing with Miyoko, and everything got so terrible for us afterward..."

Slowly, Akira nodded. "You're right... you're right. But, if you think about it, the police didn't really bother us much after Miyoko's death; it was mostly Kana. Well," she fought the urge to smile, though she couldn't help but grin as she held her arms splayed out at her sides, "who's going to pester us in her place? Kana's gone now, so..." she snickered, "she can't exactly bully us anymore, can she?"

Tomoe stared in disbelief at her friend. It wasn't just that Akira lacked any empathy for the life she took, but more that she was reveling in Kana's death; the absence of her presence.

Seeing her friend staring at her, Akira realized that she was probably a bit too expressive with her feelings. She lowered her arms, then sighed once more. "You're staring at me like I'm a really despicable bitch, Tomoe..."

She reluctantly looked away.

Exhaling sharply, Akira nodded. "Okay... fine. Yeah..." she said, offering a shrug of her shoulders. "I'm not sorry that Kana is gone," she admitted, drawing Tomoe's attention back to her. "I didn't wake up yesterday, thinking to myself, 'this is the last straw, I'm going to kill her,' or anything like that. And... even when I hit her off you with the bat, I wasn't thinking anything of the sort. But," she said, holding her index finger up in front of her, "I am *not* sorry for what happened... Kana went above and beyond, devoted days of her life to ruin mine. She was a horrible, evil bitch, and she got what she deserved."

Tomoe stared at her friend with mixed emotions.

Akira let out a deep, drawn-out sigh as she stared in desperation at her friend. "Could you say something, Tomoe? You're just staring at me, and I can't help but feel like you're judging me over what happened..."

She lowered her head. "I don't even know what to think..."

"Do you hate me?" Akira timidly asked.

Tomoe kept her head held low as so many thoughts circulated through her mind.

Akira frowned. "Tomoe?"

Her focus shifted back to Akira, staring briefly at her before shaking her head. "N-no... I don't hate you... I just..." she sighed. "I just can't believe that this happened. Both things, with Miyoko and Kana..."

Moving closer, Akira placed her hand on Tomoe's shoulder. "Hey, we're in this together, okay? The two of us. And, no matter what... I promise you that I'm not going to say a word to anyone about this," she said, though a moment of silence filled the air between them, leading Akira to feel somewhat nervous as to her friend's stance on things. "And... you're not going to tell anyone what happened, right?" she asked in a pleading voice, as she knew that everything would come crumbling down if either of them spoke of these events.

Hesitantly, she offered a brief shake of her head. "I won't say anything. I couldn't... I don't even know how to tell myself what just happened..."

Taking a deep breath, Akira moved forward, wrapping her arms around Tomoe and hugging her. "I promise... everything is going to be alright. We're going to make it through this, and when it's all said and done, we'll look back on this and... wonder why we didn't just trust and believe in one another. Everything will be fine... just fine..."

Tomoe kept her arms at her sides as Akira hugged her. It felt odd to her, being hugged, not only by someone she'd only known for such a short period but also someone who admitted to having had a crush on her; not to mention that this was the same girl who brutally beat her classmate to death as the sunset on the previous day.

Releasing her, Akira felt awkward, as if she shouldn't have done that. "I'm... s-sorry... I just thought that ya know, maybe a hug would help you feel better..." she admitted before inhaling sharply. "A-anyway! We should get to work on those chores..."

Tomoe reluctantly nodded.

"We'll, um... s-start with weeding and watering the garden. Best to do that early, before it gets hot out," Akira said as she reluctantly moved to the door, opening it and leading her friend out of her room.

As they reached the first floor, they were each given a verbal scolding by Ryoma for Akira skipping out on her chores the previous night. After he was finished, he sent them off to do all of the chores Akira would typically have on Saturday, alongside a handful of other ones as punishment for missing out on last night's chores. Akira wondered if perhaps he wouldn't be so harsh on her if he knew what she had on her mind. However, she had serious doubts that her grandfather would understand the complexities behind concealing a murder, or rather, distancing oneself from it.

Outside, the girls kept quiet as they pulled the weeds from the garden and added a bit of soil to replace what might have been lost. As they did so, Akira listened in for police sirens, of which she heard none. Fortunately, watering the garden took them no time at all, and Tomoe could at least appreciate this type of chore since her mother would often ask her to tend to the flowers at their house if she was too busy with work. After getting cleaned off, they went back inside and began tidying up.

They continued to work on their chores until Satomi invited both Akira and Tomoe to join them in the tatami room, where breakfast had been prepared for them each to sit and enjoy. Akira was, by now, starving and ready to eat, while Tomoe was hungry, though still with so much weighing on her mind that food was about the furthest thought in her head.

After washing their hands, the girls met up with Satomi and Ryoma in the tatami room, where they were each already seated and ready to eat. There were plates of grilled fish over rice on each side of the table, with a bowl of steaming hot miso soup that filled the small room with a distinct mouth-watering aroma. Akira sat down at the table, just across from her grandfather, while Tomoe sat next to her friend, just across from Satomi.

"This... looks so delicious, Miss Watari... thank you so very much for making this," Tomoe said with a bow of her head.

"Yeah, thanks," Akira said, already with a mouthful of rice.

Ryoma groaned under his breath at her.

Satomi lightly chuckled. "You're very welcome. This miso soup recipe is one that's been in my family for many generations now. It's very simple in its ingredients, but it's how you cook it that makes the difference," she said, looking to her granddaughter. "I've taught Akira the recipe before, though she's only cooked it a few times."

"I like to cook... I just don't really have the time," Akira added.

"You'd have more time to do the things you enjoy if you didn't skip out on your responsibilities," Ryoma pointed out.

Akira glared at him.

Satomi sighed, then looked back to Tomoe. "I feel as if Akira hasn't told us very much about you. Yet, the two of you seem as if you're already such good friends."

Tomoe looked to Satomi, then to Akira. Silence filled the air before Akira subtly motioned for her to say something. Taking a deep breath, Tomoe shook her head as she turned her focus back to Satomi. "Um... w-well, we've just been friends since the start of this semester. B-before then, I, uh... I had only just moved here from Fukuoka."

"Oh? That's quite some distance away. Well, how do you like it here? I'm sure it's much different than where you came from, isn't it?"

"The weather is nice. And it's really quiet... and serene here," Tomoe admitted, trying her best to keep her mind focused on the conversation rather than where it truly was, which was on the incident from last night.

"Yes, Nirasaki is a very peaceful and quiet town. We're not too far from Kofu either, so if you miss the big city life, it's just a short bus ride away. Although, I'm sure even Kofu pales in comparison to where you're from," she admitted with a light chuckle.

"I've been to Kofu, but... not for very long. Just a couple of days, but... m-maybe I'll have to go back in between school semesters and see what kind of interesting things there are to do?" she responded, trying not to be too awkward.

"You know, Ryoma and I have lived here our entire lives. Honestly, I couldn't imagine living anywhere else," she said as she mixed up some of her fish and rice. "So, what kind of work do your parents do?"

"M-my parents? Well, um... my mother works as a Japanese and English translator for a company out of Kofu," Tomoe responded.

"Is that so?" Satomi asked before looking at her granddaughter. "I'm sure you and her mother could have a lot to talk about then, Akira. Being that you're so interested in American culture."

Akira shrugged as she stuffed a large portion of food into her mouth.

"I'm guessing you must be quite fluent in English yourself then?" Satomi asked, returning her attention towards Tomoe.

Reluctantly, Tomoe nodded. "I can speak it pretty well... but not enough to make any kind of career out of it. Not... not that I'd want to sit at a desk all day anyway," she admitted, her voice lowering as she realized she wouldn't even have a career, let alone a future, if the police found out about Miyoko and Kana's murders.

Akira nodded eagerly. "I can't blame her. She's in really awesome shape. I think she'd make a great athlete," she said with a mouthful of fish and rice.

Satomi sighed. "Don't talk with your mouth full, sweetheart."

Chewing faster, Akira swallowed what food she had, then took a drink of her water. "It's true, though! I don't have gym with her, but look at her arms! I bet she's the most fit girl at school."

Tomoe couldn't help but smile at her friend. "Well, I have always been really into athletics and sports. Actually... it's sort of my dream to be a physical education teacher someday," she proudly admitted.

"Oh? I think that would be lovely. The world could always use more teachers. Someone has to make sure that the youth learn everything they need before graduating," Satomi pointed out.

"Yeah... I'm just terribly shy in front of groups, so I'd have to work on getting over that before trying to teach a class or anything," she admitted.

Satomi lightly chuckled. "Oh, I'm sure you'll be fine. I used to be quiet and shy when I was your age. But you know, the first job I ever had was working as a waitress at a restaurant here in town. It wasn't always easy, but I felt it was rewarding," she said before looking to her husband. "Ryoma worked in construction for as long as I can remember. Once we got married and had our son, I quit my job so I'd have time to raise him."

Ryoma scoffed. "Some waste of time that was..."

Tomoe looked curiously at Ryoma.

Inhaling sharply, Akira poked around at her fish and rice, trying to ignore her grandfather's words.

"Honey, please. We have a guest," Satomi timidly said to her husband.

Ryoma snorted in disgust. "The boy was fine until he went off and got mixed up with those big-city thugs and started dating that whore."

Akira slapped her chopsticks down on the table, rattling it along with the dishes. "Mom wasn't a whore!" she snapped.

He pointed towards Akira with his chopsticks. "You watch your tone, girl. I'll have you know that when a woman uses her body to make money, that makes her a whore. Stay in school, and stop wasting your youth on petty distractions, and *maybe* you won't end up doing the same," he firmly stated.

Glaring at him, Akira growled under her breath, clearly angry and wanting to protest her grandfather's every word.

Ryoma scoffed once more. "At the very least, that worthless son of mine had enough respect not to drag the Watari name through the mud," he said before looking back to Akira. "And that's the *only* thing that boy did right."

Tomoe frowned. She had no idea that tensions between Akira and her grandfather ran this high, though a part of her wasn't entirely surprised. With silence filling the air, she began to think of what she could say that would steer the conversation somewhere less hostile, as an argument between Akira and her grandfather was the last thing Tomoe felt she could endure right now.

"I, um... d-don't think I said so before, but I absolutely love your house," Tomoe said to Satomi.

"Thank you," Satomi responded, though it was unclear if it was for her kind words or for attempting to break the tension between Akira and Ryoma. "We bought this house shortly after we married. It's a beautiful home and one that has survived through the ages. That's how you know it's well built and made to last."

Tomoe smiled. "That's really amazing. So, how long have you two been married? If you don't mind me asking."

Satomi thought briefly on it. "We married in fifty-four, so that would be... forty-nine years, come this October."

"That's so wonderful. You're both so very fortunate to have one another. I hope that someday I'll meet someone with who I can spend the rest of my life," she responded with genuine delight before the constant reminder of reality brought her crashing back down, as she knew she'd likely be spending the rest of her life behind bars.

"You seem like a very bright and upbeat young woman. I'm sure you'll have no problem finding a good man when the time is right," Satomi said before looking to Akira. "I know you will too, sweetheart."

Ryoma scoffed. "Just another of many reasons why you shouldn't be a delinquent, constantly getting yourself in trouble at school and here at home," he said before gesturing towards Akira once more. "Stay in school, apply yourself, do your chores, and learn some discipline. No man would want to marry a woman who can't even manage household tasks."

Akira puffed up her cheeks in anger but kept quiet as she returned to eating her food.

Tomoe frowned, then relented and tried to eat as much as she could stomach with everything on her mind.

As things simmered down at the table, they each finished their meal, which led to Akira gathering up her's and her grandmother's dishes to wash. At the same time, Tomoe took her own and Ryoma's, if only to spare Akira from having to interact with her grandfather again. Making their way into the kitchen, they began cleaning things up, and as they did so, Akira kept looking up from the sink and out the window just above it.

Tomoe noticed her friend's strange behavior, though she checked to ensure the coast was clear before addressing it. "Aki? What are you looking for?" she asked as she continued to dry the dishes off.

Akira pursed her lips. "Not looking... listening."

"Huh?"

She looked at her. "I haven't heard any police sirens or anything. It makes me wonder if anyone knows what happened, you know?"

Tomoe's eyes drifted towards the window, which was slightly open. "I... I can't remember... did we close the gate when we left?"

Akira sighed. "I sure as hell hope not..." she said as she returned to the dishes. "If we did, then we probably left fingerprints on it, and after that cop took mine on Tuesday, I'd rather that not be the case."

Lowering her head, Tomoe kept drying the dishes off, then setting them aside to be put away.

"After our chores are done with... I want to go do what we can to cover our tracks..."

Her eyes widened briefly before her attention quickly shifted back to her friend. "Wh-what?"

Akira nodded, then turned to Tomoe. "I don't want to risk anything. If nobody knows about what happened, then we should do whatever we can to make sure it stays that way."

"B-but... Aki, no. We should just... we shouldn't do that," Tomoe said, conflicted as to what would even be the best choice for them in this given situation.

She rolled her eyes. "We did 'nothing' before, and look at all the trouble it's caused. We need to cover our tracks."

Tomoe swallowed nervously, feeling a cold chill wash over her. "Aki, please..." she pleaded, feeling her heart race as she just wanted all of this to be over.

As Akira stared at her friend, she could see how pale Tomoe had become at what she suggested. Even though she knew they desperately needed to ensure no one knew of what happened, she could tell that her idea crossed the line with Tomoe. While Akira was approaching things with a rational mind, or so she felt, Tomoe was allowing her emotions to dictate their next move. Despite knowing that history would repeat itself if they did nothing, Akira didn't wish to further alienate the girl whom she'd grown so fond of.

"You know what?" Akira said, offering a slow but steady nod. "After we're done with my chores... I could actually use a lot of help with what we went over this week in math class."

Tomoe locked eyes with Akira, finding it very difficult to figure out what she might have had planned. It was clear that she changed her mind so suddenly, simply to appease Tomoe, though that didn't prevent her from wondering if there was another aspect of Akira's suggestion.

She frowned. "Tomoe?"

"I can tutor you once we're done... yeah," Tomoe responded.

A smile quickly returned to Akira's lips. "That would be awesome. Math is, like, my worst subject. Seriously... I can barely even count to five!"

Tomoe pursed her lips. "Yes, you can..."

"Nope! Not at all. Watch," Akira said as she held her soapy hand up and began counting. "One... two... three... four... eight... four... eleventeen..."

She fought the urge to smile as she rolled her eyes. "Eleventeen?" she asked before laughing.

"What? Doesn't that come after four?" Akira asked in feigned shock.

"You said eight came after four," Tomoe pointed out. "You said four twice, Aki..."

"Twice? Is that like... more than once?"

"You are so weird," Tomoe said, laughing once more.

Akira smiled, her heart uplifted and beating steadily faster as she made Tomoe laugh. Given everything they had on their minds, this felt as if it were a truly cherished moment for her. To know that, despite the hell they had both been through and the questionable choices they made, Akira could still make this girl she had grown to like so much laugh meant the world to her. Now, all she needed to do was ensure that she could keep Tomoe's spirits high as everything no doubt began to unravel in the coming days when the police discover what happened to Kana.

Chapter 14
Lost Forever
可愛いサイコちゃん

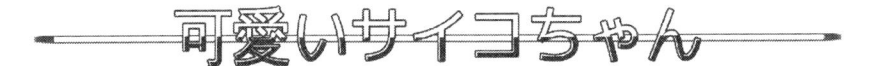

Throughout the morning, and the early hours of the afternoon, Akira and Tomoe worked diligently to tend to each of the chores that Ryoma had assigned to them. Once finished, they sat together in Akira's room, going over their math lectures in detail to help Akira know that eleven wasn't a number and that it most certainly didn't come after four. Despite feigning ignorance of how to count, Tomoe did discover that Akira wasn't lying when she claimed she was terrible at math. Even the most simplistic equations left Akira doing little more than scratching her head.

This wasn't because she was ignorant. Her mind just couldn't have been further from mathematical equations, as the only solution she was looking for was one that ensured Kana's death didn't link back to her.

With a deep sigh, Tomoe shook her head. "No. Okay, so... before we subtract or multiply anything, we have to figure out what 'X' is," she said as she erased what Akira had just written down. "To do that, we need to isolate the variable, which means we'll need to move it off by itself," she said as she looked back to her friend. "Aki, are you listening?"

"H-huh? Yeah, totally. You said that I have to... I'm trying to figure out what 'X' is, but... like, can't I just try different numbers and see which ones work?" Akira asked with a smile.

Tomoe rolled her eyes. "If you did that, then you'd be here all day. There are unlimited numbers to choose from, and even if you could figure out a range, how can you be certain it's not a decimal or fraction?"

Pursing her lips, she reluctantly nodded. "I guess that's true..." she said before hearing her bedroom door slide open. Looking over, she saw Satomi in the doorway. "Yes, grandmother?"

"Akira, could you come downstairs for just a moment?" Satomi asked.

"Uh... sure," she responded. Standing back up, she pointed to the homework. "When I get back... we're starting over. And, I promise, I'll pay super close attention to every word you say," she said as she stepped around her friend and approached her grandmother.

Tomoe sighed. "Alright... I think I know of a way to help you get a better grasp of what to do, so we'll try that when you come back."

"Sound great!" Akira said before following her grandmother out of her bedroom and towards the stairs. "So, what's up? Did we forget something with my chores, or his grandfather just trying to throw more on me to do?" she asked with a groan.

Satomi shook her head as she carefully descended the stairs. "Nothing like that, sweetheart," she responded, though, as they reached the bottom of the stairs, she turned and looked to her granddaughter. "You haven't been into any trouble at school lately, have you, Akira?" she asked in a concerned tone.

Stopping on the second step to the bottom, Akira reluctantly shook her head. "N-no, ma'am... I haven't."

"You're positive?"

She nodded. "I'm fairly certain... I, um... was late for class one day, but otherwise, I think I've been staying out of trouble," she said, fear building in her mind as she wondered where these questions were leading.

Satomi gave Akira a long, hard look, assessing whether she was telling the truth. After a moment, she sighed. "I hope that's true. I know your brother got into trouble a lot... and he'd often drag you into it. But, you should strive to hold yourself to higher standards than that."

Biting her lip, Akira nodded once more. "Yes, ma'am. But, um... what's with the serious question all of a sudden? Did I do something wrong?"

She shook her head. "Not that I know of. However, there is a man at the front door who asked to speak to you. He said that he's a detective with the police department."

Akira's heart immediately sunk. "H-he's here to... to talk to me?!" she asked, her voice cracking as she felt fear tightly grip her.

Satomi nodded. "Yes. He didn't say what it was about, just that he needed to speak with you."

"I, um... o-okay," she said in a low, shaky voice.

With a motion from her grandmother, Akira began making her way towards the front door, albeit with great reluctance. As she passed through the kitchen, she could hear two men talking. Their voices each sounded familiar to her, which led Akira to believe it was the two men from the police department who she'd ran into before, both family to Ikumi. As she drew near the front door and saw the men, it confirmed her suspicions. Waiting on the doorstep was Police Detective Yasuhida Masato and Lieutenant Yakovna Isaak.

Seeing her approach, Yakovna gestured to her with a nod, prompting Yasuhida to turn to face her.

"Miss Makai," Yasuhida said to her as she came closer.

"Y-yes, sir?" Akira responded, trying her best to compose herself, though struggling not to allow her fear to control her.

"I wanted to speak to you regarding a fellow student of yours, one whom you said you were familiar with. Miss Nakajima Kana," he said.

She nodded. "Wh-what about her?"

Yasuhida inhaled sharply. "It seems that she's gone missing. Her father reported that she didn't return home the previous night, and as of the current time, it appears that no one has seen nor heard from her," he said before gesturing to Yakovna. "My colleague here says that he had an interaction with Miss Nakajima, as well as yourself, mid-afternoon Friday. Does that sound familiar to you?"

Swallowing nervously, Akira's eyes trailed briefly to Yakovna, then back to the detective. "Yes, sir... I saw her outside of school yesterday."

"And, was that the last time you spoke to her?"

She hesitantly nodded.

"Oh!" Satomi said, drawing the detective's and, reluctantly, Akira's attention. "I nearly forgot. Miss Nakajima did come by here late Friday afternoon."

Akira grimaced. "W-wait... she did?!"

She nodded. "She came by and asked if you were home. I told her that you had gone over to your friend's house but that you would be back home later."

Akira felt her heart nearly stop, yet panic was still so very real in her mind. Kana had come by after school, ready to attack Akira in her own home. Instead, she laid in wait for them to come by, which perfectly explained why they had the misfortune of being jumped by Kana last night. Not that Akira would put it past Kana to wait all day without even knowing that she'd be home later.

Yakovna narrowed his eyes onto Akira, then diverted his focus to Satomi. "How would you describe Miss Nakajima's demeanor when you spoke to her? Was she upset, angry, or anything of that nature?"

Satomi shook her head. "Not that I noticed. Miss Nakajima appeared to be in a fair mood. I believe that she wanted to speak to Akira about something... I couldn't say for sure," she said, offering a subtle smile. "You see, she and my granddaughter used to be very good friends. They'd often spend quite a bit of time together, and so I was used to seeing her come by. Although... this was some time back," she said, looking to Akira. "As I understand it, they had a bit of a falling out a few years back..."

Akira let out a staggered sigh. *Thanks, grandmother. Anything else you want to tell them about my relationship with the girl I just killed?*

"A falling out?" Yasuhida said as his focus returned to Akira. "What was that over?"

She grimaced, then turned to him as she composed herself. "I, um... it was just a disagreement she and I had. That's all."

Yakovna scoffed. "Just a disagreement, huh? That doesn't often lead to students threatening physical harm..."

Satomi gasped. "She threatened you, Akira?"

Locking eyes with Yakovna, Akira hesitated to respond.

"What was the disagreement over, Miss Makai?" Yasuhida calmly asked.

"It was..." she said, her eyes trailing briefly to her grandmother.

Yakovna cleared his throat, returning Akira's attention to them.

Looking to Satomi, Yasuhida offered a slight bow of his head to her. "We appreciate the information you shared with us regarding Miss Nakajima coming by. However, if you'll allow it, we'd like to speak to your granddaughter alone."

Satomi frowned, though she then nodded. "I don't have any problem with you speaking alone with her. Just... let me know if there's anything I can do to help," she said before looking to her granddaughter. "Akira, you be sure and answer their questions truthfully and to the best of your abilities."

Akira sighed. "Y-yes, ma'am..."

Looking once more to the officers, Satomi bowed her head and then returned further inside the house, moving down the hallway.

Watching her leave, Yasuhida returned his focus to her. "What was the disagreement you had with Miss Nakajima?"

Yakovna crossed his arms as he awaited whatever Akira had to share that she wasn't willing to divulge in the presence of her grandmother.

Swallowing nervously, Akira turned her attention back to them, then sighed. "I'm... kind of surprised she or her friends didn't tell you," she admitted, biting her lip. "Back when we were friends, I... I kissed Kana's sister, Ina. Kana caught us kissing, accused me of doing way worse... and she's hated my guts ever since," she timidly admitted, though she then abruptly shook her head. "B-but, while Kana is a pain in the ass, all I've ever tried to do is just avoid her and her friends. I don't hate them... I just wish they'd leave me alone..."

"She accused you of murdering her friend as well," Yakovna stated.

Yasuhida glanced back at his colleague, then returned his attention to Akira. "I understand this must be a stressful time for you, Miss Makai. You're just starting high school, you're trying to make new friends, and along the way, hoping to avoid those who have been less than kind to you. What I want to do, is to help you."

Yeah, I'll bet, she thought to herself.

"As you've been made aware by Miss Nakajima, there was an incident at your school that resulted in a loss of life. It is our job to learn whether or not that incident was the result of ill intent or some unfortunate accident," he explained before closing his eyes. "Following the incident, we spoke to those close to the victim to get an idea of how things might have played out the way they had. And one friend, Nakajima Kana, was quite adamant that you were responsible for the incident."

While Akira knew this, hearing it from Yasuhida only led to her stomach twisting into knots. "Y-yeah... well, like I said, Kana hates me because of what happened."

"I could assume as much... however, your behavior when we first spoke was quite the red flag. Adding to that, there were a couple of instances on Friday where Miss Nakajima had negative interactions with you, as reported by several students at your school, as well as Lieutenant Yakovna here," he explained before crossing his arms. "And now, we come to the following day, where Miss Nakajima has had no contact with her family or friends..."

She could practically feel herself shaking. "Y-yeah? So... what are you trying to say?"

"I'm saying that the timing, unfortunately, shines poorly on yourself, Miss Makai. Circumstantial though it may be, her sudden disappearance comes on the heels of your recent negative interactions with her. It paints a nasty picture," he warned her.

Yakovna scoffed. "Perhaps you finally had enough of her and decided to put an end to her bothering you?"

Akira's eyes shot between each of the officers.

"But that would merely be an assumption based on the evidence that has presented itself," Yakovna added before motioning towards her. "Unless you had some information to rebuke these facts and the circumstances surrounding them..."

She exhaled sharply. "I... I don't know anything about anything that happened," she said, bracing herself and sorting her thoughts out in her head as best she could. "Before, when you guys pulled me aside, I was scared because I thought I had done something wrong. I'm sorry, but... the police terrify me... I know you're probably not a bad person, Mister Yasuhida–"

"Detective," Yasuhida said, correcting her.

"R-right... sorry, um... but, like... I know some cops are jerks who push people around to feel powerful. And, I guess I was afraid that you might be that way..." Akira explained before sighing. "But, you're... actually pretty cool."

Yakovna narrowed his eyes on her. "And what excuse would you feed us for why you're nervous today, hm?"

She paused, her eyes drifting between the two and seeing Yasuhida awaiting her response alongside his colleague. "It's... b-because of what happened at school yesterday. I was afraid Kana or Yuuki had finally decided to lie to you guys about what happened before. Y-ya know... about when I kissed her sister, and how she accused me of worse. I thought maybe she told you guys, so you'd come to harass me."

Yakovna glared at her, a crinkle forming across his forehead and over the bridge of his nose as he peered right through her lies, or so it felt.

Offering a slight nod, Yasuhida pulled a notepad out, then took note of what she said. "In that case... walk us through what followed after you left school on Friday."

Taking a deep breath, she nodded. "Alright, so... I left with my friend, and we went over to her house..."

"What's your friend's name?" Yasuhida asked.

"Asano Tomoe..."

He nodded. "And what is the address of Miss Asano's residence?"

"I, um... I don't remember the address. I just followed her over there. It was my first time going to her house," she explained.

Yakovna reluctantly turned and began walking back towards the unmarked police cruiser parked in front of the house.

"That's fine. We'll search for it in our database. Continue," he said.

Akira sighed. "Um... well, we stayed at her house for... a while and left a bit before sundown. We hurried back here before it got dark, and then she tutored me on math until we decided to head to bed."

"And that's all?" Yasuhida asked, sounding skeptical of her story.

Akira lightly grimaced. "I mean... she and I talked about music and pop idols too. But... I'm sure you probably don't want to hear about our argument over who is better between Jin Mako and Kaminaga Umeki," she admitted with a light chuckle, feeling somewhat more confident in her dealings with the police now. "Although, Kiya Tamae *always* has the cutest outfits out of all of them."

Yasuhida rolled his eyes. "So then you and your friend made it back here without any issues?"

"Yeah. Well, a bug landed in my hair while we were talking, and that startled me, but otherwise, we were just kind of focused on getting back here," she explained before a thought crossed her mind. "So, um... you're Ikumi's dad, right?"

He hesitantly nodded. "That's correct."

"Is she okay? Yuuki kind of hit her really hard yesterday at school... and," she lowered her head, "it was all because she was standing up for me," she said, her eyes trailing back to him. "He's hit me before... so, I kind of know how much it can hurt."

"She'll be fine," he responded before putting his notepad away, then reaching into his pocket and pulling out a business card for her. "Should you hear anything, be it positive or negative, from Miss Nakajima, give me a call."

Taking the card, Akira read over it, then nodded as she looked back at him. "I will... and, thank you for... not being a jerk, like some cops can be."

Yasuhida offered a very brief smirk. "If you're referring to Lieutenant Yakovna... you'll have to forgive his forward nature. He once served in the police force in Moscow, and they handle things a little differently than we do here."

"Ah... okay, that makes sense. I won't judge him too harshly then," she said, offering a bow of her head. "And, if I hear from Kana, I'll let you know... so long as she doesn't throw me into the canal again."

With a slight bow of his head, Yasuhida turned and began making his way back to the vehicle where the lieutenant was waiting for him. Watching him leave, Akira hesitantly closed the door. No sooner than it shut did she let out an exhausted sigh as she rested her head against it.

Fuck me... I can't believe I pulled that off as well as I did, she thought to herself before cracking a half-smile. "If she's missing... that means they haven't found her yet," she said under her breath before gasping. "Oh, shit... if I don't do something, then they'll definitely find her come Monday when those guys start working on that building again..."

"Akira?" Satomi asked as she stepped into the kitchen. Seeing her granddaughter, she frowned. "Is everything alright?"

She looked to her grandmother, then nodded. "Yeah... they just asked me some questions about, like, why Kana and I stopped being friends. I think they were just worried that she might feel bad about it," she said before shrugging her shoulders. "Next time I see her, I'll see what she wanted to talk to me about."

Satomi let out a sigh of relief. "I'm sure she just wanted to apologize for whatever happened. Kana is such a sweet girl. I just can't imagine how the two of you could have ended your friendship."

Akira shrugged her shoulders. "Just... dumb teenage stuff, that's all. I feel like we're both older and more mature now, so maybe we can work through it, ya know?"

"I hope so," she said with a smile.

"Speaking of work... Tomoe is helping me with my math homework, so I'm going to go back to grinding my head against the paper," Akira said with a playful chuckle as she passed by her grandmother. "Thanks for calling me down!" she added.

Racing up the stairs, Akira returned to her bedroom, closing the door behind her as she stepped inside. Tomoe was writing something down, though she stopped as she looked to her friend with concern in her eyes.

"Is everything alright?" Tomoe asked.

Akira nodded. "Yeah. Everything's fine."

"Wh-what did your grandmother want?" she timidly asked.

"Huh?" Akira responded before gasping. "Oh! She just asked me to take the trash out. We forgot the one in the bathroom," she said with a smile.

Tomoe stared at her in mild confusion before nodding. "Okay... I could have sworn you grabbed that when we gathered up the trash, but... I've had so much on my mind this morning that I probably just thought you grabbed it."

Akira shrugged. "I guess so. Anyway! You said you had a good idea for how to teach me to do this stuff?"

Tomoe nodded, then motioned towards what she had written down. As Akira took her seat next to her friend, she did her best to pay close attention to what she was teaching her. Despite having made no progress on ensuring Kana wouldn't be discovered by the police or that she left no evidence behind, Akira felt as if she were just happy being around Tomoe. Her talk with the police had gone far better this time than when they first spoke, and it did well to boost Akira's confidence, so much so that she began to feel as if she might even have the confidence she'd need to sway Tomoe's heart.

When Akira admitted to her friend that she had a crush on her, Tomoe made it clear that she was flattered but had no interest in women. As upsetting as that was, Akira wasn't entirely convinced. Even as a lesbian, she'd occasionally seen men on television or in movies that she felt she would possibly go for, and she couldn't help but feel that someone like Tomoe could be persuaded into trying the fairer sex, regardless of her proclaimed sexuality. After all, what else are the teenage years good for if not for testing unknown waters, be that trying new food, changing up one's lifestyle, sampling different sexualities, or even alleviating years-long problems with a well-constructed baseball bat?

Chapter 15
Another Day in Paradise

可愛いサイコちゃん

Throughout their weekend together, Akira and Tomoe did far more than the lost cause that was attempting to improve Akira's math skills. They watched a scary movie together, fixed Akira's old bicycle, helped Satomi around the house, and listened to music on Akira's computer that Tomoe hadn't heard before. And, while Akira's tastes didn't quite line up with those of her friend, one thing that did make Tomoe happy was the absolute lack of any mention of Kana, or more specifically, the incident that took her life. This, however, meant that Akira never took the opportunity to tend to any evidence she might have left behind. A foolish move that she hoped wouldn't come back to haunt her.

Taking a different route on their way to school Monday morning, Akira and Tomoe approached the entrance, each with different expectations for how the day would unfold, yet both hopeful that the day would be quiet. Entering the school, they briefly parted ways as they went to change into their indoor shoes. As Akira did so, she noticed Ikumi over by her locker, just now putting her shoes away.

"Hey, Ikumi!" Akira loudly said, drawing her attention. She waved, offered a smile, then slipped her shoes off to change them out.

Ikumi approached Akira, offering a cheerful smile, not offset one bit by the unmistakable bruising around her eye, which her makeup couldn't dream of covering. "Hey, Aki. Did you have a good weekend?"

She nodded. "I did. How's your eye?"

"Huh? Oh! It's fine. It hurts a little, but I was told it should heal without any problem," she said with a playful giggle.

"Sounds like you're very optimistic about it. That's good. Your dad dropped by my house to talk to me, and I asked about you, but he said you were doing fine. Glad to see he wasn't downplaying things," Akira responded.

Ikumi blushed. "Y-you... asked about me?" she asked before it fully hit her what Akira had said. "Hold on... why was my dad at your house?!"

"He was asking me about that girl who was trying to beat me up on Friday. The one you tried to save me from," she responded. "From what he said, she's gone missing..."

Ikumi frowned. "I hope she's okay."

"Me too. Even if she's kind of a piece of shit to me... I hope everything's alright," Akira said before glancing over at Tomoe as she approached them. "But, we should all get to class," she said as she looked back to Ikumi. "Tomoe tutored me a lot with math over the weekend, so I'm ready to ace it from here on out."

"O-oh... she's your tutor too?" Ikumi asked, her eyes trailing briefly over to Tomoe before returning to Akira. "Um, well... I'm pretty good at math, but... if you ever need help with, like, science, history, or home economics, then let me know. I'd be more than happy to help tutor you, Aki," she nervously responded.

"I'll keep that in mind. For now, let's get to class. If we're lucky, maybe we can all three sit together," Akira said, beckoning her friends to follow her as she made her way off towards class.

Tomoe watched her as she left, somewhat concerned by just how good of a mood Akira appeared to be in, despite this being the day the police would most definitely discover Kana's body.

Ikumi looked at Tomoe, seeing that she was staring off at Akira. With a sigh, she turned and followed her friend off to math class.

Reluctantly, Tomoe joined the two of them, ever cautiously optimistic that today might go well. They were fortunate enough to sit together in class, with Akira in the middle, while Ikumi was on her left and Tomoe sat behind her. This didn't allow them any special interactions with one another, as they each focused on class, though Tomoe was able to catch Ikumi throwing multiple glances at Akira. This, she felt, was likely because of something Ikumi must have heard from her father or uncle. Accusations that Akira was responsible for Miyoko's murder most likely. If not, it could have been due to what she heard Kana shout on Friday after school.

Upon finishing their class, the girls gathered up their things and parted ways, with Tomoe heading to her next class while Akira and Ikumi walked together to the gym. As they made their way to the gymnasium, Akira couldn't help but notice that Ikumi appeared somewhat distracted. Her head was held low, and she seemed focused on something. A part of her worried that Ikumi's father or uncle said something to her, but that was unlikely given her positive mood earlier.

"Is everything alright?" Akira cautiously asked.

"Huh? Oh!" Ikumi shook her head, changing her expression to a far more cheerful one, with a bright smile. "N-no! I'm fine."

Akira raised her eyebrow. "You sure?"

Ikumi nodded. "Yeah. It's nothing, I promise." Biting her lip, she looked back to Akira. "Could I ask you a question, though?"

"Uh... sure. What's up?"

Ikumi shyly smiled. "What's your, um... your favorite snack?"

Akira was caught off guard by her friend's seemingly random question. She almost felt as if she misheard what was asked. "My favorite snack? Like, candy? Or...?" she asked, hoping for clarification.

"Anything!" Ikumi promptly responded.

She held her finger to the side of her mouth as she considered Ikumi's question. "Hm, I have to admit... I really like chewy fruit candies."

Ikumi giggled. "Really?"

Akira nodded. "Yeah. Not, like, the gummy ones. But, you know? The really chewy ones, maybe like... they have real bits of fruit in them, or whatever? That kind of stuff."

"Any specific flavor?"

Akira reached up and scratched her head. "I guess probably kiwi or mango if I had to choose."

"So, if you were to buy some for yourself, would you get like... a mixed bag of flavors? Or just one kind?"

Akira chuckled. "Okay! What's with the random food quiz?"

"O-oh! No reason!" she promptly responded, offering a wide grin.

Raising her eyebrow, Akira couldn't help but wonder why Ikumi had asked her such a seemingly random question.

"My favorite is... well, I guess it's a kind of dessert. It's called a pirozhki, and while it can have a lot of different fillings, I love it with cherries or strawberries inside," she said before making a satisfied moan as if the very thought of such a dish was enough to get her mouth-watering.

Akira raised her eyebrow. "Piro-what?"

Ikumi looked to Akira briefly before awkwardly chuckling. "Oh! Sorry. Pirozhki, it's a stuffed pastry that usually either has fruit or meat inside of it. My uncle taught me how to make them, and I love them so much, even if they aren't the healthiest."

Akira nodded. "Gotcha. Well, I don't think I've ever had them before."

"I don't think they're as popular over here, although I have seen them from time to time," she admitted before raising her index finger into the air. "But! If you want a real, authentic Russian Pirozhki, then I'll gladly make you a few sometime. I bet you'd absolutely love them!" she enthusiastically stated.

Akira smiled as they continued down the hallway. "Well, they sound tasty. So, Russian cuisine, huh?" she asked, offering a playful grin. "You said your uncle taught you? He's the guy who arrested Yuuki on Friday, right?"

Ikumi smiled as she giggled awkwardly. "Y-yeah, that's uncle Isaak. I didn't want that boy to get arrested, but... well, I guess he shouldn't have hit me," she admitted, blushing lightly.

"Your uncle seems like a pretty cool guy. And, yeah... Yuuki had it coming when he decided to hit a girl," Akira responded.

Still smiling, Ikumi eagerly nodded. "I'm just glad I could help get you out of that situation. Hopefully, those two have learned their lesson."

She couldn't help but grin. "I'm pretty sure at least one of them has..."

As they entered the gymnasium, the two of them walked together towards the locker room. Glancing around, Akira didn't notice anything out of the ordinary, which further placed her mind at ease. Once inside, Akira casually tossed her half-empty backpack into the locker and began to take off her school uniform. Ikumi's locker was within eyeshot of Akira's, though it was bordering the wall nearest the entrance.

Once finished, Akira was quick to follow her friend out to the gym hall. Making their way towards the doors that led outside, Ikumi rushed a short distance ahead, pushing and holding the door open for Akira. With a bow of her head, Akira thanked her friend and proceeded outside. Ikumi followed closely behind Akira, and the two of them began running track side-by-side. They kept their conversations to a minimum while running, as they didn't want to exhaust themselves too quickly.

As with on Friday, once they finished their laps, the girls made their way over to where the water coolers were at. Grabbing two water bottles,

Ikumi handed one to Akira as they both took a seat on the bench. It wasn't exactly a hot day out, though it was warm enough that Akira broke a sweat while she was running. Grabbing a towel, Ikumi offered it to her friend, which Akira graciously accepted, using it to pat her forehead and neck.

"You really worked up a sweat, huh?" Ikumi giggled.

Akira chuckled. "Yeah. It's been a while since I've felt this good after a run."

"I'm glad you enjoyed it! It's important to stay in good health, and exercise helps with that."

Akira nodded. "Yeah... hell, maybe I should just start working out regularly? That probably wouldn't be the worst idea. At least then, it'd be harder for someone like Takashi to put his hands on me."

"Speaking of which..." Ikumi said as she gestured with a nod.

Turning to her right, Akira saw Takashi approaching them. "Go away!" she shouted at him before he even reached them.

Drawing closer, Takashi sighed. "I just want to talk, that's all."

"I don't want to talk. Go away!"

Ikumi quickly stood up and moved to stand in front of where Akira was sitting, physically preventing Takashi from getting too close. "If she doesn't want to talk, you should leave her alone."

Takashi frowned at Ikumi, then looked past her. "I just want to talk about Kana..."

Akira briefly grimaced before gritting her teeth as she glared at him. "I... I don't care about her! Get lost!"

He held his hands up in front of him, surrendering. "I'm not trying to make any accusations, I just... you know, she's been missing since, I think, Friday night? No one's seen or heard from her since then. Hideko's been really torn up about it."

Ikumi paused, then looked back at Akira. "Is that the same girl you said my dad talked to you about? The one who was threatening you outside of the school?"

Akira lightly grimaced. "I, uh... y-yeah... it's the same girl."

"I heard what she said about you on Friday. What she shouted in the hall," he admitted. "I'm worried that, with her disappearing, that people might–"

"Would you *please* go away?" she snapped.

Takashi held his hands up once more. "Hold on, Akira. I'm just worried that, like... once Yuuki finds out about it, he might think you had something to do with it. That's all. I'm just worried about you."

"I have friends to worry about me; I don't need your worries," she said.

Ikumi puffed up her cheeks. "You need to leave. Now," she said to him.

Takashi looked between the two of them in mild confusion before his eyes settled onto Ikumi. "Are you her girlfriend?" he bluntly asked.

"Wh-what?" she asked, her face turning a vivid red at his question.

Akira gasped, then stood up. "Y-you... fucking idiot!" she said, moving past Ikumi, then shoving Takashi back, albeit only a few centimeters.

"I was just curious... you know, because she's so protective of you," he pointed out before smiling. "If she is... I don't mind. I've told you before that I just want you to be happy."

"Happy is what I'd be if *you* would get lost!" she firmly stated.

Staring at Akira, Takashi frowned. "Even if you prefer girls, I'd still be more than happy to be your boyfriend as well. We wouldn't even have to do anything. I'd be pleased to just be there for you. To encourage and support you, you know?"

She began growling under her breath. *That is it! Since junior high, he's been harassing me, never listening to what I say, and always pestering me. Kana did way worse, and I put an end to her. I'm not going to let him do this to me anymore,* she thought to herself before shaking her head, then holding her index finger up. "Kenichi Takashi, if you don't get lost and leave me the hell alone, then... then I'm going to show you just how little I give a shit about you!"

A smile slowly formed across his lips as he listened to her. "You're trying to be tough for a cute girl," he said in a low voice before nodding. "You're so sexy when you act confident like that, Akira," he added.

Pausing, Akira felt sick over his words. "W-would you... just get lost already?!" she responded in a fluster.

"Just be careful, alright? And, if you need anything, you have my number," Takashi said before looking to Ikumi, who still appeared quite embarrassed over his assumption of her's and Akira's relationship. "But... my friends are waiting on me, so I'll talk to you later, Akira. Be safe," he said before turning and walking away, throwing several glances back at her.

Letting out a deep sigh, she shook her head. *At least I finally managed to get him to piss off on my own,* she thought before turning and looking to Ikumi. An awkward silence filled the air between them as neither of them knew what to say.

Biting her lip, Ikumi threw a glance over towards Takashi, then back to Akira. "I know it's... not really any of my business, but... is there any truth to what he said?"

Akira grimaced. "Um... y-yeah... Kana kind of shouted some shit about me in the hall on Friday. It... it wasn't true, but–"

"N-no... I mean, about you being, um... into girls?" she asked.

Pausing, Akira awkwardly chuckled. "Oh, um... w-well, yeah... actually, it is," she said, her face turning a bit red. "If it makes you like me less, well then, fuck it. I'm a lesbian, Ikumi..."

She stared blankly at her friend before a smile soon formed across her lips. "Really? You're not joking?"

"Uh... no, I'm not," Akira admitted before letting out a deep sigh. "I've been a lesbian since... well, since the days I first knew of romantic attraction towards others."

Ikumi nodded. "That's so awesome, Aki."

She recoiled in slight shock. "Wait... it's 'awesome?'"

"Yeah! And, I think you're really brave for following your heart," Ikumi said before sighing. "Especially with how closed-minded a lot of people can be..."

Akira scoffed. "Tell me about it..."

"So, um..." she began to say as she timidly looked back to Akira. "This might also be none of my business to ask, but... is Tomoe a lesbian too?"

Reaching up, Akira ruffled her hair as she scratched her head. "It's, uh... complicated."

"It is?"

She nodded. "Yeah, like... I'll admit, I have a huge crush on her right now, and she sort of said that she's not into girls, but..." she inhaled sharply. "I really, really like her a lot. And, dammit, if there's any chance that she might ever be into girls, I'll make sure it's with me. Because I don't care who the guy is, whatever a guy can do, I can do way better!"

Listening to her, Ikumi appeared almost upset at first, though once Akira finished, she couldn't help but smile. Reluctantly, she nodded. "I... hope that you're able to convince her then, Aki. B-because... you are really amazing, and... Tomoe would be lucky to have a girlfriend like you."

Akira offered a wide, toothy grin as she chuckled. "Thanks, Ikumi. I'd like to think I'm pretty awesome too."

"But, um... we should probably head inside and finish with our exercises for the class," Ikumi reminded her.

"R-right, I almost forgot," she admitted before beckoning Ikumi to follow as she led the way over and towards the gymnasium.

As they entered the building, they made their way over to where the exercise mats were located and resumed their workout. Despite the new knowledge Ikumi had gained of her friend, their conversations remained fairly mundane, never straying far from the various interests each of them had. This, alongside their conversation prior, did well to ease Akira's mind in trusting Ikumi. Whatever information her father or uncle might have shared with her, it didn't appear to faze Ikumi in even the slightest. This was good news, as Akira already had her hands full dealing with the impending aftermath of Kana's death.

Throughout the remainder of the day, classes seemed to only drag on, with little to no sign that anything unusual had happened. At lunch, Akira, Tomoe, and Ikumi all sat together and held a completely normal conversation, something that felt as if it was in and of itself out of place, given everything that had happened. Once the school day finally drew to an end, however, Akira parted ways with her friends and began making her way home, which was unusually quiet and peaceful, all things considered.

By the time Akira arrived back at her house, she almost became paranoid over how well things felt as if they were going. She didn't have to look over her shoulder for Kana, the police hadn't dragged her out of school asking questions, and the only other threat, Yuuki, was likely still in jail, considering he punched the lead detective's daughter in front of multiple witnesses. It almost made her laugh in disbelief over this surreal feeling of freedom she now enjoyed.

After making quick work of her daily chores, Akira then spent the rest of her evening on her computer, looking up ways to impress girls in hopes of winning Tomoe's heart. The next day, feeling eager, excited, and ready to give this potential relationship her full attention, she left bright and early, ensuring that she'd be there a little before her friend arrived. Once she got there, she quickly changed her shoes out, then waited by Tomoe's locker.

As she stood around, waiting on her friend, she saw someone who was all too familiar to her, though one she hadn't interacted with much since this hectic semester first began. Walking into the school, with her head held low, was Abukara Hideko. She was a close friend to Miyoko and

Kana, and while they hadn't been on the best of terms, Akira didn't hold any ill feelings towards this old friend of hers.

Glancing over towards her, Hideko saw Akira staring. The two locked eyes briefly before she lowered her head once more and moved to her shoe locker. Seeing how down she was, Akira knew that she must have learned of Kana's fate or that days of her friend having disappeared had her down. Thinking more on it, she couldn't help but feel somewhat bad for Hideko after having lost her two closest friends. With Miyoko and Kana out of the picture, Hideko didn't have any friends, which put her in a position that was not all that different from how Akira was when she had her falling out with them, alongside her brother leaving.

Taking a deep breath, Akira stepped away from Tomoe's shoe locker, then began approaching Hideko as she changed out of her outdoor shoes. Biting her lip, she was hesitant to speak but felt bad for her old friend and wanted to help out, at least in some way.

"Um... h-hey, Hideko... is everything alright?" Akira cautiously asked.

Pausing, Hideko looked up at her. She stared for just a moment, her mixed emotions fighting with her as she attempted to speak up. "G-go away, Akira..." she said in a low voice.

Akira frowned. "I... I just noticed that you looked really sad today..."

With her lip quivering as she fought back the urge to cry, she stood up. "O-of course I'm sad!" she said before covering her mouth as she inhaled sharply. "You... you know what happened to... to my friends... to Miyoko and Kana, don't you?" she asked, sounding almost as if she were throwing out accusations.

Akira reluctantly nodded. "I heard what happened to Miyoko, yeah... but, all I've heard about Kana was that she went missing. I haven't seen or heard from her since."

Hideko stared at her as if she were assessing Akira's every word. "You... haven't seen her?"

She shook her head. "Not since she stopped me outside of the school on Friday," she said with a sigh. "That was when Yuuki hit my friend... who's the daughter of a police officer, and got himself arrested," she admitted, feigning sadness as she frowned and lowered her head, shaking it. "I know he can be violent... but, seriously, she didn't do anything but try and help."

Hideko narrowed her eyes onto Akira through her budding tears. After a moment, she inhaled sharply. "I... need to get to class..." she said before reluctantly turning and walking away from Akira.

Watching her leave, she frowned.

"Aki?" Tomoe timidly called out from the front of the school.

Gasping, Akira turned to face her friend, then smiled before rushing over to Tomoe's locker, prompting her friend to approach. Taking the shoes out from her locker, Akira sat them down on the floor for her. "Good morning, Tomoe," she said in an upbeat tone.

"Um, good morning," Tomoe cautiously responded. "Is everything alright?"

"Everything is great," Akira responded with a toothy grin.

"Aki, Tomoe!" Ikumi called out as she ran over to them.

Akira looked at her and smiled. "Hey, Ikumi."

Tomoe glanced back at Ikumi as she approached, then returned her attention to Akira. Her eyes then trailed down to the shoes her friend had put out for her. Hesitantly, she stepped out of her street shoes, then into her indoor ones. As she did so, she saw Akira take her other pair and stow them away in the locker for her. "Um... thanks?"

Akira offered a toothy grin. "My pleasure."

Ikumi looked between the two of them before she realized what was going on. She gasped. "Oh, Aki! You're such a... uh..." she said, pausing as she cupped her chin.

Akira and Tomoe each looked at her, confused.

"Uh... what's the right word? Like, a gentleman, but for a girl?" Ikumi asked.

"A lady?" Tomoe guessed.

"N-no! I mean," Ikumi sighed. "That's correct, but... I don't know... it doesn't seem like it fits."

Akira crossed her arms. "Gentlewoman, perhaps?"

"Would that be it?" she asked, unsure of the choice of words.

"I'm confused... why are you trying to figure out which word to use? Are you trying to call Aki a 'gentleman?'" Tomoe asked.

Ikumi awkwardly chuckled. "Um... w-well, yeah... I mean... she got your shoes out for you, and... that was really kind of her. If a boy did that, I'd think he was such a gentleman, but I'm not sure if calling Aki that would be appropriate."

Akira grinned. "I dunno... although, I bet I have more balls than some guys here at school," she said with growing confidence.

Tomoe exhaled sharply. "We should get to our classes, or else we'll be late," she said, motioning to Ikumi's shoes. "You haven't even changed yourself, Ikumi."

"O-oh! Right. I should probably do that, shouldn't I?" she asked with a playful giggle. "Be right back," she said before darting across the entryway to her shoe locker.

Tomoe watched as Ikumi left. "That was so weird..." she said before looking to Akira. "I might be completely off on this, but I think Ikumi might have a crush on you..."

Akira snickered. "Um... not quite. Yesterday in gym class, I told her that I was a lesbian, and..." she lightly blushed, "I might have also admitted that I had a crush on you. So, she's probably just trying to be my wingman here... err, wingwoman, I guess?"

She rolled her eyes. "If you want to be nice to me because we're friends, then I have no problems with that. But... I told you before that I'm not really into girls. I'd never judge you... but I just don't feel the same way."

Akira frowned. "Well... I mean, there has to be a reason for that, right? Like, what do you like about guys that a girl can't achieve? I bet you that whatever it is that guys do that impresses you, I could do a hell of a lot better," she confidently responded.

Staring at her, Tomoe let out a deep sigh. "Aki..."

She grinned. "I know I might not be able to do much while we're here at school. But, I'd be totally down to, like, carry your books for you, make lunch and pack it up in a cute bento box for you, or... anything else that you might find useful," she said before holding her index finger up. "Oh! What kind of sweets do you like? I could probably make you something really tasty as a dessert if you wanted."

Tomoe stared at her, then shook her head. "The only thing I want is to not have this constant stress and anxiety..." she said, lowering her head. "And, the more I think about it... the more I feel like there's no escaping what we've done..." she added in a low voice.

Akira grimaced. "D-don't say that," she said, moving in closer and crouching down to look up at her friend. "Hey! Just leave everything to me, okay? I'm already keeping a close eye on things, so... whatever needs to be done, I'll do it."

Tomoe stared at her, unsure of how to respond to her confident claims.

"Don't be late for your classes, you two," Ikumi teased as she moved closer to her friends.

Tomoe looked to Ikumi, then moved around Akira, off to her first class of the day without saying another word.

Ikumi frowned as she watched Tomoe leave. She looked back to Akira. "Is everything alright? She looked upset..."

Akira dismissively waved her hand as she stood back up. "Eh, don't worry about it. She's just stressed out over some school stuff."

"Oh... anything we could help her with?" she asked.

"I think she'll be alright. Besides, we need to get to our classes, right?" Akira asked with a light chuckle. "I'll see you at lunch, Ikumi," she said before starting towards her biology class.

"Um... s-sure! See you then, Aki," Ikumi said.

Making her way down the hallway, Akira wasted no time before putting her attention on how she might set Tomoe's mind at ease. Things had been oddly quiet since Kana died, with no real interactions with the police outside of their questioning on Saturday, which Akira felt didn't relate at all to Kana's death, but, instead, solely on her disappearance. Whether or not this was good was yet to be determined, but at least for now, it did allow Akira to run various possible scenarios through her mind. So long as she is prepared for whatever questions the police might ask her, she can talk with them in confidence. That much, she was sure of.

Chapter 16
The Loose End
可愛いサイコちゃん

All throughout the morning, Akira wracked her brain on just how she might handle whatever questions the police might throw her way. She did fear what evidence she may have left behind, but by now, there was absolutely nothing she could do about that, but it didn't alleviate the fear she held in the back of her mind. Once her first set of classes were done for the day, she was able to sit and have a few laughs with her friends, though Tomoe hardly joined in the conversation, as it was clear that their uncertain fate was weighing heavily on her shoulders.

The latter half of her school day, Akira spent coming up with sweet gestures or kind acts that might help to change Tomoe's mind when it came to potentially dating her. She didn't want to come off too strong, as she was all too familiar with how that felt, thanks to Takashi, but at the same time, she didn't want Tomoe to think she was merely doing the things she had planned because she was just a good friend. Akira felt that she was already in love with Tomoe, so all that was left in her mind was to win over this girl she admired so much.

At the end of the school day, Akira raced home, taking the same alternative route that allowed her to avoid the construction site where she killed Kana and then jumped immediately to her chores. This allowed her yet more time to conjure up ideas that could win Tomoe's heart in the long term. By the time she laid down for the night, Akira had come up with a plethora of ways that she could impress or flatter her friend, possibly turning the tides of their relationship into far more than just a mere friendship.

The following day, Wednesday morning, Akira awoke bright and early and finished her daily routine before school. Once she got downstairs to get her food ready, however, she was informed by her grandmother that she had a friend waiting for her outside. Akira was a little surprised that Tomoe would come by again to walk with her to school, but pleasantly so. Although, this likely meant that she wanted to discuss very sensitive matters along the way, which did worry Akira slightly.

After getting everything she had left to take to school, Akira stepped outside and was shocked at who she saw waiting by the driveway. Reluctantly, she approached her old friend. "Hideko? What are you doing here?" she asked.

Looking to Akira, Hideko frowned, clearly fighting back a surge of mixed emotions. "I... I wanted to talk to you..."

"Um... okay?" she cautiously responded.

"Could we walk to school together? Please?" Hideko timidly asked.

Taking a deep breath, as she wasn't prepared to have what felt like a heart-to-heart with Hideko today, Akira nodded. "Y-yeah, sure..."

With a nod, Hideko stepped away and walked out onto the street, waiting for a moment while Akira joined her. Together, they began walking side-by-side. "Have you talked to Ina lately?"

Biting her lip, Akira shook her head. "Not really... she and I texted one another over the last break, but... well... my phone sort of got ruined, so I've been without it for a little over a week now..."

She looked to Akira, then ahead of them once more. "She's been torn up since... well... since the police came by her house on Monday..."

Akira slowly nodded.

Hideko's eyes darted to her briefly. "It's been really difficult for her," she added, looking forward once more. "She and Kana never really got along well... but they were still sisters."

She sighed. "Kana used to pick on Ina all the time. She vented to me several times about how much it bothered her."

"But, that's how siblings are," Hideko pointed out. "You should know. There were plenty of times Shojiro teased you."

"That was different. He never put me down. Kana would insult Ina's intelligence sometimes... call her names, mock her... it wasn't playful," Akira responded, shaking her head. "Maybe it's different for you and Takashi because you're step-siblings, but... I know things between my brother and I were completely different than Kana and Ina's relationship."

Hideko shook her head. "My step-brother is an idiot. All he does is sit in his room all day and play video games. Even when I tried to vent to him about what happened, he barely said anything..."

Akira glanced around as they walked, not realizing that she was leading Hideko down the path she usually took to school. They were just passing by the canal. In front of her was the construction site, with police tape still across the entryway. It made her uneasy being so near the crime scene once again, which she didn't need when she was already having an awkward conversation with someone directly affected by the recent deaths.

"Say, Akira... do you remember the day we all became friends? Like, do you remember what happened? What Kana did?" Hideko asked.

Akira looked at her, then sighed and nodded. "I... I remember. It was my first semester at a school here in Nirasaki. I'd been quiet and kept to myself the whole time because I was still hurting over the loss of my mom and dad," she admitted, biting her lip as she hesitated on the next part. "We all got stuck in a group activity together... and Kana made it her mission to get me to open up. You and Miyoko both encouraged me to join in and be more social, and... well... you guys accepted me into your group of friends."

She nodded. "Kana might have been a bit... crass sometimes, but she did have a good heart," she said as they walked along the way to school. Pulling out her cellphone, she typed up a quick message, then sent it. "You and she were close, though. Up until you... hurt Ina."

Akira looked at her and frowned. "I... I didn't hurt her."

"Yes, you did," Hideko responded.

She shook her head. "Ina told me, even after the fact, and as recent as a month or two ago, that she didn't hate me for what happened that night. It's why she still talks with me even to this day."

Hideko stopped and looked at Akira. "She still talks with you because she's nice. Don't you know that she blames herself for what happened? She said that because she let you kiss her, it's her fault that things went as far as they did... Ina's a victim."

Akira sharply exhaled as she stopped and turned to face Hideko. "All I did was kiss her... and touch a little... that's it. I didn't do anything more than that."

She put her hands on her waist as she glared. "That's enough, Akira. How would you feel if... someone like my step-brother did that to you?"

Akira grimaced. "Th-that's different... Takashi's a creep..."

"After what happened that night, all of us thought you were a creep too," Hideko retorted.

The two stared at one another in silence before Akira sighed, then shook her head. "It's not the same. Not even close. Ina and I were friends. I had a crush on her, and I was respectful to her. The night that happened, we were talking about sexuality, and I admitted to liking her. I asked if I could kiss her, and she said I could."

Hideko glared. "That didn't give you any right to put your hand up her shirt!"

Akira flinched at how loud she said that. "Th-that's... listen," she said, crossing her arms. "I apologized to Ina, and she said it was fine. She told me that she didn't blame me for how I behaved and said that if not for Kana, we could have still been friends..."

"I guess that's why you killed her, huh?" a man asked from behind her.

Pausing, Akira felt her heart sink before a hand reached around and covered her mouth, while another arm looped around her and pulled her back into a nearby alleyway that cut between several businesses. Akira tried to fight back against whoever grabbed her, though she couldn't loosen their grip in even the slightest. Feeling herself shoved harshly up against the wall, she clenched her eyes shut from the pain, then opened them to see Yuuki standing in front of her with a knife in his hand. She gasped, though with his hand covering her mouth, not a sound escaped.

"You make one noise, and it'll all be over. Do you understand me?" he asked, the volume of his anger clear in every word he spoke.

Reluctantly, Akira nodded, knowing she had no other choice but to comply.

Proceeding down the alley to where they were, Hideko threw several glances around before stopping alongside them.

As tears began to fill her eyes, her focus darted between Hideko and Yuuki, fearing what would happen next. Her heart pounded away in her chest, her mind racing as she tried to imagine how she might escape this situation, one that she didn't even know was possible. Yuuki, as far as she knew, should have still been in jail for punching Ikumi. Unfortunately, it seems he was released and was likely working with Hideko to allow this very moment to occur.

"I can't imagine there is one, but I want you to give me one reason why I shouldn't cut your throat right here and now," Yuuki said, moving his hand from her mouth and down to her shoulder, where he pinned her against the wall. In his other hand, he held the knife up, right in front of her face, so there wasn't any chance that she'd miss it.

Akira shook her head. "Y-Yuuki... please, don't hurt me," she pleaded, though knowing all too well that it was falling on deaf ears.

Hideko looked between the two of them, appearing very nervous, unlike Yuuki himself.

He grit his teeth. "Play innocent! I *dare* you! Unlike those dumbass police officers, I'm not going to buy your bullshit excuses."

She looked to Hideko. "P-please! Hideko, you can't let him do this. I... I d-didn't do anything! I swear!"

Pulling her slightly off the wall, Yuuki shoved Akira back, harsh enough that it sent her into a coughing spell as she attempted to compose herself.

Biting her lip, Hideko didn't respond, instead choosing to simply watch the two of them.

Yuuki's hand moved from Akira's shoulder to the front of her shirt, twisting the fabric around in his fingers as he tightly held her. "Game's over, Makai."

"W-wait! I... I didn't hurt Miyoko or Kana, I swear!" Akira responded.

He moved the knife up against her neck. "Shut the *hell* up! I'll buy that you didn't mean to kill Miyoko. But you beat the fuck out of Kana! When the police found her, they..." he paused, tears forming in his eyes. "They could barely even identify her... she was that brutally beaten!" he said as his tears ran down his cheeks. "You mutilated her! What you did... you didn't just kill her... you destroyed every semblance of who she was. And now, you're content with just living out your everyday life as if *nothing* happened?!" he shouted, pressing the knife against her throat.

Feeling the blade already cutting into her skin, Akira gasped. "It... it wasn't me, I swear!" she responded as tears ran down her face.

Hideko gasped as she moved in closer. "W-wait, Yuuki! You told me that we were just going to make her confess. You... you're not actually planning to... to *kill* her, are you?!"

Yuuki threw a brief glare at her. "She murdered Miyoko and Kana... you're damn right I'm going to kill her. The police haven't done shit, aside from that asshole Russian arresting me!"

She stood speechless, unsure of how to respond. It was clear by her demeanor that she had no intentions of things going this way.

With her mind scrambling on what to say to get out of this situation,

Akira knew she had to come up with something, or else this would be the end of her. "It... i-it was Asano Tomoe! She's the one who did it," she reluctantly said.

Yuuki turned to look at her, staring in brief disbelief before he hesitantly withdrew the blade, just off the surface of her skin. "What?"

With her heart pounding away in her chest, Akira looked to Yuuki as tears ran down her face. "Asano Tomoe is the one who... sh-she pushed Miyoko down the stairs," she said, feeling her whole body shaking. "I... I stumbled across her and Miyoko arguing. Tomoe has... she's a psycho... she's *insane*. Miyoko and Kana were trying to bully and harass her, and... and Tomoe had enough. She shoved Miyoko down the stairs; I was there, I saw it! And... and once she realized that killed Miyoko, she wanted to kill Kana too..."

Yuuki's eye twitched in irritation as he listened to her. "That's bullshit!"

She shook her head. "N-no! It's true! Tomoe said that either of us could be blamed for shoving Miyoko, and... w-with the police looking so much at me, rather than her, she knew that if she kept me around, that she could blame everything on me if all else failed," she said, swallowing nervously. "A-and, when Kana jumped us on the way home... T-Tomoe just saw that as a perfect opportunity to..." she inhaled sharply, shaking her head. "Oh... God... the blood... there was so much blood," she said, closing her eyes as her tears continued to flow. "I was so scared. I'd never seen anything like it... not since... not since my parents..."

Growling under his breath, Yuuki withdrew her from the wall, throwing her back up against it to silence her. "Enough! I'm not here to listen to your lies!"

Hideko looked to Akira, a wild mixture of emotions coursing through her as she listened to what her old friend had to say.

He pressed the tip of the knife against the bottom of Akira's chin, forcing her head up, else the blade dig into her flesh once more. "Spin whatever tale you want, Makai. But, no matter what you say, I know in my heart that it was you and you alone that killed Miyoko and Kana. The fact that you'd try and blame it on the one girl who's dumb enough to stand by you throughout all of this... it just goes to show how fucked up you are."

Swallowing nervously, Hideko stared at Akira, seeing the genuine fear across her face. "Y-Yuuki, wait," she said, moving in closer.

"What?" he snapped.

"I... I think she's telling the truth," Hideko said.

Akira's eyes shot open, shocked that of all people to side with her, it was Hideko.

Lowering the knife, Yuuki turned his attention to her. "You can't be serious."

Hideko nodded. "Even... even if we're not friends anymore... I knew Akira for a long time. She was always a really... *really* terrible liar. Like, it was always so obvious when she was trying to hide stuff," she said, her attention settling solely onto Akira. "But, what she's saying... it makes sense... and, she doesn't seem as if she's trying to deceive us at all."

"You're kidding, right?" Yuuki asked before stepping back slightly, though keeping his hand on Akira, holding her against the wall. "You can't honestly believe that some new girl, who was teased and picked on for a few weeks or whatever, would do that to Kana, can you? The police said so themselves... whoever did it passionately hated Kana... no one fits that description better than Makai."

"P-please, Yuuki. I'm telling the truth, I swear it," Akira pleaded.

He turned his focus back to her, glaring as he grit his teeth.

Hideko moved in closer, placing her hand on Yuuki's arm that pinned Akira to the wall. She frowned at him. "If she's telling the truth, then what we're doing is wrong."

"And if she's lying through her teeth?" Yuuki asked.

"She's not," Hideko said.

Akira stared in disbelief at her. *Hideko... is defending me?*

He sharply exhaled as he struggled with his intense feelings towards blaming Akira, just as Kana had done before, and the very slight chance that Hideko is right about Akira telling the truth, thus he would be wrong in taking her life. He turned and gave a long, hard stare into Akira's eyes.

Akira stared back at him, genuine fear on display for him to see, though hoping in the back of her mind that he didn't see the deceit that lingered behind that fear.

Growling under his breath, he released his grip on her, then stepped back, pacing around in frustration.

Holding her hand up to her neck, Akira could feel the sharp pain of the cut. Examining her hand, she saw the blood.

Hideko moved closer to Akira, placing a hand on her shoulder. "Are you okay?"

Reluctantly, she nodded. "Y-yeah... thank you... thank you for believing me..."

Hideko hesitantly offered a smile, then turned her attention to Yuuki.

Pacing around, he threw a glance their way, then gestured with his knife towards Akira. "If what you say is true... then your friend is messed up in the head."

"I... I think we should go tell the police," Hideko said.

Akira immediately grimaced at that idea.

Yuuki shook his head. "No... the police think Makai did it, and so I doubt they'd trust her word," he said before scoffing. "We'll just do this same little song and dance with Asano Tomoe. If she's the one to blame, then her true colors should come out once she's at the end of her rope."

Hideko frowned. "I'd... prefer that nobody else has to get hurt."

"We're beyond that now. That ship sailed the moment I heard what happened to Kana," he firmly stated before glaring at Akira. "And, I'm half-tempted to beat you within an inch of your life just for not coming clean sooner... if you're telling the truth. I don't believe you one bit, if we're honest. You're suspicious as hell to me."

Biting her lip, Akira reluctantly nodded.

Hideko turned to her. "You're telling the truth... aren't you, Akira?"

She nodded. "Y-yeah... I've just been... terrified of sharing it up until now, but..." she exhaled sharply, "I don't want to die, just to keep her secret..."

Exhaling sharply, Yuuki put the knife away, then approached Akira, prompting her to back up until she had her back pressed against the wall. "Alright then... here's the deal. You are going to bring Asano Tomoe along with you to your house, and we'll take care of things then," he said, throwing a glance at Hideko before returning his focus to her. "And she's coming along with you both. Then, once I have Asano, Hideko will make sure you don't try anything funny. She'll also stay with you the whole day, making sure you don't rat our plan out to Asano. Do you think you can remember that, Makai?"

"I–"

He slammed his hand against her shoulder, pinning her once more against the wall. "If you fuck this up... I *will* kill you the next time I see you. Don't think that I won't."

Swallowing nervously, Akira nodded. "I... I-I understand..."

"Good," he said, pushing off from her. He threw a glance to Hideko. "Both of you go to school, and don't let her out of your sights."

"Um... b-but, we don't have all the same classes," Hideko admitted.

Yuuki groaned. "Don't let her be alone with Asano or that blonde bitch. Not that I imagine the detective's kid is in on this."

Hideko frowned, then looked to Akira. Taking a deep breath, she returned her focus to Yuuki, then nodded. "I'll figure it out."

Scoffing, Yuuki reluctantly turned and began walking away, saying nothing more as he got out onto the street and disappeared.

Watching him leave, Hideko turned to face Akira. "I... had no idea that he was going to do something like that..." she admitted, grimacing at the thought of it.

Akira let out a deep sigh as she checked and saw there was still blood from the wound on her neck. "We need to get to school... we're already late..."

She nodded, then checked her book bag briefly. From inside, she pulled out some tissues, then offered them to Akira. "Here... I don't know how much this will help the bleeding, but it'll at least keep the blood from staining your uniform."

"Thanks..." Akira said, taking the tissues from her, then holding them against her wound. "F-fuck, that stings..."

Hideko frowned. "I can put some makeup over it once we get to school; that way, nobody notices. But, we'll have to stop the bleeding first."

She shook her head in disbelief. "I can't believe he'd pull a knife on me like that..." she said under her breath.

Glancing around for a moment, Hideko looked back to Akira. "I have an idea. Wait here," she said before running off to the far end of the alley.

Akira watched her leave, then exhaled sharply. "This is so fucked up... Yuuki wants me dead. I had to blame everything on Tomoe just to live... and now Hideko is trying to help me," she said before holding her hand against her forehead. "What the fuck?!" she groaned.

Slumping down, she sat in the alley as she waited for Hideko's return. Her mind scrambled with how she was supposed to handle this unintentional mix-up. In all of her plans, she'd completely neglected to consider Yuuki or the chaos he might bring to the table. She did murder his girlfriend, so it should have been something she considered. Now, she'd thrown Tomoe into his crosshair to save her own hide and had less than eight hours to find an alternative solution. If she had her phone, she could text and warn Tomoe, but she had no opportunities to do so as it stood.

Before long, Hideko returned to the alley with a few items to assist

Akira's injury. The first was a topical cream meant to seal minor wounds, which Hideko applied to the hairline cut across Akira's neck. The next was some makeup to blend the discoloration around her injury with her natural skin tone, and finally, a cute ribbon that Hideko tied securely around Akira's neck, akin to a choker, that would ideally further conceal the injury from prying eyes. It wasn't ideal but worked in a pinch. Once her wound was sufficiently covered, the two left for school, already nearly half an hour late for their first classes of the day.

Chapter 17
Unexpected Planning

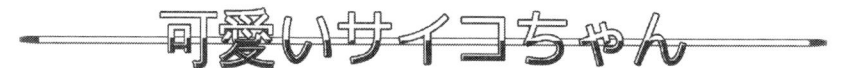

可愛いサイコちゃん

As the two old friends made their way to school together, intent on only making it to their second class of the day, one they shared, Hideko came up with an idea that would suffice for allowing her to keep an eye on Akira. At least to the point that Yuuki would likely be satisfied. Hideko would walk with Akira to each of her classes, and afterward, Akira would wait for Hideko to come by and walk her to the next class. This would ensure she never had time alone with her friends outside of class. Akira agreed to this simply because arguing against it would likely win her no favor.

Upon arriving at the school, they quickly changed their shoes and took their time walking to gym class. Hideko attempted to discuss just what type of person Tomoe was, but Akira insisted that they shouldn't talk at school about it. By the time they got to gym class, they were about ten minutes early, and it showed. There was virtually no one else in the gymnasium or locker rooms other than themselves. Their gym teacher was present, as were a small handful of students, but otherwise, it felt eerily devoid of activities.

Akira took her time changing into her gym uniform as her mind raced to figure out what she should do. The easiest solution would be to be as vague as possible and insist that Tomoe stubbornly refuse to go with Akira, no matter how much she begs or pleads. However, this all hinged on Akira's chances of speaking alone with Tomoe.

Hideko saw that Akira had been sitting on the bench for some time, now with only her clothes changed out, but not even wearing her gym socks or shoes. She approached her and moved around in front of where she sat. "Are you alright?"

"Huh?" she responded before lightly gasping. "O-oh! Yeah... yeah, I'm fine..." she said, offering a deep sigh. "I'm just... I'm trying to think of the best way to ask Tomoe to walk home with us that won't sound kind of suspicious to her..."

Hideko pursed her lips as she seemed to think on it as well.

"Aki? There you are!" Ikumi said as she walked into the locker room with the flow of other students. Approaching her, she frowned. "We didn't see you in math class. Tomoe and I were both worried about you. I was going to text you, but I realized that we hadn't exchanged numbers yet," she said, though as she spoke, her eyes kept drifting over to Hideko.

Akira awkwardly chuckled. "Y-yeah... I overslept. That was my bad," she said before noticing Ikumi's attention shifting. "Oh, um... this is Abukara Hideko. She's, uh... a girl who went to my old school."

"Oh! Well, it's nice to meet you," Ikumi said with a slight bow of her head. "My name is Yasuhida Ikumi."

Hideko stared at her. "It's nice to meet you as well... so, um... you're Detective Yasuhida's daughter?"

She immediately lit up with a smile as she eagerly nodded. "Uh-huh! You know my dad?"

"I've, um... heard his name before, yeah..." Hideko responded.

Grabbing her socks and shoes from her locker, Akira hastily threw them on as the two of them went back and forth. She then stood up. "Say, Ikumi... it's, um... been a while since I last talked with Hideko. You don't mind if I exercise with her, do you?"

"Huh? Well... no, of course not. But couldn't we all exercise together?" Ikumi asked.

"W-well, I mean... I, uh..." Akira began to say, unsure of how to excuse herself from exercising with her friend.

Hideko cleared her throat. "I wanted to ask Akira for some advice on a... very personal situation that she's been through herself. I don't mean any offense, but... I'd just rather not–"

"O-oh! S-sorry," Ikumi said, bowing her head. "I didn't mean to, like... no, it's fine," she said, putting on a bright smile. "If you two need to talk about something personal, then I don't mind. I just... y-you know what? It's not important," she said with an awkward giggle. "I'll see you at lunch, Aki," she said before bowing once more, then reluctantly heading off to her locker.

Watching her leave, Akira looked to Hideko. "Uh... thanks."

Hideko nodded. "She seems nice."

"Y-yeah... Ikumi is really nice."

"Does she know about Tomoe too?"

Akira shook her head. "Not a chance. She's only been my friend for a few days now. Honestly... I don't even know if she has any idea about what happened to Kana."

Hideko frowned at the mere mention of her friend's name as if it were a quick reminder of just how her best friend met her end. Taking a deep breath, she looked to Akira. "We... should go do our exercises..."

She reluctantly nodded. "Okay..."

Together, Akira and Hideko went out into the gym hall and began their exercises, following what little routine Hideko had managed to make in her few days here at school. As they did so, Takashi seemed to watch them from afar, hesitant to approach, even though Akira was now with someone who was less hostile towards him than Ikumi had been. Perhaps he knew what was going on? Akira felt it was unlikely, as much like Kana relentlessly bullied Akira, Yuuki tormented Takashi regularly.

The two had never gotten along well in school, as far back as Akira could remember. Yuuki always harassed Takashi about his masculinity, or supposed lack thereof, because he didn't play sports but instead kept to his video games, anime and manga. Akira was keenly aware of this, as Takashi often vented to her about it regardless of how willing she was to listen. This was likely due to how she was kind towards him, always listening to his frustrations when they first met before she knew he was such a creep.

After Akira and Hideko finished their exercises, they met back up with Ikumi in the locker room, and each changed back into their school uniforms. Akira questioned whether or not Hideko was going to sit with them during lunch. If she didn't, then that would be her opportunity to warn Tomoe about what Yuuki was planning, though she'd still have to be cautious discussing such matters around Ikumi. Once they finished, Akira was slightly irritated by Ikumi's immediate proposal for Hideko to sit with the three of them during lunch, even more so when she accepted Ikumi's offer.

Together, they walked to the cafeteria, with Ikumi asking Hideko dozens of random questions to get to know her better. This didn't surprise Akira, as she knew from personal experience that Ikumi was very friendly and talkative. But it annoyed her because she didn't want Hideko around more than was necessary. Before, she harbored a bit of remorse for how Hideko must have felt following Miyoko and Kana's deaths. But, now... Akira was looking forward to whenever she and Tomoe could figure out a solution for Hideko and Yuuki.

Arriving in the cafeteria, Ikumi led the way to the table where Tomoe was sitting at. As they approached, Tomoe looked to them, relieved to see Akira but surprised by who accompanied her. As they arrived, Ikumi took her seat next to Tomoe while Hideko and Akira sat on the other side of the table.

"Um..." Akira began to say before gesturing to Hideko. "Tomoe, this is Abukara Hideko... she's, uh... an acquaintance of mine from Nirasakinishi Junior High."

Hideko hesitantly bowed her head, though she kept her eyes locked on Tomoe as she did so.

Staring momentarily at Hideko, Tomoe's eyes reluctantly trailed over to Akira, who wore an uncomfortable, forced smile. It was clear by Akira's demeanor that something unusual was going on, but Tomoe could only guess what it could be.

"So, did you two often share classes at your old school?" Ikumi asked.

"We, uh..." Hideko began to say, pausing as she thought about it.

Akira glanced down to the far end of the cafeteria, then back to Ikumi. "Hey, you might want to get your food, Ikumi. It looks like a decent line is already forming."

Ikumi lightly gasped. "Oh! Right. I almost forgot. Thank you, Aki," she cheerfully responded before scooting her chair back, then rushing off towards the line of students.

Watching her leave, Akira turned back to her friend. "So, how have your classes been, Tomoe?"

With her eyes drifting between Akira and Hideko, it took a moment before Tomoe responded. "They were... good. I suppose..."

"Awesome! I'm glad to hear it," she said with a light chuckle.

An awkward silence filled the air as Tomoe and Hideko stared at one another, neither one wishing to maintain consistent eye contact.

"S-so, um... Tomoe. Do you think you could help me out with the notes from math class?" Akira asked.

"Huh? The notes?" Tomoe responded.

She nodded. "Yeah... because I missed class today..."

"Oh! Um... sure, yeah... one second," Tomoe said as she turned and got her notebook out, then flipped it over to today's lesson. "They're on these two pages," she said as she laid the notebook on the table.

"Thanks!" Akira cheerfully responded before looking to Hideko. "You're so quiet... you should tell her a bit about yourself. Tomoe's not even from around here, you know?" she said, encouraging the two of them to interact with one another.

Hideko lightly grimaced at Akira, then sighed. "I, um... okay. Well, I've... I've lived here my whole life, and... I don't know..."

"Uh... w-well... what kind of hobbies do you have?" Tomoe nervously asked.

Taking the notebook, Akira pulled her own notebook and pencil from her backpack, then began writing down the equations. She caught Hideko looking her way briefly before returning her attention to Tomoe. While she wasn't looking, Akira scrawled down a message in English, warning Tomoe that no matter what she says later in the day, to not walk home with her and Hideko, adding that she needs to call her mother to pick her up from now on. As she finished copying down less than a quarter of the equations, she added to Tomoe's notebook that she'd come by tonight and explain everything.

Closing her friend's notebook up, Akira smiled at her as she slid the book across the table. "Thanks, Tomoe! I appreciate it," she said before tapping her finger on the cover. "You miscounted on one, though. But I corrected it for you," she said with a confident grin and a light chuckle. "I guess your tutoring is already helping."

Tomoe looked to Akira, then reluctantly nodded. "I, um... I'm glad," she said before feeling her friend nudging her leg under the table with her shoe.

Akira mouthed the words "read it" before continuing to smile. She turned and gasped. "Oh! That was fast," she said as Ikumi returned to the table.

Sitting her tray down, Ikumi shook her head at Akira. "I think you might need glasses, Aki. The line wasn't that long at all."

"Eh, I'd look super cute with glasses, but I know I'd probably lose them," she admitted with a light chuckle.

Ikumi nodded. "They would look really cute. It'd depend on the frames, though," she said before motioning towards her. "Speaking of looking cute. I love your little ribbon choker, Aki. It's absolutely adorable."

Akira awkwardly chuckled. "Oh... um, thanks. I thought I'd try something a little different today, and... I don't own any chokers, so I made one out of this ribbon."

Hideko looked to Akira with slight suspicion, though her attention was then torn away once Ikumi began bombarding her with friendly questions and carefree conversation. Meanwhile, Akira kept her attention on Tomoe as she checked the message, then looked at her in shock. Akira offered a nod, then got her bento box out to begin eating lunch, not that she felt all that hungry.

Throughout their lunch period, there was an unsettling feeling between three of the girls, with Ikumi being the only one to not feel as if something were up. Once they finished, they each left off for their next classes, with Hideko walking Akira to and from each of her's. Fortunately, whatever suspicions Hideko held towards Akira, she didn't have an opportunity to bring them up, as any time they met, there were far too many students around for any meaningful conversation to be had on such a sensitive subject.

By the end of the day, they walked together, through the crowds of students, towards the main entrance. In Hideko's eyes, this was the chance they had to lure Tomoe into a trap, though after their brief back and forth in the cafeteria, Akira could tell that Hideko doubted Tomoe's guilt when it came to the deaths of her friends. After they each changed into their street shoes, Tomoe approached Akira, cautiously watching Hideko as she did so.

Akira smiled at her. "Hey, Tomoe. I know we haven't been doing it lately, but do you think you could walk with me back to my place?"

Tomoe tore her eyes away from Hideko, turning her attention solely to her friend. "I... I can't..."

She frowned. "What? Why not?"

"B-because, I... I promised my mom that I'd help her after school. She needed to go pick up some planters for the garden, and they're heavy, so... I said I'd help her," Tomoe explained, quickly coming up with what Akira felt was a very believable excuse.

Akira grimaced. "Uh... b-but, can't you just walk with me and then go back to your place to help your mom?"

Thinking briefly on it, Tomoe shook her head. "The place closes soon, so if I'm late, then we won't be able to go get them. I'm sorry, Aki..."

Hideko watched the two of them from a short distance away, keeping a close eye on how they talked.

Ikumi approached them, standing next to Hideko, and smiled. "Even if Tomoe can't walk home with you, Aki. We can walk with you, right, Hideko?" she asked with a playful giggle.

Akira looked to them and scrambled to think of how to salvage this situation in such a way as to exclude Ikumi so that she wouldn't get hurt. She lightly gasped as the perfect idea hit her. She awkwardly chuckled. "One second, Tomoe," she said before rushing the short distance over to Ikumi, then leaning in close. "I'm trying to get a moment alone with her so I can do some romantic things. You know... drop some poetic lines? Shower her in praise? That sort of stuff," she said in a low voice, though ensuring Hideko could also hear her.

Ikumi gasped. "O-oh!" she said, covering her mouth.

Akira nodded.

Ikumi awkwardly laughed. "Silly me. I forgot... my uncle has been coming to pick me up, so he'd probably be upset if I ditched him after he drove all this way to give me a ride home..." she said, which would have been partially true, as her uncle had been here the days before to pick her up.

Turning to face Tomoe, Akira grinned widely. "So, you really can't walk with me? Please..." she pleaded, though her eyes showed just how disingenuous she was being.

Reluctantly, Tomoe once more shook her head. "I can't. I'm sorry. But, I'll see you tomorrow, okay?" she said before moving around them and heading towards the exit.

Watching her leave, Akira frowned. "D-dammit..."

Ikumi watched Tomoe as well, then turned back to Akira. "I'm sorry, Aki. Maybe you can get her to walk with you tomorrow?" she suggested before offering a bright smile. "But, I'm sure my uncle wouldn't mind if I did walk you home. Or, maybe he'd even be willing to give you a ride?"

"Nah... thank you, though, Ikumi. I appreciate it," Akira said before gesturing to Hideko. "We don't live far from one another, so we'll just walk together and... I don't know, reminisce about the 'good ol' days,'" she said with a light chuckle.

She frowned. "Well... alright, if you're sure," she said before looking to Hideko, then offering each of them a bow of her head. "I'll see you two tomorrow."

"See you, Ikumi," Akira said as her friend turned and left. With a deep sigh, Akira looked to Hideko. "Someone's not gonna be happy..."

Hideko did her best to maintain her composure before turning and heading towards the exit.

Akira found it odd how she was behaving and began to worry that she saw right through Akira's plan. Following her out, they walked together in the direction of Fujimi.

"I can't imagine she'll have another excuse tomorrow, so... I bet we'll be able to get her then," Akira said.

Hideko kept walking, her head held low as she appeared lost in thought.

Akira frowned. "Is everything alright?"

Stopping, she stared at the ground briefly, her eyes holding no focus as if she were completely blanking out.

Turning to face her, Akira leaned down to see her better. "Hideko?"

Her eyes shot to Akira, then after a brief moment, Hideko abruptly turned and began running away, back the way they came.

Akira stared in disbelief before reluctantly chasing after her. "H-hey! Hideko, where... where the hell are you going?" she called out.

With no response, she continued to run, not even looking back at Akira. Fortunately, she wasn't nearly as fit as Kana or even Tomoe, so Akira had little problem catching up with her. Closing the distance, she moved around in front of Hideko to try and stop her as they ran down the street that bordered the canal.

"Wh-what the hell has gotten into you?" Akira asked.

Hideko shook her head as she backed away. "G-get away from me!" she said, staggering back. "You're... y-you're a liar... you lied to me!"

She stared in disbelief, unsure as to what was going on. "What the hell are you talking about?"

Hideko took shallow breaths as she held a timid, though defensive stance at least three meters from Akira. "You said... y-you said you didn't do anything... that... that you were innocent. But... I can tell. I can tell that you were lying," she said, her eyes swelling with tears. "You... you killed my friends, didn't you? Admit it!"

Inhaling sharply, Akira glanced around, seeing no one in their immediate area, though with the time of day it was, she knew there would no doubt be others not too far away. She returned her attention to her old friend. "No. I didn't. I told you before that she's crazy. She's *really* good at playing innocent. How do you think she's fooled everyone into believing she didn't do anything? You have to believe me, Hideko... I didn't hurt anyone."

With her heart pounding in her chest, Hideko shook her head. "No, I don't believe you. I saw how confused she looked. She didn't have any idea what was going on," she said, pausing as she wiped her tears away. "Does... d-does she even know what you've done?! Or that you blamed her for everything?!"

Exhaling sharply, Akira closed her eyes. *Goddammit... now what?! What am I supposed to do here? If Hideko doesn't believe I'm innocent, then she'll tell Yuuki, and he'll kill me the next time he grabs me. But, what the fuck could I say to convince her?*

Hideko grimaced before reaching into her bookbag, then fumbling around for a moment before pulling out her phone.

"Huh?" Akira said as she noticed Hideko on her phone, vigorously typing something out. "What... what are you doing?" she asked, to which Hideko offered no response. *"H-hey!"* she said, realizing that she must have been sending a message to Yuuki.

Rushing over, Akira reached out and grabbed onto Hideko's phone, trying to pry it away from her. Hideko struggled to pull the device back, though, despite Akira's lack of physical prowess, she was still far stronger than Hideko. Wrenching the phone from her old friend's grasp, she checked the screen as she stepped away and saw the message that had been typed out but not yet sent. She turned and glared back at Hideko.

"You were going to tell him that I was the one who killed them?!" Akira angrily asked as she grit her teeth. Turning to face her, she stomped her foot on the ground. "Hideko... Yuuki had a knife to my throat! He was going to *kill* me! What do you think he'd do if he saw this message?!" she said, trying her best not to shout.

Swallowing nervously, Hideko backed further away. "Y-you... you did kill them... I know you did. And... and the police aren't going to do anything, so... so what choice do I have?"

Akira exhaled sharply. "You want me to die? You want Yuuki to slit my throat, then watch me beg for my life on my hands and knees while I bleed out?" she asked, tears forming in her eyes. "Are you going to be there to watch? Because that's what he's going to do to me..."

With her lip quivering, Hideko collapsed onto her knees, then sat on the pavement as she cupped her face in her hands and began crying. She muttered amidst her tears that she simply didn't want anyone else to get hurt but that she misses her friends so much.

Hesitantly approaching her, Akira kneeled and placed her hand on Hideko's shoulder. "H-hey... don't cry," she said, prompting Hideko to look up. "I know they were both... horrible towards me after what happened, but..." she sighed. "As much as I hated them, I'd never... do that to them... I promise," she said, struggling to lie about something like this to Hideko's face, given their history together.

Staring at her, Hideko's lip quivered as she searched for the words to say what it was she felt. "Akira... I have... I have to know," she said, inhaling sharply as she braced herself. "D-did... did you kill Miyoko and Kana?"

Locking eyes with her, Akira went to speak up, though she hesitated. Closing her eyes, she shook her head, then looked back to Hideko. "No... I didn't. But, I did see it happen... and I'm *still* horrified by what I saw..." she said, feigning disbelief.

Hideko took a moment as she sized up Akira's response, then swallowed nervously before nodding. "Okay, I... I believe you. S-so... Tomoe did it then?"

She nodded.

"And... she was just feigning confusion at school today?"

"I think she was confused as to why you were with me. I think that made her behave the way she did," Akira explained, sighing. "I know you and Yuuki don't trust me... but, unless I can talk alone with her, I don't think we'll be able to get her somewhere alone where he can... do... ya know... his thing," she said, wishing to avoid talking about killing the girl she loved.

Hideko shook her head. "N-no. Akira, listen," she said, wiping her tears away. "We need to figure out some way to let the police know. Like... in a way that they'll know she did it. I don't want anyone else to get hurt, and I know you don't either. So... maybe you can find some evidence to use against her?"

Akira grimaced before standing up and crossing her arms as she stepped back to give Hideko some space. "Um... I'd have to think... maybe I could get her to confess on a recording?"

Hideko stood up as well, then eagerly nodded. "Th-that would work! Just bring the topic up, and... I don't know. Ask her questions. If you could record it, then... then you could play that back for the police, and they'd have the evidence they need to arrest her."

"Yeah, but... I don't exactly have a way to record her. I mean, I could do recordings on my cassette player, but... that got ruined last week when...

well, it doesn't matter. All that matters is I have no phone or cassette player to record anything on," she admitted.

Hideko pondered it briefly before slowly nodding. "I have an idea," she said as her focus returned to Akira. "I know your grandparents don't give you any, like... allowance or anything, so it's not as if you can afford to purchase a phone for yourself. So, on the way home, we'll stop by a convenience store, and I'll get you a new phone. We'll make sure to get one that can record messages too."

Akira recoiled in slight shock. "You'd buy me a new phone? Seriously?"

"If it helps us bring Tomoe to justice for what she's done, then yes," she said before forcing a smile. "I'm... I'm sorry I didn't see through her lies, Akira. We used to be close friends, and like I said before, I've never known you to be the type to lie. Well... successfully, anyway," she said with a light, albeit awkward chuckle.

Akira reluctantly smiled. "Thanks, Hideko..."

She nodded. "Let's get going then. I'll get you that phone, and then we'll talk about how we might get her to confess, okay?"

"We'll have to talk about it later. Or else I'll end up grounded by my grandparents. Besides, I think I have a great idea," Akira said as she beckoned Hideko to follow. "I'll tell you on the way to my place."

Following alongside Akira, Hideko walked with her back towards Fujimi as they discussed the plan that Akira had just come up with. It was fairly simple yet effective in the way she intended to play it off. She would propose the idea of a sleepover this weekend with Tomoe, and that would allow her to ease into the topic of murder. This prompted Hideko to ask about what Akira said to Ikumi about wanting to flirt with Tomoe and whether or not Akira had feelings towards her.

This hadn't even crossed Akira's mind since they left the school, and so she had to quickly explain away what she said. She claimed a partial truth, that Ikumi knew she was a lesbian, as did Tomoe, but that Akira didn't have any romantic feelings whatsoever towards her friend. Not since she became the scapegoat for Tomoe's brutal murders. Akira then fluffed up the remainder of their conversations as she reminisced about how odd it felt for Miyoko and Kana to be gone and how she, in a way, missed them pestering her.

Hideko shared with Akira just how upset Ina was over everything and that she was refusing to leave her room after Kana's death came to light. This made Akira feel worse, as she genuinely still cared about her old crush but knew that she had to push through these emotions, else she might find herself giving in to the temptation to confess the truth of what happened. Akira had made her bed, she knew this, and after everything that happened, she was prepared to sleep in it. More specifically, she was ready to fight tooth and nail to allow herself and Tomoe to come out of this in one piece and with their freedoms fully intact.

Chapter 18

Impact of Malice

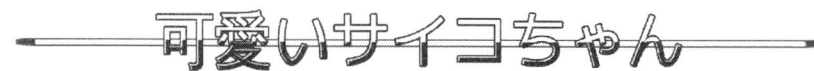

可愛いサイコちゃん

After purchasing a new cellphone for Akira to use to record Tomoe's supposed confession, Hideko parted ways with her so that she could get home before her grandfather accused her of being too late. Meanwhile, Hideko promised to talk with Yuuki to buy them time. Akira wasn't optimistic that he would want to allow them to go through with this alternative plan, but it did give her a chance to figure out precisely what it was that she needed to do.

Upon arriving back at her house, Akira wasted little time before adding Tomoe's number to her cellphone, then shooting a quick text message to her friend, informing her of the new phone and that she'd call her later so they could talk. Akira then began work on her chores. As she did so, she couldn't stop thinking about how she'd handled things since the start of all of this.

In the beginning, when Miyoko fell down the stairs, Akira didn't assume she was dead, only unconscious. Her goal was to avoid Miyoko's anger, and by extension, Kana's. But, after becoming aware of her death, Akira's focus then became ensuring that Tomoe, her only friend, didn't get into trouble for something that wasn't even her fault. Now, with Kana's death at Akira's own hands, something that was done to protect not only herself but Tomoe as well, Akira found that she was handling everything in a far different way than she imagined, or even that she could accept.

Kana's death didn't bother her. However, knowing that she was now emotionally manipulating Hideko, using her, and now possibly planning something terrible as a solution to their new problems with Yuuki, it was simply too much for her to stomach. Everything Akira had done until this point was to protect herself and Tomoe and felt entirely justifiable in her eyes. Now, she had to plan what she'd need to do, and the very thought of that left her stomach in knots.

By the time she finished all of her chores, she didn't have the time nor desire to relax in her bedroom, listen to music, or anything. And once her grandparents turned in for the evening, Akira's stress and anxiety had reached such a head that she knew she needed assistance in relaxing. Her grandfather always kept a case of beers in the refrigerator, of which he'd drink one or two each evening. As it stood, he had a case with eight beers left inside. Akira took the entire case from their refrigerator and brought them outside with her, alongside a nearly full pack of cigarettes.

Sitting on the stone border of their garden, she cracked open a beer and threw it back, persevering through the disgusting taste of the cheap alcohol as she polished off nearly half the can in one go. Setting it aside, she then lit her first cigarette and took long, hard drags off of it, spitting the smoke out in front of her. Leaning forward, she rested her elbows on her knees as she hung her head low, closing her eyes as she held her hand against her forehead in frustration.

The fuck am I even doing? She wondered as she shook her head in disbelief. *Even though she didn't do shit while Miyoko and Kana made my life a living hell, Hideko is... she was my friend. Now, I'm lying to her and... contemplating this?! But, what choice do I have?*

Exhaling sharply, Akira reached over and grabbed her beer, finishing it off, then tossing the can aside. She opened a second beer, downing several gulps of it before stopping as she coughed and gagged on the cheap beverage. Wiping her mouth off on her arm, she stared down at the can in her hand.

It's the only way. If Yuuki is so intent on killing one of us, or hell... maybe even both of us... then I don't really have a choice. But, then Hideko will know it was me, and she might tell the police, she thought before closing her eyes. *Am... am I really going to have to kill both of them, just to ensure Tomoe and I are safe? But then what? Where does it end? If... If someone like Ikumi became suspicious, would I have to kill her too?*

Opening her eyes, she stared at the ground, then shook her head. "No... I like Ikumi too much. She's too kind towards me, too understanding," she said, sighing, then taking another long swig of her beer. Finishing off this second can, she belched, then threw it a short distance in front of her.

"Yuuki has to die. That's a fact. Hideko... maybe I can do something else. She shouldn't die. She's not a threat... not a physical one, anyway..."

Reaching up, she ran her hand through her hair. "Fuck! Why have I let things get this fucked up?!" she groaned as she leaned back so far that she fell off the border of the garden and down into the soil, crushing a few of the flowers under her weight. Staring up into the night sky, she took short, shallow breaths. "I can't let it end like this..."

Seeing the beautiful sky above, the stars only barely visible through the sheen of reflections from the city's lights. The night air felt cool, crisp, and pure, as if there wasn't a worry in the world, at least outside of Akira's mind. Surrounding her was little more than the sounds of the night itself. Crickets chirping, leaves rustling in the breeze, cars driving down distant streets, and a dog barking far off in the neighborhood.

Akira exhaled slowly into the air above her as she wore an emotionless expression. "I can't let Tomoe go to prison for shit Miyoko started. I can't go myself, simply because Kana was a fucking unhinged lunatic..." she said, inhaling sharply. "And, if Yuuki is so set on killing Tomoe or myself, then I have no choice. I have to kill him too. As for Hideko... I'll kill her if I have to... but I'd rather not," she said before biting her lip. "There's the police too... *fuck!*"

Although slightly startling at first, Akira felt something land on her face, just on the tip of her nose. As her eyes focused on it, she saw a small cricket sitting there. It rubbed its hind legs together, producing that same familiar chirping sound that filled the night air, though once Akira began to move as she breathed, it jumped off and continued on its way. Pushing herself back up onto the stone border, she brushed the soil and mulch off her clothes and out of her hair.

"There's only one solution to the police. I'll have to do the same shit I did on Saturday. When they ask me questions, I'll have to respond with confidence. I have to get my story straight, and I have to make damn sure that I have answers for every question they ask," she said as she reached out and grabbed another beer. "I just need to avoid coming off as too arrogant or confident, or they may see through it. I'm a victim here... that's what they need to believe," she said as she popped the tab on the can, then let out a deep sigh. "I might not like it... but I don't have any other choice."

Staying up far later than she expected, Akira kept drinking beers and smoking cigarettes back-to-back with few signs of stopping. She didn't concern herself with what repercussions there might be for her behavior, only that it helped ease the pain of what her life had become. After having polished off five beers, more than she'd ever had before, Akira felt as if it were long since past time for her to clean up and head to bed.

Unfortunately, she found it incredibly difficult to walk, feeling as if she could barely keep her vision straight. With the assistance of the fence, she stumbled back inside of the house, then staggered her way down the hallway until she arrived at the bathroom, where she intended to get cleaned up and head to bed. At this point, though, she just wanted to use the toilet, then go to sleep. Though she wouldn't make it that far as the moment she approached the toilet, she felt sick to her stomach and quickly fell to her knees.

If the beer tasted terrible going down, Akira would agree it was more flavorful than the taste associated with it coming back up, if she were even enough in her right mind even to recognize what was going on. At this point, her mind had become so muddled by the alcohol she forced herself to drink that she barely even knew what was going on. Collapsing down onto the floor, she could scarcely tell that she was staring at the side of the toilet bowl before passing out.

Having lost consciousness thanks to her indulgence in alcohol aside, Akira soon learned that the bathroom's cold, hard tile floor was about the furthest she could get from a comfortable night's rest when she was awoken with aches and pains in her side and back. Though it wasn't the pain that woke her, it was the loud, dull sound of her grandfather beating his hand against the bathroom door.

"Makai Akira! Get out here, now!" Ryoma shouted.

Groaning, Akira slowly pushed herself up until she was sitting just in front of the toilet. She had an unspeakably terrible taste in her mouth, her nose felt clogged up, and she could still feel the burn of vomit in the back of her throat. Coughing, she spat into the toilet, which was still a mess from the night before. Her head throbbed with pain, made worse with Ryoma's continued beating on the door.

"O-one moment!" Akira shouted as she flushed the toilet, then used the bowl to steady herself as she stood up.

Staggering over to the sink, she looked at herself in the mirror. She was visibly exhausted from what it looked, her hair a matted mess with dirt and mulch still stuck in it. She still had vomit on her mouth and around her nose, and she even had a bruise across her cheek, likely from where she hit the edge of the toilet when she passed out. Splashing water on her face, she tried to make herself at least somewhat presentable. Not an easy task when she was clearly as messed up as she was now.

Beating yet again on the door, Ryoma shouted. "Makai Akira, you come out here right now!"

Groaning, she approached the door, unlocked and then slid it open. The light from the hallway blinded her, though she barely had a moment to recoil and shield herself from it before Ryoma grabbed hold of her and pulled her out into the hall. Pushing her up against the wall, Ryoma stood in front of her, examining the absolute mess she was.

"Do you want to explain yourself?" he angrily asked before gesturing towards the front of the house. "I found multiple empty beer cans outside, alongside several cigarette butts!"

Akira squinted at him and recoiled slightly at the sound of his voice. "Could... you not yell?" she groggily asked.

"What?!" he responded, prompting her to flinch. Reaching out, he grabbed onto her arm, then used his other hand to pat the pockets on her shorts, finding the pack of cigarettes and lighter she had inside. Pulling them out, he crushed the pack in his hand, then thrust it in her face. "Where did you even get these?! Did you steal them?"

"I didn't steal them!" she snapped.

He scoffed. "You don't have money, so how did you pay for them? What are you doing? Having boys at your school buy them for you?"

Reaching up, she held her forehead. "Can I please go to bed?" she asked, feeling as if she could barely stand.

Ryoma glared at her. "Bed is where you should have been hours ago. Instead, you decided to drink until you passed out on the bathroom floor. You're lucky that's all that happened with how many beers you just drank! I knew you were stupid, but this is astonishing, even for you!" he shouted.

Closing her eyes, Akira felt as if her head was heavy on her shoulders.

With a firm shake, he woke her back up from her momentary daze. "Oh no. You had your chance to sleep. You have school in two hours. But, before then, I'm going to make sure you learn your lesson when it comes to such delinquent behavior," he said before pulling on her arm, forcing her down the hallway. "For each beer you decided to steal and down, you are grounded for a week. For every cigarette butt I find out there, you can tack on another week," he said as they stopped by the stairs. He turned to face her, then pointed to the stairs. "Now, go upstairs, get changed out of those clothes you ruined. Once you get back down here, I'll tell you what you'll be doing. And don't you dare be tardy."

Squinting, Akira stared at him in confusion.

"Go change clothes, then get back down here! You have three minutes, starting now!" Ryoma shouted.

Turning to the stairs, she began climbing them slowly, with every step more difficult than the one that preceded it. By the time she got to the top, her head felt like it was going to explode from the throbbing pain inside of it. She'd never drank so much before in her life, and this hangover, mixed with the lack of sleep and disgust from having lost herself last night, gave her a horrible feeling that she knew she wouldn't soon forget. Stepping inside of her room, all she wanted to do was collapse into bed and sleep, but she knew doing so would only worsen things for her.

"Fuck my life..." she groaned as she approached her dresser. Grasping onto the drawer's handles, she struggled to open it. "Someone... just fucking kill me," she added as she tried to even remember what she was doing.

Eventually, she pulled some clothes out, then began to change. It took forever for her to finish getting into new clothes, which weren't even her school uniform. She then made her way back downstairs, even slower than before, which only served to add to Ryoma's irritation with her. In the kitchen, he gave her a short list of chores, already far more than she knew she could finish before it was time for school, and yet he promised to add more. He swore that there would be no end to the chore she'd have while she was grounded, and being that she only just recently got over being grounded for something else entirely, she knew he wasn't bluffing.

With her morning off to a terrible start, things were only set to worsen for her as time drew closer to school. After cleaning up and changing into her school uniform and still feeling exhausted and sick to her stomach, Akira left her grandparents' house to head to school. A part of her just wanted to skip out and spend the day resting, though she knew the consequences for doing so would far outweigh the benefits.

Arriving at school, Akira had to practically drag herself up the steps and over to her shoe locker, where Tomoe was waiting for her. As she drew closer, Tomoe could see just how exhausted and messed up Akira was, though she didn't appear surprised in the slightest by her friend's unusual display. Turning to the locker, she took Akira's indoor shoes out, then sat them on the floor.

"Thanks..." Akira said as she yawned.

"Do you feel better now that you got some sleep?" Tomoe asked as she wore a concerned frown.

Akira looked oddly at her friend. "Better? Um... well, I didn't really get much sleep, but... was I off or something yesterday? I don't remember..."

She grimaced. "Well, you were. Mostly with everything regarding Hideko, but... I mean, since we talked last night."

"We talked?" Akira responded with genuine surprise.

"You don't remember?" Tomoe asked. With a sigh, she shook her head. "Aki, you called me at like... two in the morning, and... I don't know how to put this. But you were completely incoherent. You couldn't remember how much you drank, but it was really obvious that you were completely intoxicated."

Akira frowned. "I... I called you while I was drunk? What did I say?"

"I don't even know. I could barely understand a word you were saying," she responded before sighing. "I kept telling you to just go to bed, and... at some point, you said you would, and that's when we ended the call. But it doesn't look like you got any sleep."

Scratching her head, Akira shook her head. "I think I got an hour or two... but they were on the bathroom floor after I threw up and blacked out."

Tomoe gasped. "Oh my goodness! Are you alright?"

She lightly blushed at her friend's concern, then nodded. "I'm better now. But... I'm still really exhausted. And, my grandfather grounded me for, um... three months?"

"Geez... because he caught you drunk?"

"That, and he saw that I'd been smoking. Luckily, he didn't check my other pocket because he'd of found my phone and took it away," Akira said as she pulled her cellphone out of her skirt pocket.

Tomoe sighed, then smiled at her. "A small blessing, I suppose. But, was there any reason you decided to drink so much?"

She awkwardly chuckled. "Yeah... sort of has to do with all of the shit we've been through lately. But, I'll have to tell you about it later," she said, putting it away. "For now... we'd better head to our classes before we're late..."

"We're already a little late. But, you still need to change your shoes," Tomoe said, gesturing down towards Akira's street shoes.

"Oh! R-right... yeah, that would probably be a good idea. Goddamn, I'm tired..." she said as she slipped out of her shoes, then into the ones Tomoe laid out for her.

Parting ways, Akira and Tomoe each went to their classes. In Akira's first class of the day, biology, she had Hideko with her, though the two didn't sit near one another. Likely a good thing for Akira, as she almost immediately fell asleep in the middle of class. She was eventually awoken by her teacher, who was more concerned than upset at her for having slept through the entire class. Akira lied about why she was so tired, then ran off to her next class. She was, fortunately, able to avoid Hideko, thanks to the teacher speaking briefly with her. She made it through half of her next class before nodding off once more, repeating in her third class for the first half of school.

This was the last thing Akira needed, as this was her chance to figure out how best to eliminate Yuuki as a threat and ensure Hideko didn't become a more prominent threat herself. As it stood, she had no plan and limited time at her disposal. As lunch period rolled around, she had to practically drag herself to the cafeteria, where she took a seat across from Tomoe. Crossing her arms in front of her, she laid down on the table, closed her eyes, and almost immediately fell asleep.

Tomoe sighed, then shook her head at Akira. Pulling her bento box out, she began preparing her meal while her friend proceeded to snore just across from her.

Approaching the table, Ikumi looked curiously at Akira before taking her seat next to Tomoe. "Um... is there a reason Aki is sleeping?"

"It's a long story," she responded before shaking her head. "Essentially, she didn't get much sleep, and fought with her grandfather, so now she's grounded."

Ikumi frowned. "Aw... that sucks. Well... let's not disturb her," she said before pulling her books out and preparing to do some homework.

"Are you not going to eat, Ikumi?" Tomoe asked.

She smiled. "I had a big breakfast this morning. It's my dad's birthday, so I woke up early to cook him a spectacular breakfast so he'd have the best start possible for his busy day," she said with a playful giggle.

Tomoe grimaced. "Um... busy day?"

Ikumi nodded. "Yeah, they've been talking over the phone a lot with others from work about this big case. I think it's mostly been with the chief of police, their boss."

Akira grumbled, then leaned up, wiping her eyes.

Ikumi gasped as she covered her mouth. "Oh no! I didn't wake you, did I, Aki?"

"Huh?" she asked as she looked at her friend in confusion. She shook her head. "No... at least, I don't think so..." she said, holding her head as she groaned. "Fuck me... my head is killing me."

"I have some medicine in my bookbag if you think it'll help at all," Ikumi offered.

Akira chuckled. "Does it fix hangovers?"

She frowned. "Um... no, I don't think so. Do you have a hangover?"

"A little bit..."

"You should drink plenty of water. And, try to eat foods that are filling, like rice," Ikumi suggested with a smile. "Uncle Isaac told me that whenever I drink on holidays and during celebrations, that I should have a small glass of water between each of my beverages so that way I don't get dehydrated."

Akira snickered. "Yeah... that would have been a smart idea."

"More importantly, he told me not to drink until I'm old enough," she said, gesturing towards Akira. "Which you are not."

Akira stuck her tongue out at her friend. "So what? What are you going to do? Tattle on me?"

Ikumi pursed her lips, then shook her head. "No. I wouldn't do that. But maybe this hangover is a good enough punishment to discourage you from over-drinking again? Next time, you should make sure to have someone trustworthy around to watch over you, encourage you to drink more water, and make sure you stay safe."

Akira nodded. "Yeah... it'd probably be best to have someone there to keep you out of trouble. Or at least vouch for you that the trouble wasn't entirely your fault," she said with a laugh before an idea crossed her mind. "Say, Ikumi... are you free this weekend, by chance?"

"Huh?" she responded before thinking briefly on it, then nodding. "I should be. Other than having some homework to do."

"Awesome!" Akira cheerfully responded, feeling more energetic now that she had a great addition to her existing idea. She looked to Tomoe. "What would you two say about a sleepover this weekend? Maybe at your place?"

Tomoe recoiled in slight shock. "A... sleepover?"

Offering a wide, toothy grin, Akira eagerly nodded. "Yeah! I think it'd be a lot of fun. And, it'd give us all three a chance to hang out together outside of school."

"I think that would be a lot of fun," Ikumi said, though she then frowned. "But, didn't Tomoe say that you were grounded? I'm guessing for drinking?"

Pausing, Akira awkwardly chuckled, then threw a brief glare at Tomoe. She then looked back to Ikumi. "Did I say sleepover? I meant... weekend study group! Yeah! That's what this is. And I'm sure my grandparents won't have any problem with something like that," she said with a snicker.

Ikumi rolled her eyes. "You're so sneaky, Aki... but you're probably going to get yourself into more trouble."

She scoffed. "I'm always in trouble, so nothing new there."

Tomoe sighed. "I'll... have to check with my mom."

"That's fine. We'll talk about it more after school..." Akira said, feeling a surreal surge of energy, to the point that she barely even felt tired anymore. Opening her backpack, she pulled her bento box from it, then placed it on the table. "No more sleep for me. I'm starving now," she said with a wide grin.

Tomoe stared at her, still confused as to what she was planning. Between the oddities yesterday with Hideko, Akira's heavy drinking, and her now being grounded, things felt as if they were all coming unraveled behind the scenes. This was terrifying because she could have no idea just how bad things might be until Akira decided to share that information with her. Far as Tomoe could have known, her friend could be at her wit's end and prepared to turn her in to save face. It didn't feel as if that were something that Akira would do, but Tomoe had to admit, up until the previous Friday, bludgeoning someone to death also didn't feel as if it were something Akira would do.

Chapter 19
Tomoe's Gambit
~~可愛いサイコちゃん~~

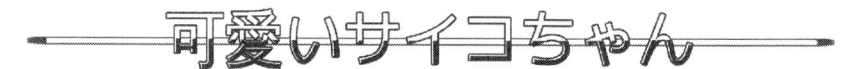

Throughout the remainder of the school day, Tomoe tried to wrap her mind around everything that had been going on since Kana's death. Her primary concern had initially been Akira's lack of remorse for killing the girl she had once been so close to. Since then, things had been quiet, to the point that it was unsettling. Neither of them had been accosted by the police, as far as she knew, nor had they endured any further troubles from other students. Things had simply been going too well for them since such the brutal encounter that ended off their first week as friends.

As her final class came to a close, Tomoe hastily made her way out of the classroom to meet with Akira. She hoped to better understand why her friend so abruptly wanted them to have a sleepover, especially after being grounded for binge drinking. Stepping out into the hallway, she wouldn't have to go far to meet up with her friend, as Akira called out to her the moment she left her classroom.

Akira eagerly waved to her. "Hey, Tomoe!"

Spotting Akira, Tomoe began walking towards her, letting out a deep sigh as she drew closer. "Please don't yell, Aki..."

"Sorry, I'm just eager to talk to you about this weekend before my grandfather gets pissed off at me for not rushing home," she responded before glancing around. "Let's go somewhere we can talk."

I was afraid of that... please say things aren't worse, Tomoe thought to herself before nodding. "Most of the students will be heading down to the first floor, so if we go upstairs, we'll mostly be alone."

Akira grinned. "Perfect! Let's go," she said, leading the way as she darted towards the stairs.

Following behind her, Tomoe frowned. "You seem like you have a lot more energy than before..."

"Oh, I don't. This is just adrenaline," she said with a laugh as she ascended the stairs.

Adrenaline? She has a lot of energy because she's excited about something, then? Maybe... it's something positive? Tomoe wondered as the two of them reached the third floor.

Glancing around, Akira saw it was mostly empty up here, as this was where most of the clubrooms and teacher's offices were located. She turned and smiled at her friend. "Okay, so..."

Tomoe braced herself for whatever Akira had to share with her, hopeful that it was something good, yet fearing that she'd be discovering some horrible new turn of events.

"Don't freak out, but..."

Oh no...

Akira sighed. "We need to kill Yuuki," she said in a low voice.

Tomoe's eyes widened. "Wh-what?!"

"Shh! Keep your voice down," Akira said before throwing a panicked glance around.

"Aki, are you out of your mind?!" she asked, her heart racing at the very thought of them taking yet another life.

Akira turned back to her. "Yuuki grabbed me on the way to school yesterday. He held a knife to my throat and said he was going to kill me," she said, pulling her makeshift choker down enough to show the cut across her neck.

Tomoe gasped as she held her hands over her mouth.

Akira nodded. "I had to tell him something, so... I told him you were the one who killed Miyoko and Kana."

Tomoe fell a step back as her eyes went wider, far more than before. "You told him what?!"

She flinched. "K-keep your voice down, geez..." she said before shaking her head. "Listen, he was about to kill me. I had to tell him something. But, listen. You're going to be fine."

"Is this why you told me to have my mom start picking me up from school?" Tomoe asked, her heart racing as she sat on the verge of tears.

"Yeah... but, just listen. Here's the plan, okay? We have ourselves a sleepover, just you, me, and Ikumi. And, once Ikumi falls asleep, I'll sneak out to meet with Yuuki, but I'll go prepared and try to get the jump on him and kill him," she explained with questionable confidence.

Tomoe stared in disbelief at her, unsure of how to respond. "You... Aki, no. You can't do this. Wh-what if... what if you're caught, or hurt, or worse?"

Akira lightly blushed at Tomoe's concern. "I'll be okay. I just have to be focused. And, before you ask... the reason we need Ikumi over is so when the police ask questions, we can just be like... 'oh, no, officer, I was at my friend's house having a sleepover. Just ask the detective's daughter. She was there too,'" she said with a grin.

This can't be happening. She can't seriously be suggesting this. There has to be some way to talk her out of hurting someone else, she thought before abruptly shaking her head. "That... h-how are you going to... you know. Be at my house for a sleepover while your out doing... this? Ikumi could wake up and see that you're missing," she said, hoping that poking holes in her friend's plan might serve to dissuade her.

"That's easy! I just crush up some sleeping pills, put them into a glass for Ikumi to unknowingly drink, and once she falls asleep, I'll kill him, then return before she wakes up. Far as she'll know, I'll have never left," Akira responded.

She's going to drug Ikumi?! Has she lost her mind? I... I can't let her do this, she thought as her mind scrambled to think of how else she might dissuade Akira from attempting something so horrible. "It's... it's too dangerous. He's a lot stronger than either of us. If you tried anything, he'd overpower you," she explained.

Crossing her arms, Akira sighed. "You're right... he is significantly stronger than I am. But, as I said, I'll have to get the jump on him. I'll bring a kitchen knife or something with me."

Lowering her head, Tomoe could scarcely believe that Akira would come up with such an evil and immoral plan.

Akira let out a deep sigh, then checked her phone. "My grandfather is gonna be pissed if I don't get home soon, so I'd better go," she said, looking back to Tomoe. "Listen, I know you're worried about everything... I am too. But, trust me, I'll take care of this. Yuuki wasn't this big of a problem for us until Kana... and that's on me. I'll handle him, and I promise I won't get myself hurt, or worse," she said, offering a far more confident smile than before as she reached out and placed her hand on

Tomoe's upper arm. "We're going to get out of this. I swear it. You and I are in this thing together, and we're getting out together. I won't sell you out, and I won't stop until we're in the clear."

With a brief wave goodbye, Akira made her way over to the stairs, then descended back down towards the second, then first floors of the school. While Akira's speech about her handling everything was likely meant to reassure Tomoe that things would be alright, the truth was that she felt as if their lives were taking a dark turn that they may never return from. Less than one week ago, Akira had bludgeoned a girl to death in cold blood, then very casually returned to her daily school life as if nothing had occurred. Now, she intended to kill someone else, and while her motivations were understandable, violence shouldn't be the first thought in her mind.

Feeling discouraged from this sudden abrupt turn of events, Tomoe reluctantly made her way down the stairs. She did have her mother here at the school to pick her up, though she had struggled to come up with a legitimate reason to need such accommodations. Therefore, the explanation she provided was one of partial truth, now more than before. Some students were bullying Akira, and Tomoe stood up for her, and now they were trying to bully her. She'd already vented her frustrations with the teasing she received before with her mother, so this wasn't a complete surprise to her.

On the short drive home, Tomoe kept quiet, thinking to herself what she could do to change Akira's mind. Every idea she came up with felt as if it would simply fall flat with a bit of improvisation from her violently resourceful friend. Mari noticed how quiet she was and even inquired about it, though Tomoe brushed her mother's concerns away by simply exclaiming that she was tired and would likely turn in early for the night. She didn't enjoy keeping secrets from her mother, but what she held now was a secret she didn't want anyone knowing.

That, for Tomoe, was the most painful part out of all of this. The fastest and most effective way to prevent Yuuki's death, or even Akira's if she were to get herself killed in this horrible plan of hers, was to go to the police and simply turn herself in. Doing so would undoubtedly devastate her mother and even her father once he heard of what happened. But, it would also destroy Akira's life, as Tomoe wouldn't wish to take the blame for Kana's death, as it wasn't her fault. If anything, Tomoe had tried her very best to prevent a conflict between those two from culminating in violence.

No sooner than they arrived back at their house did Tomoe climb up the stairs to her bedroom, then fall against her bed, her mind exhausted from processing what Akira had shared with her at school. Staring up at the ceiling, she felt frustrated, hopeless, defeated but also as if she had simply allowed this to all drag on for far too long. Before, she wasn't opposed to just turning herself in and facing judgment for her mistake. But now, the thought of living years of her life, especially during her youth, behind bars terrified her. To know that every hope and dream she ever held would be swept away, should she divulge the truth, was enough to keep her lips sealed.

I can't let her do this... Tomoe thought to herself as she shook her head. *I don't want anyone else to die or even get hurt. But, what could I do? If I beg her to leave him alone, she'll just come up with a ton of reasons why she thinks this is the only solution.*

With a groan, she rolled over and buried her face in her pillow, wanting nothing more than to cry her frustrations away, though knowing that would accomplish very little. Peeking up from her pillow, she stared at the headboard of her bed, her mind still churning out potential ideas, each of which felt as if they would fall completely flat. However, one idea stood out to her, one which was very simple yet difficult for her to accept or even consider.

She swallowed nervously, then reluctantly nodded. *If I tell her not to go, because I don't want anyone to get hurt... she'll do it anyway, because it's just me asking her as a friend. But, if I beg her to stay... because I don't want her to get hurt, then tell her it's because I...* she paused her thoughts as she closed her eyes, then shook her head. *Because I 'love' her... and want to be with her, but don't want her to risk her life for this... then, I think she'd be willing to stay,* she thought before shuddering. *I don't want that... but I can't think of any other way. I can't let her do this. I can't let her kill Yuuki simply because she wants an easy way out. There has to be another way.*

Pushing herself off from her bed, Tomoe stood up and wiped tears from her eyes. "If we have this sleepover... I'll tell her then. I'll drop it on her at the last second, just before she leaves. Then, she won't have a chance to come up with any alternatives. And, if that doesn't persuade her," she looked to her bed, "I'll invite her up here to... cuddle, or something," she said, shivering as she thought about having to get intimate with someone like Akira.

It's alright, Tomoe... you can do this. It's either this, let people die or go to prison for the rest of your life... I can fake a relationship... that's no problem, she thought to herself before turning and making her way out of her bedroom, then downstairs. *I just need to ask my mom if it's okay. I hope she's fine with it because otherwise, I'll have to figure out another way to do this.*

Looking around, Tomoe could hear her mother in the kitchen, likely preparing dinner for the two of them. Stepping into their quaint little kitchen, she put on a smile. "Something smells good."

Mari looked to her daughter and smiled back at her. "You say that no matter what I cook," she said with a light chuckle. "But, I'm making harusame tonight. If you're still hungry afterward, we do still have some cake in the refrigerator."

"I'm sure the salad alone will be fine," she said as she drew closer to her mother. "So, um... I wanted to ask you... would you have any objections to me inviting a couple of my friends over this weekend for a sleepover?"

Mari pursed her lips, then shook her head. "No, none that I can think of. I am curious, though. I've only met your one friend, Akira. You made another who you'd already like to invite over?"

Tomoe nodded. "Yeah, her name is Yasuhida Ikumi. She's the daughter of a detective who works for the police department, so... she's really mature and responsible. You can tell that her father's work really inspires her," she said, speaking highly of her to help set her mother's mind at ease.

Mari's smile soon returned. "She sounds like a very reliable friend to have. Well, I'd love to meet her as well, so feel free to invite her and Akira over."

She gasped, then bowed her head profusely. "Thank you so much!"

Mari lightly chuckled. "You must have had your heart set on this. I'm glad I could make your day. So, will they be staying until Monday?"

"Uh..." Tomoe rose back up and thought briefly on it. "I think... maybe just Friday night? Aki said she has a lot of chores and homework this weekend, so... probably just for this one night, if that's okay."

"That's fine. Feel free to invite them over again in the future if they're able to stay longer. It's been a while since I've been able to cook a large meal for you and your friends, and I kind of miss it," she said with a playful grin. "I suppose you could say that seeing you and your friends together reminds me of my youth when I used to spend time with my friends," she said, motioning to her daughter. "These are your glory days,

Tomoe. You should spend them growing strong relationships with others, networking with people at school and in whatever field you're interested in, and devoting your energy to your studies. Don't squander these days."

Tomoe let out a deep sigh. *They'll definitely be squandered if the police do end up finding out the truth...* she thought to herself before nodding. "I won't, mom. I promise," she said before bowing her head once more. "I'm going to text Aki and Ikumi the good news. Thank you again!" she said before hastily making her way back upstairs to her bedroom.

Pulling her cellphone from her bookbag, she promptly sent a text message to Akira, letting her know that Mari was fine with the two of them coming over for the weekend. She then sent a message to Ikumi, whose number she'd picked up on Tuesday. While Akira didn't respond, likely due to being swamped in chores, Ikumi quickly replied with a mind-boggling number of cheerful emojis. Clearly, she was excited to spend time with the two of them, even if it was only for one evening.

For the time being, Tomoe was essentially facilitating this confrontation between Akira and Yuuki. If her plan to seduce and persuade Akira to stay failed, then Tomoe would be out of options, aside from resorting to brute force and perhaps trying to restrain Akira to prevent her from leaving. Though, making someone she was terrified of, such as Akira, her enemy, hardly felt as if it would be beneficial to anyone. Tomoe needed to be smart when it came to handling her deranged friend. If she could seduce Akira and engage in a relationship with her, then Tomoe would have the pull to prevent her from hurting anyone else, at least until she can figure out a better solution that doesn't end in anyone's death.

Chapter 20
Change of Plans

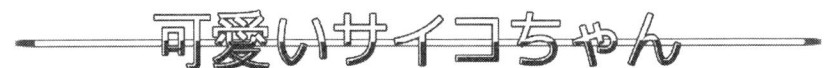

可愛いサイコちゃん

After having gotten home herself, Akira began working on the long list of chores her grandfather had for her as punishment. A list so in-depth and detailed that she knew there was no way she could get them done before the end of the night, and that was no doubt by design. If she had any homework from school, it hardly mattered, as her mind was far too focused on how precisely she would handle Yuuki. Momentary distractions, such as her grandfather yelling at her, or her grandmother trying to comfort her, or inquiring as to why she even drank and smoked so much last night, were bumps in the road to finding answers she desperately needed.

It wasn't until she laid down in bed that she saw the text message from Tomoe, informing her that they were good for tomorrow night, that she felt as if things might actually work out for her. Yuuki's strength would still be a significant factor in how she approached this situation, and she'd still need to ensure she could meet with him to execute her plan. To facilitate this, Akira sent a text message to Hideko, asking for Yuuki's number. She provided it, then asked why Akira needed it. A question Akira didn't bother answering.

Sending a message to Yuuki, Akira promised that she would have a sleepover with her friend and that she'd meet him late at night to give him a voice recording of Tomoe confessing to the murders. She also provided her apologies for not being able to lure Tomoe to him, stating that she was overly cautious after having seen Akira and Hideko together. He didn't respond before she fell asleep. However, by the time she woke up, she had a confirmation of a time and place for them to meet. This was perfect, as it was in a nearby park, away from any potential witnesses to the murder she intended to commit.

After completing her morning chores, then preparing for school, she left home, eager to get this day started and then over with so that she could finally see her plan to fruition. Along the way, she felt oddly upbeat and optimistic about how things would play out today. She still had no idea how she'd stand up to someone like Yuuki, who was so much stronger than Akira was, though she was confident that she'd eventually have a brilliant idea pop into her head of how to handle him.

Arriving at the school, Akira was just changing out of her street shoes when she was approached by, of all people, Hideko. She wore a look of concern, which told Akira that she most likely didn't hear from Yuuki what was planned for tonight. All the better, as she'd be one less potential witness who could rat Akira out to the police after she kills him.

"Hey, Akira?" Hideko called out as she drew closer. "I never received a response from you about why you needed Yuuki's number," she said, throwing a glance around. "You're not... planning to actually let him do what he said, are you? I thought we were going to go a more peaceful route?"

She turned to her and smiled. "Still peaceful. I need his number so I can send the recording of her confessing to him."

"You told him about our idea?" Hideko asked in shock.

Akira nodded. "Yeah. Why? What did you tell him the day we didn't show up like he wanted?"

She grimaced. "I told him that you weren't able to convince her to walk home with you and that she seemed super suspicious of things... and that you and I had a few ideas to make things work out. But, I never gave him any details."

Akira shrugged. "Then this all works out fine."

"If... if he hears her confess, though, how do you know he'll give it to the police, rather than just using it to fuel his anger? He might try attacking her here at school if that's the case," Hideko fearfully explained.

Akira shook her head. "I don't see that happening. Besides, I'll send you a copy of the recording too. Then you can take it to the police if he decides to stick with his original plan."

Staring at her, Hideko appeared somewhat suspicious. "You seem... very confident that things will be alright..."

"Good morning Aki," Ikumi said in a cheerful tone as she approached, wearing a wide grin. She then looked to Hideko. "And good morning to you too, Hideko."

Throwing a glance her way, Hideko sighed. "I need to get ready for class," she said, turning and walking away.

Ikumi frowned as she left, looking back to Akira. "Is everything alright?"

Akira nodded. "Yeah, I wouldn't let her mood bother you. That said... I think she was faking being our friend," she admitted with a sigh. "She's friends with that boy and girl who attacked Tomoe and me outside of school on Friday," she said, her focus trailing to Ikumi. "I think we should just try to avoid her."

"Wow... yeah, if she's friends with those two, then definitely," she said.

"Hey, you two," Tomoe said, sounding somewhat upbeat as she approached them.

"Good morning, Tomoe!" Ikumi cheerfully responded.

Akira smiled. "How did you sleep?"

"Fine. Aki, did you get my message about the sleepover? My mom said it was fine," Tomoe said.

She gasped. "Oh! Shit... I must have forgotten to respond. Yeah, I got it. Sorry, I was dead-ass tired last night after my chores..."

Ikumi turned to Akira and frowned. "That reminds me... how is a sleepover going to work if you're in trouble at home?"

"I'll, um... just be staying one night. I'll do all of my chores, then go over to Tomoe's house this evening. We'll all hang out late into the night, crash, and then I'll get home late Saturday morning," Akira explained.

Ikumi pursed her lips. "You have permission from your grandparents?"

Akira grinned widely. "Eh, I'm more of an 'ask for forgiveness than permission' kind of girl, so... I'm sure it'll be fine..."

She sighed. "You're going to get into even more trouble, Aki..."

Akira scoffed, then dismissively waved her hand. "Don't worry about it. I'll be fine."

Tomoe gently placed her hand on Ikumi's shoulder to draw her attention. "We should get our shoes changed out for class. We don't want to be late."

With a nod, Ikumi moved to her locker to get her shoes changed.

"H-hey, Tomoe... plans aside, I'm psyched to hang out with you two tonight," Akira said to her friend before she walked away.

Tomoe reluctantly smiled at Akira, almost as if the plan Akira had in mind soured the very idea of them having a sleepover.

Akira felt a degree of remorse from her friend's hesitant smile, though she knew what had to be done. If Yuuki weren't dealt with, he'd become a progressively greater threat until he finally got the opportunity he wanted to kill them both.

Once the girls were ready, they walked together to their class. Taking their seats, Akira noticed Hideko skeptically watching her from a distance. It felt as if she could already see through Akira's plan, though it was difficult to know for sure. As their math class ended, Akira noticed that Hideko was quick to bolt from the classroom, making her way off towards gym class. Parting ways with Tomoe, Akira and Ikumi began walking to the gym as well, with Ikumi leading the conversation about what all they could do tonight.

She suggested that she could bring some board games for them to play or movies to watch, and Akira simply agreed to everything, being that her mind couldn't have been further from the conversation. Even once they reached the gym, Akira found herself scrambling to ensure everything was in order, at least in her head. Hideko likely wouldn't know or have anything that would point the police squarely at her, and while Yuuki might, she just needed to make sure that she took or destroyed his phone after she kills him tonight.

During gym, Akira and Ikumi found no interruptions. Akira did see an odd sight, however. Hideko was exercising with her step-brother, Takashi, likely as she talked about how suspicious Akira was now behaving. If it kept Takashi from bothering her, though, she was fine with Hideko telling him whatever she wanted to. The remainder of Akira's day was every bit as peaceful, as she had no further interactions with Hideko or Takashi and didn't even see Yuuki at school at all. A part of her wondered if he was choosing not to come or if he had been expelled somehow.

After school had ended, Akira raced home and began work on her chores. She kept busy, so her grandfather wouldn't harass her, which worked about as well as one would expect, as he made sure she knew that she'd be busy with chores this entire weekend. Unfortunately, she had other plans, and once her grandparents turned in around their usual time, Akira was getting ready to ride her bike over to her friend's house to join in the fun of a sleepover before finalizing her plan to murder Yuuki.

Arriving at Tomoe's house, Akira parked her bike out by Mari's car, then made her way over to the back door. She knew Ikumi had already been here for a couple of hours, which made her happy, as that meant the two of them could get to know one another better. Tomoe's experience with Ikumi had been limited only to their interactions at school, and those were fewer and further between compared to Akira's. Knocking on the back door, Akira eagerly waited for her friend to answer.

It only took a moment, but soon Ikumi opened the door and gave Akira a huge grin. "You're late!" she teased.

Akira pursed her lips. "Can't be late when the party doesn't start until I arrive. Where's Tomoe?"

Ikumi giggled. "She and Miss Mari are making snacks for us. I was decorating them, but my hands were clean, so I ran to answer the door," she said, showing her hands off to Akira.

"I see. What kind of snacks?" Akira asked as she stepped inside.

"We have dango, coffee pudding, and I also brought a bag of chewy candy... I remember you saying those were your favorite," Ikumi said, a light redness forming on her cheeks.

Akira chuckled. "Yeah, they are. But dango and pudding sound delicious too," she said as she made her way down the hall, then peeked into the kitchen. "Sorry, I'm here so late. Got super held up with chores."

Tomoe turned to her and smiled. "It's okay. I'm glad you made it."

Mari glanced over her shoulder at Akira. "You should be careful. You know there's a curfew at eight, don't you?"

Akira wore a wide, toothy grin as she snickered. "Which is why I raced over here as fast as I could on my bike. I only broke curfew by a few minutes... I'm sure they'll forgive me."

Ikumi moved past Akira and returned to decorating the dango. "Honestly, the curfew might be at eight, but my dad's always said that they don't bother enforcing it until ten. And by then, most everyone is asleep unless they work late."

She motioned towards her friend. "See? *See?!* I have proof that I'm fine. And Ikumi knows because her old man is a cop."

"Detective," Ikumi corrected her.

"Isn't a detective a cop?" Akira asked with a snicker.

Ikumi puffed up her cheeks, feigning irritation.

"Alright, don't start fighting, you two," Mari teased.

Ikumi giggled. "I'm not. I'm just playing around."

"Same," Akira said as she moved over towards where Tomoe was rolling the dango dough into balls. "Two o'clock, by the way..." she said as a whisper.

"Two?" Tomoe asked, keeping her voice low.

She nodded. "Yeah... you know..."

"Oh..." Tomoe responded, turning back to the dough she was rolling in her hands. She sighed, then nodded. "Alright."

Akira stared at her for a moment before looking at Mari. "Thank you for letting Ikumi, and I come over."

Mari nodded. "You're both more than welcome here whenever you'd like," she said, throwing a glance back at Ikumi. "Especially Miss Ikumi. Tomoe was still cleaning up when she arrived, and she didn't waste any time jumping in to help," she said with a light chuckle. "Anyone who cleans my house for me is welcome here anytime."

Ikumi blushed, then bowed her head. "W-well, I didn't want to just sit around while she did all of the work... I would have felt terrible."

Akira grinned. "Yeah, well, she deserves the help. Tomoe has helped me a few times with my chores whenever she comes over."

"If I didn't, you'd never have any time to hang out," Tomoe responded.

She rolled her eyes. "That's true..."

Mari smiled at her. "Don't scoff too much at your chores, Akira. When I was your age, I hated doing chores around the house for my parents. But, once I grew older, and especially after having Tomoe, I was grateful for that discipline my parents instilled into me."

Akira couldn't disagree more, as she knew that the chores were intended as little more than punishment for her from her grandfather. "Yeah... I suppose you're right, Miss Mari..." she said before moving over and to the table where Ikumi was using seaweed and other various edibles to decorate the dango. "Can I help?"

Ikumi giggled. "Of course!" she said before motioning to the seat next to her. "I'm falling a bit behind anyway."

Sitting down, Akira took one of the sticks that had three dango balls already skewered onto it, then began gathering edibles to decorate it with. As she did, she had many laughs with both her friends and Mari, as the girls all shared various short stories with one another or gossiped about the shows they watched. Akira even went off on a bit of a tangent on the music genres she loved so much, prompting a brief conversation between Mari and her in English, which gave Akira some well-needed experience speaking the language in casual conversation.

Once they finished making all of the snacks, the girls moved to the living room to watch a movie that Ikumi had brought over. It was a scary movie, of which Akira wasn't the biggest fan, while Tomoe was indifferent. It was about a woman who was murdered, then her spirit possessed her granddaughter, before waiting years to manifest so that she could exact revenge against the man who killed her. There were some truly disturbing aspects to certain scenes of the movie, but nothing was as unsettling as the event Akira had planned for tonight.

As midnight struck, Mari decided to call it a night on the documents that she had been working on, then bid farewell to the girls as she retired upstairs. Akira saw this as the perfect opportunity to plant the drugs into Ikumi's drink. As it stood, her friend had a small bottle of fizzy fruit soda, which she was almost halfway finished with. Akira already had a double dosage of sleeping pills crushed up in a plastic bag in her pocket, so she knew she could add the drugs whenever she wanted, but she needed to be subtle with it.

Ikumi stared at the television, completely zoned in on the movie she was watching. Reaching over, she picked her soda up, then took a short drink before setting it back down. With her so intensely focused on the movie, Akira just reached over and took the bottle without Ikumi noticing a thing. Pulling the small bag from her pocket, she began dumping the powdered medication into the liquid. She kept a close eye on her friend as she did this, then gave the bottle a firm swirl until the powder was well mixed in with the beverage.

She then returned the bottle to the table where Ikumi had it. This drew her friend's attention, though Akira just offered a wide grin and claimed that she had stolen a sip. Ikumi reminded her that she too had a drink, so she didn't need to steal her's, then went back to watching the movie. Akira kicked back and relaxed as Ikumi steadily worked her way through the rest of the bottle, and within the last third of the movie, began showing signs of just how sleepy she was.

With a deep yawn, Ikumi adjusted her position on the couch to lay her head on the couch's armrest. She didn't say a word about feeling tired, but by the time the credits were rolling, her eyelids weighed heavily on her, and it wasn't long after that before she began subtly snoring as she dozed off. Akira gave it a moment, at least until the movie was entirely through the credits before she got up to check on her friend, seeing that Ikumi was peacefully snoozing away.

Akira grinned. "Out like a light..." she eagerly said, though making sure to keep her voice low. Stepping away from her, she hastily made her way into the kitchen.

Watching Akira leave, Tomoe quickly stood up and followed her. "Aki..." she said as she trailed shortly behind her.

"Alright, so... I'm gonna need a knife, and somewhere to hide the knife... oh!" she said, stopping as she turned and went to go back into the living room. "I can just use my backpack."

Blocking the way, Tomoe frowned. "Aki, wait."

"Huh? What's up?" Akira asked, somewhat confused by her friend blocking her way.

She sighed. "Do... do you have to do this?"

"Uh... yeah? If I don't, then Yuuki is going to kill one or both of us. The guy's lost his fucking mind," Akira explained as she frowned, fearing that Tomoe was going to oppose the idea.

She lightly grimaced, then lowered her head. "Have you, um... figured out how you're going to do it? Since... you know... he's so much stronger than either of us?"

Reaching up, Akira scratched the back of her head. "I had a few ideas... I think I'll probably have to improvise, though..."

Tomoe looked back at her. They stared for only a moment before she inhaled sharply. "I... I don't want you to go."

She sighed. "Don't think that I want to do this. If he weren't threatening both of us in his own way, I wouldn't even consider anything like this. Hell, I didn't even think about him until he had a knife to my throat."

"No, Aki..." Tomoe said as she shook her head. "If you go, and do this... and get hurt, or worse... I don't know..." she said, struggling to find the words to express what she was trying to say.

Akira frowned. "Please, don't say that you feel like this is all your fault. I don't want you blaming yourself anymore... I'm the one who pissed Yuuki off, so I'm the one who should–"

Rushing forward, Tomoe placed her hands on Akira's cheeks, gently holding her as she delicately pressed her lips against her friend's.

Akira's eyes went wide as Tomoe abruptly kissed her, locking their lips together. Her mind swirled and spiraled through an array of feelings, all of them positive, all of them wonderful. Though it felt like it lasted forever, their innocent kiss was only for a few seconds before Tomoe slowly pulled back. Akira stared at her friend in utter disbelief, unsure of what to say in response to such an out-of-the-blue action.

Wh-what the fuck?! Akira though to herself as her mind scrambled to make sense of what happened.

"P-please, don't go, Aki... I don't want you to get hurt, or worse..." Tomoe said, appearing as if she were struggling not to cry.

Akira continued to stare, speaking only after a few awkward moments had elapsed. "You... y-you just... kissed me?"

Biting her lip, Tomoe nodded. "I've been... struggling with my emotions, Aki. I've never felt this way towards anyone before. The way I feel about you, I mean," she said before sighing, then reaching down to take Akira's hands in her own. "I couldn't bear to have anything happen to you. The very thought of it makes me want to cry..." she said, inhaling sharply once more. "Akira, I... I r-really... *really* like you... and, I want you to stay here... with me. *Please?*"

Akira's mind wasn't so much racing as much as it was scrambling to even operate in any real capacity. This girl she loved, who had told her not all that long ago that she wasn't interested, had just kissed her and was now pleading with her to stay here.

With a momentary grimace, Tomoe tried to maintain her composure as Akira silently stared at her. "Um... Aki?"

"Ba–" Akira began to say before abruptly shaking her head. "Wh-what?" she asked, snapping out of her confused daze.

Tomoe eyed her with concern. "Will... will you stay here with me?"

Feeling her heart racing in her chest, Akira knew she needed to take care of Yuuki, or else things would become infinitely more difficult for them. But, on the other hand, she wanted to stay here and explore these feelings with Tomoe. More than anything, she wanted to stay here with the love of her life.

Tomoe bit nervously at her lip, hesitating as she began to speak up. "If... if you stay... we could, um... go upstairs to my room, and..."

Akira perked her head up, listening to every word that left Tomoe's lips.

She sighed. "We could cuddle in bed together and... fall asleep in each others' arms," she suggested as she began to blush.

Slowly, Akira's face began to turn from a light reddish hue to a vibrant, burning red as embarrassing thoughts filled her mind.

Tomoe swallowed nervously. "Is... is that too much? I just thought–"

"N-no!" Akira loudly proclaimed, hastily covering her mouth as she realized she shouted. She shook her head. "No, no... it's not. I just..." she exhaled sharply. "J-just stop. You don't have to... I... n-never mind! I'm staying. I'm not going anywhere," she said as she moved a bit closer. "I don't care wh-what we do... Tomoe, I just... I want to be here... with you."

"So, you won't put yourself in harm's way by... trying anything stupid?"

Akira offered a nervous, toothy grin. "Is kissing you stupid? B-because, I'd really like to try that again..." she said as she felt her heart throbbing heavily in her chest, threatening to pound straight out, should her nerves not ease up.

Tomoe lightly giggled, then leaned forward and kissed Akira again, with no hesitation. Pulling back, she smiled at her behind a veil of what appeared to be nervousness of her own.

Akira felt as if her knees were weak from Tomoe's lips pressed against her's. Lightheaded from how love-struck she was in this moment, a huge, goofy smile formed across her lips before she laughed in disbelief.

Tugging gently on Akira's hands, Tomoe gestured with a nod towards the stairs that led up to the second floor. "Come on... let's go," she said with mild reluctance.

"O-okay," Akira promptly responded, her voice cracking slightly due to her rush of adrenaline and euphoria.

Guiding Akira behind her, Tomoe led the way upstairs to her bedroom, feeling a mix of knots in her stomach. Akira felt similarly, though for far different reasons, as her mind scrambled to deduce whether or not this was really happening or if she just imagined it all. As they stepped inside Tomoe's bedroom, Akira had a completely different feeling than the last time they were here. It almost felt as if it were forbidden for her to be in here, akin to something very taboo that she should avoid.

Tomoe walked over to her closet and dug around for a moment. Akira, meanwhile, just stood awkwardly nearby, unsure of what her friend was searching for but mildly intimidated by what she must have been thinking as she sifted through her clothes. Pulling out two pairs of shorts and some comfortable-looking t-shirts, Tomoe turned and offered one of each to Akira.

"If you want, you can change in here. I still need to go brush my teeth before bed, so I'll change in the bathroom," Tomoe said.

"Uh... o-okay..." Akira said in confusion as she took the clothes.

Tomoe threw her a cheerful smile before making her way out of the bedroom and just down the hall.

Watching her leave, Akira's eyes soon drifted down to the clothes in her hands. *I brought my own clothes... although my backpack is still down in the living room...* she thought to herself, wondering if she should go and get it or just wear what Tomoe had picked out for her.

Looking over to the closet, she approached it and began timidly searching around. She was trying to find a tank top, which fortunately didn't take long to find. Staying out of sight of the open door, Akira took her shirt off, along with her bra, then slipped the tank top on over her head, securing it loosely on her small frame. She then took her shorts off to exchange them for the soft cotton ones Tomoe had offered her. Waiting around for a moment, Akira picked her phone up from the pocket of her shorts, then meandered over to the bed, hesitantly taking a seat on the edge of it.

Akira couldn't help but feel incredibly nervous over this. As she had shared with Tomoe, this wasn't her first time kissing a girl, nor even sneaking into bed with one. Although, this was decidedly different than her brief foray into her previous friend's arms. Tomoe initiated this, and she had already confessed her affections towards Akira, feelings that she must have been suppressing all along as she desired nothing more than to conform to what others consider normal. And yet now, she's decided that she wants to follow her heart, a concept that sent an excited shiver down Akira's spine.

After around five or six agonizingly long minutes, Tomoe returned to the bedroom, a content smile across her lips as she closed the door. She then looked to Akira, cocking her head curiously at her friend but then shaking off whatever caught her off guard. Tomoe turned the lights off before moving around to the other side of her bed from Akira. This left only the faint moonlight to illuminate the room as the girls began settling into bed under the thin sheets.

Taking a deep breath, Tomoe turned onto her side, facing Akira, and smiled. "So, um... just cuddling, okay?"

"Huh? R-right, yeah... and, uh... kissing too, right?" Akira timidly asked.

"A little... but, it is late. We should get some sleep," Tomoe said before scooting a bit closer to Akira, then running her arm under her friend's neck, around to her back, and pulling her a bit closer.

Akira's heart felt as if it jumped as Tomoe brought her over and into her arms. Her friend was so much stronger than she was, and this helped put that on clear display. Akira rested her head on Tomoe's shoulder as she scooted closer, while Tomoe laid back down onto her back. Draping one leg over her friend's, Akira closed her eyes and nuzzled her cheek against

Tomoe's shoulder and upper chest. Being held like this and with their bodies so close, it felt like heaven to her. Whatever plans she had tonight merely melted away as she enjoyed the warm embrace of her beautiful, strong, and charming friend.

Chapter 21
Escalating Problems

可愛いサイコちゃん

The following morning, Tomoe awoke to little more than the sunlight leaking in through the window, bathing her in its radiance as she slowly began to realize where she was, or more specifically, who she was with. Laying next to her, albeit slumped down further than where she started, was Akira. She was loosely clung to Tomoe's side, one leg draped over, while her head rested against Tomoe's chest, no different than if it were pillows on the bed for her. It was clear that she was in a deep sleep, so Tomoe knew her friend wasn't up to anything perverse, but it still troubled her that this was how they awoke.

Cautiously, Tomoe squirmed away from Akira, at least enough that her head fell to rest on her arm.

"Hm? Wha?" Akira groggily said before rolling over and onto her back, deeply yawning as she reached up and rubbed her eyes. It took a moment for her to remember where she was, though once she did, a gracious smile formed across her lips as she looked to her friend. "Um... h-hey, Tomoe. How did you sleep?"

"I slept alright, I suppose," she said as she scooted over to the edge of the bed and stood up. Checking her phone, she saw the time and glanced back at Akira. "It's already eight. We should probably go check on Ikumi."

Akira blushed. "Um... say, Tomoe? Does... does this mean that you and I are... w-well, I mean... you know, because we kissed and, like... yeah..." she began to say before sighing. "Are we... girlfriends now?"

Biting her lip, Tomoe reluctantly nodded.

With a gasp, Akira practically jumped up in bed. "*Yes!* I actually have a girlfriend! This is so–"

"Aki, shh!" Tomoe snapped.

"Oops... sorry," she responded, covering her mouth.

Tomoe exhaled sharply. "I don't know how my mom would react to me having a girlfriend... but, also," she said, holding her index finger up. "I'll only be your girlfriend under one condition."

Akira swallowed nervously. "And that is?"

She placed her hands firmly on her hips. "I don't want you to do *anything* that might put yourself, or me, in any kind of danger. No matter what. I... I l-love you, and I don't want anything bad to happen to you. So, promise me that you'll stay out of trouble and not get hurt."

Akira stared blankly at Tomoe. "You... you said you love me..." she said in a low voice as her smile began to grow.

"I do... but, *promise* me."

She nodded. "I promise, and... I love you too, Tomoe."

Sighing deeply, Tomoe moved closer to the bed, placing one knee on it as she leaned in and kissed Akira on her lips. "Come on. We need to get downstairs and check on Ikumi."

Akira felt her heart flutter as their lips touched once again. She nodded. "Lead on... I'll follow you wherever you go, beautiful."

Tomoe rolled her eyes, then pulled back as she moved to circle the bed.

Pushing the covers back, Akira got up and followed her girlfriend out into the hallway. Together they descended to the first floor, where they were surprised to see that Ikumi wasn't on the couch where they had left her. Akira did hear some talking in the kitchen, which sounded as if it were from Mari, then a response from Ikumi. However long she slept, she was already awake.

Tomoe grimaced, then turned to her new girlfriend. "We should have woke up way earlier. Now, what are we going to tell my mom and Ikumi about why you slept in my room?"

Akira frowned, then thought briefly on it. "Ikumi won't really care... but, as for your mom... why not just say that we tried to wake Ikumi up so we could all go up to your room and crash, but she was so out of it and tired that we just gave up?"

"My room isn't that big. Where would each of us have slept?"

She scratched her head. "Uh... on the floor? Maybe one on the floor and two in the bed? But, since Ikumi was down here, we both slept in the bed?"

Tomoe sighed. "My bed's barely big enough for–"

"Tomoe? Akira? Is that you?" Mari called out from the kitchen.

The two of them turned in the direction of the kitchen.

"Y-yeah, we just woke up," Tomoe said before looking back to Akira. "Just act cool..."

"No worries. I've kept my sexuality a secret from my grandparents for years," Akira confidently stated.

Making their way into the kitchen, they saw Mari was preparing breakfast while Ikumi sat at the table, drinking some fruit juice.

"Good morning," Ikumi said in a cheerful, upbeat tone.

Tomoe bowed her head to her friend. "Good morning, Ikumi."

"Hey, Ikumi, did you sleep well? You were out like a light last night," Akira teased.

"I know... I feel like I slept like a rock. I guess school has really taken its toll on me with the semester," she responded with a deep sigh.

Mari turned and looked at Tomoe. "How did you two sleep?"

"Oh, um... we slept fine," Tomoe responded.

She smiled. "I'm glad. You two looked *very* cozy when I went to wake you up earlier. I had thought that since Ikumi woke up early, you and Akira would want to wake up and spend time with your friend. But, I wasn't sure if I should 'interrupt' the two of you," she said, hinting strongly at the fact that she saw them cuddling together.

Akira and Tomoe's faces each turned red.

"Y-yeah, Aki had a bad dream, and so... she and I, we... we talked and..." Tomoe began to explain, though her mother could see through her paltry attempts to lie.

Akira grimaced as she looked away.

Exhaling sharply, Mari shook her head. "We'll talk about it later," she said before turning around to continue tending to breakfast.

Biting her lip, Tomoe lowered her head.

Breakfast was, the say the least, awkward following Mari calling Akira and Tomoe out. It hadn't crossed either of their minds that Mari would have checked on them in the bedroom, although they each could agree that they shouldn't have just abandoned Ikumi downstairs. This became more clear when Akira and Ikumi left, each to go home, though Ikumi stopped to ask Akira what happened and why they left her in the living room alone.

Akira was honest with her friend, telling Ikumi that she and Tomoe kissed and cuddled, but nothing more. This clearly appeared to bother

her, and when Akira apologized, Ikumi shared that she felt as if she was just a third wheel for the sleepover, and it was more so intended for the two of them to hook up. This almost brought her to tears, though Akira was quick to promise that wasn't true, and even proclaimed that the moment she was no longer grounded, they would all three have a weekend-long sleepover that was full of fun, games, and plenty of laughs.

This did well to improve Ikumi's mood, and the two of them parted ways, with Akira riding her bicycle back home, where she knew she'd be chewed out by her grandfather for disappearing in the middle of the night. And, that's precisely what happened when she arrived back at her place. She was scolded, had her punishment doubled, meaning she'd likely spend the rest of this semester grounded, and even her grandmother was disappointed by her behavior. Despite all of this, Akira felt it was all worth it because she now, finally, had a girlfriend to call her own. Nirasaki was, at long last, not so lonely anymore.

Once Akira laid down to sleep, she sent Tomoe a few heartfelt messages, which she returned in kind. It did make Akira feel as if she were truly special in Tomoe's life. Although that was when her mind drifted away from the paradise she found herself in and began to think about the threat that pushed Akira to betray her grandfather's orders and go to Tomoe's house in the first place, Yuuki. He had messaged her before the sleepover, but she hadn't recalled any new messages. She checked, and sure enough, he hadn't messaged her at all.

Nervous as to what this could mean, as she essentially stood him up when it came to their plan, Akira wasn't sure what to do. She could try to lie and set up another time to meet, but then she'd need a new alibi, he'd likely be more suspicious, and it'd also put her in harm's way, which would go against what Tomoe pleaded her not to do. It was truly a difficult situation, and she wasn't exactly sure how she would handle it. Feeling that she had to do something, Akira called Yuuki's phone. She would try to give him some kind of excuse and attempt to gauge his reaction, then go from there.

The phone rang a few times, but there was no answer. It went to voice mail far sooner than Akira would have suspected, and that worried her. Yuuki likely saw her calling and decided to decline her call. Wanting some idea of how things were, she tried calling Hideko's number, which went directly to voice mail. Either her phone was off, or she had blocked Akira's number. Laying in bed for a moment, Akira was pleasantly surprised when she received a text message, though it was just from Tomoe. Not that she didn't appreciate the affection from her girlfriend, but right now, she needed comfort that everything was alright.

Throughout the weekend, Akira attempted to contact Yuuki a few more times, though each was unsuccessful. This progressively began to worry Akira more and more the longer she was left with nothing but silence between herself and those two. Hideko seemingly blocked her entirely, while Yuuki was simply not answering her calls. She sent them each a few text messages, though she still received no response. By Monday morning, she was genuinely fearful of what might happen, as Yuuki already threatened her before, and now he might very well make good on that. Fortunately for her, with her bike now back in working order thanks to Tomoe's help, Akira at least had one safe way for her to get to school. Or so she hoped.

Never in her life had she raced so quickly to school, pedaling as fast as she could to try and outrun Yuuki, should he be lying in wait for her. Akira was astonished that she was able to arrive at school without any difficulty, and once she did, she parked her bike, then raced inside, hoping to avoid any run-ins along the way to the school's main entrance. After changing her shoes out, Akira sent a text to her girlfriend, who she discovered was almost here and was being brought by her mother. This was a huge relief to Akira, though she knew she probably needed to be upfront with Tomoe about this possible threat.

As she was waiting around, she noticed Hideko walking into the school. She threw a glance Akira's way, though otherwise ignored her. Pursing her lips, she stepped away from her girlfriend's shoe locker, then approached Hideko. Composing herself, she tried to conceal her true fears and emotions as she drew closer.

"Hey, Hideko... I tried calling you over the weekend, and... I texted you, but you never responded," Akira said.

Slipping her indoor shoes on, Hideko put her street shoes away, then turned to Akira. "I'm sorry, Makai. But I don't talk to murderers," she plainly stated, making no effort to keep her voice down.

Akira recoiled back in slight shock. "Wh-what?"

"You heard me," she responded before glaring. "And, if you don't like it. I guess you'll have to *kill* me, just like you did to Hachi Miyoko and Nakajima Kana!" she loudly proclaimed before turning and walking away. "If I end up dead... we'll *all* know it was you, Makai!"

Staring in disbelief, Akira couldn't even find the words to respond. Other students nearby watched her, some whispering to one another, more than a few commenting to their friends about how another girl said the same thing about Akira and that they hadn't seen that girl in over a week. Akira nervously moved back to Tomoe's locker, though with everyone watching her, she couldn't stand to wait here in the hall and instead decided to head to class.

Keeping her head down, Akira took her usual seat. She then leaned forward and held her hands over her head, her mind scrambling about what she should say or do about Hideko screaming the same things Kana had before. She knew her old friend wasn't the violent type, so she wasn't a threat. But it'd still come back to severely hurt Akira if rumors like these began circulating freely here at school.

After a few moments, Tomoe and Ikumi stepped into class and made their way over to where Akira was seated. She was still holding her head, and it was clear that she was frustrated.

Ikumi frowned as she saw her friend in distress. "Aki? Are you okay?"

"Hm?" Akira responded as she looked at them both, seeing that they were each staring at her with concern. "I, uh... y-yeah, I'm fine," she said, forcing an awkward chuckle. "I was... just holding my head. I have a bit of a headache, that's all."

Ikumi looked briefly to Tomoe, seeing that she too didn't believe Akira's excuse. Returning her sights to her friend, she nodded. "If you say so. But, if there's anything you want to talk about... we're here for you."

Tomoe nodded. "Yeah... and, if it's not something you know 'how' to talk about... or something you want to keep private, just text me. Okay?"

"Alright, I will... thanks," Akira responded.

Reluctantly, Tomoe and Ikumi each took their seats next to Akira just as the class began. While her friends had their focus split between their worries for her and the class itself, Akira's mind was entirely focused on what all must have happened since she canceled her original plans. Hideko's opinions of her had at least changed over the weekend, and being that she stood Yuuki up, it was safe to say he wasn't her biggest fan either.

Once class was over, Akira and Ikumi departed for gym after a brief talk with Tomoe, where she reassured Akira that whatever was bothering her wasn't worth worrying about and that they could talk about it later. It was all too obvious to Akira that Tomoe knew precisely what was bothering her, or at least an aspect of it. Her girlfriend likely believed that it was all about Yuuki, but while he might have been the greatest threat to her, Hideko's antics out in the main hall proved to be a more immediate danger.

As they entered the gym hall, Akira didn't notice Hideko anywhere around. She knew she needed to be on guard for whatever might come next, as well as figuring out a solution to now two problems she likely had to deal with. Walking with Ikumi into the locker rooms, Akira noticed Hideko, though it appeared that she was very hastily getting changed, then leaving to head back out into the gym hall itself. A part of Akira began to wonder just what was going through her mind now that she was trying to effectively live up to Kana's standards for bullying Akira, with her trying to shout out to everyone that Akira was supposedly responsible for what happened to Miyoko and Kana.

With their gym uniforms on, Akira and Ikumi went out to start their exercises, choosing to start with indoor ones, if only to break up their routine a little. As they began their sit-ups, though, Akira noticed Takashi staring at her from afar. This wasn't unusual, though he appeared to be watching her with a more worried expression than she would have expected from someone who often eyed her like she was some prize to be won. With visible reluctance, he began approaching the two of them, seemingly undeterred by Ikumi's presence.

Noticing him, however, Ikumi exhaled sharply. "Again with this guy?" she asked, sounding disappointed that he still hadn't learned his lesson. Ikumi then stood up and moved once more between him and Akira, who was still sitting on her exercise mat. "I will go and get Mister Masaru if you keep harassing her like this," she warned as he drew near.

Takashi frowned. "I just wanted to talk to her... it's kind of important."

"You should have considered that before you continually harassed her simply because you 'like' her," she said, crossing her arms. "The next time you like a girl, I suggest you become her friend, get to know her, treat her with respect and then go from there. Definitely don't grab onto her against her will, like I've caught you doing to Akira, twice."

He lightly grimaced, then looked to Akira. "Um... w-well, it's about–"

"I don't care what it's about! I have enough shit to worry about without you adding to that," Akira snapped.

Ikumi nodded. "You should leave."

He sighed. "But, it's about Yuuki, he–"

She stomped her foot. "Leave now, or else I'll call Mister Masaru over here," she firmly stated.

Scrambling to stand up, Akira moved to Ikumi's side. "H-hold up..." she said, now curious as to what Takashi had to share about Yuuki.

Ikumi looked at her friend in confusion.

Pausing, Akira cleared her throat, then composed herself. "If it's really so important, then fine... I'll hear what you have to say," she said before turning to Ikumi. "I'll hear him out, then be right back."

She frowned. "Okay... if you want to. But, if he puts his hands on you, I'm yelling for the teacher."

Akira nodded, then looked to Takashi. She gestured off to the side. "Come over here, and tell me whatever it is that is so important," she said, feigning irritation as she led the way several meters away from Ikumi, far enough away that she'd be unlikely to overhear their conversation. Once they were far enough away, she threw a glance over at Ikumi, who was closely watching them. She then turned her attention to Takashi. "So, um... what was that about Yuuki?"

Takashi scratched his head. "Um, well... over the weekend, I found out that he was talking to Hideko a lot, and... I wasn't sure why, until she came to me and asked, no, insisted, that I stop talking to you."

She lightly grimaced. "Uh... why's that?"

He frowned. "She said that you and your friend, the cute one with the black hair, had something to do with her friends' deaths... I mean, she was really emotional about it, but... it sure seemed like she believed it."

Akira rolled her eyes. "She's just spreading rumors. Now, what was that about Yuuki?"

"Well, um... the way Hideko made it sound... it seemed almost like he intended to really hurt you. Like... maybe I'm exaggerating here, but I genuinely think he believes you had something to do with Kana's death and wants to... *kill* you in return," Takashi reluctantly shared.

Closing her eyes, she lowered her head. She already assumed that he wanted her dead after Hideko's abrupt change of tone, and it appeared that she was right. She looked back at him. "You're overreacting."

"I don't think I am," he said before taking a step closer and reaching out to take her hand.

She took a half step back to avoid him as she glared.

He sighed. "I'm really worried about you, Akira. You know you mean the world to me. I don't want anything bad to happen to you."

"I'll be fine. All I have to do is avoid Yuuki. It should be easy since I don't share any classes with him, and my bike is working again, so I can get home before he has a chance to try anything," she responded.

"You won't have to worry about him here at school," he said with a subtle smile. "From what I heard, he got expelled."

Akira recoiled in slight shock. "Expelled? For what?"

"According to Hideko, it was some cop who harassed the school over it. Apparently, Yuuki punched his kid or something, and he got mad about it. So, he strong-armed the principal into expelling him," Takashi said.

She pursed her lips as she thought about it. Her eyes trailed over to Ikumi. *If I had to take a wild guess... I'd say it was her uncle, not her father, who argued for Yuuki's expulsion. Not that it matters. If he's not here at school, though... that means he could be waiting for me anywhere.*

Takashi glanced back at Ikumi, then at Akira. "Hideko told me how Yuuki described the girl. That's her, right? Your friend?"

Akira sighed, then looked to Takashi. She nodded. "Yeah. She's the lead detective's daughter. But I think the guy who bitched at the principal was probably her uncle. Guy's pretty intimidating, so I could totally see it."

He smiled. "If you're such good friends with the daughter of a detective, then it's kind of hard to believe Hideko or Yuuki either one thinks that you could have hurt anyone. I mean..." he chuckled, "you'd have to be pretty dumb to try and get away with murder when your friend's dad is a cop."

Reluctantly, she nodded, then even chuckled herself. "You're not wrong," she said, realizing that she was having a relatively normal conversation with Takashi without him creeping on her in any way. He'd said a few unnerving things, but nothing compared to how he usually was. She cleared her throat. "Well, thanks for letting me know about Yuuki. But, I'm going to go back to exercising with my friend," she said, starting back towards where Ikumi was at. "Oh, and... don't talk to me anymore. I appreciate the heads up, but you're still a creep, and I don't want anything to do with you."

He frowned at what she said, though she stepped away before he could respond. Returning to Ikumi's side, she reassured her friend that everything was fine and that he was just letting her know that Yuuki had gotten himself expelled. Ikumi asked how, worrying that it was somehow her fault, but Akira reassured her that it was his own doing. As they went back to their exercises, Akira began to work out in her mind how she would handle things. She had to alleviate her problems with Yuuki, but that was now made more difficult because Tomoe didn't want her putting herself into harm's way.

    This left Akira with only one real option. She had to eliminate Yuuki as a threat without exposing herself to any danger. Hideko could be handled later, but Yuuki had to be tended to immediately. Her best shot was probably to get him arrested again, although the only crime he'd likely commit at this point would be murder, and that wouldn't gel well with her intentions to keep herself out of harm's way. She continued to wrack her brain throughout gym class, and Ikumi knew she was deep in thought by how quiet she was. She needed answers to her problems, but while she knew what she needed to do, figuring out how to get it done was another step entirely.

Chapter 22
Unintended Planning

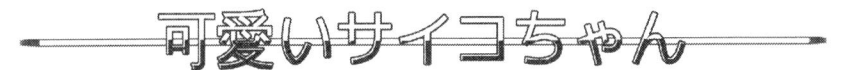

可愛いサイコちゃん

As they neared the end of gym class, Akira and Ikumi wrapped up their exercises and prepared to head into the locker rooms to change. They weren't bothered again by Takashi since Akira spoke to him, though that didn't stop him from watching her from a distance. The information he shared was valuable to Akira, though that didn't change her opinion of him in the slightest. The further he was from her, the better. Although, she knew that she'd enjoy things more if he weren't peering at her from across the gymnasium.

Entering into the locker rooms, Akira and Ikumi approached their lockers, though as Akira opened hers, she noticed that it was empty. Her backpack and all of its contents were missing. She stared for a moment before she immediately knew what happened; Hideko. Throwing a glance around the locker room, she spotted her old friend at her own locker, just now getting ready to change into her school uniform. Closing her locker, Akira began to approach her, anger building as she drew near.

"Abukara Hideko, what the fuck did you do to my backpack?" Akira asked as she stood behind her old friend.

Hideko glanced back at her, then scoffed. "I could ask the same thing of you, Makai. Although, my concerns are for human life, not some stupid belongings."

She glared at her. "I'm getting really tired of this bullshit, Hideko... where the *fuck* is my backpack?"

With a scoff, Hideko ignored Akira and went back to changing.

Reaching out, Akira grabbed Hideko by her arm, shifted her slightly to the side, then roughly shoved her back against the locker next to her's. "Where is my goddamned shit, Abukara?!" she shouted, drawing the attention of nearby girls, including Ikumi.

Hideko nervously glared at her. "Wh-what are you going to do? Kill me over... your stupid bag?"

Growling, Akira clenched her free hand tightly into a fist.

"Aki, what are you doing?!" Ikumi asked as she ran up to her friend.

Akira looked briefly to Ikumi, which did well to temper her anger, at least enough to prevent her from boiling over. "Hideko stole my backpack that has all of my stuff in it, and now she's refusing to tell me where it is."

"I'll admit where your backpack is once you admit to the *murders* you committed, Makai," Hideko responded.

Turning to face her once more, Akira grit her teeth.

Ikumi sighed. "Aki, just hold on. Are you sure that–"

Not waiting for her friend to finish, Akira threw a punch directly into Hideko's abdomen. "Where did you put my bag?!"

Reeling from the hit, Hideko maintained her composure, muttering only more insults from under her breath.

"A-Aki, stop it!" Ikumi said.

Akira once again threw another punch into Hideko's abdomen, then grabbed her by her hair, pulling her from the locker and forcing her down onto the floor against the edge of the nearby row of lockers that stood in the center of the locker room. "Where is my stuff?!" she screamed, now fuming from her anger.

Hideko, never one to tolerate much pain at all, quivered as she looked up to Akira, tears already in her eyes as she realized just how furious she was. "I... I... it's in... th-the showers... I threw it in there and... and I turned the water on. Please, don't hurt me," she said amidst her tears.

Ikumi moved closer to her friend, placing her hand gently on Akira's upper arm to dissuade her from continuing her assault. "A-Aki... just, go get your backpack," she said in hopes of ending this confrontation.

Exhaling sharply, Akira stepped around Hideko and began making her way over towards the showers. While she was gone, Ikumi kneeled to check on Hideko, though even despite offering aid, Hideko had no interest in talking to anyone who was friends with Akira. Inside the showers, Akira easily found her backpack, soaked from the water, with almost all of the contents ruined, including her phone. Cursing under her breath, Akira returned to the locker rooms as she pulled her school uniform out of the bag.

Moving back to where Ikumi and Hideko were, Akira threw her soaked uniform down and into Hideko's lap. "There! You wanted to ruin my clothes? You can fucking keep them," she said before turning to Hideko's locker and grabbing her uniform from it.

"H-hey!" Hideko said in protest as she leaned forward.

Akira threw a furious glare at her, silencing her immediately. "If you fuck with my shit again, I *swear* I'll..." she said, shaking her head. "I'll give you a *legitimate* reason to be afraid of me. Rather than the bullshit that keeps coming out of your fucking mouth," she said before walking past Ikumi and Hideko as she returned to her locker.

Sighing, Ikumi threw only a glance back down at Hideko before following her friend. "Aki..."

Akira groaned. "I know what you're going to say..."

"That you shouldn't be fighting other students?" Ikumi asked as she stood nearby her friend, arms crossed.

Sighing, she turned to face her. "She ruined all of my shit. Even my cellphone."

"Then she should pay for that... financially. Not physically," Ikumi said, her stern expression relaxing into a more sympathetic yet supportive form. "I know you're upset. I can tell that you've been stressed out lately. But, how is what you just did any different than what that girl did to you outside of school?"

Staring at her friend, Akira began to realize more and more that she really shouldn't have done that, especially in front of Ikumi. Biting her lip, she lowered her head slightly as she began to worry about Ikumi telling her father or uncle about these violent tendencies she was now showing.

Reluctantly, Ikumi offered a comforting smile as she leaned down enough to look up at Akira's face. "I know you're not a bully, Akira. That's just not you... you're kindhearted, caring and friendly. So, I know what just happened... that's not like you," she said before leaning back up. "Just leave it to me. I'll explain the situation to Mister Masaru so that way he knows the full story and doesn't have to listen to Hideko's side versus your own."

"So... you're going to tell on me?" Akira asked as she lightly grimaced.

"What you did was wrong, Aki. But, what Hideko did was wrong too. Neither of you were in the right, but that doesn't mean it should just go unreported. I don't think he'll do anything, so long as you promise that it'll never happen again, and you say you're sorry," Ikumi said.

She scoffed. "But, I'm not sorry..." she admitted, though, in retrospect, she knew she should have just kept that to herself.

Ikumi giggled. "Well, just say you are. It'll get you into less trouble."

Akira stared at Ikumi, a bit surprised by her response but relieved that she wasn't disgusted by the lack of empathy she had towards Hideko now.

"Come on. Let's get changed, and then we'll go talk to Mister Masaru," Ikumi said before stepping away to go over to her locker.

Akira smiled as she watched Ikumi leave. Her friend might have leaned more towards the lawful side of things, but she at least was smart enough to know things were more than just black and white.

Changing into the uniform she stole from Hideko, Akira left her backpack in her locker, then left with Ikumi. Together, they went straight to Masaru, where Ikumi explained what happened while Akira repeatedly apologized for her part. Masaru appeared as if the situation irritated him, though they could tell that he was relieved to see that it wasn't something that would reoccur. He warned Akira, then said he'd speak with Hideko about it. Otherwise, it appeared as if Akira was free of any repercussions for what happened.

A part of her thought back to times when Kana or Miyoko bullied or harassed her. How they always got away with everything, outside of the heat of the moment, it appeared as if most teachers just found it easier to ignore conflicts between students rather than prying deeper to find a solution. Before, this was a huge hindrance to Akira, but now, it felt as if it were a boon.

Throughout the remainder of the day, there was no mention of Akira's assault against Hideko, and likewise, Akira made no mention of the dangers Yuuki posed. She still needed to come up with a solution, and so long as Tomoe was getting a ride home from her mother, that was all that concerned Akira. Although, a new concern would soon be at the forefront of her mind as she concluded her last class of the day, then went to meet with Ikumi and Tomoe at the main entrance.

As she approached her shoe locker, she was irritated to find Takashi standing nearby, looking worried, just as he was earlier in gym class. As she drew closer, she glared at him. "Is there some reason you're next to my locker?"

Takashi looked to her and awkwardly chuckled as he stepped aside to allow her room to get to her shoes, though he then quickly got them out for her and sat them on the floor.

Exhaling sharply, she continued to glare. "Could you leave me alone?"

"Um... well, I just wanted to let you know that–"

"You again?" Ikumi asked as she and Tomoe approached them.

Akira glanced back at her friends, happy to see them, though now mildly curious about what Takashi might have to share with her. She looked to him, then returned her focus to her friends.

Ikumi pursed her lips as she narrowed her eyes onto Takashi. "You'd better be behaving yourself."

"I... I am," Takashi nervously responded.

"Aki? Is everything alright?" Tomoe asked in a low voice.

"Uh..." Akira began to say, worrying that what Takashi might have to share with her could be about Yuuki. "Y-yeah, everything's fine."

Tomoe looked doubtful at Akira's words, though she didn't seem to question her response further.

Akira smiled. "Takashi told me some stuff during gym class, and... I guess he found something else out. It's no big deal. I'll talk to you about it later. I promise," she said, keeping her voice low.

"Okay... if you say so, but..." she began to say before sighing. "Just, don't get into any trouble, alright?"

"I won't, I promise," Akira said, forming a wide, toothy grin. "If you and Ikumi want to head out, I should be fine. I rode my bike to school, so I'll just cruise back home the same way I came," she said, raising her voice back so Ikumi could hear as well.

"Are you sure, Aki? We can wait for you if you want," Ikumi offered.

Akira shook her head. "Nah, you both have family members giving you rides home. I don't want to keep them waiting. I'll be fine."

Ikumi nodded. "Alright... well, we'll see you tomorrow morning then, Aki," she said with a bright smile before turning and moving to her shoe locker.

Tomoe reluctantly began to move to her own, though she glanced at Takashi, then back to Akira.

"I'll be fine. I promise," Akira reassured her girlfriend.

"I... I trust you, Aki..." Tomoe said before continuing past Takashi and over to her locker.

Watching them both move away, Takashi turned back to Akira. "So..."

Akira held her index finger up, prompting him to wait until her friends both left. Once they were gone, she looked back to Takashi. "Alright, out with it... what's going on?"

"I saw Yuuki outside of the school earlier today. It was right around lunchtime. I was on the second floor, sitting next to a window while I played on my Game Boy," he explained before frowning. "Hideko was out there with him, talking to him. He looked pretty angry, and then I saw him, um..." he paused, thinking of how to phrase whatever it was he had witnessed.

"Out with it, what did you see?" Akira impatiently asked.

He sighed. "I saw him messing around with a bike outside, and... it looked a lot like the one you used to ride. You mentioned having taken your bike to school today, and so... I was just worried he might have done something to it."

Pausing, Akira groaned. "Are you serious?!" she asked before walking past him and out of the main entrance.

"A-Akira, wait. You didn't even change your shoes," he said as he grabbed her street shoes off the floor and chased after her.

Outside, Akira approached the row of bikes, which were just across from the secluded alleyway, and saw her bike amidst the plethora of other bicycles. The first thing she noticed was that her chain had been removed and that her tires were both now flat. But, beyond that, she saw the confusion amidst other students. Her bike wasn't the only one messed up, as it appeared all of the tires had been slashed. Swallowing nervously, Akira turned to Takashi.

"Yuuki... he did this..." she said in a low voice.

Takashi frowned. "Looks like he got all of the bikes. Man... that guy is such a jerk..."

She groaned. "He probably did it, so I couldn't just nab another bike and go home that way... *fuck!* What am I supposed to do now?" she asked as she grabbed at her hair.

He offered a comforting smile to her. "If you want, I could walk you home," he said.

Akira gagged. "*No*, thank you," she said before starting back towards the school. *I am so fucked right now... I have to figure out a way to get home that Yuuki won't see me. But, who knows where the hell he's lying in wait for me?!*

Following her, Takashi sighed. "If it'd help, you could use my cellphone to call your grandparents to come pick you up. Or, maybe we could ask one of the teachers if they'd give you a ride home? That might work."

She closed her eyes as she held her forehead, stopping just near the shoe lockers as she felt a headache coming on. *Him calling my grandparents would likely cause my grandfather to assume I'm up to something, and I'd get grounded for even longer. And these teachers are fucking worthless,* she thought to herself as she groaned. *Fuck! I just need to figure out a way to get Yuuki out of my life. If I could just do that, then I could...* she stopped, opening her eyes as a brilliant idea crossed her mind. She looked back to Takashi, a subtle smile forming despite her apparent frustrations.

Takashi noticed this and smiled back at her as he pulled his cellphone out. "I don't mind at all. I think I still have your grandparents' phone number in here..." he said as he began to check his contacts.

That... could work... if Takashi walks me home, and Yuuki jumps me... then, I can have Takashi intervene to 'protect' me, and then Yuuki might kill him out of rage. It'd get Takashi out of my life entirely and give the police a reason to arrest Yuuki. Hell, they might even think Yuuki was the one responsible for the other murders! This is perfect! She thought to herself as her smile grew.

"Ah! Here it is," he said, showing his phone to her as he wore a bright smile. "See? I knew I had it."

Akira moved closer to him as she smiled back. "I think my grandparents are running errands today, so they wouldn't be home to answer. But, if you'd like... you could walk me home. I know Yuuki is really scary, but I trust that you'll keep me safe if he tries anything," she said, her voice falling to an almost flirtatious tone as she spoke.

Takashi lightly blushed as he put his phone away, then nodded. "Uh, sure! Yeah... I don't mind walking you home."

Akira forced a wide, gleeful smile as she giggled. "Let's get going then."

He held her street shoes up in his other hand. "Don't forget to change into these."

Pausing, she looked to the shoes, then sighed. Swiping them out of his hand, she tossed them down onto the floor, then swapped her shoes out. She then hastily ran over and tossed her indoor shoes haphazardly onto the shelf of her shoe locker, then returned to him.

"Let's go," she repeated, her eagerness clear in her voice as she beckoned him to follow.

Trailing a short distance behind her, Takashi soon moved to walk alongside her as they began making their way back towards Akira's house.

Normally, she'd choose some alternative route to avoid Yuuki, but now, she was looking forward to running into him. When she did, she'd have Takashi engage against him while she ran. She'd then call the police and frantically explain what happened. Regardless of whether or not Takashi lives or dies, it should be enough to send Yuuki to jail, at least until Akira figures out a better solution to her problem. A small part of her did feel bad for throwing Takashi's life on the line like this, but she just reminded herself of the creepy things he'd done over the years and how much of a pain his step-sister had been to her. This was nothing more than repentance for him in her eyes.

As they walked down the canal together, Akira kept discussions to a minimum as she watched her surroundings. However, Takashi kept trying to strike up a conversation between the two on various topics. None of which garnered much attention from Akira. Eventually, he did get the hint, and as they neared the bridge where Kana had thrown Akira off, her focus was torn away as she saw there was still police tape up on the construction site. Her mind trailed to what they might have found there and what kind of evidence she possibly left behind.

The police already had her fingerprints, and she most definitely touched quite a few things there in her panic. For one, she knew she had pushed the gate open, and she also handled the baseball bat and maybe even touched the railing of the bridge from where she dropped the bat. If they found her prints or the bat either one, Akira felt as if she would be completely screwed. However, her attention was soon torn from her fears when she felt Takashi grab onto her arm.

"H-hey! Let go of me," Akira responded.

Takashi's focus was ahead of them, intensely staring at something. This prompted Akira to turn and follow his vision, where she saw Yuuki approaching them from where he'd been hiding, just behind a nearby row of buildings, across from where the construction site was. As he drew closer, he passed by the bridge Akira had been thrown off before by Kana and had his eyes narrowed onto the two of them. Akira could see a pocket knife in his hand, the same he had used against her before.

Akira staggered half a step back as Takashi released his grip on her arm. "Sh-shit..." she said under her breath as she felt her heart race.

Yuuki glared furiously at her. "You know, Makai... I'm not sure what disgusts me more... the fact that you could stomach the lies you told me... or that I, even for *one* goddamn minute, believed a word you said."

Takashi held his arm out in front of Akira, trembling nervously as he tried to be brave.

She looked to him, then to Yuuki. "W-well...?" she asked, her own nerves clear in her voice. "Aren't you going to protect me?"

Looking to her, Takashi swallowed nervously, then nodded. "Y-yeah..." he said with shaky confidence as he looked back to Yuuki. Taking a deep breath, he lowered his arm and stepped forward. "You, um... y-you need to leave Akira alone..."

She sighed. *Wonderful confidence. I'm sure Yuuki is shaking in his boots.*

Yuuki scoffed. "Get lost, Kenichi, you pathetic excuse for a man," he said as he continued to approach them.

Takashi continued to shake with fear, though he took a step closer towards Yuuki as he braced himself. "I'm... I'm not g-going anywhere. Akira is a nice girl. And, I'm not going to let you hurt her."

He narrowed his eyes onto him. "Have it your way... but nothing is stopping me from making her pay. *Nothing!"* he shouted as he began charging at them.

Akira staggered several steps back as she grimaced.

Takashi tensed up, his mind scrambling as to what he should do.

Upon reaching Takashi, Yuuki grabbed him by the shoulder, gripping his uniform tightly before plunging his knife into Takashi's stomach. He doubled over and let out a loud groan in pain, coping with a feeling he'd never had before. Meanwhile, Akira felt her heart pounding away in her chest as she tried to figure out where she could run to. Glancing around, she quickly decided that her best bet would be to sprint home as fast as possible. She wasn't all that far away, and if she was lucky, she might make it close enough to scream for help.

Moving past the two of them, Akira narrowly avoided Yuuki reaching out to grasp at her. He then shoved Takashi aside before racing after Akira as she fled towards the bridge. Moving to cross over the canal, she threw a glance back and saw him closing in on her. Practically tripping over her own feet, she stumbled across the bridge. He was getting so close, and she knew he'd kill her if he got his hands on her, so she did the only thing she could think of in the heat of the moment. She turned to the railing of the bridge, then quickly climbed over it and jumped.

Just as she went to leap, Yuuki reached out and grabbed hold of her leg, causing whatever hope she had of landing gracefully to go out the window as she fell from his grasp and plummeted upside down into the meter-deep waters below. With a loud splash, she sunk to the bottom, bubbles spewing forth from her mouth and nose as her mind scrambled to figure out what just happened. Breaking the surface of the water, Akira gasped for air in between coughs as she tried to regain her composure.

She was so distracted by just trying to get a handle on her current situation that she narrowly missed the splash behind her. She wouldn't even have a chance to turn around, however, as she felt Yuuki's arm wrap around her neck. Instinctually, she reached up to pull his arm away from her, but she was hopelessly weaker than him and stood no chance of prying herself free of his grip.

"Do you think I have anything left to lose, Makai?! Thanks to you... the only thing I have left now is revenge," he said as he tightened his grip, progressively choking the life out of her. "If I didn't think I'd get stopped before I could kill you, I'd of walked right into your house or the school and slit your fucking throat," he warned before offering a menacing grin. "Although, maybe this would be a bit more horrifying for you... I want you to relish in these final moments. Understand the pain you've brought, not only to Hideko or me but to Kana and Miyoko's families as well. Breathe it in... then *fucking* die."

With that, Yuuki released his grip of her neck, then took a firm handful of her hair. Without hesitation, he forced her forward, shoving her head deep under the water until she was pressed against the floor of the canal. She barely had a moment to get a breath of air from when he released her to when she was forced under, and now that wasn't exactly an option. As fear filled her mind and her heart began to race, Akira struggled to get free, pulling against him or trying to pry herself free, even going as far as trying to rip her hair out to escape him, but nothing was working. Yuuki's grasp of her was too tight, and underwater like this, what little strength she had was minimal at best.

Yuuki narrowed his eyes onto her as she thrashed underwater, attempting to free herself, to no avail. "You're not getting away, Makai... not this time. And, if I make it out of this... I'll tend to your fucked up little friends too... both of them."

Fuck... fuck! What the hell am I going to do?! Akira asked herself as she continued to struggle. *No, not like this... please... please!* She pleaded in her head as she clenched her eyes shut.

Try as she might to hold her breath, her body desperately needed air. Once she could no longer bear it, feeling that her mind was beginning to drift, her body forced her to at least attempt to breathe, causing her to swallow the horribly putrid water. In her final moments of life, Akira heard a vague, almost distant plunge into the water that echoed around her. She was then abruptly shoved forward before her consciousness betrayed her, and everything fell to black.

Chapter 23
Calm After The Storm
可愛いサイコちゃん

Following those final moments underwater, where Akira was denied even the opportunity to draw her last breath, she felt as if it were all over for her. That was the end, and there was no escaping the hand fate had dealt to her that late afternoon. There was so much in those final moments that she wished she had done, so many wrongs in her life that she needed to right, so many people she wanted to spend more time with. But, more than anything else, she was heartbroken that she didn't have more time to enjoy her first relationship, the one she had formed with Tomoe. If life had only given her a second chance, she knew their love for one another would breathe into Akira's life, a joy she had never felt before.

Akira's eyes slowly crept open, feeling as if she was awakening from a restless night of fighting off some terrible cold or something. It was difficult to explain, but she was most definitely miserable. She could hear some noises, and they sounded as if they were coming from a television. Various cartoony, almost childish sound effects played in front of a catchy tune. Looking around, she didn't recognize where she was, but she did feel that she was lying in a bed, one that she was unfamiliar with.

Reaching up, she scratched her head as her senses steadily returned to her. Glancing around, she saw she was in what looked to be a boy's room, with posters on the wall of skimpily dressed anime girls, most of who were far too well-endowed for their small frames. Her eyes then trailed towards the sounds she was hearing and saw Takashi sitting on the floor, playing some kind of game on his television. This prompted her to gasp as she leaned up in bed, realizing she was in his bedroom.

"Wh-what?! Where... wh-why am I...?" she began to ask, her mind racing.

Takashi promptly paused his game, then looked back at her. He smiled as relief washed over him. "Akira, you're awake!" he cheerfully said before standing up.

Feeling her heart race, she kicked the covers off, feeling gross even being in the same bed as where Takashi slept. That was when she noticed that she was wearing an oversized t-shirt, alongside basketball shorts that barely clung to her petite frame. She was wearing his clothes.

Moving through the mess that was his floor, he stood near the bed. "How are you feeling? Can I get you anything?"

Akira grit her teeth as she glared at him. "Why the hell am I in your bed?! And where the fuck are my clothes?" she angrily asked before something hit her. "Sh-shit... Yuuki..." she said in a low voice.

Takashi frowned at her. "You'll have to forgive me... but your clothes were soaked from the water in the canal. So, I..." he blushed, "took them off and slipped some of mine onto you. I was worried you'd catch a cold or something."

Her eyes widened. "You... you *undressed* me?!"

He flinched. "Shh... not so loud. I had to. Otherwise, you'd of been lying on my bed in smelly, wet clothes. Don't worry; I promise I didn't do anything to you while you were out," he said, although it did appear his mind trailed off as he possibly thought of what he could have done.

Akira shivered in disgust. She felt sick to her stomach that he'd do that to her. But, also, she didn't know what happened to Yuuki. Her eyes trailed to the window, seeing it was dark out. "Wh-what time is it?"

"Huh?" Takashi asked before looking at the clock on his nightstand. "It's almost nine. You were out for a while. You woke up coughing for a bit, but then I think you fell back asleep, or whatever," he explained.

Scooting over to the edge of the bed, Akira stood up and began looking around the room. "I have to get home. I am *so* fucking dead..."

"Can you stand alright? I can help you walk if you need," he asked as he reached out to grab her by her arm.

She abruptly pulled away. "N-no! Don't touch me..." she said, feeling her heart racing. "I... I have to go," she said as she moved towards the door, narrowly avoiding the clutter of odds and ends on his floor.

Takashi began following her, wishing nothing more than to help her, or so it seemed.

Opening the bedroom door, she stepped out into the hallway and saw a door that appeared to head outside to her left. She started that way but heard a voice behind her.

"Wh-what are *you* doing here?!" Hideko asked in shock.

Pausing, Akira glanced back at her.

She took half a step back in horror. "And... why are... why are you wearing Takashi's clothes?!"

Akira's face burned red from embarrassment and shame for having been spotted like this. Without saying a word, she bolted towards the door, opened it, and ran outside.

Takashi stepped out of his room just as Akira left and frowned.

"What did you two just do?!" Hideko asked her brother in disgust.

Looking to her, he lightly grimaced. "I... w-we didn't... it's not what you think, Hideko. I was just helping her," he said, though she simply turned and ran back down the hallway to her room, where she closed and locked the door behind her.

Meanwhile, outside, Akira hastily walked down the street, holding the shorts up as they risked falling off her due to their size. She was barefoot, though that didn't slow her pace as she quickly remembered where she was in town and began making her way home. In her haste to leave, she didn't even ask about Yuuki, as the last thing she remembered was him holding her head underwater. She could still vividly recall those horrific moments, which made her tremble at the thought of them. Did Takashi somehow prompt Yuuki to abandon his plans to kill her? That made little sense, as he was so bold in his assault that avoiding capture was likely low on his priorities.

One fortunate aspect of this evening was that Akira knew, from her prior friendship with Hideko, that she wasn't far from her grandparents' house. Crossing a few streets, then down an alley or two, Akira arrived on the south side of the street she lived on. As she drew closer, she noticed a sight that made her pause. Outside of her house, parked in the street, was a police car. It didn't look as if it were the same one the detective and lieutenant rode in; however, she wasn't sure if she wanted to chance it.

That said, she knew she needed to get home. And, in all likelihood, the police car was there for her, in one way or another. Tempering herself and trying her best to develop an excuse that would fit her situation, she continued on her way towards her house. As she did so, she could hear her grandfather speaking. He sounded angry, which wasn't unusual, though as she got closer, she could hear him describing how she looked and where she went to school.

No sooner than she came into sight did her grandfather promptly notice her and glare. "There she is!" he shouted, prompting the two police officers to turn and looked towards her. "Do you have any idea what time it is, young lady?"

Akira sighed but didn't respond to her grandfather as she made her way towards the front door. She wasn't ignoring him but more so striving to avoid the police.

"Hey! Don't ignore me when I'm talking to you!" he snapped. He turned to the officers. "You're welcome to arrest her for being out past curfew. A night or two in a cell might actually teach that girl about respecting the rules of others."

One officer looked to his partner, who shrugged his shoulders. His focus returned to Ryoma, and he shook his head. "It's still early enough that curfew isn't really an issue, sir. But, if there are any other problems, you're free to give us a call."

Ryoma scoffed at the officers, then turned and made his way inside, following his granddaughter.

Inside, Akira stood in the kitchen with her grandmother as she tried to explain what happened and where she'd been. She, unfortunately, didn't have many options in terms of excusing her absence without being caught in some type of lie, though telling the truth appeared as if it were a gateway to a whole other world of problems.

"Makai Akira!" Ryoma shouted as he approached her.

Akira turned to him, then backed away slightly as he approached.

"You're going to explain yourself right now. Where were you? Did you forget that you're already grounded for what you pulled before?" he snapped before looking her over. "And just what are you wearing? Are those boys' clothes?! What? Did you sneak off to some boy's house?" he asked, his anger building.

Satomi looked to her husband. "Ryoma, please... allow her a chance to answer..."

"Well?!" he snapped.

Akira exhaled sharply, already hating herself for using this excuse. "I... went over to a friend's house after school..."

"A friend? Damn well doesn't look like it was your friend you spent the night with before," he said, gesturing towards her. "Unless she wears young men's clothes or has a brother, in which case I'd still like to know why it is you're wearing his clothes?"

She rolled her eyes. *He's not going to believe whatever I tell him. I might as well play into his assumptions, so he feels like he's right and just punishes me. I can't take this back and forth right now...* she sighed. "It wasn't Tomoe's. I went over to Kenichi Takashi's house."

Ryoma recoiled as if he were shocked that she'd so quickly tell him what he already believed. "So you did sneak off to some boy's house?" he asked before scoffing. "Considering who your mother was, I'm not surprised..."

Akira glared at him. "Fuck you!"

"You watch your damn mouth, girl!" he snapped back.

"Even if I did go over to some boy's house to do that, it's none of your business!" she responded.

He took a few steps closer to her, threatening in his demeanor. "As long as you live under my roof, whatever you do is my business!"

She grit her teeth as she growled under her breath.

Ryoma pointed off towards the hallway. "You're to go straight to your room. When I wake up in the morning, you'd better be there because you are going to be doing chores until it's time for school, and then I will be driving you there and then bringing you home," he said before scoffing at her. "And if you keep up this type of behavior, then we'll see what law enforcement thinks about you being every bit the delinquent your brother was."

Akira continued to glare at him, so many thoughts of what she'd love to say to him all swirling around in her mind.

"Your room. *Now*," Ryoma demanded.

Exhaling sharply, she turned and made her way down the hall, passing by her grandmother, who looked upon her with both sympathy and disappointment, as she no doubt knew there was more to Akira's behavior than simply a girl acting out against her grandparents. Climbing the stairs, she continued to her bedroom, where she slid the door closed, then turned the lights off and practically fell down onto her bed. Staring up at the ceiling, she had far too much on her mind to even begin to think about how things were.

Abruptly, she began coughing, feeling almost as if she wanted to vomit as she could taste some of the putrid water from the canal on her breath. She should have been dead. Yuuki had her held underwater, and there's no force Akira could imagine that would convince him to let go of her. She then woke up in Takashi's room. There was only one explanation, but it made no sense to her no matter how she considered it. But, barring the possibility of some form of divine intervention, it was the only answer to her question.

"Takashi... saved my life..." she said to herself in a soft voice as she stared up at her ceiling. "But... did he kill Yuuki to do it?"

As she laid in bed, thinking about how things might have played out, she felt similarly to how she did on that first Tuesday at school when Miyoko died. There was just no way around it; Yuuki had to be dead. Otherwise, Takashi would never have been able to rescue her. But, how and why would he go that far? Was it because of how much he cared about her? The thought of him being that dedicated to her was somewhat disgusting, even more so now that she had a girlfriend. Although, that did remind her that she needed to bring Tomoe up to speed on what was happening.

Lingering awake for long enough to hear her grandparents head to bed, Akira gave it another half-hour before she snuck downstairs and picked up the phone in the kitchen. Using it, she called Tomoe's cellphone, knowing that she'd likely be waking her girlfriend up, but also knowing that she needed to share what all happened, especially being that Akira was nearly killed by Yuuki today. It was no surprise that it took a moment for Tomoe to answer, and when she did, Akira took a seat on the counter and braced herself for an emotional roller coaster of a conversation.

"Hello?" Tomoe sleepily answered.

Akira sighed. "Hey, Tomoe. It's Aki... I'm calling from my house's phone... I'm sorry I woke you up."

"That's alright... is something wrong?"

Reaching up, she scratched her head. "Yeah... well, I mean... sort of."

"What... what happened?" Tomoe nervously asked.

"This is going to be a little... shocking, but... some shit happened when I left school yesterday," she admitted. Exhaling sharply, she threw a glance down the hallway before continuing. "Yuuki slashed my bike's tires, along with every other bike in front of the school. He was making sure that I didn't have a way to get home easily..."

Tomoe audibly gasped. "I can't believe he'd do that... but were you at least able to get a ride home or something? I mean, you're okay now, right?"

"Yeah, I'm fine, but... I had to walk home, and," she briefly gagged, "I had to ask Takashi to walk with me, just to be safe. And... it's a good thing I did because Yuuki jumped me on the way home, not far from where Kana stopped us that night... and, well... amidst the chaos, I kind of fell unconscious."

"B-but... you're okay, right? You didn't get hurt?" she nervously asked.

Akira awkwardly chuckled. "He almost killed me..." she admitted in disbelief. "But... when I came to, I was in Takashi's room at his house. I don't know what the fuck happened after Yuuki knocked me unconscious, but I sort of... I sort of think that Takashi might have killed him."

"Wh-what?! But, why do you think that? Why would he?" Tomoe asked in disbelief.

"To protect me? Takashi is obsessed with me, and I'm pretty damn sure that Yuuki wasn't about to spare my life no matter what. He attacked me in broad daylight and had every intention of killing me," she responded before sighing as she shook her head. "My instincts were right about Miyoko being dead... and now they're telling me that Yuuki's dead too. There's just no other way that Takashi could have saved me."

A moment of silence filled the phone call before Tomoe spoke up. "You... didn't purposely put yourself in harm's way, did you, Aki?"

Akira scoffed. "Oh, yeah! I totally decided that I'd cut my tires and force myself to walk home," she sarcastically responded before rolling her eyes. "I'd of been plenty happy if Yuuki would have left us both the hell alone. I didn't intend to be jumped by him on the way home. I'd think him nearly killing me would be proof of that."

"I'm... I'm sorry, I didn't mean to insinuate anything like that. It's just... I know that before, you were... you know..." Tomoe began to say.

She frowned. "You asked me not to put myself in harm's way because of how much you care about me. I wouldn't knowingly put myself into a position like that. I promise," she admitted before cracking a half-smile as she playfully scratched a finger against her cheek. "Although, if he is dead, then that means we don't have to worry about getting rides to and from school now," she said with an awkward chuckle.

Silence once again filled the phone call.

Clearing her throat, Akira hopped down from the counter. "But, I just wanted to call and let you know what happened and that I was safe," she explained, forming a smile across her lips. "Just... so you know... I'd never do anything to upset you or break your heart, Tomoe. I care about you so much... if I ever even so much as made you frown, I'd really beat myself up over it," she said, blushing lightly. "I love you, Tomoe..."

"I... I love you too... Aki..." Tomoe hesitantly responded.

Taking a deep breath, she nodded. "I can tell you're still really tired, so I'm going to let you get some sleep. Oh! And, I'm in more trouble with my grandparents because of some stupid shit regarding me not coming straight home. I can't tell them Yuuki tried to kill me, so... I'm probably grounded for the rest of my life. But, I promise that won't cause any problems in our relationship. I just might have to rush home after school, and I doubt we'll be able to have many sleepovers," she said with a light chuckle.

"Okay... goodnight, Aki," Tomoe said.

"Goodnight, Tomoe," Akira cheerfully responded before hanging the phone up. She smiled. "Well, that went a lot better than I expected."

Nodding to herself and feeling rather good about how Tomoe took such shocking news, Akira moved down the hallway and went to return to her room but recalled that she was still wearing Takashi's clothes. Feeling disgusted at this, she detoured instead to the bathroom so that she could get cleaned up. Feeling the water across her skin did give her a few sparse flashbacks to when Yuuki plunged her head underwater, though these only reinforced her feelings that she was grateful for him to be dead. He tried to kill her under the presumption that she was responsible for Kana's death, which she was; however, he had no way of knowing that for sure.

Chapter 24
Questions Abound

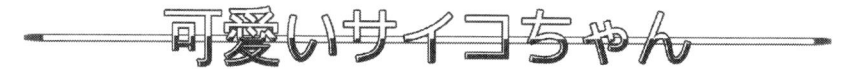

~~可愛いサイコちゃん~~

Akira, once she was finally able to get to bed, was deprived of the sleep her body desperately needed after such a horrific experience, as her grandfather woke her up at six in the morning, right after he and Satomi had awoken. Half-asleep and with almost no energy, Akira was given a long list of chores, which Ryoma demanded she finish before it was time for her to go to school. It was a losing battle, as she had just under two hours to get everything done and still get ready for school itself.

She did her best to keep up with everything throughout the morning, though her mind was hardly in the right space for chores. She was in the utility room, folding the laundry as she pulled each piece from the dryer when she thought she heard talking at the front of the house. It was as if her grandfather was speaking to someone, but with her grandmother taking a shower, she knew it couldn't have been with her. Akira kept to herself, folding the clothes, before hearing her grandfather call out to her.

"Makai Akira!" Ryoma shouted from the front door of the house.

She groaned. "I'm never gonna get shit done if he interrupts me," she complained under her breath as she sat the clothes down, then started towards the kitchen.

"Makai Akira!" he called out yet again.

She growled under her breath. "I'm coming! I'm coming! Geez..." she responded.

Drawing closer, she could see he was speaking to someone at the front door, and who it was caused Akira's heart to sink. The same duo that she'd learned to watch out for stood speaking to her grandfather, the lead detective, Yasuhida Masato, and the lieutenant who always seemed to accompany him, Yakovna Isaak.

"Ah, Miss Makai," Yasuhida said. "We apologize for interrupting you and your family on this fine morning. However, we'd like to talk with you regarding matters that recently came to light."

Swallowing nervously, she drew closer. "Um... wh-what do you mean?"

"I'd be happy to elaborate... would you be willing to come with us down to the station to answer a few questions?" he asked.

Akira grimaced. "I, um..."

"Yes, she would," Ryoma responded.

She looked at him. *Why would you just volunteer me?! You have no idea what they want to talk to me about,* she thought, feeling as if she were on the verge of tears.

Yasuhida stepped aside, then gestured towards their cruiser. "If you don't mind then, Miss Makai."

Taking a deep breath, Akira slipped on her street shoes, then stepped forward, walking between the two men, throwing a glance up at each of them. Yasuhida seemed to look at her concern, while Yakovna appeared as if he were already hurling accusations her way. When she woke up this morning, she knew today would be terrible, but she suspected that due to her lack of sleep and being swamped in chores. She hadn't considered finding herself in an interrogation with the police.

After thanking Ryoma for his time, Yasuhida and Yakovna brought Akira over and put her into the back seat of the police cruiser. The ride over to the police department was eerily silent, without a single word spoken between anyone. Once they arrived at the station, Akira was escorted inside. As they led her through the halls of the police department, her mind scrambled to sort out precisely what she might tell them. Were they going to ask her about Yuuki? If so, should she tell them the truth? She didn't kill him, after all. But what if they asked her of Kana's death? It felt as if so much time had passed since Miyoko and Kana died that Akira just knew this had to be about Yuuki.

Leading her into a small, nondescript room with only one table and two chairs, one on either side, Yasuhida motioned towards one of the chairs. Akira had never in her life been in an interrogation room before, and yet here she sat with two intimidating men, poised to ask her potentially endless questions regarding the now three deaths Akira found herself associated with.

Standing off to the side, Yakovna locked his eyes onto Akira as he crossed his arms.

Taking the seat across from her, Yasuhida stared, peering into her eyes, before he spoke. "It appears as if we keep coming across one another, doesn't it, Miss Makai?" he asked before sighing. "If you would be willing to do so, I'd like to make this as easy and painless as possible." He gestured towards her. "Would you like to tell us why you're sitting here with us this morning?"

Biting her lip, Akira lowered her eyes, breaking away from her focus on him. "B-because you guys asked me to come in?"

"I think you and I both know there's more to this than that," he said.

"Your grandfather filed a report that you had gone 'missing' last night," Yakovna stated. "Conveniently lines up with something else that occurred that same night."

She swallowed nervously.

Yasuhida leaned forward, resting his elbows on the table. "In all of my years serving this fine city... I have only experienced five homicides. In over twenty years... five," he stated before allowing a brief silence to fill the air. "In this month alone, there have been three deaths. One of questionable circumstances, another that appears to have been a crime of passion, and as of late last night, one that leaves many questions unanswered... even with the compelling evidence we've discovered."

Akira's eyes reluctantly trailed back to Yasuhida.

"Three people are dead. Each a child from a family who will be mourning their loss for decades to come," he explained, allowing a moment for the significance of the damage done to sink in. "I trust you are at least familiar with the individuals in question, yes?"

Feeling her heart pounding in her chest, she once more lowered her head.

"Would you tell me their names?" he asked.

Letting out a staggered sigh, she hesitantly spoke. "Hachi Miyoko... she was the first. I know that because Nakajima Kana blamed me for what happened to her..." she said, pausing as she chose her words carefully. "And then... Kana herself, I guess, was the second? Someone at school told me about her... and you guys came by and asked about her, saying she had disappeared."

Yakovna scoffed. "You're a terrible liar."

She looked to him, fearful that he saw right through her efforts to appear as if she knew very little.

Yasuhida motioned for his colleague to wait. "Do you know the name of the third one?"

Akira returned her attention to Yasuhida, staring at him as she contemplated telling the truth.

He nodded. "I can tell by that look in your eyes that you do. What is their name?"

Swallowing nervously, she lowered her head once more. "I don't know."

Yakovna moved closer, slamming his hand down on the table, causing it to rattle as Akira practically jumped in her seat. "What is the name of the boy who died last night?!" he snapped. "We fished his *goddamn* corpse up out of the canal ourselves. You know who he is. His name. Now."

She felt her heart pounding in her chest as her mind scrambled. This man, Yakovna, terrified her. Yasuhida at least spoke to her with a sense of mutual respect, but Yakovna felt as if he would be content with locking her up and throwing away the key, with or without substantial evidence.

"Well?" Yakovna asked.

Her eyes trailed to Yasuhida, seeing that he too was waiting for her response. She took a deep breath, deciding that at this moment, the truth was all she could reliably fall back on. "Was... w-was it Taichi Yuuki?" she timidly asked.

Yakovna scoffed as he leaned up from the table. "Looks like her memory isn't as bad as we thought..."

Yasuhida nodded. "Mister Taichi was discovered in the canal by a passerby. The location was near your residence," he said as he interlaced his fingers together as he leaned in closer to her. "We want to know what happened last night that led to Mister Taichi being murdered, then discarded into the canal. You went missing that same night... that is no mere coincidence."

She nervously looked between each of them.

"Game's over, Makai. Start talking, or else this vice is only going to get tighter," Yakovna warned her.

Taking a deep breath, she set her focus on Yasuhida. "Yuuki destroyed several bikes at school... he did so to make sure I couldn't ride home. He blamed me for what happened to Kana, and he threatened to kill me. I managed to get away from him the first time... but, since then, I've been living in fear of him," she explained, feeling as if she were genuinely on the verge of tears. "I asked the only person I knew who was still at school to walk me home, and–"

"What was that individual's name?" Yasuhida asked.

"Um... it's Kenichi Takashi," she responded.

He nodded. "Continue."

"So, uh... Takashi walked with me back to my house... but, along the way, Yuuki jumped us. Takashi tried to fight him, and I ran away. Yuuki chased after me, and..." she exhaled sharply, then wiped some of her tears away. "In desperation to get away from him, I jumped off the bridge and into the canal. I didn't think he'd follow me..."

Each of them listened closely to every detail she shared, though neither of them bothered to take notes. Likely because hanging on the wall behind them was a camera, recording her every word.

"Yuuki jumped down into the canal with me... then held my head under the water," she said, feeling a cold shiver wash over her as she recalled that horrific moment. "I thought I was going to die... but, after I blacked out, I..." she paused, hesitating on the next part, "I woke up in Takashi's room at his house. He didn't tell me what happened, just that he saved me..."

Yakovna narrowed his eyes onto her.

"So, you're telling us that Taichi Yuuki attempted to drown you in the canal's waters. You then fell unconscious and awoke in Kenichi Takashi's residence?" Yasuhida asked.

Akira nodded.

He looked to Yakovna. The two stared at one another for a moment, almost as if they were silently discussing her story.

She nervously looked between them both. *Are... are you serious? I'm telling the truth... are they really not going to believe me?*

Yasuhida returned his focus to her. "Tell me about Kenichi Takashi. He's one that we've not come across as of yet."

Biting her lip, she nodded. "Um, well... he's someone I've known since junior high school. I met him through Abukara Hideko... his step-sister. For as long as he and I have known one another, he's had a huge crush on me. He's always flirting with me at school, grabbing onto my hands and..." she shuddered, "saying some really disgusting stuff to me..."

"It sounds as if you're not on the best of terms with him then," Yasuhida said. "Why then would you ask for him to walk you home?"

She sighed. "Because I was scared for my life. Yuuki wanted me dead. I didn't have anyone else to turn to."

"Could you not have called for a ride? If you are as opposed to Mister

Kenichi as your demeanor suggests, I would assume you would exhaust any other option aside from accepting his help."

She reluctantly nodded. "I would have liked to... but I was already in trouble with my grandfather for sneaking over to a friend's house, so I wanted to get home before I got into any more trouble."

"And so you put your trust in a boy whom you feel uncomfortable around?" he asked.

"It's dumb, I know..." she said before shaking her head. "But, even if he is an absolute creep... I don't think that he would do anything to me."

Yakovna scoffed. "And I don't believe for even a moment that you're that naive, Makai," he said before leaning down, his hand placed firmly upon the table once more. "You aren't as pure and innocent as you wish to portray yourself. There's more to this than you're letting on."

She hesitantly looked at him. "I don't know what you mean. I needed to get home before I got into even more trouble, and so I asked him to walk home with me."

"You said so yourself. You felt Mister Taichi threatened your life, so why would you then put your well-being in the hands of someone who you don't trust? That makes no sense," he said, leaning in uncomfortably close to her. "What aren't you telling us, Makai? Perhaps that you had no intention of simply walking home?"

Akira locked eyes with him, tears forming as she listened to him dismiss her story, despite it essentially being the truth.

Yasuhida held his hand out, placing it on his colleague's shoulder. "Lieutenant..." he said, prompting Yakovna to take a step back. He then looked to Akira once more. "We want to help you, Miss Makai. Work with us, and I can promise you that you will receive the best possible outcome for you, regardless of your given situation," he reassured her. "Now, this Kenichi Takashi... describe him in greater detail to us. Does he seem as if he is a violent individual? Perhaps someone who you might suspect would lash out at others?"

She hesitated with her response, as she didn't want to jump ahead in their questioning and volunteer information. "Um... that I'm aware of, no."

"Did he have any reason that he might have intended harm towards Mister Taichi, aside from defending you?"

"Well, Yuuki bullied him a lot at school. But, I don't know if that would cause him to do anything crazy," she admitted.

"Mister Taichi was harassing Mister Kenichi?" Yasuhida asked.

Akira nodded. "Yeah... he bullied him a lot. Takashi would always try to vent to me... even though I didn't wanna hear about it."

Staring at her briefly, Yasuhida looked to Yakovna, then slid his chair back as he stood up, then returned his attention to her. "Excuse us for one moment, Miss Makai," he said as he began to make his way out of the room.

Yakovna reluctantly followed him, keeping an eye on Akira for an uncomfortably long time.

As the two of them left the room, Akira let out a deep sigh of relief as if she could breathe once more. "Fuck me... being in the same room as those two is stressful as hell," she said under her breath. Staring down at the table, she tried to calm herself down. *I don't know what all they have against Tomoe or me, but... all I know is that I need to speak confidently with them. If I show my fear, they're just going to see right through me. I can't let my worries dictate my behavior... I can do this.*

Several minutes passed, dragging on longer and longer as she sat there waiting, her confidence fading in and out as her self-doubt began to grow. Soon, however, the door opened, and Yakovna stepped back inside. With the door closing behind him, he walked over and sat down in the seat where Yasuhida had been before. Akira didn't like being in here alone with him, but it appeared as if she had no choice in the matter.

He narrowed his eyes onto her. "You said you used to be friends with the victims, yeah? Hachi and Nakajima, they were friends of yours?"

She reluctantly nodded.

"Then they began to bully you," he quickly said. "What did they do to you? And I want specifics."

Staring at him, she went to speak, though he cut her off.

He leaned in closer. "We know what they've done to you... witnesses have already come forth. So, consider this a test of your honesty."

Pausing, she felt her heart stand still for a moment. It was almost as if it were difficult to breathe, though she knew it was simply her nerves getting the better of her. "I, um... they humiliated me in school," she said, trying to tell him the truth, though remaining somewhat vague. "Kana would beat me up occasionally, while Miyoko spread rumors at school about me. They both destroyed my belongings and... mocked me in front of others. No one ever stood up for me either..." she admitted, feeling as if, perhaps, she should have left that last part off.

"That must have pissed you off quite a bit, huh? Ever get to the point that you might just want to... put an end to their harassment?" he asked.

She swallowed nervously. "I tried skipping school a few times, but... that was a temporary solution at best..."

"Murder was a more permanent one then, hm?"

She shook her head. "I didn't hurt anyone. I don't understand why everyone wants to blame me for everything."

He slammed his hands down on the table, causing it to rattle as he stood up. "Because you have the motive *and* the opportunities to commit the crimes!" he snapped. Glaring down at her, she could tell by the expression that he wore that this was no game to him. "We found evidence with your fingerprints on them, we have DNA evidence that links you to the murders. If you'd like to continue to try and bullshit us, then you're welcome to do so. But, I *warn* you... it will only make matters worse."

She had to resist the urge to glare back at him. She knew he was lying; he had to be. If they had all of that, then she'd be in a jail cell right now, not sitting at a table being asked vague lead-up questions.

"Why'd you do it?"

Akira shook her head. "I didn't do anything."

"It might take me a moment, but I'd be happy to bring the murder weapon in here for you to see," he said, a sly smirk forming across his lips. "Or, did you think we wouldn't find a blood-soaked baseball bat in the canal waters?"

Try as she might, she couldn't fully conceal her shock at the knowledge that the police had the bat she used to kill Kana. Her body involuntarily shivered with fear, and her mouth suddenly felt as if it were bone dry, all while she struggled to maintain eye contact with Yakovna.

He leaned in closer, uncomfortably so. "Start. Talking."

"Wh-what do you want me to do? Lie? I've..." she swallowed nervously, "I've told you everything I know," she said, tears forming in her eyes.

"Bullshit!" he said, slamming his hand down on the table. "Let me share something with you, Makai. Consider this your free lesson in criminal law. We have the right to detain, for questioning, any suspicious individuals whom we believe may be concealing pertinent information to an ongoing investigation for up to three weeks," he said before pulling back, standing tall in front of her as he grinned. "So, unless you'd like to spend the next twenty-one days here in this room, with myself and Detective Yasuhida questioning you from dusk until dawn... I suggest you start talking."

Akira felt her heart throbbing, almost painfully, in her chest. She wasn't entirely sure if he was telling the truth or not, but based on his confidence and how she knew police were able to easily abuse their powers if they wanted, she truly didn't put it past him being able to hold her for so long. At the same time, she had nothing she could give them to get them off her trail.

"Wh-what do you want me to say? I'm telling the truth, I don't know anything about what happened to Miyoko or Kana... other than what people have told me," she desperately explained.

Yakovna slowly nodded. "Very well then..." he said before turning and making his way over towards the door. "I'll leave, so you have a chance to think about it," he said before checking his watch. "I'll be back in ten hours to see how you're doing."

"T-ten hours?! But... b-but, I have school, and–"

"You will be excused," he said, throwing a glance back at her. "You need only worry about telling the truth. Perhaps this moment of solidarity will provide some incentive to be honest for a change..." he said before turning and stepping out of the room.

Watching him leave, Akira was in disbelief. Was he truly going to leave her in here for ten hours straight? What about food? She hadn't had breakfast yet, and she most certainly didn't pack a lunch for this. Was making her suffer his intention? Hoping that would break her and cause her to confess? If she stuck to her guns, then there, simply put, was nothing for her to confess to. But, he mentioned the baseball bat. Did they have her fingerprints on it? There were so many unanswered questions Akira had.

Leaning forward, she crossed her arms in front of her as she rested her head against them. Their intention of leaving her here alone was to break her resilience, but what they didn't know was just how perfect this was for her. This allowed her time to put together and think of a logical explanation for everything. Ten hours in solitary confinement? That was ten hours for her to piece together a story to get them off her trail. Or, at least, that was her initial plan.

As she laid her head on her arms against the table, her mind sorting through every detail she knew and what she assumed the police knew, Akira found her fatigue catching up with her. Ryoma had woke her up hours before she would have normally gotten out of bed, and now she was in the peace and quiet of this little room. It wasn't difficult at all for her thoughts to drift off as her exhaustion got the best of her, and she ended up falling asleep.

With no concept of time, it was hard to say how long she was asleep before she felt a nudge against her arm as if someone were poking her with the corner of a book. As her eyes crept open, she looked up and saw Yasuhida standing over her. She leaned up and sat properly in her seat as she gave him her full attention.

"You would do well to not sleep in here. Knowing my colleague, he will find something in the books that defines this as an illegal action," he said before taking the seat across from her. "I have a few more questions for you, Miss Makai."

"Um... okay?" she groggily asked as she began to wake up.

"I'd like you to think back to the first time we spoke. I believe it was at the very start of your school's semester, yes? On a Tuesday, if memory serves," he said as he opened a folder, then began sorting through the pages of the document.

Akira hesitantly nodded. "Y-yeah... I think it was..." she said, knowing full well which day they first spoke.

"If you would, please walk me again through what happened that day," he said as he pulled an ink pen out from the breast pocket of his coat.

Swallowing nervously, she thought briefly on it. "Um... like, from the beginning, or...?"

"From the beginning," he responded.

She sighed. "Well, I went to school and then to my classes. I, uh... guess you don't really need the details of what we went over in class, but... after my second class of the day, I..." she began to say before pausing.

Thinking back on it, she couldn't recall exactly what she had told them that day. She mentioned she was late, but she couldn't remember what excuse she used. Her mind immediately scrambled to try and think of what it was.

Yasuhida stared at her as he saw her falling deep into her thoughts. "Miss Makai? Feel free to keep going," he said.

Swallowing nervously, she nodded. "R-right... well, um... I was a bit late for my third class, but I did tell my teacher, and she let me into class. But then I–"

"Why was it you were running late for your class again? I apologize; I know I asked you this before, but... things have been a bit disorganized here, and I misplaced the notes I took from that day," he explained.

Bullshit... you just want me to tell you something else so you can catch me in a lie. I remember you and some other cop were both taking notes of everything I said. I doubt you lost both of them... she thought to herself, though, recalling that moment, it hit her what she had said. "O-oh! Um... I think I was late because my teacher in my, uh... oh! My business ethics class. Yeah, he held me a bit late because I," she awkwardly chuckled, "I wasn't really paying attention in class."

Yasuhida slowly nodded, then wrote something down. "I see... and what happened after that?"

"Um... well, there was a weird announcement at school, telling everyone to stay in their classes. We were in there for... it must have been like, an hour or two, and then they sent everyone home," Akira explained before frowning. "I found out... a day or two after, thanks to Kana, that Miyoko had died at school," she said, feigning sadness over her former friend's death.

"It was brought to my attention that Lieutenant Yakovna had seen you and another girl outside of school that day. I believe, based on what he has told me, it was Miss Asano Tomoe," he said, to which Akira timidly nodded. "He described you both as... distressed that day. Even going so far as to say that Miss Asano collapsed onto the ground, appearing as if she were having a mental breakdown of sorts. Could you elaborate on what that was about?"

Akira fought to maintain a neutral face as he asked that question, as she hadn't even considered what excuse she might use at that moment. What made it worse was if she lied and offered some perfect excuse, then he could simply bring Tomoe in and ask her the same question, exposing Akira's lies.

"It, um..." she began to say, trying to think of what she could say that would be simple enough not to raise suspicions but sound enough to prevent them from further inquiring about that moment. "W-well... it's kind of embarrassing, and... I don't know if Tomoe would want me to tell a, well... grown man about it."

"Miss Makai, these questions regard an ongoing investigation... refusing to share information is actively hindering the investigation. I'd strongly advise against withholding anything simply because you feel it might be 'embarrassing,'" he stated.

Akira lightly blushed, almost cracking a half-smile, as he clearly didn't know what excuse she had come up with. "If... if you're sure. Um... so, that day, Tomoe wasn't feeling so good. And when we left school, we stopped to talk about why we thought school let out early. But, while we were talking, she got some really bad cramps, and that's why she wasn't looking as if she was very happy. Or, she looked 'distressed,' I suppose," she said with an awkward chuckle. "I guess her's are worse than mine, though, because she almost started crying."

Yasuhida continued to listen to her, oddly not caught off-guard by her excuse, which she almost expected. Reluctantly, he wrote something down. "Let's talk about the evening of that same week. At the end of the school day on Friday, you were assaulted outside of school by Mister Taichi and Miss Nakajima, correct?"

"Uh... they bullied me, yes, sir."

"Do you recall that interaction well?" he asked.

Akira pursed her lips. She recalled it vividly, though she shrugged her shoulders. "That day, I was scared since Kana had already been threatening me throughout the week. She blamed me for what happened to Miyoko, and... I'll be honest, that entire scene played out like a blur to me. One moment Kana had me up against the wall, and the next, that lieutenant guy was there arresting Yuuki for hitting Ikumi," she said, laughing in disbelief. "I don't even know what all happened."

Yasuhida looked down at his notes. "When we spoke to you the following day, you didn't appear to have much difficulty recalling it then."

"That was the very next day... right around noon, I think? It was still really fresh in my mind, but now... I can't recall many details."

He exhaled sharply at her response, clearly not buying her excuse. Writing something else down, he looked to her. "I'd like to discuss a few topics unrelated to your time at Nirasaki High School. According to our records, you've had several run-ins with law enforcement before..."

Swallowing nervously, she nodded. "My brother and I did... yeah..."

"Let's talk about that," he said as he prepared to take yet more notes.

Akira could feel her stomach turning and twisting into knots. She and her brother, Shojiro, had gotten into a lot of trouble when she was younger. For most of her life now, she felt as if much of that trouble was just dumb fun kids were having and that it wouldn't matter as she grew older. In fact, she didn't even care all that much about it, even then. But now, with the police investigating her for three murders, one of which she did commit, Akira felt nervous about sharing her past with them.

It was all documented within the police department; it always had been.

However, talking about it now provided a direct connection between the delinquent behavior and violent tendencies she and her brother shared and the blood that now stained her hands from taking Kana's life. This connection was one she wanted no one but Tomoe to know about, most especially the police. With everything well documented, however, she had little choice but to be as honest and forward with her past as possible. At the very least, this could potentially lead to Yasuhida believing that she was honest about everything else.

Chapter 25
Aftermath

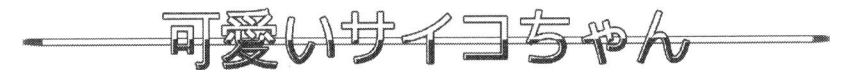

可愛いサイコちゃん

For hours, Akira sat and spoke with Detective Yasuhida, sparsely with Lieutenant Yakovna when he would join them, and divulged every ounce of information about her past to them. It pained her to do so, but virtually everything of interest would be well known and documented by police. After spending nearly an entire day in this room, answering many questions, and offered only small snacks as food, so long as she continued to cooperate with them, Akira was relieved when, at long last, Yasuhida stated that she could go.

Despite all the information she'd given them, and how she danced around having any knowledge of Miyoko or Kana's deaths, they were allowing her to walk free. Much like before, something told her that this wasn't the type of freedom she was hoping for. They had evidence against her; Yakovna repeatedly taunted her with such. A part of her believed it must have been a bluff, though she knew they must have had pieces of the puzzle that only she or Tomoe would know of, such as the weapon used against Kana being a baseball bat or that it was discarded in the canal.

Once she was free to go, her grandfather arrived at the station to pick her up. The ride home was filled with her grandfather ensuring she knew that this was the path she was going down and that if she didn't change her act, she'd end up just like her father. He threw a few good jabs at her brother and how he constantly got into trouble with the police, yet also praised him compared to Akira, as he at least seemed to be doing better in his life now. She kept to herself the entire ride home, even when her grandfather called her out on her silence, accusing her of ignoring him.

Upon arriving home, Akira made her way inside and was greeted with a warm dinner from her grandmother. Though, she was promptly reminded by Ryoma that there was still time left in the day for her to do her chores. Despite her hunger, it wasn't easy to keep her food down when she knew her life could be steadily creeping down a path that would soon find her locked behind bars. She had already told Tomoe what happened with Yuuki but completely missed speaking with her girlfriend today. Now, she had to share the information that the police took her in and interrogated her all day long, threatened and even warned of supposed evidence they had against her.

Her evening consisted of chores, fears, and many doubts that she'd even have a future to worry about in the coming days. Up until now, she had convinced herself that things would be alright or that she could persevere and make it through all of this. But since being taken in and questioned by police on everything, with her every word recorded on audio and her nervous demeanor on video, she wasn't quite as confident that she would make it out of this.

The following day, she was torn from what little rest she got and thrown back into her cycle of doing chores. She couldn't help but fear that the police might come back for her today, just as they'd done the previous morning, though she was fortunate enough to make it through these early hours undisturbed. She was then brought to school by her grandfather and warned that she'd better be out on time or else he'd start extending her sentence, a poor choice of words when she could be facing several decades behind bars if convicted of murder.

Approaching the main entrance to the school, Akira found it difficult to have enthusiasm for anything except seeing her friends. Her education and performance in classes had never been a huge priority in her life, but now, it felt as if it weren't even a consideration in her mind. Making her way inside, she was relieved to see both Tomoe and Ikumi hanging out near her shoe locker, as they each arrived early, something Akira often did when she wasn't being brought last minute to school by her grandfather.

Ikumi gasped as she saw her. "Aki!" she cheerfully called out, waving her hand in the air enthusiastically.

Tomoe appeared far more reserved with her excitement, likely because she could tell that something terrible must have happened. "H-hey, Aki... how are you feeling today?"

"Um... less sick than I was yesterday," Akira reluctantly admitted.

Ikumi frowned. "Is that why you weren't at school? Because you got sick?"

Akira lightly grimaced, then nodded. "Y-yeah, that's it... I sort of risked it and ate something that had been in the refrigerator for a while the night before, and... it just didn't work out."

"Aw... I'm sorry to hear that. Well, do you feel better today?" she asked.

"Kind of..." Akira said, her eyes trailing towards Tomoe.

Ikumi glanced back at Tomoe, then to Akira. She smiled. "Um... I'll go make sure our seats aren't taken in class. But, it's about to start, so don't you two linger too long, okay?" she said before stepping away to give her friends a chance to talk alone, as she knew they had just recently started dating one another.

Watching her leave, Akira sighed, then moved closer to her girlfriend.

"Aki? What's wrong?" Tomoe asked, her fears clear in her voice.

"The... the police took me in for questioning yesterday... I was there *all* day," she responded, her voice breaking as she nervously looked around.

Tomoe's eyes widened, her complexion going pale as she heard her friend speak. "Th-they did?!" she asked in shock, though she kept her voice down.

Akira nodded. "They asked me everything... even about, like... my past and shit. They asked about my parents, the things my brother and I did, my relationship with my old friends, *everything*... and that's not even the worst of it," she said, tears forming in her eyes. "Tomoe... they found the... the bat... the baseball bat..."

She staggered half-a-step back as she covered her mouth. She shook her head. "D-do they know what you... what you did? Do they know what *I* did?"

Akira swallowed nervously, then shook her head. "I don't know. They could be bluffing... but, they said they have evidence that puts me at the scene of the crime. I don't know if I believe that because they let me go. I think they were just hoping I'd cave and confess to shit, or something..."

Tomoe nervously glanced around. "We shouldn't talk about this here..."

"We can't talk any other time. We share like, one class together, and Ikumi is right next to us. I can't come to school early, or stay late, because my grandfather is giving me rides since I didn't come straight home... you know, the night Yuuki tried to kill me," Akira explained before reaching up and running her fingers frustratingly through her hair. "I just want to scream. Tomoe... I don't know what to do. I have *no* idea how to fix this."

Lowering her head, Tomoe stared down at the floor, many fears crossing her mind as she contemplated just what would come to pass if, or rather when, evidence was brought against them for the crimes they committed.

Akira glanced nervously around the area before moving closer to Tomoe and leaning in to kiss her on her cheek, even despite them being in public and at school. This prompted her girlfriend to look at her, surprised by her boldness. Akira forced a smile. "If... if everything falls to shit... I don't want you to worry. If they have evidence against me for what happened to Kana... I'll..." she paused, hesitating as fear tightly gripped her. "I'll tell them that it was me... who shoved Miyoko..." she whispered.

Tomoe stared in disbelief at Akira, almost as if she hadn't entirely heard what she said.

Akira nodded. "So, no matter what, I don't want you to worry. I'll... do whatever it takes to take care of... and protect the woman I love."

Her mind swirled with a veritable miasma of emotions, knowing full well that she had lied about her feelings towards Akira, and now based on those supposed mutual feelings, Akira was willing to take the fall for everything.

Seeing no response from her girlfriend, Akira lightly blushed as she awkwardly chuckled. "Was... that a bit much? S-sorry, my only real, I guess, romantic experience is from reading it in books or manga, and I know those are usually super cheesy, or whatever," she clumsily explained.

Tomoe reluctantly shook her head. "N-no, it's not that it's... th-thank you, Aki. But... I don't know what to say."

"Um... how about..." she began to say, pausing to think of whether or not she should say what she was imagining. "Just, uh... s-saying that you love me too?" she nervously suggested.

Tomoe timidly smiled. "I... I love you... too, Aki."

Akira forced a wide, toothy grin. "Then, I don't have anything to fear. So long as I have Asano Tomoe in my life, I know everything will work out..." she said, her confidence quickly fading away.

"We, um... should probably get to class..."

"Right. I bet we're already running late," she said with another awkward chuckle. "Um, let me change my shoes real quick, then we can go," she said as she hastily moved to her shoe locker, then changed out of her street shoes.

Walking side-by-side, each consumed by a wild array of emotions, Akira and Tomoe made their way to class. They almost missed it, as the teacher had just begun to slide the door closed. He warned them to be early for their classes, or else they'll be late, same as they would experience in the workplace, but then let them in. Taking their seats next to Ikumi, neither girl could even pay attention during their teacher's lecture or follow any of the equations he went over. Instead, they were each lost in thought over what was transpiring in the world around them.

Akira found herself staring out of the classroom window, passed the hedges that bordered the building, and out onto the grass that decorated the schoolyard. It wasn't the foliage that drew her attention; it was the knowledge that the beautiful outdoors and quiet little city that she lived in, and experienced at least a degree of freedom within, would soon be nothing more than a distant memory. If she took the fall for everything, then she knew she'd be looking at over three decades behind bars, she felt.

The idea of Akira being in a prison cell until she was forty-six years old was terrifying. If that were the case, she'd almost prefer to be dead herself, as being that old was akin to her life already being over, at least in the short sight that she had at her age. Thinking more on it, Akira couldn't help but begin to wonder about other possibilities. She still had her freedom, at least for now. For a fleeting moment, she considered running away and hiding. Doing so would mean abandoning the life she now had, one that she was beginning to enjoy up until Yuuki attacked her.

Ikumi was a wonderful friend, and Tomoe was the girlfriend Akira had always dreamed of. She didn't want to abandon it all, but she also didn't want to watch her life rot away inside of a prison cell. All Akira wanted was a way out of this corner that she backed herself into. Although, it was beginning to look as if there wasn't another way out. She'd have to either surrender or flee, neither of which provided her much solace. After all, it wasn't as if Tomoe would be keen on the idea of running away with her fugitive girlfriend.

As their math class ended, Akira parted ways with Tomoe and began walking to gym class. It was difficult for her to hide from Ikumi that something was wrong, though her friend simply assumed that Akira's stomach must have still been upset from whatever she ate. Ikumi was a kind girl, Akira knew that, and she always seemed to accept the excuses she was given without any questions. Her devotion and reliability were both traits that Akira found herself really appreciating.

Entering the gym hall, Akira was still lost amidst her thoughts when she heard someone call her name.

"A-Akira!"

Stopping, she and Ikumi each turned around and looked behind them, seeing Takashi approaching. It appeared as if he were waiting by the door, most likely for Akira herself.

Ikumi pursed her lips. "Should I call for Mister Masaru?" she asked, directing the question at both Akira and Takashi.

Akira reluctantly shook her head. "N-no... Takashi was... he was nice to me the other day. He, um..." she began to say before looking to Ikumi. "It turned out my bike had a flat tire, and... he carried my bike all the way back to my house. Isn't that right, Takashi?" she asked.

Pausing and lightly blushing, he laughed, then eagerly nodded. "Y-yeah! It was kind of heavy, but I didn't mind."

Ikumi stared at him, almost as if she were judging him, as she had every right to do so.

"Um, Ikumi... I know he's been... less than great in the past. But he's been trying to be better. I'd like to give him a second chance," Akira said.

Turning to her friend, Ikumi appeared conflicted over the decision, though she reluctantly nodded. "You have a really good heart, Aki... so, if you want to give him a second chance... then, I think that's fine," she said, snapping her attention back to Takashi as she narrowed her eyes onto him. "And, I'm sure he will see how kind that is and respect your personal space from now on... right?"

"H-huh? I, uh... y-yeah... yeah, I will," Takashi confusingly responded.

Akira placed her hand on her friend's shoulder. "I'm going to see what it is he wants. He... might not say, if you're standing here," she said in a low voice with a light, albeit awkward giggle. "I think he's scared of you."

Ikumi scoffed. "He should be. Men should respect women, not treat them like objects," she responded.

Akira offered a wide, toothy grin. "You're damn right they should. I'll make sure he knows that going forward."

She sighed. "Alright... well, I'll go ahead and get changed. But... once I'm done, I'm coming back out here to check up on you... okay?"

"Alright," Akira responded.

Throwing a glance at Takashi, Ikumi narrowed her eyes squarely onto him, an expression that warned him not to do anything cruel to her friend. She then reluctantly walked away, looking over her shoulder several times at him to ensure he behaved.

Watching her leave, Takashi sighed. "Your friend is... kind of scary."

Akira turned back to him. "Takashi, I have to know..."

"Huh?"

"Yuuki... is... is he?" Akira began to ask.

Takashi grimaced before glancing around.

"We can talk out in the hallway, come on," Akira said, beckoning him to follow as she left the gymnasium.

Trailing a short distance behind her, Takashi walked along with Akira, much further than he suspected they'd go. By the time she stopped, they were out of the direct line of sight of the gym hall.

She turned and looked at him. "Is he dead? Did... did you kill him?"

He sighed. "Geez... do you have to ask so bluntly?" he responded before frowning. "You weren't here at school yesterday... are you okay? You left kind of fast after you woke up."

She pursed her lips. "I left in a hurry because someone stripped me down against my will and threw me in his bed."

Takashi reached up and scratched at his messy hair. "I said I didn't do anything... besides, your clothes were wet, and they smelled terrible."

Akira swallowed nervously. "You saved my life... for that, I owe you. But, there's a lot of questions I have. You want to know why I wasn't at school yesterday? It's because the police took me down to the station and kept me there all day, asking me an endless barrage of questions about where I was when Yuuki died."

He frowned. "What... what did you tell them."

"The truth!" she responded as she reached up and pulled at her hair. "I didn't know what the fuck else to say because I didn't know what they might know. But now, I know Yuuki is dead, and I'm fucking positive that I was in no position to fight back. You were the only one there, so... what the hell happened?"

"I don't know if I want to talk about this at school, Akira..."

She moved closer to him, something that usually would have brought him joy, though the desperation on her face, her desperate need for an answer, almost forced him to fall back a step. "Takashi... I need to know... now. I don't know if the police are going to blame me for something I didn't do, or what... but," she shook her head, "please, just tell me what happened."

Takashi let out a deep sigh, then nodded. "Okay, okay... I'll tell you. So, when you ran off... Yuuki stabbed me, then ran after you. It took me a moment to even realize what happened, but then, when I saw Yuuki jump down into the canal, I saw you were down there too," he said, throwing a nervous glance around. "So, I grabbed the first thing I could, and I climbed down into the canal using one of those... it's like, I guess a service ladder or something? Kind of how they'd climb out of the canal after doing–"

"Takashi, could you focus? I don't give a fuck what it's called," Akira responded, her irritation mounting.

"Oh! Uh... r-right, my bad. Well, I had grabbed this, like, metal post thing? No clue what it was used for, but... I saw he was holding your head underwater, so I just moved up to him as fast as possible and swung it at him. He fell into the water, and... he didn't get back up, so I grabbed you and carried you out of the water," he explained, awkwardly chuckling. "You were... heavier than I thought. N-not that I think you're fat, but, it's just... you know, the water and everything, I..."

She exhaled sharply.

"Right, right... stay on topic. Uh... well, like, after I got you out of the canal, you weren't breathing, so I..." he paused, his face turning a bit red. "I performed CPR on you. You coughed up some water and groaned a little, but you were still unconscious. I didn't know what to do, so I took you back to my house," he said, scratching at his messy hair once more. "I was so lucky because my parents weren't home, and Hideko was taking a shower. I know they would have asked a lot of questions, but... man... Hideko was really mad when she saw you later on..."

Akira gagged. "That's because she thought we fucked, and she hates my guts," she said, feeling less repulsed by that idea that she typically would, because between sleeping with a creep or going to prison for the rest of her life, one terrified her more than the other. "So, you knocked Yuuki out and left him in the canal?"

Takashi nodded. "Yeah... it didn't occur to me under after I got you back to my place that... he'd probably, um... die without air, but... hey! He deserves it! He treated you and me like shit, and he tried to kill you."

She stared at him, offering no response.

"Uh... s-sorry, was that bad of me to say?" he asked.

"No... I mean, yeah... but..." she began to say before shaking her head. "You don't feel bad for killing him... because he deserved it?"

"Huh? Well... I mean, I guess it feels really weird. But, if I didn't do something, then he would have killed you. And... I like you a heck of a lot more than I liked him," he admitted with an awkward laugh.

Akira stared at him in disbelief. Takashi killed Yuuki to protect her and harbored no remorse for his actions. Akira herself had killed Kana, and she did so to protect Tomoe and also held no remorse for the life she took. Two sides of the very same coin, and while she hated that they shared this similarity, it gave Akira at least a mild reassurance that her feelings on the matter were justified. And that she wasn't alone in that regard.

"Uh... you're just sort of staring at me, Akira..." Takashi responded, blushing slightly.

Abruptly, she shook her head. "S-sorry," she said, taking a half-step back as she lowered her head. *He killed Yuuki... and he didn't even intend to. But, he also doesn't feel bad about it*, she thought to herself before her eyes widened. *I told the police that he was there... they're going to figure out it was him that killed Yuuki.*

"Akira?" Takashi asked as he looked oddly at her.

She gasped. Hold on, the police will know he killed Yuuki, but they still won't know about Miyoko and Kana.

He raised his eyebrow. "Uh..."

She turned her focus back to him. "You... you killed Yuuki... to protect me? B-because you care about me, right? That's what you said, yeah?"

Takashi lightly cringed at her so boldly declaring his actions but nodded. "Yeah... I did."

"I..." Akira began to say, pausing as she chose her words carefully. "To protect my friend... because Kana was going to kill her... I killed Kana," she reluctantly admitted.

He recoiled back in slight shock. "Y-you... you did?!"

She nodded. "That's why Yuuki was trying to kill me. Well... he was trying because he thought I had killed her... but he was right," she said before shaking her head. "But, just like you, I... I don't regret it. Kana spent every moment of her life making me miserable, and then she tried to kill my friend because she blamed her for Miyoko's death. I had to protect the person I cared about, so I..." she sighed, "you know..."

Taking a deep breath, Takashi reluctantly nodded.

An awkward silence filled the air as Akira expected him to respond, at least with more than a mere nod. She lowered her head. "I'm scared... Takashi... I'm terrified that the police are going to know what we did."

He swallowed nervously, though he continued to listen to her silently.

She sighed. "Thanks to me being a complete idiot... they probably know you killed Yuuki. They're probably just getting evidence together now to prove it. But, they'll eventually find out that I killed Kana and probably blame Miyoko's death on me too," she said before feeling weak in her knees, prompting her to collapse down onto the floor as she cupped her face in her hands and began to cry. "I don't... I don't want to go to prison, Takashi..." she sobbed.

Hesitantly, he moved closer and kneeled to her. "Akira... please, don't cry."

"I can't... I can't help it," she said, looking at him through her tears. "You know what kind of trouble I got into when I was little... you know who my parents are. People like me... when we break the law, the police want to lock us up forever... they think, just because I was troublesome when I was a kid, and my parents were criminals, that I should rot behind bars," she said, cupping her face once more. "You're lucky... at least with you, they'll be gentle with your sentence because you've never been in trouble before... and you still have both of your parents, and they're not criminals like mine!"

Takashi frowned as he listened to her. "I... I don't really know much about any of that, but... won't they be easier on you since you're a girl?"

"N-no! They'll be worse," she said, looking to him. "They'll lock me up for the rest of my life... Takashi, I'll never see daylight again. And, for the first time in years, I was finally starting to feel happy..." she said, lowering her head as she sighed. "I was already thinking about how I wanted to improve at school, go to college and become a teacher..." she did her best to try and blush, though it was difficult. "To be a wife... a mother... to someone who... who really cares about me, you know?" she said, looking back to him. "Someone who's always cared about me..."

He stared at her, clueless for a moment before it hit him. "Um... d-do you mean... me?"

Akira subtly let out an irritated sigh as she closed, then rolled her eyes before looking back to him and nodding. "I know I... haven't always really been kind towards you, like... at all. But... you saved my life. What's more, you got stabbed, then killed a man to protect me."

He began to blush, though he grimaced at her reminding him that he killed Yuuki.

"Takashi, I..." Akira began to say.

"Akira?" Ikumi called out from down the hallway.

She lightly flinched. *Goddammit... ya know, sometimes having a reliable, dependable friend is more of a hindrance than I'd expect it to be,* she thought to herself before groaning. A glance around, she noticed the restrooms nearby. She promptly pointed towards the boy's restroom. "Takashi, hide in there, or else Ikumi is gonna yell at you," she demanded.

"I, uh... o-okay," he said in a panic before moving to the bathroom and stepping inside.

Shaking her head, Akira exhaled sharply, then began walking back towards gym class. As she came around the corner, she saw Ikumi around ten meters down the hall.

"Oh! There you are," Ikumi responded.

As she drew closer, Akira awkwardly chuckled. "Yeah... my stomach is still acting up. I had to run to the bathroom after I got done talking to Takashi," she said as she met back up with her friend. "Come on, Ikumi. Let's get back to gym class. Maybe a bit of exercise will tell my stomach to shut up."

Ikumi smiled at her friend, then began walking alongside her back to their class. "You seem like you're in a better mood, so I'm glad. But, just don't push yourself too hard, okay?"

"No promises," Akira responded.

Making their way back to the gym hall, she couldn't help but curse under her breath at Ikumi's timing. All things considered, it made sense for her friend to come looking for her. But, Akira needed more time to talk to Takashi, something she never thought would cross her mind. He killed Yuuki, and he had no remorse for that. Akira was already on the cusp of being caught, so her telling him she'd done the same to Kana had few consequences. However, if she could convince him that things would be far worse for her, should she go to prison versus him, and also used the feelings he's had for her for years against him, then perhaps there might be a way out of this for her.

It was all that she came up with on the spot, and maybe Ikumi's interruption was merited after all, as it gave Akira more time to put her plan into practice in her head. Simple though it might be, she needed to choose her words carefully. Convince Takashi that she's secretly harbored romantic feelings for him all of this time, she was just afraid to show them because of some reason, and that if she is convicted of these crimes, she'll go to prison forever, while he'd only go away for a short while. If he truly loved her, then her hope was, he'd be willing to take the fall for her.

Takashi confessing to the crimes, providing the police with information that only the killer would know, would get the police off Akira's trail and have the bonus of eliminating Takashi from her life as well. Unlike how she once felt for Hideko, after having killed her friends, Akira didn't care at all about ruining Takashi's life. He'd been a horrible creep towards her for years, and she saw these horrific acts as justified. Tomoe likely wouldn't agree, at least at first, but Akira had little choice. It was either this or take responsibility for her actions, and she wasn't quite prepared for the latter of those options.

Chapter 26
Pleas For Help

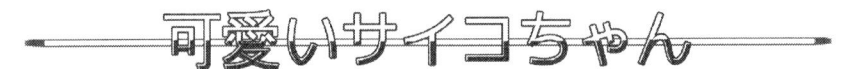

可愛いサイコちゃん

All throughout gym class, Akira considered how she might convince Takashi to take the fall for her, just how far she might have to go, up to and including actually physically portraying a relationship with him. The thought of him touching her, let alone them kissing or anything beyond that, disgusted her. However, Akira already had it firmly planted in her mind that she would do whatever it might take to convince him to do this for her, up to and including declaring him her boyfriend.

This did require a degree of subtlety as Ikumi was already somewhat suspicious of Akira spending time around someone she had proclaimed to hate, even if she did say that she was offering him a second chance. Still, if Ikumi's probing questions during gym class were anything to go on, she was skeptical at best of Akira offering Takashi even one moment of her time. Once gym was over, the girls made their way to the locker rooms. Akira had seen Takashi staring at her from a distance throughout gym class, undoubtedly wanting to speak to her again. An impossibility, given Ikumi was with her throughout the class.

After they washed up in the showers, then began changing into their school uniforms, Akira brainstormed how she might ditch Ikumi, and realistically, there was only one opportunity she had. Walking with her friend out of the gym and towards the cafeteria, Akira had to think of how she could slip away from their lunch period long enough to speak with Takashi. Approaching their usual spot, Akira saw Tomoe already with her textbook out and doing some homework.

"What are you studying, Tomoe?" Ikumi cheerfully asked.

"Huh?" Tomoe responded, looking to her friends. "Oh, um... this is just my biology homework. I know what chapters we went over in class today, but... I had other things on my mind, so it was difficult to focus during the lecture," she explained.

Akira sighed, then nodded. "That was me during gym class," she muttered under her breath as she took her seat.

Ikumi looked between each of her friends, then frowned. "You two have both seemed kind of... I don't know... sad today. Is everything alright?"

"E-everything's fine... well, for me, it is," Tomoe responded before forcing a smile. "I just stayed up too late studying last night, and now I'm really tired."

"Oh... well, alright then," she responded, her focus shifting back to Akira as she sat down. "What about you, Aki? Is anything wrong?"

"No, I'm... just bummed out over getting grounded extra hard for the sleepover we had. I mean," Akira awkwardly chuckled, "don't get me wrong, it was totally worth it since Tomoe and I were able to finally share our feelings with one another, but... being grounded for, pretty much, the rest of the school semester is kind of shitty."

Ikumi smiled. "If it makes you feel any better, my dad made me promise not to date anyone until I was done with school," she said before letting out a disheartened sigh. "It kind of sucks, because, well..." she shook her head, "i-it's not important."

Akira snickered. "Sucks why? Because you already found someone you like?" she teased.

Blushing, Ikumi shook her head once more. "N-no... I'm just a very, um... romantic person, I guess. What I mean to say is," her blushing intensified, "I like romantic stuff. Like, I read romance novels a lot, and I really just... want to find that special someone..."

Tomoe's eyes drifted from Ikumi back to Akira. She stared for a moment before sighing, then closing her biology book. "Aki, can I talk to you about something?"

"Uh... sure?" Akira confusingly responded.

"In private?" she added.

Ikumi looked to her friends, then smiled. "I need to go get my food anyway. So, I'll... just take my time," she said before standing back up, then stepping away to give them a moment alone.

Tomoe sighed as she left. "I sort of meant outside of the cafeteria..." she said to herself before looking around to see if anyone nearby was paying attention. She then returned her focus to Akira. "I... I'm really worried about what you told me earlier. Have you, like... I don't know... decided what you're going to do?"

Reaching up, Akira scratched playfully at her hair. "Sort of. But, I need more time to figure out the details and to make sure it works. And, Ikumi is sort of making that difficult."

"Huh? How so?"

She laughed. "Because she's way too good of a friend. I'd rather wait to explain the details once I've actually... ya know, figured out if this will work, but–"

"You're not going to hurt anyone, are you?" Tomoe hesitantly asked.

Pausing, Akira sighed. "Not physically, no..."

"Wh-what does that mean?" she asked, fearful of what Akira might have been planning.

"I promise, if my plan works, then no one will be hurt, and neither of us will be in trouble. And, hopefully, it'll be foolproof," Akira reassured her.

Tomoe held her head in her hands.

Pausing, Akira stared at her girlfriend in confusion. "Um... Tomoe?" she asked before hearing her begin to cry. Frowning, Akira leaned forward and reached across the table, placing her hand on Tomoe's arm. "Please... please don't cry..."

Feeling Akira's hand on her, Tomoe shook her head, then stood up and hastily walked away from the table, making her way out of the cafeteria.

Watching her leave, Akira wasn't sure what to say. She felt devastated at seeing Tomoe cry, likely over the fear of one or both of them going to prison over everything that's happened. It merely reinforced in Akira's mind that she needed to ensure their safety above all else. Standing up, she looked around the cafeteria, searching for Takashi. She managed to spot him, sitting at a table with his step-sister. They weren't that far away, and so Akira wasted little time before walking over towards them.

"Takashi," she called out as she drew near. "I need to talk to you. *Alone*," Akira firmly stated.

Hideko looked up at Akira and glared. "You need to leave me *and* my brother alone, Makai," she warned.

"Shut the fuck up, Abukara," Akira responded.

She sneered at her. "I told our parents about what happened. About how you snuck over and slipped into my brother's room. They don't want you anywhere near him."

Moving closer to her, Akira reached down and took her bento box of food, then dumped it all over the front of her uniform and down into her lap. "I said for you to shut your *fucking* mouth," she snapped.

Hideko gasped in shock at Akira's actions. Looking down, her food stained her uniform, possibly ruining the pristine white fabric of it.

Akira turned to Takashi. "Come on," she said with a wave of her hand as she beckoned him to follow as she began to leave.

Takashi stared at his sister for a moment before he stood up and began following Akira.

"T-Takashi!" Hideko called out.

He threw a glance back at her but then continued to follow Akira.

Making their way out of the cafeteria, Akira led Takashi down a nearby hallway, a fair distance from the entrance to the cafeteria itself. Stopping, she prompted him to stop as well. Keeping her back to him, she took a few deep breaths as she braced herself.

"Um... Akira? Is this about what we talked about earlier? B-because, I wanted to tell you that I-" he began to say before his words were cut off.

Abruptly turning around, Akira moved to Takashi, gripping the front of his uniform as she pushed herself up onto her toes to reach him so that she could press her lips against his. She held their brief, unsettling kiss for a few seconds before she pulled back, concealing her disgust as she stared deep into his eyes.

"I love you, Kenichi Takashi..." Akira blatantly stated.

Staring in disbelief, he stammered in his response. "I... I-I love you too... Akira..." he said, taking staggered breaths.

Appearing as if she were going to cry, she lowered her head. "I just... I wanted to tell you that... because... I'm certain that before long, we're both going to get arrested, and we'll never see each other again," she said, reaching up to wipe away her fake tears. "I'll go to prison for the rest of my life, and... by the time you got out, I don't even know if you'd still care about me... or if they'd even allow you to come to see me..."

Takashi reached out and took her hand. "Akira, I... I will always care about you. I've loved you since the day I met you. And... that'll never change."

Akira did her best to push her disgust back, which became progressively easier for her following the kiss they just shared. She offered a soft smile to him before she lowered her head, appearing defeated. "I just... it could be years before you'd get out and come visit me. If... if there was some way for me to not go to prison... I know I'd visit you every chance I could. Every week, day... hell, I'd visit you every hour if they'd let me," she said, blushing shyly. "I could even wear stuff to cheer you up. Maybe some cute cosplay of some of your favorite girls from the manga or anime you like?"

Takashi lightly chuckled. "It'd... be amazing to see you dress up for me. I bet you'd look so cute."

She sighed. "I wish I could... it'd be a lot of fun. But... by the time I get out of prison, I'll just be some wrinkled old hag... the best parts of my life gone forever..."

"Um... maybe there's something we could do to keep you from having to go? M-maybe we could both run away? That might work?" he asked.

Akira grimaced. *No, you idiot... you're supposed to take the fall for me.* "But, then we'd be on the run, and our entire lives would be lived in fear. I don't want to be a fugitive, running from the law, Takashi... I want to live a normal life. I already lived the past three years in constant fear of Kana... would you really make me live the rest of my life in fear of the police?"

Scratching his head, Takashi frowned. "I... I guess not..."

Moving to the nearby wall, Akira slumped back against it. *Why is he taking so long? You always talk about wanting to make me happy, right?! Fucking volunteer to take the fall already!*

Approaching where Akira now stood, Takashi let out a deep sigh. "So... earlier, you said you told the police what happened? That means they probably already know I killed Yuuki," he admitted before glancing down the hallway towards the main entrance. "I wonder why they haven't come for me yet?"

"Takashi..." she said, her impatience growing.

"Yeah?" he responded as he looked at her.

She teasingly bit at her lower lip. "I was just thinking... and I know this is asking a lot, but..." she exhaled sharply, "since it's likely the police will catch both of us, you for certain, and then myself very soon... what if you were to, I don't know..."

"Take responsibility for killing Kana?" Takashi asked.

Pausing, she looked at him in shock.

He reluctantly smiled. "That's what you were going to say, wasn't it?"

At least he could see that much. It means he's not a total dunce. She lowered her head. "It's too selfish... I couldn't ask you to do that..."

He forced himself to grin. "I always said that I'd keep you safe, right? And... how can I back out of that when you just confessed your feelings to me?" he asked before taking her hand once more in his. "I love you with all of my heart, Makai Akira. I don't care about your flaws, your faults, none of it. I love you for who you are, and I'd give my life to keep you safe."

"T-Takashi..." she responded in a gentle tone.

"I'll tell the cops that I killed Kana. Then, they'll leave you alone," he said with wavering confidence.

She timidly smiled at him. "That's... so sweet of you, Takashi. Truly," she said before moving to embrace him. As they held one another for a moment, she pursed her lips. "But, um... you'll need to know a few things," she said as she pulled away. "So, you need to tell them shit only the killer would know, okay? That means you need to tell them that Kana was bullying me, and so you wrestled her baseball bat from her, then beat her to death with it. My fingerprints might be on the bat, so I could tell them that I'm the one who threw it into the canal," she explained before cupping her chin. "Is there anything else I need to add?"

Takashi swallowed nervously. "Um, so... are you going to talk to them too?"

Akira nodded. "We'll go to them together, and you'll tell them that you murdered Kana and Yuuki to protect me... oh! Miyoko, too, you shoved her down the stairs because she was harassing me."

He grimaced. "W-wait... I'm confessing to *all* three?!"

She frowned. "If you don't... then, I might..." she said as her tears began to well up.

"I-I... okay, okay... I'll tell them I shoved Miyoko too. Um... was there anything else?"

"We need to go over roughly when all of this happened. I think Miyoko was around eleven? Maybe a bit before? It was on the second day of this school semester, on that Tuesday. Kana was... shit, it was like seven or eight at night. This was over at a construction site near my house. You remember where the old record store used to be?"

He hesitantly nodded.

"Yeah, that one. They're rebuilding it, and Kana chased me there to beat me up, and you killed her," she said, giggling awkwardly. "And, uh... oh! That was on Friday, the end of the first week here at school."

"O-okay... so, um... Miyoko at eleven on Tuesday? And then Kana at like, seven on Friday?" he asked.

She eagerly nodded. "That's right. Oh! And if the police try and bullshit you, just stick with this story. Don't let them convince you to change it. If we go there together, they'll probably, like, split us up and talk to us. They'll lie and say like, I'm telling them something completely different. Just stick to this story; I'll do the same. They do that so you'll change details of what you said before, and they'll just pick and choose whichever one gets them the biggest sentence to throw at you."

He frowned. "You sure do know a lot about this kind of stuff, Akira..."

"I've seen a lot of crime movies, TV shows and read a few books. I know they're not authentic, but there are overlapping themes that have to be spot on," she explained.

"Oh, I see... so, um... when should we do this?"

Akira cupped her chin. "Hm... As soon as possible, I think that way they close the case and don't find any more evidence against me. But... I don't know. Would you be alright going down to the police station with me now?"

"Like, right now?" he nervously asked. "Uh... couldn't we like, go maybe... what about this Monday? Then we'd have the rest of the week, and the weekend to... ya know, at least go out on a date or something?"

She exhaled sharply. "We'll be lucky if we make it to the end of the day before they show up to arrest us..."

An awkward silence filled the air between them.

Akira closed her eyes. "I'll tell you what," she said before looking back to him. "How about we go to the police and confess everything together this evening... and, since that's more important than anything else right now, we can just ditch school and go on our date."

"Um... you mean go on a date now?" he eagerly asked.

She nodded. "Yeah. We'll go to the mall, or maybe go see a movie or something like that."

"I'd love to take you out to a movie. Oh! How about we get a bite to eat first? I didn't start eating my lunch yet," he said.

She smiled. "That's fine. I hadn't started either. If we can, I'd love to get some-"

Interrupting her, the intercom system chimed on. "Attention, students, would Makai Akira please come to the principal's office? Miss Makai Akira, you are needed in the principal's office," a man's voice called out.

Glaring up at the ceiling, Akira held her middle finger up towards the nearest intercom. "*Fuck off*, I don't care," she said before looking at Takashi and forcing a wide grin. "I'm about to go out on a romantic date with my new boyfriend," she said, gagging mentally at her own words.

Beckoning Takashi to follow, urging him to do so as she offered her hand for him to take, Akira began leading him towards the school's main entrance. As much as she despised this, one afternoon of tolerating Takashi would alleviate all of her problems, as well as remove him from her life for good. It was the perfect solution for a problem she thought she'd never find an answer to. It, however, wasn't the only thing that was perfect, as Akira's timing couldn't have been better, at least for someone else.

As she approached the main entrance where the shoe lockers were, she stopped when she spotted Lieutenant Yakovna and another officer standing nearby.

Immediately he saw her and moved with the other officer to approach her. He wore a cocky grin, one that told Akira that he finally got what it was he was after.

"Makai Akira," Yakovna said as he reached to his side and drew his handcuffs. "I need you to turn around and place your hands behind your back. I'm also supposed to discourage you from offering any resistance, but to be perfectly honest with you... I'd prefer it if you did resist."

Akira swallowed nervously. "Wh-what? But, why?"

"You're under arrest for the murder of Nakajima Kana. Now, I'm required by law to request only once more that you put your hands behind your back... after that, I have the right to use force," he stated, apparently eager to dole out some of the same justice he served Yuuki the day Ikumi got hurt.

Akira looked to Takashi reluctantly, then pulled her hand from his, though he only let go after she tugged a few times. Biting her lip, she turned around and held her hands behind her back, trying her best to conceal her emotions, as she hoped there might still be time for her plan with Takashi to work out.

"Pity..." Yakovna said before moving forward. He threw one cold glare at Takashi. "Mind your distance, boy. Unless you'd like to spend a night behind bars too," he said as he grabbed Akira's arm, then latched the shackle around her wrist, then the other, binding them both together.

Takashi's eyes shot between Akira and the lieutenant, unsure of what to say. "A-Akira... should I... what should I do?" he asked in a whisper, clearly lacking any confidence in the situation.

She looked to him with pleading eyes. "Don't let them take me away... please," she begged in a low, meek tone.

With a forceful tug, Yakovna pulled Akira away and then began guiding her towards the entrance. He looked to the other officer. "Radio Detective Yasuhida and let him know we spotted her attempting to flee the school. Just another item to add to her running list of crimes."

"Yes, sir," the officer responded.

"W-wait!" Takashi said as he ran to catch up with them.

Yakovna threw one glance back at him, then glared. "Do yourself a favor, boy. Get back to your class or whatever and leave us to do our job. If you interfere with us even once more, I'll have your ass locked in a cell, living off cold rice for a month straight," he warned.

Swallowing nervously, Takashi shook his head. "A-Akira didn't... she didn't kill Kana. I did!" he said, his voice cracking as he spoke.

Yakovna narrowed his eyes onto him before diverting his focus to Akira. "Goddamned little succubus..." he said under his breath, though she could clearly hear him.

"P-please, she didn't do anything. It was me. A-and, I shoved Miyoko down the stairs too! And, I killed Yuuki!" Takashi explained.

Akira closed her eyes. *You fucking idiot... could you make it any more obvious that you're making this shit up on the spot?!*

Exhaling sharply, Yakovna looked to the officer. "Take her to the squad car, and get her down to the station. We'll be right behind you."

The officer nodded. "Yes, sir," he said before moving to Akira, then guiding her out and towards a police cruiser that was parked just in front of the school.

As she was forced to leave, Akira glanced back at Takashi, seeing Yakovna speaking to him. With even an ounce of luck, he might be able to convince them that he took part in some of the crimes, but a part of her knew he'd mess everything up, and she'd be stuck serving time behind bars for the rest of her life. She needed to get out of this, and her only option now was to commit to the plan she had made with Takashi, the plan to ensure he went to prison for her crimes, and she was able to walk free.

Chapter 27
Final Words

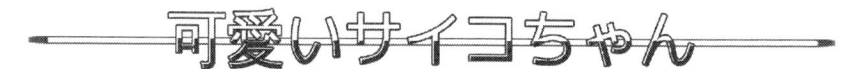

可愛いサイコちゃん

Throughout her entire life, Akira had always felt as if the world itself was against her. First, her parents were taken from her at such a young age, then she lost her friends for simply following her heart, her brother abandoned her, and now here she sat, cold and alone in a bright room, awaiting what could be the end of her life. It's the second time this week that Akira found herself in the police department's interrogation room, though she was far more scared this time. They had officially arrested her, ready to charge her with the crime of murder, and likely slap her with the harshest sentence a judge would allow.

Surprisingly, it had been an incredibly long time since she was first brought in here. She'd been handcuffed to a metal hoop on the table, preventing her from even so much as scratching her leg, let alone getting away, and now she was beginning to worry that they were merely allowing her time to go insane with thoughts in her head. It was starting to work. The one upside to this was Akira figured out precisely what she would say to the detective and his lieutenant once she spoke with them, though she knew it would put her limited acting skills to the test.

Hearing voices from the other side, Akira's attention shifted to the door. That was when she saw the doorknob twist and turn, then the door opened. Stepping inside were the exact two men she expected, and as with before, Yasuhida took the seat across from her while Yakovna stood nearby.

"I trust you were informed as to the reason for your arrest today, Miss Makai?" Yasuhida asked, maintaining an air of professionalism as he spoke to her, even if he should have believed by now that she was a criminal, a murderer.

"Um... h-he told me..." Akira timidly said, hesitantly looking at the lieutenant.

"You were arrested under suspicions of murder. We're here to discuss that with you," Yasuhida said before opening a folder he had with him. "Now, Miss Makai... we discovered a discarded baseball bat in the city's central canal system. On this bat were several fingerprints. Among the prints that were present were those of Nakajima Kana's and your own."

She swallowed nervously.

"On the railing of the canal, we discovered bloodied fingerprints which matched to the ones we had of you on record. In addition, on the night of Miss Nakajima's death, nearby residents reported the sounds of arguing or yelling. The voices in question sounded to all parties as if they were from two young women," Yasuhida said, looking to Akira and seeing how pale she was. He then looked back to the papers.

"I... I was... was there..." Akira said, her voice cracking.

Pausing, Yasuhida looked back at her. "We have hard evidence to prove that, Miss Makai. If you're willing to cooperate with us, tell us the full story, paint us a picture of what happened... we might be willing to do what we can to lessen the charges against you," he said before sighing. "This would be in your best interest. In all of my years serving this police department... I have never once seen anyone staring down a maximum sentence of this size before. Were you not a minor, you might even be looking at capital punishment for your crimes."

Taking a deep breath, she nodded. "Can... I start from the beginning?"

Yasuhida motioned for her to begin.

"So, it all started when I was... around thirteen. I was friends with four girls, Miyoko, Hideko, Kana, and Kana's sister, Ina. We were all close, and we hung out together all the time," she said before frowning. "But, I developed a crush on Ina, and... well, I told you two about that before..."

"Go ahead and tell us again," Yasuhida said as he took notes.

"Um... well, I had a crush on Ina, and so I convinced her to kiss me during one of our sleepovers. Kana saw us kissing, accused me of far worse, and–"

"What were the accusations?" he asked.

"O-oh, uh..." Akira grimaced. "Kana... accused me of molesting her sister..."

Yasuhida nodded. "Continue, as you were."

"So, um... after she accused me of that, she and all of her friends kicked me out of their circle and then told me to stay away from them, especially Ina. But, Ina was still friendly towards me. I apologized, and she was fine with staying my friend. This made Kana even angrier, and so she started bullying me at school. At first, it was to teach me a lesson, and then it was... I guess just because she hated me," she explained.

Writing that down, he looked to her. "How severe was the bullying?"

Akira grimaced as she thought about it. "I don't really have anything to compare it to... but it made me absolutely miserable. There were times when I... I felt like I didn't even want to go to school anymore, or wasn't even sure I wanted to... keep living..." she admitted as she dropped her head low once more.

Yakovna lightly scoffed at her.

Biting her lip, she looked to Yasuhida. "Kana made my life miserable. I hated every day because of her..." she said before looking away. "The only person who was ever really nice to me back then... was Kenichi Takashi."

"That was the young man who was with you when Lieutenant Yakovna placed you under arrest, correct?" Yasuhida asked.

Akira nodded. "I always thought he was... kind of creepy. Like, a stalker or a guy who just never took 'I'm not interested' as an answer. I tried everything, but he... he'd never take the hint," she said, taking a deep breath. "But, things changed this semester. I've... I've been too afraid to tell anyone, but..." she sniffled as tears began to form in her eyes. "I don't want to throw my life away, and... maybe the police can protect me from him... if I tell you what happened?"

"I can't make any promises until you finish explaining everything," he warned her.

"O-okay... I understand," she said, swallowing nervously once more as she took a staggered breath. "On the first week of school... Miyoko caught me in between classes. She was bullying me and making me late for my next class. I asked her to let me go, but she refused. That was when Takashi saw us. He asked her to leave me alone too, but she just insulted him. I... I don't know why, but I called her a... a bitch, and she got so mad at me. She began pulling on my hair and trying to scratch me... and then, Takashi shoved her..." she said, purposefully pausing as if to give the detective a moment to take in what she said.

"You're telling me that Kenichi Takashi pushed Hachi Miyoko?"

She nodded. "Yes, sir... and when he did, she fell down the stairs. I thought she was hurt, and so I nervously ran off to my classroom. I knew once she woke up that she'd tell Kana, and they'd both beat me up..." she said, biting her lip nervously. "The next day, I discovered that Miyoko had actually died from her fall..."

"You expect us to believe that?" Yakovna asked.

"Let her continue, Lieutenant," Yasuhida responded.

He scoffed. "It's a waste of time..." he muttered under his breath.

"Continue, Miss Makai," Yasuhida said.

"Um... so, the next time I saw Takashi... he told me that he heard what happened and that he didn't care that she died. He just said that he wanted to protect me, to keep me safe. I was scared, and so I didn't say anything to anyone. But, Kana... she kept harassing me. She thought I had shoved Miyoko down the stairs... she blamed me for everything," she said, shuddering as best she could to emphasize how disturbed she was at the thought of her taking the life of another. "And... then came Friday..."

Yasuhida crossed his arms in front of him on the table as he listened, more so than took notes.

"Takashi called and asked me how I was... and I told him I was scared that Kana might try something. He offered to walk me back to my house, and... I took him up on his offer," she said, hesitating as she tried to recall what the police already knew. "Along the way back to my house, Kana jumped us with a baseball bat... she hit Takashi, then chased after me. I ran to the construction site in hopes of finding someone who would protect me from her, but no one was there... she attacked me, and... and Takashi came to my rescue," she said, closing her eyes as she inhaled sharply.

Yakovna rolled his eyes at her theatrics.

"He took the bat from her... and began hitting her with it..." she said, feeling her tears running down her cheeks. She was relieved, as she feared she wouldn't be able to force herself to cry. "He kept hitting her... again and again... there was... so much blood," she said, losing herself for a moment in her tears. She leaned down to once more wipe more tears from her eyes. "By the time he stopped, he was covered in Kana's blood. I was so terrified, I could barely speak..."

"So, Mister Kenichi was responsible for the murder of both girls, and you were a witness to each?" he asked.

Akira nodded. "Yes, sir..."

"Why did you not report this to the police? Even when we spoke to you that next day, you lied to us and stated that you had not seen Miss Nakajima. By your own words, you saw her when she was murdered."

"I... I did lie... I'm sorry. I didn't want to," she said as she lowered her head once again. "I hate lying... I'm not even good at it. But I was just so scared... I was terrified. After Takashi killed her, he came over to me and hugged me... he hugged me with his clothes and hands soaked in the blood of a girl I considered like a sister to me at one point," she said before she began to sob.

Yasuhida watched as she cried profusely, her tears appearing genuine. He looked to Yakovna, who remained steadfast and unconvinced.

As her tears subsided, Akira sniffled, then wiped her eyes. "He gave me the bat and told me... told me that I could hit her too if I wanted. I didn't. I urged him to leave, and in a panic, I ran to the bridge and dropped the bat. Looking back, I know it was wrong, but I was terrified. If I made one wrong move, what was stopping Takashi from killing me next? I... I didn't want to die... but I was afraid of who else he might hurt..."

"Have you ever heard of obstruction of justice, Miss Makai?" Yakovna asked.

Akira wanted to glare at him, despising how he was so unapologetic towards her plight, as if he saw right through her.

"You assisted in concealing Mister Kenichi's first and second murder, and were far more complicit the second time," Yasuhida stated before he narrowed his eyes onto her. "We brought you in for questioning after Taichi Yuuki's death, and you neglected to share all of this information while you did point us in Mister Kenichi's direction. Would you care to explain your rationale during that?"

Her focus returned to the detective. She lowered her head in shame. "I... I wanted to tell you everything then, but... I was just too scared. I was afraid Takashi might lash out at me if I tried to turn him in. I was afraid he'd hurt or kill me... or my friends."

"Sure appeared as if he were eager to turn himself in once we slapped the cuffs on you. Hardly the trait of a man who's murdered three people," Yakovna pointed out.

She turned her attention back to him. "Takashi's had a huge crush on me for a really long time... and, before now, I've always rejected him. I've been too afraid to be around him lately, but... a part of me was hopeful, after he killed Yuuki, that I might be able to give in to his feelings and then later convince him to turn himself in. I didn't expect that you guys would arrest me for his crimes, or that he'd willingly admit to them to save me," she said before sighing. "I... I don't care what happens to him. He's a monster, a sick, demented monster. He's tormented me for years, and... and after he killed Yuuki... the next thing I remembered, after having blacked out, was waking up naked in his bed," she said, shivering in disgust. "I just want him to leave me alone..."

Yakovna groaned.

Yasuhida took a few more notes down, then looked to her. "Was there anything else you wished to share with us, Miss Makai?"

"Um... just that I'm really... *really* sorry that I didn't do the right thing in coming to you sooner. I should have trusted in you more... I mean, aside from being a detective, you're also my best friend's father," she admitted before forcing a subtle smile. "Looking back, I know you would have helped me... and maybe Kana and Yuuki would still be alive..." she said, lowering her head once more.

With a deep sigh, Yasuhida stood up. "If you'll excuse us then, Miss Makai. We'll be back momentarily," he said before gesturing for Yakovna to follow him as he left the room.

Watching the two of them leave, Akira slumped forward and buried her head in her arms as best she could, as she was still shackled to the table. *Please... please say that Takashi stuck to what I told him. If he didn't, then the only daylight I'll probably see again will be from a prison yard.* Inhaling sharply, she stifled her genuine tears as she felt like her entire life, her entire future, rested on the decisions of one boy. She was trusting in someone she hated and treated terribly for most of her life to throw his own life away to save her.

It felt as if hours were slowly passing her by as she waited almost sixty agonizing minutes. Her stomach was in so many knots that she could barely even imagine sitting down to eat with her friends. Friends she thought she'd likely never see again. She missed them so dearly, Tomoe, her lovely girlfriend, the love of her life, and the greatest treasure she'd ever found. And Ikumi, a moral compass of a friend who was always so upbeat, cheerful, and positive, something Akira desperately needed in her life and needed it in spades. However, her wait would soon be over as she heard the door open and saw Yasuhida reentering into the room.

Perking her head up, she looked to him with cautious optimism.

"How are you faring, Miss Makai?" Yasuhida asked.

She lightly grimaced, then frowned. "My stomach is in knots... I still can't believe I let things get this bad..."

With a sigh, he raised a document up, flipped it open in his hand, then began to read. "As of this moment, the charges that stand against you are as follows," he said, taking a short pause as he read through them mentally, then shared them with her. "Obstruction of justice, destruction of evidence, and attempting to conceal a murder," he said before his eyes trailed back to her. "You knew of the murders committed, be they accidental, intentional or premeditated, went through a degree of efforts to conceal or destroy evidence, in your case, throwing the murder weapon into the canal. Finally, you, by your own admission, assisted in covering up the murders," he stated.

Akira stared blankly at him. *Um... I noticed a distinct lack of 'you killed Kana' in that list... did he really confess?!* She shook her head. "B-but, I–"

Yasuhida held his hand up, motioning for her to wait. "While you did not speak to us until you were arrested, you did volunteer a significant amount of information, which served well to answer most every question we still had regarding the investigation. Before, the evidence we had pointed to yourself as the assailant in our primary case. With the clarity that you, and Mister Kenichi, have offered, we will be able to close the book on not one but three ongoing investigations."

Biting her lip nervously, she nodded. "I'm... glad I could help. Um... hopefully, Miyoko, Kana, and Yuuki's families can... find peace in knowing what happened. I feel like I owe them a huge apology for not saying something sooner..." she admitted with a deep, remorseful sigh.

"I will leave you to do that on your own time. That said, while various charges stand against you... I am content in only pursuing one due to your cooperation on the matter. And that is the charge of obstruction of justice. A significant amount of damage could have been prevented, as well as lives saved if you had been honest from the start," he said, shaking his head. "Namely, when we spoke to you at your school on that first Tuesday. If you had been forward with us then, Miss Nakajima and Mister Taichi would both still be with their families."

Sniffling, Akira hung her head in shame as she weakly nodded.

A moment of silence elapsed before he spoke again. "I'm going to process your paperwork, and then you will be released into the custody of your grandparents," he said as he closed the folder he had.

She hesitantly looked at him. "W-wait... I'm able to go home?"

"For your cooperation, yes. We will notify you about your court date, and depending on what Mister Kenichi pleads, we may require you to testify against him. Given the circumstances, I would suspect you to receive a light, suspended sentence," he stated.

"R-really?" she asked in disbelief.

He nodded. "Wait here, and I'll go handle the paperwork, as well as notify your grandparents of the situation," he said before turning and starting towards the door. As he took the handle, he turned and looked at her. "Thank you for your cooperation on this matter, Miss Makai. Since she met you, my daughter has spoken highly of you. I was worried when the evidence began to direct us towards you... I'm relieved to see that there was more to this story than appeared on the surface."

Akira timidly smiled. "Th-thank you as well, sir. And... I'm glad Ikumi thinks so highly of me. I'll... I'll make sure I live up to her expectations in the future."

"She's a smart girl. If you ever need help or someone to speak to... you can trust her," he said before opening the door. "I should be back here for you in about twenty minutes."

She nodded, then watched as he left. *Did... did he just essentially let me off easy because Ikumi and I are friends? He seriously let me off easy?!* she joyously thought to herself.

It took every fiber of her being to resist the urge to jump in excitement in her seat. She was still on recording, so her celebrating this victory would likely come off as a bit strange; she knew that. But, to know that Takashi really did stick to their plan and that she and Tomoe were now completely free of consequences for what happened was such a huge relief to Akira. She was genuinely eager to tell her girlfriend of the good news and of how they were completely in the clear now.

A small part of her did feel bad for Takashi, though she knew this remorse would quickly fade once she was able to see her friends again, especially Tomoe. Sitting here in this quiet room, with only the hum of the air conditioning, she was already daydreaming about her girlfriend's beautiful face. Nothing would stand between them now, and for the first time in what felt like years, Akira was about to begin a truly normal life, one without the insanity of concealing murders or the anxiety of always looking over her shoulder.

Upon Yasuhida's return, Akira had her handcuffs finally removed, and she was then escorted out to meet with her grandparents in the main lobby of the police station. Satomi was incredibly grateful to see her and immediately embraced her, offering comforting words of reassurance. It was clear that Yasuhida had already informed them of just what happened, or supposedly what happened. Akira took this opportunity to profusely apologize to both of her grandparents, especially Ryoma, as she secretly hoped he would reduce or even eliminate her punishment.

By the time Akira left the station with her grandparents, it was already nearly six in the evening. She had a court date set and was reassured that so long as she went to court and stayed out of trouble, that her life should continue as if none of this had ever happened. From the legal side, of course, as there was no way for Akira to forget the feelings she had when she took her destiny into her own hands and ended Kana's life, putting a stop to the years of torment she had caused. Much had changed in Akira's life, and she was now far more confident and outgoing than she was at the start of this semester. A net gain in her eyes.

After arriving home, Akira received the wonderful news from her grandfather that he would be allowing her to walk to and from school on her own if she wanted to and that she was no longer grounded. This was encouraged by Satomi, who felt that, more than ever before, Akira needed the support of her friends. It was strange for her to know that they were aware she had witnessed three people die, and even more so when they were each so sympathetic to how she must have felt. Satomi even suggested Akira see a therapist, though she reassured her grandmother that she'd be fine, so long as she had Tomoe and Ikumi to vent to.

That evening, after her grandparents had retired, Akira did just as she did before and snuck downstairs to the kitchen so she could call and talk to her girlfriend. Sitting on the countertop in her nightwear, Akira waited eagerly for her girlfriend to answer. She joyfully kicked her legs in the air just in front of her as they dangled off the counter's edge. She bobbed her head from side to side and hummed a cheerful tune to herself.

"Hello?" Tomoe cautiously answered.

Akira smiled brightly. "Hey, beautiful. I didn't wake you up, did I?" she excitedly asked.

"Um... no, not really. Aki?"

She laughed. "Who else calls you at, like, ten at night?"

"I suppose that's true. Are you okay? What happened? You disappeared during lunch, and neither Ikumi nor I heard a word from you. I did hear the principal call for you, but... I don't know. Did they send you home or something?" Tomoe asked.

Akira happily waited as her girlfriend asked all of her questions, wearing the same upbeat smile as she listened to each word. *Goddamn... I really love her voice. It's so soothing to hear...* she thought to herself before letting out an exasperated sigh. "If I'm completely honest, I stepped out to talk with Takashi, but then the police dropped by the school and arrested me," she said before laughing. "Don't worry, though. This isn't like my one phone call from jail or anything."

"Wh-what happened?" Tomoe asked in shock.

Leaning back, Akira rested her head against the cabinet as she stared up at the ceiling. "Takashi confessed to all of the crimes so they'd arrest him instead of me. But they took us both in. I sort of spun this story that explained everything as Takashi killing Miyoko, Kana, and Yuuki in an attempt to protect me and win my heart over. I cried, played the victim, and..." she giggled, "Ikumi's dad actually believed me. Isn't that crazy?" she asked, practically gleeful with excitement over narrowly avoiding jail time.

A brief silence filled the call as Tomoe struggled to speak. "W-wait... you mean someone else is going to... to prison... for our crimes?"

She nodded. "Yeah! This means, one, he won't be creeping on me anymore, and two, you and I won't have to look over our shoulders at every turn anymore. We're off the hook *completely*, no strings attached! Well... my grandparents think I have, like, trauma from watching Takashi kill people, but..." she scoffed, "I'm just eager to hang out with you and Ikumi again. Oh! Which, by the way, I'm not grounded anymore."

As Akira spoke, Tomoe had been sitting in her bed, talking on her cellphone to her girlfriend. She was worried about Akira, as well as for herself, but now, hearing this supposed good news, Tomoe couldn't find the words to respond. She simply held her phone against her ear as her hands wouldn't stop shaking.

"So, since I'm not grounded, and I'm 'in need of my friends' support,' I thought that maybe we could have another sleepover? It'd be really cool if it were at your place, ya know? I mean... it could be at my place, but... your bed is way more comfortable than my bed," Akira said with a brief chuckle. "Oh! Which reminds me... is your mom still upset about us like... you know, sharing a bed? She seemed pretty irritated that day about it. It was pretty awkward..." she said, though when she received no response, she spoke up once more. "Hey, Tomoe? You still there? You didn't fall asleep on me, did you?"

Lowering the phone down, Tomoe sat it face down on her bed as she pulled her covers up to her face, using them to muffle her tears as she began to cry.

"Tomoe? Hello? Ah... well, I guess you must have fallen asleep to the sounds of my voice, huh?" Akira asked, giggling playfully afterward. "Well, I'll let you get your beauty rest, not that you need it, and I'll see you tomorrow at school. Love you! Pleasant dreams," she added before blowing a kiss through the phone, then ending the call.

Inhaling sharply, Tomoe continued to sob into her bedsheets, muffling her tears not only to hide them from Akira but from her mother as well. The very first friend she made here in Nirasaki, at her new high school, a kind and funny, albeit awkward girl, turned out to be a terrible, borderline evil monster. She remorselessly killed a girl who she once saw as a dear friend. She lied to their mutual friend and even drugged her, intended to kill a boy at school who was simply distraught over the death of his girlfriend. And now, Akira was overjoyed after sending a young man to serve the rest of his life behind bars for their crimes.

No matter how Tomoe tried to paint her to make herself feel better, Akira was a monster. She might have been able to hide it from some, but Tomoe could see her for the psychopath she truly was, deranged into believing that her evil acts were justified simply because of her greed. And now, Tomoe was a part of her horrific cycle of pain and suffering. It was too late to attempt to wash her hands of this, to out Akira as the terrible person she was. But, it wasn't too late to protect others from her. She'd already committed to starting this relationship with Akira, and now she knew that if she didn't continue it, others could very well die. So, she would keep loving Akira, at least on the surface, if only as a form of leverage to prevent her from harming anyone else.

Epilogue
可愛いサイコちゃん

In the weeks following Akira's initial arrest much had happened. She attended her court hearing, where she was sentenced to serving a five-year suspended sentence for her inaction concerning the murders. Tomoe had attended the hearing, as did Ikumi, each of them there to support their friend, albeit for significantly different reasons. Tomoe knew from this point onward that Akira needed to stay out of trouble, or else she'd risk facing an actual prison sentence. And, while the idea behind her behind bars would mean she couldn't hurt anyone, Tomoe was more fearful of what crime Akira might commit, should she stray from the law.

The court had given Akira the opportunity to see a therapist and strongly encouraged her to do so. She did for a while, though eventually, she assured everyone that she was fine and that all she needed was the support of her friends. With the people who made her miserable now gone from her life, an amazing girlfriend, and a genuine friend she could trust, Akira felt as if for the first time since her last friendship fell apart, her life was truly returning to a state that she would consider normal. Whether or not that would last was still to be determined. However, for now, life was quiet and peaceful for Akira, Tomoe, and Ikumi.

On a beautiful Friday afternoon, the girls left the school, each with exciting plans for their weekend. Akira and Tomoe looked forward to the weekend they'd be spending at Tomoe's house, while Ikumi was thinking of what all she'd need for the vacation trip she had planned with her father and uncle. They wouldn't see one another again until Monday morning, and so they said their farewells to one another before parting ways.

"Just make sure not to eat too much junk food on your trip," Tomoe advised her friend.

Ikumi giggled. "I'm more excited for the sights than the food. Although, I do *love* seafood..."

Akira smiled. "Being right there on the water will be nice. Be sure and snap a lot of pictures for us too. I mean, I, for one, have never been to Hiroshima, even if it's not all that far away."

"It's probably less impressive to someone who grew up in Tokyo... after all, Tokyo is such a big city," Ikumi responded.

"Eh... I don't remember a lot about it if I'm honest. I was pretty young at the time," she admitted with a shrug of her shoulders.

Ikumi's smile steadily faded as she sighed. "A part of me would still kind of prefer to stay here and have a sleepover with you two... but I haven't done anything with my dad and uncle since the start of the semester, and... nothing is more important than family, right?"

"That's right," Tomoe responded.

"Speaking of family..." Akira said as she looked past her friend.

Turning to follow Akira's sights, Ikumi saw her uncle approaching them. She smiled, then threw him a cheerful wave.

"I can tell you're already itching for this vacation, Ikumi," Yakovna said as he drew near.

She eagerly nodded. "I am. It's going to be a lot of fun."

"I agree. And, as promised, I did take off work early today so that I could take you to run those errands before the trip," he responded.

Ikumi wore a big smile as she giggled. "Thank you, Uncle Isaak," she said before looking to her friends. "I have to go get a haircut and buy a couple of things before the trip. Especially a camera. Without that, I won't be able to take pictures for you two."

Akira pursed her lips. "Your hair's already pretty short, Ikumi... how much were you planning to get cut off?"

"Oh, just a little bit. I guess it's more of a touch-up than a haircut, but I'm still excited about it. It's going to feel so much better without my hair on my neck at the beach. I can't wait to feel that cool breeze," Ikumi said with a deep, exasperated sigh.

Tomoe frowned. "That's why I wear my hair in a ponytail... but now I'm sort of jealous. I want to go to the beach too..."

Yakovna gestured with a nod towards his car. "Ikumi, why don't you run ahead..." he said, his eyes trailing towards Akira. "I'd like to have a moment alone to speak with your friend... see how she's been doing after everything that happened."

Ikumi nodded. "Yes, sir," she said before looking to her friends. "I can't wait to see you guys on Monday. Have a great weekend!" she said as she began racing off towards the vehicle.

"You too!" Akira responded.

Watching her leave, Yakovna returned his sights to Akira. "You seem to be holding up well, Miss Makai..."

She nodded. "I am... it helps to have the support of my friends."

"Ah, yes... no doubt," he responded before lightly scoffing. "Well, the ones you *haven't* killed, I'm sure," he said as his eyes narrowed onto her. "Considering you've painted yourself as the victim, it's a bit of a surprise to see that you've so hastily transitioned back to life as normal. I hear that you're not even attending your therapy anymore."

Taking a deep breath, she looked to Tomoe, then back to him. "Well, with my friends... I don't feel as if I need to talk to a therapist anymore."

"Of course not. After all, there's no need for that when you lack even *one* iota of empathy or remorse for the lives you've taken, the families you left broken," he said before crossing his arms. "For most, even so much as seeing a dead body leaves them scarred and traumatized. You witnessed three individuals, each killed before your very eyes. You recall the state Miss Nakajima was left in, yes? Thank goodness she had identification on her, else we'd of never known who she was."

Staring at him, Akira bit at her lip before sighing. "Um... listen, I have chores I need to do at home, and Ikumi is waiting on you, so... I should probably go..."

He scoffed. "Oh, by all means. Feel free to simply walk away... *but*, before you leave, there was one thing I wanted to ensure you're made aware of," he said before holding his index finger up. "One... just one. That is the number of times you need to break the law before I'm able to arrest you, take you before a judge, have your suspended sentence revoked, and watch you rot for the next five years, or more, behind bars. Perhaps not for the crimes you actually committed... but even a small justice is still justice."

Swallowing nervously, she glared at him. "I was a victim here... as a police officer, aren't you supposed to protect victims, not harass them?"

"I cannot protect corpses, Makai... and those are the only victims here. Aside from the families of those victims, of whom I am diligently serving," he said before taking a step closer. "You know... before moving here to

Japan to be closer to my sister and her family, may her soul rest in peace, I served as a police officer in our home city of Moscow. And let me assure you, we play none of these 'political' games in Russia. No... when we find a murderer... we take care of them. We don't waste time on petty matters of a public image or ensuring everything is tied together like a bow atop a gift box... none of that. We protect our citizens from those who wish them harm. People like yourself, Makai," he warned her.

Glaring at him, Akira grit her teeth as she almost growled under her breath.

He narrowed his eyes onto her. "One other thing. I am well aware of just how... enthusiastic Ikumi is to have the two of you as her friends. Her father and I each hear almost every day about how much she enjoys school because of you two," he explained before scoffing. "As much as I'd prefer she come to her senses and see the truth, she appears devoted to the fantasy you've painted for her. Regardless, it would be remiss of me not to tell you flat out... if anything happens to her, I will find you, no matter where you flee or where you hide. And I will hear you plead for death before I even consider granting you such mercy."

She could feel a vicious mix of emotions as he even suggested that she would never hurt her best friend. "I... I would never, *ever* do anything to hurt Ikumi... and, if anyone else hurt her, I'd..."

"Careful there, Makai... a threat of physical violence made in front of an officer is a minor offense, but an offense nonetheless," he said.

Akira scoffed. "I wouldn't let *anyone* hurt Ikumi... and I damn well wouldn't hurt her myself."

Tomoe reached out and placed her hand on her girlfriend's upper arm. "Aki... let's just go," she said in a low voice.

Yakovna grinned at her. "Yes... go. Runaway, Miss Makai. And keep running. Because once I return from this... family outing of mine, I'll look forward to seeing just how long you can go before you cross the line once again. After all... you've had the taste of blood. It surely can't take long before you crave it once again," he said before turning around, then walking off towards his vehicle.

Watching him leave, Akira grit her teeth angrily. "F-fucking asshole..."

Moving around in front of Akira, Tomoe blocked her view of him. "His threats don't matter, Aki. Because... you're not going to do what he's accusing you of. Everything that happened... it's all over, and we're *never* going to have to relive that nightmare again, right?"

Exhaling sharply, Akira nodded. "Yeah. It'll be annoying to have him breathing down my neck twenty-four-seven, but..." she forced a smile. "He'll just be wasting his time. The only things I care about now are spending time with my friends."

"And school," Tomoe added.

She rolled her eyes. "Yeah... and school," she said with little enthusiasm.

Tomoe sighed. "Alright, come on. Let's get back to your house so we can do your chores and pack up for this weekend."

"Sounds good. And, maybe we can cuddle and fall asleep again?" Akira asked as she turned and began making her way down the secluded alley.

Walking alongside her girlfriend, Tomoe reluctantly nodded. "Yeah... we can. My mom did say she'd give us privacy, so long as my grades don't decline, and... they haven't, so..."

Akira offered a toothy grin. "Thank goodness she doesn't care about my grades because those are fucking abysmal!" she said with a loud chuckle.

Continuing on their way to Akira's house, the girls had very little to concern themselves with, at least on the surface. While things may have appeared pristine and wonderful between the two of them, for one of them, Asano Tomoe, she was left feeling doubt and uncertainty over how everything had played out. A young man was serving twenty-six years behind bars for crimes he didn't commit, while the ones responsible were left with only the burden of choosing a movie for their sleepover. The weight of knowing she was partially responsible for this was crushing for Tomoe.

However, as she looked to the ever cheerful, psychotic girl with whom she was engaged in a loveless relationship, Tomoe knew that at least in some small way, she was serving a long-term sentence of her own. With any luck, she hoped that it would not end with a death sentence for anyone involved, though she knew that with someone as volatile as Makai Akira, it was only a matter of time before the fuse lit and burned down to meet the gunpowder. Until then, she could only do her best to reciprocate Akira's emotions and twist those to ensure she didn't inflict harm on another person again. A daunting task, but one Tomoe hoped that she'd be up for.

Printed in Great Britain
by Amazon